Tri Moons: Hidden

Book 1

Yanette Mantro

Print ISBN: 9781732409200

For more info contact:

Purplefly Press, LLC

3225 North Hiatus Road #450158

Fort Lauderdale, FL 33345

purpleflypress@gmail.com

https://landing.mailerlite.com/webforms/landing/m9i7n1

Cover Illustration by Amalia Chitulescu Digital Art
© 2018

Editors: Charlotte Stanley and Wild Obsidian Press, LLC

Formatted by: Wild Obsidian Press, LLC

Contents

Stay proud, be bold and continue to take those big leaps. Remember to always keep those dreams alive. Live it up!

Write. Tell. Author it.
~ Yanette Mantro

Prologue

Jasinda

Six months ago…

I sat in my car trying to gather myself before going inside. In an instant, my life had completely changed. I'd never realized just how much a few simple words could alter reality. Two small words had changed everything. *You're pregnant.* My doctor told me an hour ago that I was twenty weeks pregnant. *How the hell had I not noticed?*

I'd asked her that. She'd said it happens sometimes in a first pregnancy. I didn't notice any changes in my body and my periods were still coming, except lighter than usual. My annual checkup had turned into a pregnancy announcement. It hadn't felt real until she'd handed me the sonogram with three different images of my baby.

Mine and Elier's baby. *How was I going to tell him? Would he be happy?*

Elier said he had a special date planned for us. Maybe I'd tell him then. It would make the date even more special. I turned the car off and walked inside my house.

After dropping my keys and a handful of pamphlets on prenatal health on the counter, I went straight for my tea kettle. As the water heated, I leaned against the counter and placed my hands on my belly in wonder. *Would Elier ask me to abort the baby?* We've been together for four years, yet that subject never came up. *Could I handle being a mother?*

A knock at my door had me bolting upright while wondering who it could be. Elier wouldn't be here for another hour or two. I walked over to the door and peeked through the peephole above my lock. My dad thought it was a good idea to put the peephole there, hidden in the actual lock. A beautiful blonde woman with hot pink lipstick on very thin lips stood outside my door.

Who the hell was she? Maybe she was lost.

Unlocking the door and opening it just enough for me to lean on the doorframe, I crossed my arms over my chest. "Can I help you?"

I noticed she was in a short white dress with pink heels. Her long legs were bared to the world. The smirk on her face made me want to cringe. It appeared almost sinister. No, it *was* an evil one, I decided as I stared at it longer. Goosebumps rose on the back of my neck.

What the hell?

She didn't say anything as she stood there sizing me up. Her eyes roamed my entire body then settled on my belly. Anger flashed in her eyes. She mumbled something under her breath. She must have the wrong house because I had no clue who she was. She finally looked me in the eyes and plastered on a fake smile.

Oh, how I wanted to punch that smile right off her face. But she still hadn't spoken. I dropped my hands to my hips and gave her a daggered look. I'd grown up with the Mitchell brothers. They'd trained me well enough in martial arts to wipe the floor with her, so I wasn't worried about the hostility in her eyes.

I cleared my throat and repeated myself, "Can I help you?"

Her smile widened as she stood straighter. "Jasinda?" she asked.

I kept quiet. I didn't like how she said my name.

"You're dating Elier, right?" My senses spiked, and I stood to my full height.

"Right. What can I do for you?" I bit out.

She held out her left hand for me to shake. "My name's Miranda and I'm Elier's fiancée. Nice to meet you."

My jaw dropped. I left her hand hanging as I stared at her empty ring finger. I couldn't speak. No words formed to ask her about her lack of an engagement ring.

What the hell? This had to be a joke, right? My eyes darted around for a hidden camera but came up empty.

She laughed. "Sorry. I thought you knew about me."

Nope, not a joke.

She dropped her hand and placed it on her hip. "You're nothing like us, babe. I mean, I'm trying to figure out what he sees in you. I have to say, I don't see it. No offense."

I stood there motionless, my fingers twitching with rage as I fought the urge to gouge her eyes out.

Engaged? How could I have been so clueless?

She was rambling on about something else, but I couldn't hear her anymore. The ache in my heart was too much to bear. His *fiancée* had come here to hurt me on purpose! *Bitch!*

"Anyways, playtime's over for Elier. I need him to start concentrating on our wedding, rather than playing around with his little *toys*," she taunted. "You were just entertainment for him. I'm sure it was fun, but fun doesn't last." She twirled her body away and sashayed towards her car.

I gawked at her departing back, completely dumbfounded. *How in the world had Elier Sky been engaged while being in a four-year relationship with me? How had I not caught on?*

Slamming the door in anger, I marched straight for my phone. My fingers stabbed at his name, which was saved as the number one contact in my speed dial. *Not anymore, buster.* While I waited for his number to dial, I tried to figure out what I'd say first. He answered the phone on the first ring.

"Dewdrop—" he tried to say, but I interrupted him quickly.

"Please tell me that you are not engaged to a woman named Miranda. Please tell me she's some skanky ex that is trying to break us up over jealousy and I have nothing to worry about?" I wailed.

"Let me explain, Jasinda."

"Explain? Are you serious? Who the *hell* has a fiancée *and* a girlfriend at the same time?" I shouted. "Why was she here, Elier? And what the hell did she mean when she said I'm nothing like you guys?"

"Wait, Miranda was *there*?" he asked, horror evident in his tone. *Was it horror at being busted or horror at something else?*

"Yes, she was *here*. She was at my damn door, Elier! *How?* How does she know where I live?" I yelled. I took a deep breath and continued without giving him a chance to answer anything. "How could you be engaged *and* be in a relationship with me? Do you even *love* me?" I croaked out and hung up the phone. I didn't want to hear him say *yes*. I didn't want to hear him say no either, especially not *now*. But there was no way I could handle him saying yes.

I had to get out of there. No way in hell was I going to be at home when Elier decided to drop by and attempt an explanation. Snatching up my keys and my purse, I stomped to my car. Squeezing my eyes shut, I counted to ten before reopening them and drove the five minutes to work. I needed the distraction. The turns made me relax a little. After I pulled into the plaza's parking lot, I parked, applied some lipstick as armor, and walked into work. I said my hellos to the few staff and motioned Angie, my best friend, towards my office. The look on her face was one of confusion. I knew what she was about to ask me.

"I thought you were hanging with Elier today," she pointed out and closed the door behind her.

I kept my face blank and tried my hardest not to have a meltdown in my office. "Not anymore. His fiancée showed up at my door this morning to rub their engagement in my face." I weakly told her. I couldn't look her in the eyes. Her shoulder was as close as I could get right now.

"What!?" she bellowed. "You're joking. Where's Ashton hiding? You're pranking me, right?"

"I wish I was." I slumped my shoulders. "That's not the worst part."

"Did she put her hands on you?"

"I wished she had, so I could've punched the smirk off her face," I said angrily.

"She had the *audacity* to smirk?" Angie asked.

"Yup." I finally looked Angie in the eyes. "I'm pregnant. It's a boy. You're going to be an auntie," I flatly spilled.

"What? No way!" she whispered. I nodded at her. "Shit. Are you ok?"

I loved how she didn't just jump for joy. It wasn't a joyful time for me. "No, but I'll figure it out and I'll be ok," the crack in my own voice was unbearable.

She pulled me into her arms and rocked me as I opened the floodgates to my pain. She pulled me on the loveseat in front of my desk with her. "We'll get through this together, girl. I've got your back. That little boy is going to be spoiled by the best auntie in the whole wide world," she gushed.

That got a smile out of me but it didn't do anything to ease my pain.

My phone rang, and I knew it was Elier. He'd been trying to call ever since I'd hung up on him. I'd picked up a few calls and immediately hung up so that he'd know how angry I was. I felt Angie's body move towards my purse and knew she was looking for my phone. I was about to tell her that it was just Elier, and that I didn't want to speak with him when the ringing stopped.

"You're a piece of shit, you know that? What the fuck is wrong with you? How the fuck can you act like you're so in love with her while you're engaged to someone else? You two deserve each other since she's a piece of shit herself for showing up at Jasinda's door." Angie didn't stop her tirade there. "You better warn your precious fiancée, that if she *ever* shows up at Jasinda's door again, I'm going to fuckin' pound her to the ground. She'll be a part of the sidewalk!" She yelled that last part.

She dropped the phone on my desk as she huffed out a breath. Now, that's what best friends are for.

*T*wo *weeks later…*

"Jasinda, stay with me. You're going to be all right," a soothing voice urged me as I tried to gather air into my lungs. My eyes were closed. I didn't know who he was. There was a slight familiarity to his voice, but with all the pain, my mind couldn't focus on the mystery of who the voice belonged to. My body was jerked up. A hard ridge of muscle rippled under my cheek, and a strong, masculine scent filled my nostrils. I was cradled against someone's chest and that someone was running, bouncing me with each step.

"Don't move. Be still and breathe."

The pain in my abdomen was excruciating, and I was trying my best to stay as still as possible, as he'd indicated.

"I've got you. I've got you. We're almost there."

Voices filled my ears and were getting louder. They were joined by the wailing of sirens from an ambulance. *This wasn't good.*

"I need help, now!"

"What's her name?" an unfamiliar voice asked.

"Jasinda."

"What happened?"

"She was attacked and suffered a blow to her belly. She's pregnant and bleeding," my rescuer spoke in a rush.

How did he know I was pregnant?

My body was lowered onto something soft. My eyes remained closed, because I was too afraid to look at anyone and see concern on their faces. I didn't want to be here. I shouldn't have waited to tell Elier that I was pregnant with his son. I'd been waiting to calm down from his betrayal and from the pain he caused me. I was going to invite him to dinner in a public place and tell him within the next few days. Now he'd never know because I knew I wouldn't be leaving here with a baby still in my belly. The wetness between my legs told me so.

Chapter One

Jasinda

*P**resent Day...***
    I gripped the leather seat as Angie stopped the car a few feet away from the valet. My heart thumped against my rib cage, and I wished it was from excitement. It had been months of work putting the charity event together. I wanted to enjoy tonight, but—

"Did you hear me?" Angie's voice broke through my thoughts.

"Huh? Sorry, what?"

"I asked if you were ok." She frowned. Brown eyes filled with concern.

"I don't know." My voice wasn't as steady as I wanted it to be. "Elier is supposed to be there."

Her eyes softened for a moment, before hardening at his name.

I put a hand over my flat belly. Except it shouldn't be flat. It should have been nearly nine months round with a thriving baby kicking my ribs when I ate ice cream. The memories of the attack pushed on my mind, but I couldn't remember who, didn't know why...and Elier didn't know he would have been a father. The fiancé I hadn't even known about showed up at our door effectively ending things between Elier and I before I'd had a chance to tell him.

"You'll be fine." Angie squeezed my arm.

"Sounds promising," I bit back.

"You know what I mean, girl."

Yes, I knew what she meant, but it didn't help tamp down my nerves. In fact, this charity event was causing said nerves to scatter my mind. And to top it all off, this was the first client who Anthony, my business partner, was in charge of handling on his own. It was a big deal for our company.

I glanced down at my lavender dress, laced with white flowers. It had a V-neck and stopped two inches above my knees. Nude heels and a silver clutch completed the look. I gripped my purse and took in a breath.

"How do I look?" I asked, trying to forget about Elier.

"For the tenth time, you look fantastic! That dress was made for you." She waved her hand up and down.

Looking into her brown eyes, I saw nothing but sincerity.

"Hey," she whispered and put her hand on my lap. I blinked a few times, and she continued, "You look fuckin' sexy. I mean *fuck me right here, right now* kind of sexy. If you run into Elier, just smile and say hello. Go with the flow. Besides, I don't think he'll try to talk to you tonight. At least not about the breakup."

I exhaled the breath I'd been holding. "You're right, I'm just freaking out over nothing."

"That's it. Now, are you sure you want to keep that same old jewelry on?"

Automatically, my hand gripped the beautiful emerald-green butterfly pendant at my chest. A gift from my mother before she disappeared.

"What's wrong with it?" I asked defensively.

"Well, you could've worn something a bit fancier with that dress," she says with a shrug.

"Angie, you know how much this jewelry means to me. Besides, I don't care for all that expensive stuff."

"Are you sure? I brought my grandmother's expensive jewelry just in case."

"Thanks. I'll be fine."

"Fine. I had to try," she huffed.

She smiled at me and drove right up to the entrance door. Taking one last glance in the mirror, I checked my makeup, adjusted the honey brown hair pinned together at the nape of my neck and took a breath. I could do this, even if my confidence was a little shaken lately.

"All right. I'm going."

"Later," Ang said.

I got out of the car, and in the light of the doorway, my caramel skin stood out in contrast with the lavender dress.

As I walked up to the entrance, a lovely white butterfly passed by me. I was drawn to it for some odd reason. My gaze followed it as I stood in line and waited. It was rare to see a butterfly at night. "Remarkable!" I said to myself. Then, it disappeared into the sky. Almost as if only I were meant to see it.

The man greeting the guests as they entered smiled at each one like he knew them all. Until I reached him. His face then took on a mask of professionalism and was devoid of any friendliness.

He studied me for a minute before he spoke, "This is a private charity event. I believe you're at the wrong place."

I looked at him for about five seconds and decided not to let his stupidity get the best of me.

I mean, how the hell could he just assume I was at the wrong event?

I smiled and decided to try and be polite.

"You didn't even ask for my name, so how do you know that I'm at the wrong event?" I tilted my head slightly to the side.

His eyebrows shot up, but I continued before he could respond.

"That's a bit rude, don't you think?" Then the smartass in me took over, "Jasinda Santana, and I *am* on the list. And yes, I know this is a private charity event. I am with JNS Event Planning. That's why I'm here. Thank you very much."

He looked at me with annoyed eyes as he paused for a second and looked down at his clipboard. His eyes moved up and down the sheet, stopping at my name a few times. His eyebrows shot up in surprise each time he read my name.

"Yup that's me, J-A-S-I-N-D-A-S-A-N-T-A-N-A," I nearly shouted.

His annoyed gaze met mine, causing his eyebrows to furrow and nostrils to flare. He didn't like me looking at his clipboard. He must have been so focused on trying not to find my name on the list that he didn't even notice me hovering over him.

A small laugh sounded behind me, and I looked back into a pair of brilliant green orbs. They were so green they glowed like glittering gems. Everything stopped at that moment. I was so enthralled my heart dared not even beat. Wow. He gazed right back at me and smiled. A hint of a smile formed on my face in response, but I knew my eyes showed something different. I felt a bit queasy. My stomach twisted and churned like I was racing downhill. I didn't even bother to look at the rest of him. His eyes had undone me.

"Ms. Santana, right this way," a voice said, but I couldn't move. He'd cast me under some sort of spell. It took me a few more seconds to break free and compose myself.

"Ms. Santana?"

"Yes, I'm ready," I said, while still staring at those damn beautiful eyes.

He was still grinning as I slowly turned back to the tall, dark man holding the clipboard. Confusion clouded the clipboard man's features, but he sent me in the direction of a handsome teenager. At least he looked like a teenager. He offered his arm for me to hold onto as he escorted me inside. I had this crazy urge to look back, but I thought it best not to.

The hall was huge and beautiful. Miniature white candles held in circular glass votives suspended from the ceiling. They appear to be floating. I searched for strings, but I couldn't find any. I'd have to ask Anthony how he managed to hide them all. If the power failed, the hall would still be perfectly illuminated by hundreds of flickering candles. Simple, yet elegant.

I was enamored with the atmosphere, and I knew it was all Anthony's doing. When he'd presented the idea to me, I'd immediately fallen in love with it. Seeing his vision come to life was breathtaking. Each table had a purple tablecloth adorned with a long glass holder, filled halfway with water. Floating candles and purple rose petals were scattered on the water's surface. The purple was a deep, dark color. Beautiful. Romantic. Simple. Tonight's charity fundraising was to benefit Hope in Children. Purple symbolized hope. And that was exactly what they were fostering.

This particular charity was known for getting children off the streets and into loving homes. They even had a building they'd turned into a shelter.

I'd volunteered there with Anthony on nights they'd held dances or holiday parties for the kids. It had always been fun.

"Miss Santana is here," the teen boy said.

I hadn't realized we'd stopped. I started to answer him, but realized he was talking into an earpiece. My eyes darted around as I waited for him to take me to my seat. Unease came over me as my gaze locked with a pair of sharp grey ones. Elier was handsome as ever with his wide shoulders, squared chin and pointy nose. He stared at me with such intensity. I clutched the young man's arm as if he was my lifeline.

He must have noticed my tightening grip. "Miss Santana?"

Slowly I looked up into his beautiful, golden eyes. He was certainly handsome.

"Please call me Jasinda." I beamed.

He nodded at me. "Ok. Jasinda, Anthony will be here to escort you to your table. He has a special seat for you."

"Thank you." I said and looked back over to see if those grey beauties were still looking at me.

Yup. Still fixed on me.

Elier stood like a dog waiting to pounce. He fidgeted with a button on his suit. When he took a few steps in my direction, I shook my head at him to stop him from coming any closer. He froze, and pain filled his face. For a moment I felt bad but it died when I saw Miranda, the fiancé I never knew about, being escorted to his table.

I did *not* want to talk to Elier Sky right now. We hadn't spoken in four months. The first month after things ended hadn't been good. I yelled and cried whenever I answered his calls but didn't *speak* with him. It was the worst feeling. After committing four years of my life to him, I thought we'd had something. At least until my unexpected visit from Miranda four months ago. What a sucker I'd been. Well, no more. As far as I was concerned, Elier and the bitch deserved each other.

She *was* beautiful, almost like a Barbie doll—blue eyes, blonde hair cut to her chin, and an oval face with thin pink lips. She also had beautiful long legs and pale skin. She was wearing a dress that showed off her legs.

As I remembered how it ripped at my heart to hear the words she enjoyed telling me, it stabbed at my insecurities. I quickly shook off the feeling when I noticed she was tugging on Elier's arm and he wouldn't budge. *This too shall pass*. I repeated the mantra over and over in my mind.

Chapter Two

Jasinda

Anthony finally arrived looking sharp as always, black dress slacks and a lavender shirt. He beamed at me, his eyes gleaming with excitement and happiness. I loved when he was happy.

Putting a hand on my hip, I cocked my head to the side. "Did you match me on purpose?"

He put a hand to his chest feigning surprise, wide eyes gleaming with excitement. "Would I have the opportunity, means, and absolute talent to do so?"

"Yes."

"You're right." He grinned and walked over to me, adjusting the G-shock watch on his hand. "Hello. *Ojos qué brillan*," he greeted me in Spanish.

Eyes that sparkled. That was his normal greeting for me. My eyes didn't feel particularly sparkly, but I'd take the compliment. My fragile ego needed it after seeing Miranda.

Anthony tapped a kiss to my lips and enveloped me in a warm hug. With a tug, he gently removed my hand from the young man's arm so I could hug him back properly. Pulling away, he smiled at me, looking me up and down.

He looked over at the man who had escorted me. "Thanks, Trent. I'll see you later."

"Thanks," I said as he walked away, a sheepish smile on his face.

Anthony twirled me around once and cleared his throat. "These white flower patterns are beautiful on the lavender dress." Once fully stopped, his lips tipped up. "You look sexy! Natural as hell! You always know how to put yourself together without any effort."

"Thank you. So, do you. Mr. Matcher," I accused.

"Truth is I saw the dress hanging on your closet door the other day and thought it would be good to match with you for this event."

"You mean, since you're working right now."

"You're overseeing me. Besides, we might get a couple of new clients after tonight."

"Well, they'll be yours to handle. So, be ready," I warned. I was the only one who typically brought clients into our business and Anthony wanted to expand on our clientele. He mentioned he could get special clients that had money to spend on anything. Learning to draw them in was his goal.

He nodded at me and looked toward Elier. A concerned look crossed his face. Pain sliced at me from catching a glimpse of Elier again. I braced myself for Anthony to speak his mind like he normally did.

"Jasinda, just talk to him. Let him explain everything," he said in a pleading tone. "There must be *more* to this. I *know* how he feels about you, and he wouldn't let *her* get in the way of that."

Inwardly, I pouted. That was Anthony, always seeing the best in others. But some things couldn't be sugar-coated, like lying and cheating.

He held my hands in his, keeping me from turning away from eyes that saw too much when they looked at me. "I know he wronged you, but just hear the man out. He still loves you. At the very least it'll be fun to watch him grovel."

"He has a funny way of showing it." I was so sick of having this conversation. He repeated the same thing several times before.

"I'm not going to pretend that I know why he pulled the crap that he did... But he was never going to marry her. Hear him out."

Every time he tried to reassure me of that, there was a knowing glint in his eyes. Just like now. Almost like he knew something and he wasn't telling me.

"What's there to explain, Ant? He's a cheater and a liar. *And* he failed to mention a few key points. Like his fiancée! Who does that Ant?" I said angrily.

My outburst drew the attention of people around us. Feeling sheepish, I lowered my voice. "This really isn't the place for this discussion."

He nodded. "Yeah, I know. I just thought you two could be friends somehow."

"Maybe one day," I said, hoping he'd drop the Elier subject.

"You should at least go say hello to him," he said softly.

Elier still stood by his table, waiting while staring in my direction with sorrowful eyes. I took in a breath and smiled at him. He smiled back and the sorrow turned to hope. I waved at him and looked over towards Miranda. She was angry, *really* angry and that pleased me. It was petty, but today I didn't care. Turning back to Anthony, I noticed he was hiding a grin. That too, satisfied me.

"So, where are you seating me?" I asked, trying to steer the convo from my cheating ex.

He shook his head a little and put his arm out for me to loop mine in his. With a broad smile, he turned us away from Elier. We set off at a slow stroll so that I wouldn't trip over my heels. At six feet tall, Anthony had to shorten his strides in order to match my five foot four steps. That was fine with me as it meant that I got another look at Trent. I may not be looking for a relationship, but that doesn't mean I can't appreciate a fine specimen. Trent is not on the level of the man with the stunning eyes, but he's beautiful in his own right.

"You know he's only eighteen. You should be ashamed of yourself," he said with a mischievous smile.

"What?" I adopted an innocent tone.

"Trent. I saw the way you were looking at him."

"Oh, that? He's just eye candy," I said sternly.

"Sure, whatever." he said as he nudged her.

Laughing at the banter, we stopped in front of a table on the other side of the hall. I glanced back and grinned when I took in our location. It was directly across from Elier's table. He'd have to walk across the dance floor to get to me. Tension radiated off him, enough that I could practically feel it even all the way across the dance floor. But what did he and Anthony expect? I wasn't going to talk to him. Especially not with that bitch at his side.

"Are you all right?" Anthony questioned, with his famous smirk.

"Fine." And I *was*, because I wasn't sitting next to Elier. *Asshole.*

Chapter Three

Jasinda

Anthony studied me for a minute, then turned me slightly to face a man who was standing by patiently holding out a chair. Oops. He was waiting for me to sit. I froze when my gaze met his amused look. It was the man who had been behind me at the front entrance. He'd laughed at what I'd said to the man checking guests in.

"Jace Hunt, meet Jasinda Santana."

He reached to shake my hand, but I didn't move. I was too shocked to even blink. I was sitting next to the man that captivated me at the entrance. He grinned at me and I wanted to hide from the heat spreading across my cheeks.

"It's a pleasure to meet you," Jace said.

Oh, that voice. That deep bass sent tingles across my skin like a caress. Anthony nudged me slightly forward, thrusting my hand into his. Jace turned my hand over and kissed it.

"Pleasure," I managed.

Different currents of lust and warmth were running through me. My reaction to Jace was so unexpected. His face was beautiful, and so was his body but there was something more there, too. He looked at me with mirth and perhaps kindness. Being near him made me feel serene. He appeared genuinely pleased to meet me.

Clearing my throat, I finally found my voice, "I hope you don't mind sharing your table with me?"

He was the only one seated here.

"Not at all. I like a wiseass here and there." He winked.

So, he *had* heard everything that had gone on at the entrance.

"What's he talking about, Jasinda?"

I gave Anthony a devilish smile but remained silent.

"Jasinda?" he scolded.

"The guy at the entrance checking in guests was a bit rude about me being on the list. I just pointed it out, in a...polite way." I was hoping that incident wouldn't make it back to Anthony.

Jace coughed. "She was a little audacious, which was well deserved. Frank was being rude in his disbelief that she was on the list. It was quite entertaining if you ask me."

I beamed like a little girl in the middle of the biggest candy store in the world. I couldn't help it.

Anthony rolled his eyes and smirked. "So, you think it's funny?"

"Obviously, you do," I pointed out to him.

He laughed and turned to Jace. "Would you be so kind as to keep her company? Oh, and keep an eye on her as well?"

"Um...I'm not a child in need of a babysitter." I leaned closer to Anthony to whisper, "Even if he is a good looking one."

But I was pretty sure that Jace heard me anyway, because his lips turned up into an immense smile that showed all his pearly white teeth.

"Ant—"

"I'll keep her company," Jace said cutting me off. "*And* I'll watch her if you're telling me she's your girlfriend and I need to make sure no other man steps in. If she's not your girlfriend, then she doesn't need watching in that way." He winked.

Ant looked back at me. "No, she's not my girlfriend but I want to make sure she's ok." The words came out clipped, his shoulders tensing with anger. "So that's what I'm asking of you."

Jace placed both hands into his pockets and arched his back, standing taller. I watched them both. *What the hell was I missing?*

"Ok, I'll look after her," Jace clipped.

Anthony finally killed the silence. "I trust only you, Jace. Thanks." He kissed my cheek. "Gotta run. Don't give him too much of a hard time."

I gasped dramatically, bringing a hand to my chest and inserting a playful tone in my voice. "Who *me*? Now, why would I do such a thing?"

He shook his head and walked off.

Jace pulled out a chair for me. "Have a seat."

"Thanks." I sat, immediately turning to him as he sat on my left. "Just so you know, I'm not sorry for the way I acted at the entrance. He was rude."

His eyebrows shot up, but he smiled. "Frank *can* be rude. Sometimes he doesn't realize the vibe he's putting off. But he's harmless and means well. He pretty much knows everyone here, except for you. He was in protective mode."

I stared at him for a minute, lost in his eyes and his voice. He smoothed out the long black ponytail that practically shined against his olive skin. It stood out because of three bands that each had three emeralds glinting in the light. I didn't know if they were real or not, but it didn't matter. They paled in comparison to the chiseled jaw accented with a black goatee, smooth and perfectly groomed. That amazing body decked out in an almost platinum colored suit, screamed 'touch me'. *Oh, yeah. I wanted to touch him all right.*

"Jasinda?"

I blasted those thoughts away and snagged a glass of wine from a passing waiter. "I understand and to be honest I'm over it. I've said my piece, and now I'm here. It's all good. I don't know the guy well enough to hate him or anything. I just wanted him to know he was being rude." Taking a smooth sip of wine, I winked at him this time.

His smile widened. "Good to know. I was hoping that wasn't the reason I saw you upset earlier."

The wine turned bitter on my tongue and burned in belly. I didn't know what to say. What guy wanted to know about another man cheating on you in the first ten minutes of meeting? But I didn't want to lie to him. At least not totally.

Tracing my finger around the rim of my glass, I leaned in closer to him. "Honestly, I didn't want to sit next to my ex."

He raised an eyebrow. "Your ex is here?"

"Yes." I took another sip of wine to chase away the anxiety that bubbled in my chest.

He made a move as if to ask something, but then stopped.

"What?" I finally asked.

"Who's your ex?"

Lying was a consideration. Or telling him it was none of his business. Except the way he looked at me, the earnestness in his eyes, I *didn't want to* lie to him. "Elier Sky."

His gaze darkened, moving between where Elier sat and back to me.

"I thought he was engaged to Miranda?" confusion peppered the question.

I drained my wine glass before answering. "That's why he's my ex," I murmured.

"No judgement," he said in an easy voice.

"*Wait,* so you think that what I did deserves no judgement?" I snagged another glass of wine before it could pass me by.

"That's correct." He raised an eyebrow at my astonished look. "Did you know that he was engaged?"

If I'd known that important little detail, I'd never have gotten involved with him to begin with.

"No, I didn't," I said, shifting in my seat.

"If you didn't know he was engaged, then there's definitely no judgement here."

Well then, I was pretty impressed. *Maybe men didn't really judge like women did.*

"I wish I'd known though. I mean, that's serious, don't you think?" I said it more as a question to myself. "How could you be engaged to one woman and dating another? I just don't understand. I was a fool. For years."

"Maybe he had his reasons for not telling you or Miranda. Did you ask him?"

Hell no, I didn't ask him.

I couldn't even remember all the things he'd said to me. The pain and anger overwhelmed everything.

"Jasinda?" Jace's quiet voice brought me back to the present.

Damn, I wished I had more wine.

I sighed. "No, I didn't ask. I didn't care to know the reason."

His eyes searched my face, stopping at my lips, before drifting back up to my eyes. "What if he followed…a certain way of life and was afraid to tell you?"

I frowned and he continued.

"There are all kinds of… customs in the world that could explain things," he said. "I mean, some families give their daughters away to the men they choose, as is done in arranged marriages. Some treat marriage like a business transaction, or a merging of families for mutual benefits. Other families teach the males to take more than one wife and make it work."

Yeah, I knew those situations did exist. But normally those beliefs were mentioned early in a relationship.

"What *are* you getting at?"

He smiled at me, then looked at my lips again. "What I'm saying is, what if Elier has a tradition that he follows? One that he was afraid to tell you about. Perhaps he thought you were the *one* but was terrified that you wouldn't accept his traditions? Wouldn't accept *him*. So, he tried to keep it a secret and it backfired on him."

I didn't care. If Elier had thought I was *the one* or had cared enough about me, then he would've been honest with me. And told me everything to see if I could handle it.

"Ok, what *if* what you're saying is true? Why not say something, and see if I could handle his traditions?" I rambled on. "He said he loved me, but not enough to tell me about his culture. It's worse finding out he'd lied from his *fiancée.*"

"Did Elier ever tell you that you two were exclusive?"

"Uh… I mean…well, no," I stuttered. "But who wouldn't be exclusive after dating for *four* years? And he would *certainly* not have been accepting of me two-timing." *What the hell?*

"Some guys need to shop around looking for their mate, I mean *match*. So, they try out several serious relationships at once to see if any of them happen to be the *one*."

"That's absurd. You mean to tell me that he may have been seeing more women besides Miranda and me?"

"I'm not sure. I am trying to wrap my head around why he would keep her." He nodded towards Miranda. "And not you. It makes no sense to me."

Those words almost made me smile. "So, being a cheating scumbag is his dating tradition?"

Chapter Four

Jace

I didn't want to encourage her to forgive Elier or take him back. But I did want her wounded pride and heart to heal. Understanding was probably key to that. "Something like that."

Wow. She was beautiful *and* smart. I saw why Elier had fallen for her. He was a damn fool to let her go, though. She was special in a way I couldn't understand.

Yet.

It sparked my interest. The moment I'd heard her being sassy with Frank at the entrance, I knew there was something unique about her. The way her eyes sparkled when she smiled. How amazing she looked in that simple dress. Her scent was intoxicating...and familiar, though I couldn't place how.

Her nervousness added a tanginess to the air around me. When she'd first come over with Anthony, she'd been comfortable. But the moment he'd left, her nerves had fluttered, stirring the beast within me to reach out and calm her. I straightened in my seat, stunned that my beast had risen *now* of all times. I wanted to shift right here into my wolf form so I could lay my head on her lap. To let her know that I was here to soothe her.

Her eyes were avoiding mine as she pursed her beautiful lips. They were almost too perfect to kiss. They screamed for my attention, and I had the hardest time not staring at them. *Maybe a kiss would calm her nerves.* It had been years since the beast's voice echoed in my head. I was almost tempted to lean over and kiss her as he suggested, but thought it best to stay put. My beast grumbled but agreed I should be patient.

Good, wolf. Don't you move yet. You'll get your kiss soon enough.

He howled back in reluctant agreement.

Tearing my gaze from her lips, I caught her looking at me expectantly. *Shit, did she ask me something?* Her light brown eyes were filled with curiosity.

"It's fine if you don't want to answer," she said.

"I'm sorry, ask me again."

"How long has he been engaged?"

"I believe almost six years now."

Her face paled. *Fuck.* I probably just made it worse!

'Who cares? You'll eventually make it better,' the wolf answered.

"Wait," she gasped with a mixture of pain and anger in her voice, "you mean to tell me that they've been together for six years?" She sat back and folded her arms across her chest.

I sighed. "Actually, they've been together for seven years and engaged for six of them. But most of that time they've never been exclusive. Even though they were together, they weren't *only* together." She opened her mouth and then closed it. Her shoulders slumped in disappointment.

"You seem to understand a lot about them. Are you and Elier...friends? You knew all of that and I didn't. I didn't know him at all," she sighed, her lip trembling.

"Elier and I were close once," I said, trying not to sound too dry.

How did I explain the relationship that I had with him through our families?

She wouldn't understand that our packs were allies and had shared business interests. And she wouldn't comprehend that as much as I didn't want to have anything to do with him anymore, my position as alpha demanded I tolerate him. "We were always together when we were kids. But we've drifted apart for the past six years or so. We still talk but not like we used to." *Now we only talked when we had to.*

Her eyes fixated on me like she could see right through me. But she remained silent, so I continued, "I lost some of the trust I used to have in him. Now the only trust I have is with our business relationship and our families."

She tilted her head to the side a little. "Did he deceive you too?" Pain laced every word.

I liked how she asked me about it but didn't demand details. She respected my privacy, which only made me want her more. "Yes, he did."

"Did you forgive him?" she asked.

The ass was lucky I hadn't ripped his heart out after his betrayal when he slept with Priscilla, my ex. "Yes, I forgave him. Even if it was against my better judgment. I knew we still had to work together and be civil when our families gathered."

She raised her eyebrows. "Are you two related?"

If Elier had been blood, the betrayal would have been worse. Initially, I couldn't stand to be in the same room with him.

He shook his head. "No. Not by blood anyway. Our families have just been close for a very long time."

"So, you do know him better than I do." She pointedly accused.

I nodded and watched the jolt in her stare.

She brought her head a little closer and whispered, "Do you understand why I can't sit next to him?"

Pain so bright and palpable, came off of her in waves. Even a foot away from her, the air was thick and heavy with Elier's betrayal. She missed him, but not in the way that meant she wanted him back. It felt more like the mourning of a friendship. It was bizarre to be in tune with her. My senses were on fire.

"I understand, but eventually you'll have to decide if you're willing to forgive him," I said, hoping she understood that facing him sooner rather than later would be better.

She folded her hands on the table. "Yeah, I know. I guess I wanted him to suffer a little. But now, I don't know how to face him. I'm afraid to."

Slowly, she turned her head in Elier's direction. Surprisingly, or maybe not so, he seemed to be watching her too. Jasinda looked away quickly, turning back to me. *There was something else she wasn't telling me. Or maybe not telling him?* I felt a tremor of loss. Sadness. A tentative smile curled her lips as she drummed her nails against the tabletop.

"Being afraid is a good thing. It shows how much you care about a person. You're still wary enough to protect yourself," I said, trying to see where her head was.

She laughed. "I'll always care and want nothing but the best for Elier, but that's all I feel right now."

Well, that settled it. She was mine for the taking, and I would take her for myself.

Chapter Five

Jasinda

"Let's go for a walk and get some fresh air. Maybe some more wine." He stood and held out his hand.

"That would be great," I whispered and slid my hand into his.

Warmth flowed through me at this touch. I closed my eyes and felt it travel the length of my entire body. It was strange but comforting. So much so, that my body went slack. Jace gripped my elbow and pulled me against him, steadying me. A sound, almost like a growl, rumbled through me. Startled, I pulled, certain that I was going to find an agitated animal somewhere in the room. Jace hadn't seem to hear it, still holding me in his arms.

His eyes shone, almost unnaturally, as he stared at me intently. I gasped softly and tried to stand up straighter, but couldn't. He slid away a bit, giving me some space, but dropped his hand to the small of my back as he led me towards the back balcony.

Once outside, I inhaled deeply in an effort to clear my head. I felt like I was coming down from a high. Like being tipsy and having it fade quickly. When I felt more like myself, I chanced a look at him. There was a question in his eyes.

"Are you ok?" he asked, concern etched wildly in his voice.

I nodded.

"Want to tell me what happened back there?" he prodded.

"I...I just felt a little lightheaded that's all," I managed, surprised at my raspy voice.

He smirked a knowing look at me. "Are you sick?"

"No, more lightheaded than anything. Do you think you can get me some water?"

"Sure."

With his warm hand settled at the small of my back, he guided me towards the tables. He encouraged me to sit before walking away. As soon as his touch left me, I started to tremble uncontrollably. *What the hell was happening to me?*

I stood, then quickly sat back down, because my legs felt weak and wobbly. It didn't make any sense. Cramps hit my lower abdomen and sides, causing me to double over. I'd been stressed since my breakup with Elier. Maybe seeing him tonight had triggered this.

Closing my eyes, I took a few short breaths—inhaling through my nose and exhaling out of my mouth. On my last big exhalation, the feeling went away. Just like that, I felt nothing.

My period. That had to be it. It was about a week and a half away. That could explain the cramps. It was the only explanation. Tears stung my eyes at the reminder of what I'd lost. Of what could have been a life in my arms right about now. A life that I was excited about, until it became more pain than anything I've imagined. I rapidly blinked them away. This was not the place to have a break down. The double doors swung open, and Jace reappeared. Our eyes met, and warmth filled me from the inside. *Weird.*

"Drink," he whispered, handing me the water.

I took a quick sip to test the water. It was room temperature, but it'd have to do. I immediately gulped it down.

"Thank you," I said, once the glass was empty.

His thumb slid down the corner of my lip, wiping away the droplets of water that I was too sated to wipe myself.

He smiled an uneasy smile. "Would you like for me to take you home?"

Oh, you can take me home and have your way with me. I'll submit, quickly.

"No," the word rushed out. My thoughts surprised and unnerved me. "I feel much better now. I think coming out here helped, thank you. Besides, I'm enjoying the fresh air."

Jace stood near the edge of the balcony, staring off into the waterfall. After a few moments he turned and smiled at me like he had some secret that I didn't know about. His intoxicating stare left me in a daze.

"Jasinda?"

"Hmmm."

"Are you up for taking a walk through the waterfall?"

I stood sluggishly, and he grabbed my elbow to help. "What do you mean walk through the waterfall?"

Jace led me to the ledge by my elbow and settled closely behind me. His breath tickled my neck. I shivered and took in a slow steady breath, as he gently put one hand on my hip and the other on my shoulder to turn me slightly to the left.

"Do you see each side of the waterfall?"

"Yes," I muttered and was taken aback by the outstanding view of it.

Tall rocks that reached over 8ft tall were covered by a flow of glistening water that softly splashed into a pool surrounded by more rocks. Stems of Dahlia's peaked out from the rocks, bringing life to them.

"If you look closely, you'll see an entrance on either side. It allows you to walk through a small path leading to the other side."

I squinted my eyes and leaned forward to get a better view. He was right. There was an entrance on both sides. Vines served as an outline of some sort, marking a difference in that area. I turned back towards him slightly with an excited grin. He was so close, too close. But I didn't care. He smirked and entwined our hands as we walked towards the entrance.

"How do you know Anthony?" he asked.

"I met him at a party, and we hit it off. Friendship at first sight."

"He does like a good party."

"Yeah, he does. I usually have to drag him out by his legs."

He squeezed my arm gently and pulled me a little closer. "He's very protective of you. He's never approached me the way he did tonight. I thought you were his girlfriend."

"Ha! We could never be lovers. It would be incest. We're practically like siblings."

"Good to know," he said, as a smirk appeared on his face.

"Why?" I asked.

"Because, I'd like to take you out on a date."

Heat touched my cheeks. I was surprised at the shift in conversation. An internal squeal sounded in my mind. He wanted to take me out. It had been months since Elier and I had broken up.

Was I ready for this?

Yes, it felt good to be wanted. "A date sounds great. But how do you know I'm not some crazy, psycho serial killer?"

He laughed. "And how do you know I'm not some psycho killer who's obsessed with beautiful women and wants to cut them up into little pieces?"

"Well, I'll be damned. A man after my own heart. Literally," I teased.

We laughed as we walked through the entrance of the waterfall. I couldn't believe that this rock had a cave carved into it. Glistening water trickled from all the rock walls inside. Rails on both sides provided a safety barrier between the walkway and the edge of the pond.

"Look down," he breathed right into my ear.

I glanced down and gasped. The entire walkway was glass. "Holy waters! This is incredible."

Jace squeezed my hand gently. I'd forgotten that our hands were still entwined. "Keep walking but continue looking down."

He let go of my hand, and I continued along the path. Along with each step the water beneath me rippled, exposing shiny objects like seashells, emeralds, rocks, and pearls. The precious stones appeared and disappeared after a few seconds.

"Who designed all this?" I waved my hands to gesture towards all of it.

Jace observed me from a short distance with his hands in his pockets. "A very good landscaper. He managed to recreate the rainforest theme that I wanted, without the animals." He winked at me still grinning and continued, "I wanted it to be magical and very captivating. It took six months to get it right, but he did."

"You were the mastermind behind all this?" I was surprised that it was too magical.

His smile wavered a little. "Yes, Jasinda, I..." He paused and chuckled to himself. "I own this place. Almost all events are done here, because of the backfield. People love the beauty of it, just like I do. This used to be a private school. When it went up for sale I got this idea to buy it, remodel it, and rent it out for special events like this."

Not only was he good looking, but he was generous in ways that mattered. This was good. Impressive, even. "Does everyone know about this?"

Jace drew in close to me. "Only family and special individuals get a private tour. I usually don't let others enter without someone accompanying them."

The man was close enough that if I leaned in just a little bit, our mouths would touch. I wanted that in the worst way. To feel his lips against mine. To feel his body pressed against me.

Like I'd telegraphed my thoughts, Jace leaned in and kissed me. It was very delicate at first, until I felt a small spark— a tiny shock of static electricity in my mouth — then he rushed in. His tongue overran me in blissful waves. My arms slid around his neck. His hand gripped my waist, pressing me against him. His other hand settled between my neck and earlobe, softly caressing me.

I was willing to let him take me here. I couldn't ever remember being this lost in my emotions that I didn't care I'd only known him for all of about an hour or two.

Breaking the kiss, he stepped back slowly, causing displeasure to surface within me.

"We should get back before Anthony thinks the worst of me," he said.

Smiling, he took my hand and looped it in the crook of his elbow to escort me back to the hall. The displeasure left me, remembering that we were at an event and that he was right. We should get back before Anthony thought the worst of me, not him.

This was exciting, but *so* unlike me. Angie would be proud. She always lived in the moment, and tonight I'd done that myself. I hadn't let Elier kiss me on our first date. Not even a peck. Not until the fourth date did we kiss, and Angie was the one going crazy about it.

As we walked out the other side, an angry-faced woman, dressed for the gala stormed our way.

"Jace, what the hell?" she hissed.

She turned her enraged eyes at me. *Really? What did I do?* Jace stopped, tightening his grip on my hand. It was as if he was warning me to stay calm.

"Priscilla," he said it so coldly that I had to look at him.

The tenderness of his face had transformed into a menacing look, eyes filled with a scathing look. I was grateful it wasn't directed at me.

"Who is she and why is she even here?" she asked with authority in her voice.

"She's none of *your* concern. Maybe you need to go back to the party. Don't you have a date to entertain?" he said in a firm tone.

Her mouth dropped open, but she quickly closed it. "She's not one of us. I don't understand—"

"Another word and I'll ban you altogether," he said, effectively cutting her off.

We both flinched at the harshness of his words. She looked back at me and stormed off.

"Girlfriend?" I cautiously asked him, slighting putting distance between us without letting go of his hand. I couldn't handle any more secret girlfriends scurrying out of the woodwork. Especially after kissing him.

"Nope. She's the ex that I can't seem to shake off," he retorted.

Chapter Six

Jace

I didn't expect my night to turn out this way. When Anthony brought her to me, I was already smitten from earlier. Priscilla's timing, as always, was awful. No matter how many times I told her that I wasn't interested, she kept trying. "Sorry about that. She can be a little too dramatic at times, and it was rude of her to disturb us."

"It's all good. She's not my problem." She winked at me.

"You should consider yourself lucky." I winked back.

"Trust me, I *am* lucky. After that, I think I should give you all of my luck for the future." She laughed softly and winked again.

The winking game. I liked it. It was sexy when she did it. I was cheesing like a kid as we walked. I was both confused and amazed that she wasn't giving me hell about Priscilla. Most females were quick to judge and assume. She'd handled it better than I expected.

It made me want her even more.

We were rounding the corner to go up the steps when I felt his presence. Heat radiated from him and he wasn't even visible yet. Once we hit the last step and turned the corner, Elier Sky stood there, anger raging in his eyes.

She tensed at my side.

"Elier," I said.

"Jace," he returned flatly.

We glared at each other before he finally decided to speak, "I need to talk to Jasinda, will you excuse us, please?"

Strain was evident in his voice.

Jasinda's body went rigid, tension flowing off of her. She took a deep breath and shook her head.

"Can this wait another day, Elier?" Annoyance tinged her tone, which pleased me.

He scowled at me, "No, it can't. You've avoided me long enough, and it's time we talked."

He was firm, but hopeful at the same time. She sighed, then looked over at me, placing her hand on my forearm and gently squeezing it. "Do you mind giving us three minutes?"

This woman was something. I laughed inside. She was only giving him three minutes of her time, yet she didn't look pissed. But I sensed how uncomfortable, angry and hurt she was right now.

I tilted my head towards the bar and said, "Sure, I'll be at the bar over in the far corner."

"If you don't mind could you get me a drink while you're there?"

"Wine?" I replied.

"No, I'd like a pineapple juice with Pirate Bay, please."

I nodded and began to walk off as she spoke again, "That should be enough time."

I looked back at her and smiled, then continued to the bar. I ordered a drink for myself first just to give her time. Plus, I wanted to listen in on what he had to say.

"What do you want, Elier?" she snapped.

Elier visibly tamped down the impatience and anger that bubbled up.

"Why didn't you sit next to me tonight? Anthony told me he would arrange for us to sit together, instead you're sitting with Jace."

Wrong thing to say, bud. That only pissed her off more than she already was. It was amazing that I could sense her anger from here. So easy to read.

"Is Jace engaged? Or no, let me guess, he's already married? Is that why you want to talk? Are you here to warn me about what a lying, sniveling, cheating bastard he is?"

Elier closed his eyes and inhaled. With my sensitive hearing, I heard his teeth grinding.

"No, nothing like that. I just wanted us to talk. I hate that *this* is *us* right now. You have to know how much you mean to me."

Quickly, I ordered her drink, hoping the three minutes were almost up. Her pain and anger were thick in the air.

"There is no us! If I'd truly meant something to you, then why weren't you honest about your fiancée?"

Clutching her drink, I strode over. Elier was still searching for an answer when I joined them. Jasinda turned towards me and smiled as I handed her the drink.

"Thank you." Then she looked back at Elier. "I don't want to talk anymore, especially not right now."

"You never gave me a chance to explain."

She looked over at me and grabbed my hand. The sensation had me wanting to wrap my arms around her body pulling her tightly against me. She began walking, tugging me along, as she spoke over her shoulder, "No explanation needed now. I don't want it."

She was a tough one, and he was royally pissed off.

"Enjoy the rest of the evening, Elier," I said.

And with that, we made our way back into the hall.

We settled back at our table finding the auction already underway. It looked like it was almost over, which was when I'd normally give my donation or take part in the bidding. I hadn't decided which to do yet, because she'd completely thrown my night off the moment Anthony sat her at my table. I'd *never* taken a woman inside the waterfall. There'd been women in the group tours I'd given before. But never in private one like tonight.

My actions shocked the shit out of me. Knowing it was the secret entrance to my world, I guarded it fiercely. In my world, I didn't have to hide who I was or be careful around humans. Honestly, it was a world I hoped she could enter one day and not be afraid. Though, I felt a little lost regarding her. She seemed human, but I wondered if she could be one of us. A half-breed maybe?

"Are you OK?" I managed to ask, trying to rid myself of these thoughts.

"Yes, I'm sorry about Elier."

"Don't be. You handled him well. It seems as though you have some unfinished business with one another."

"It seems so, but I just don't know how I'll finish it," she said, sounding conflicted

"What do you mean?" I urged her on.

"Well, I don't know how to tell him--"

"Jasinda, I need a huge favor," Anthony rushed over, cutting her off. "I mean 'enchiladas every other weekend for two months' kind of favor."

She laughed. Laughter filled her eyes in an exotic way. She covered her mouth with her hands to stifle the melodious sound, even though it was already loud in here.

"What's up?" she asked trying to be serious.

"Can I auction *you* tonight?" he asked.

She stopped smiling and looked at him. "What?"

"Correction, I meant can you model for some really expensive jewelry up for auction? You'd be perfect, and there are plenty of men here who'd drop a few grand just because you're the model."

She remained quiet as I sat here hoping she'd say yes. Because if she said yes, I was going to be the highest bidder tonight.

"I...I... I can't. I can't be responsible for some expensive jewelry," her whisper was low as if she didn't want me to hear. But I heard it all loud and clear—her words, her stuttered breathing, her heartbeat pounding in her chest like an enraged gorilla.

"Please, Jasinda. I really need this. I've never come close to raising this kind of money for a charity." He pleaded.

It seemed she was a sucker for that puppy dog look. I felt her emotions shift from irritation to sympathy. He went in for the kill, "Don't forget, it's both our names on this event as the planners. If they see you involved, then they'll know you have my back and support teaming up with them."

"I hate you right now," she muttered.

"I knew I could count on you. I'll make it up to you, I promise."

She pointed her finger at him and scolded, "Oh, you better make it up to me. I want the works."

He gave her a weak smile, but shook his head and put his hand out. She grabbed it and looked over at me.

"Excuse me, while I go lend myself to modeling expensive jewels." She nodded toward Anthony and walked off.

I smiled. The woman was a goof. Different from everyone else I'd ever dated, and I was finding that I liked that. Jasinda modeling the jewels tonight was the perfect ending to the auction. Normally I didn't stay to the very end. I liked to make an appearance, donate and leave before the dance floor got too crowded. These things usually bored me to tears, but Jasinda had kept me entertained tonight. As I watched her sashay behind the curtains, Anthony took the stage.

A few moments later, she joined him on stage. The men cheered and whistled, as she stood there smiling, and blushing. Anthony grabbed her hand and walked closer to the edge of the stage.

Hmmm.

She was shy in front of a crowd. A complete contrast to the sexy, eager woman who'd kissed me beneath the waterfall.

Heat burned behind me. Without looking, I knew it was Elier. He pulled out the chair Jasinda had been sitting in, but I stopped him. No way in hell was I going to let his scent mix in with hers. He moved quickly to the opposite side of me.

"What do you want, Elier?" I slowly turned to face him.

"Jasinda," he bit back. His eyes glowed like a fluorescent light.

"Can't claim her if she's made it clear that she doesn't want you."

"She's different Jace. *Very* different than what you're used to."

We stared at one another while Anthony continued to talk in the background. I was missing the auction, but this was important. Elier was hiding something.

"I know," I whispered, hoping he'd spill something more about her.

"You *don't* know, Jace. Which is why I *need* to be with her. I have to be around her even if she doesn't want me." Fear rolled off of him. Fear that spread through me, causing my hairs to spike up.

"What am I missing, Elier?" I asked as the crowd went wild. I looked over my shoulder toward the stage.

Everyone cheered and clapped as Anthony let go of Jasinda's hand and took a few steps back, leaving her in the spotlight. Having not been focused during my argument with Elier a few thoughts of the men around me filtered in my mind.

'I'd like to make her mine forever, one thought wistfully.

… date her,' another hoped.

'Wasn't Elier with her? Why the hell did he leave that?' I shared his opinion on the stupidity.

'If she was one of us, I'd fuck her on stage right now.'

A growl simmered in my mind at the vulgar suggestion.

Most of the men here wanted her, but they weren't going to get her. She was mine. I waved Trent over and gave him a number to bid on the jewels that glittered against her skin. Then I turned back to Elier.

"Talk," I demanded.

"She's special. *Very* special, and I love her."

"I already know all this," I said flatly.

"It's complicated, Jace. Hard to explain and more that I'm not able to tell."

I raised an eyebrow at him, now wanting to know more.

"Jace, I don't know how to explain this without saying things I'm bound by blood *not* to say." His voice was laced with pain as he continued, "I'd tell you everything if I could. *All* of it."

The truth of his words poured off him.

"Then show me instead," I suggested.

"It won't work. That's how strong this secret is. No one can know. Only *she* can uncover it."

What the fuck was he talking about?

"For the crown to be given, the piece must stay hidden. Until time is a given, the crown is long living."

"A fuckin' riddle, Elier?"

"That's all I can say. All I'm able to say."

"A hundred grand, huh?" Anthony said from beside me, interrupting us. "You just made my career, boss."

He shook my hand as Elier stood, virtually swelling with anger. I glared at Elier, a silent warning for him to back off. He hesitated for a fraction of a second, then walked away.

"Now the rules," Anthony chimed with glee.

I gave him a look of incredulity. "I don't need any rules, Anthony. It's just jewelry."

"Well, since you bid that much on the jewels, you get to take her home with you."

I blinked in confusion. "What?"

"She'll be going home with you, so you can put the jewels in your private safe. Which also means you owe her dinner." He tilted his head towards the stage. "I told her that it'd be your treat as a thank you for helping me. You know, wine and dine her for me as a favor, which brings me to my *one* rule."

I raised a questionable eyebrow at him but nodded for him to continue.

"Show her a fuckin' good time. I don't care what it is. Just make sure she enjoys it. She'll seem a little closed off at first. But once she opens up, you'll never want to let her go." He walked off without another word.

Lupkin was our realm, and Borru the name of our pack. I knew almost everyone in it. I'd always liked Anthony. Sometimes I didn't understand his ways, but they always made sense in the end. We'd spoken about personal matters before and of people outside the Borru, but never about anyone close to him. Tonight was the first time he'd ever brought someone from the outside into our circle. A human. I'd known that he had a close relationship with *someone* and I'd assumed he was courting her. But now I knew he'd been protecting her the whole time from people like *us*. People like me. He cared for her like she was his little sister. His protective scent was all over her.

Jasinda's tinkling laughter pulled me out of my thoughts. I searched the crowd until I spotted her salsa dancing with Anthony. He was showing her off. She looked so fuckin' good on the dance floor, moving with rhythm and raw sensuality. Watching her hips move was making me hard. The other men around were just as aroused.

Anthony turned her then, pointing her face in my direction. She looked at me and almost lost her step but recovered herself instantly. Her smile stayed on her face, but something flashed in her eyes. Nervousness. Excitement.

'*Go,*' my beast roared inside me, demanding that I go to her and pull her into my arms. I had to close my eyes and concentrate on holding the beast back. In all my life, my inner beast had never been risen by anyone other than me. But now, I could hardly hold him in check at the thought of having her.

I was still fighting him when shouts and screams echoed in the hall. *What the fuck?*

Chapter Seven

Jasinda

"**E**veryone, hands where I can see them. Nobody moves and nobody gets hurt," a voice shouted.

Panic struck me.

I tried to see what was happening, but Anthony shielded me as he looked towards the commotion. I was shell-shocked and couldn't move to save my life.

"I'm looking for Jasinda Santana. I know she's here," the familiar voice said.

Slowly, I looked over and saw Darrell. His gun was drawn and he was coming toward me. Dayne and Devon were on either side of him.

Why were they crashing the event looking for me?

They'd always been a bit overprotective, even when we were kids, but this went far beyond their normal macho protectiveness. Now that they worked for my dad, though, it had been dialed up a notch.

"What's going on?" my shaken voice drifted from behind Anthony's protective stance.

Dayne look directly at me and relief filled his eyes.

What were they doing? I thought they were on duty tonight.

They were in their Mystic Force Agency uniforms, looking like a swat team, except in black and green. As members of that government task force it was their job to deal with the supernatural cases. The MFA was technically above the law. Dayne was the leader of the three-man team, who all happened to be brothers and my childhood playmates. But I couldn't understand why they were *here*. An upscale charity event was hardly a hotbed of supernatural activity. It had to be some sort of mix-up. Or they were screwing with me.

"Too much to explain here. We need to go," Dayne responded.

I fought the urge to ask more questions. Dad had drilled proper protocol into me since I was little. I could hear him in my head now.

'One, when a member of MFA tells you something, don't ask questions. Two, follow the MFA to somewhere safe. Three, understand the alert codes to assess the danger.'

He was always cautious and worried that his enemies might target his family.

The brothers kept looking around as if they expected something to pop out and grab them. I was so confused.

"You couldn't just *call* her? You had to barge in here, waving your guns around and get everyone all spooked?" Anthony bit out.

Oh damn, he was pissed.

All three brothers peered at him and then at me. A look passed over their faces, and I knew they were trying to figure out what to tell him.

Dayne stepped forward looking directly at him with menace in his eyes. "Anthony, when it comes to *her*, we'll tear this whole place down just to keep her safe. Right now, she's in serious danger. Do us the damn favor and get out of the way so we can get her out of here."

All right, this was serious. When I stepped from behind Anthony, Dayne relaxed a little.

"How bad Dayne?" I asked.

"Code SD RED," he said softly.

I gasped as I recognized the threat level associated with the code. Never did I ever imagine that I'd be a part it, since I don't know anything about the supernatural.

This was supernatural related and apparently, I was in danger from it. I'd never had any encounters with the supernatural. Or maybe I had and just hadn't known it. The world teemed with magic and was filled with supernatural species. I could feel it. But for some reason I'd never met any. I probably wouldn't even know what one looked like. I truly had no clue about things of that nature, so how could I possibly be in danger? It had to be related to Dad, not me. I'd just have to follow protocol and feed into their belief that there are supernatural beings out there. We all believe in the impossible, don't we? I'm starting to.

A memory crept into place. One of an older woman talking to a little girl about unicorns. The faces were blurred; I was not able to recognize them.

"Are they real?" The little girl asked excitedly.

"Of course! They stay away from prying eyes to keep their magic preserved and to stay safe," the older woman told her.

"But have you seen one before?" the little girl continued.

"No. But they are only seen by those who do not seek to do them harm. It is rare that they come around anyone outside of their own kind. It's how they keep themselves alive."

"Tell me more? Please, grandmother." The little girl squealed.

"Where are you taking her?" Anthony chimed in, bringing me back from the memory.

"A safe house. Somewhere no one can find her," Dayne said.

Anthony looked at me and then back at Dayne. He studied him and his brothers for a long minute and finally spoke, "Then I'm going with her."

"Yeah, that's *not* happening, bro," Darrell emphasized.

Anthony growled beside me, really growled like some enraged dog.

"Not here, Anthony. This isn't happening here," Darrell stated calmer than before.

"What isn't happening here?" I interrupted, looking between them while I waited for an answer. But they kept staring at one another as if I was nonexistent. "Um…remember me? Hey, I'm right here," I said as I waved my hands and wiggled my body a little. The move helped defuse the situation, depleting Anthony's anger as he gave me a handsome smirk.

The Mitchell brothers on the other hand still had that stoic look going on. So, I gave in with a sigh. "All right, I'll go with. Your seriousness is starting to kill the mood anyway. Let me go get my clutch."

As I walked away, a jolt coursed through my body, causing my step to falter. Continuing towards my table, the jolt zapped me again, stopping me dead in my tracks. I'd felt the jolt before, months ago right before I'd been attacked. Slowly, I turned around toward the brothers.

"What is it?" Dayne's concerned voice cut through the haze I was getting lost in.

"I...I..." But I couldn't speak. I didn't even know how to explain it.

Dayne closed the distance between us. He looked at me and gave me a nod, urging me to speak.

"I felt something. I felt some sort of jolt. Like static or something," I managed to say with a frown.

"It's time to leave," he said firmly.

I looked over at Anthony and gave him a small smile. "I'll call you later. Right now, I need to go with them." I didn't give him a chance to respond as I turned away with the brothers beside me.

"Promise?" Anthony's agonizing voice cut through me.

I couldn't help but smile as I spoke over my shoulder, "Promise," and continued on my way.

A strong hand wrapped around my elbow, halting me in place. Turning my head, I faced Dayne. "Dayne, what the—" A deep growl cut me off.

Slowly, I turned toward the sound, and my soul nearly leapt from my body. I gasped at the four beast-like creatures, towering over as they growled. Saliva dripped from bared teeth and they had sharp claws at the end of their hands.

The color leached from my face as I stood paralyzed by fear.

"What are they?" I finally asked.

"They're Dracolupus. A mix between a dragon and a wolf. Magical creatures that can be either evil or good. They're the third strongest creatures, next to dragons and wolves. Most are good, because they're used as protectors," Darrell explained. "Now, slowly move back, princess. No sudden movements. Nice and slow." I looked around to see fear etched on some of the guests that were visible to me. "This is why we are here." Dayne gritted out. "This is the danger we were sensing."

I did as he commanded. As I took my first step backwards, the creatures growled in unison, and I froze. *Shit.*

I didn't want these things furious with me, or anyone else for that matter. *Hell no, no way!*

"Guys…I think moving even a fraction of a step is going to make things escalate with them. So, let's just figure out a plan. Who wants to get eaten first?" I said.

"Now isn't the time for jokes, Jasinda," Devon scolded.

Usually, he was the quiet, calm one and just followed orders. But today his usually stoic face was tense with fear. "These creatures are ruthless, and they can kill just about anything and anyone. They're difficult to fight."

"Then what do you want to do?" I asked through gritted teeth.

"Just stay calm and still," Devon requested.

"Easier said than done," Dayne muttered.

"I agree, but did any of you *really* looked at them?" Darrell asked. "They're not growling at *her*, they're growling at *us*. Their eyes are focused on the three of us." Curiosity got the better of me, so I looked back at the creatures and noticed that Darrell was right. I *wasn't* a focal point for them.

"And that means what guys?" No one said anything. "Hello…an explanation would be helpful."

"It means that they're not here to hurt you, but rather to hurt anyone else who might get too close to you. It's almost like someone sent them to keep you here in the open and not out of sight like we want you to be," Devon reasoned in a tone that hinted at him knowing something that I wasn't allowed to.

"Huh?" I said.

The brothers exchanged looks.

"Is anyone going to tell me what the hell is happening?" I couldn't contain my frustration any longer.

The growls rumbled through the air in front of us again as one of the creatures took a step forward.

Dayne moved closer, shielding me. Darrell had said the creatures didn't seem to want to hurt me. So, maybe if I shielded them instead, the creatures wouldn't attack at all.

Before I could test my theory, the creatures leaped towards Dayne.

I threw myself in front of him without even thinking, using my forearm to protect my face. "Jasinda, no," Devon yelled.

"STOP!" I waited for the pain of teeth and claws, but nothing happened.

Slowly, I peeked over my forearm. All four beasts were seated before me. I didn't dare move or speak. They stared at me, as if waiting for another command.

Taking a few deep breaths, I pushed my heart back into its place and lowered my arm. Keeping my eyes on the creatures, I stepped back slowly, pushing Dayne with me.

"What just happened?" I murmured.

No one moved or said anything. Silence surrounded me like the Dead Sea. They were keeping something from me, and I wanted to know what. A loud whistle sounded, the notes forming some melody. To my surprise, the creatures formed a single-file line. My gaze darted around searching for the source of the whistle. My breath caught in my throat as Elier approached them. None of the creatures growled at him.

What in the hell?

"Does somebody want to tell me what the hell is going on?" I pointed my glare at Elier, but he remained stoic. "Seriously!? Nothing?" I threw my hands in the air about to throw a tantrum like a crazed teenager. "Ugh. This is unbelievable. How can you guys pretend that all of this is ok?"

They all passed looks among one another like a hot potato. Then, all the fine hairs on my entire body went rigid.

Chapter Eight

Jasinda

A blast of light flashed in the middle of the dance floor. Most people in my line of sight used their hands to keep the light from blinding them, but the light didn't bother me. I enjoyed the royal blue burst of light that shone with sparks like fireworks in the sky. Then a thump sounded and we were all thrown back.

At least, I *thought* I was being thrown back. My eyes flew open while in mid-air and I found myself being jerked forward. I hit the floor, but not as hard as I expected. Closing my eyes, I laid there a few seconds to orient myself.

What in the world just happened? Fear made me want to keep my eyes shut, but I had to see what was going on. After counting to ten, I stood with my eyes still closed. Afraid, I braced myself as I cracked my eyelids open and looked around.

Everyone stood pressed against the walls as if something was holding them in place. They were a blur from where I stood. I couldn't make out anyone in particular. Leaning down, I took off the one shoe that I still wore, while trying to figure out what the hell had just happened. This damn light was so bright that it left my vision blurry. After a few seconds of turning in place, I noticed a large figure in the middle. It was huge, at least seven feet tall and hefty like a linebacker. My eyes squinted in an effort to see what it was, but I couldn't.

I took a step closer not thinking or assessing the situation.

That's when his deep low voice filled the air, "Don't move."

I froze. Something in his voice sent a slight chill through me and then a calmness.

"Close your eyes and take a deep breath. Your vision should clear."

As odd as it sounded, I did as he told me. His voice calmed me. The sound of it scratched at something in my mind. After a few seconds, I opened my eyes to see him as a blur and then his features resolved.

My vision was back, but my sanity was gone. The figure before me was a dark brown wolf-dragon of some sort. A beast on steroids with pointy ears, like a wolf. His body was wolf-like, but he stood on two furry legs like a man. The claws on him were big, long and extremely sharp. His snout was big with sharp teeth and seemed to have a mix of wolf and dragon features. And the tail wasn't long like a dragon's, but it was scaled with tiny spikes along it.

He's not real. He's not real, was on repeat in my head.

Staying as calm as I could, I walked around him to analyze him. I was amazed at what I saw.

He looked a bit scary and I should've been scared. But the way he'd spoken to me made me relax, made me bold enough to explore him. So, I made a full circle around him.

"Holy waters," I blurted. "What the hell *are* you?"

He stared at me hard, making me doubt my boldness. I took a step back, and he took a step forward.

Uh oh. I'd said the wrong thing.

I wanted to run, but something inside told me that wasn't a good idea. So, I stayed.

He frowned at me in confusion. "I'm a wolf-lord. The lord of my people." I stared at him dumbfounded. What was I supposed to say to that? He gave me a questionable look and continued to speak, "This isn't funny, Jasinda."

Startled by my name coming out of his mouth, I had to ask, "How do you—"

He cut me off, "Focus, princess. I need to ask you something."

I was curious as always, and curiosity always seemed to get the best of me. Besides, he was someone I didn't want to piss off.

"Ask away," I said this and began to walk around him again.

"What are you doing?" he whispered with a confused look that almost had me laughing.

"Checking you out," I told him bluntly.

He tilted his head to the side. "Checking me *out*? Is this a game, Jasinda, because I do not have the patience for this."

I didn't answer, because I had no idea why he'd think it was a game.

"Where's your mother?"

Well, that was the million-dollar question. "Your guess is probably better than mine. Why are you asking me about my mother?"

I should've been scared out of my mind with the way he glared at me.

"Jasinda, enough with the games. I need to speak with your mother."

The sarcasm took root and I couldn't stop it. "*Really?* So, do I."

The tips of his claws started to glow. He closed his eyes and sniffed the air.

Not the reaction I was expecting.

Everyone was still pressed against the walls, but I didn't see Anthony, Elier, or Jace. The creatures were out of sight too. What I did see were the three brothers, my childhood protectors. There angry glares aimed at the wolf-lord before me. I gasped as I noticed that where their hands should've been were claws too.

Darrell's features had been transformed by a snarl with his canines over his lips. He caught my glance and then looked away as if ashamed.

I took a few steps toward them but stopped when the wolf-lord spoke.

"You don't remember?" He scoffed in disbelief. "I guess her magic is more powerful than I thought. I hoped you'd recognize me at the very least." He sounded hurt. "It seems I'm going to have to help you remember what was forgotten."

I turned towards the wolf-lord and paused mid-step.

"What? What are you talking about?" I asked in confusion.

A whip appeared in each hand, sparks of royal-blue flames dancing on it. Inwardly, I screamed to myself to run, fear becoming the focal point.

"Her magic is too powerful for me to reverse what she's done to you," he said.

Her magic? What in the world?

"I don't understand."

He took a step closer, but I stood my ground despite the urge to flee.

"You're afraid of me. I don't like that. You never were before."

"We've met before?"

He smiled, his gleaming sharp canine teeth showing. "We know each other."

"That's impossible. I'd remember."

Anger reached his eyes as he responded, "Four months ago, you were attacked. I am the one who rushed you to the hospital."

I teetered in place, my mind racing. *How did he know I'd been pregnant? I don't recall my rescuer being a beast.* Only Angie knew that. She'd only found out because I'd needed bedrest for a week after losing my baby. She'd told my father and anyone else who'd called that I'd come down with the flu and wasn't available.

"How do you know about that? Only one person knew, and I doubt she's told anyone," my voice trembled as I questioned him.

"I was there when you were attacked. I was the one who killed your attacker and carried you to the hospital. The smell of loss in your womb filled my nostrils, so I knew the child you carried would be stillborn."

I took a faltering step back, trying to stifle my tears. My mind drifted back to the worst day of my life…

"Hold on… Everything's going to be alright," a voice in the darkness said.

I fought to drag the memory forward.

I was walking to my car after work late one night. A man approached me, grabbing me by the arm.

"You should stay with your own kind," he growled in my face.

Shock froze me in place. Fighting back wasn't something I could even consider. Despite being pretty far into my second trimester, I had only known about my pregnancy for two weeks. In that moment my only thought was protecting my unborn son. "Take whatever you want, I—" He moved so fast, and I tried to shield myself, but his fist slammed into my belly. Pain* *exploded in my abdomen and the force of the hit knocked me into the car. Stars danced in front of my vision before I backed out.*

No matter how hard I plucked at the memory, all I remembered about my attacker was his smirk. The memory train trudged forward with halting jerks, giving me only flashes from that night.

The severe pain in my abdomen jolted me back to consciousness. The wetness. The fear. I could barely move. A sensation of being cradled to someone's chest. Then a voice. His voice. Telling me I'd be all right. Telling me to breathe. Telling me not to move.

"I don't remember much after the man…" I trailed off and decided not to tell him I remembered a voice that kept me calm until I was in the hospital. I thought it best to keep that out since I still didn't trust him. So, I whispered instead, "You rescued me that night and killed my attacker?"

"Yes, that was one of the worst days of my life." The raw pain in his voice was too clear.

"Mine too," I confessed, holding back the tears that threatened to spill over.

We stood there staring at one another until he finally took two steps closer.

His eyes bore into mine as he spoke, "If I told you that I knew the woman who sent that man after you *and* that you knew her, what would you say?"

My body tensed. Anger heated my face.

"I'd say show me who this low-life bitch is." I tried to sound confident, but part of me was nervous. A bigger part was furious that someone I knew would do this—that they would take an innocent child's life.

He took in a deep breath and exhaled. "She's here. Right in this very room."

The world spun, and I steadied myself as best as I could on bare feet. I only knew *one* woman here. One who I didn't *want* to know. Realization hit, along with a mixture of nausea and fury.

"Miranda," I whispered.

I bowed my head in defeat and closed my eyes as it all came together. When she showed up at my house telling me that I was Elier's play toy and that she needed him to focus on their wedding. That smile when she'd walked away from me after telling me about Elier and her. It was an evil smile. Now, I understood it all. She'd known I was pregnant. *How was that possible?*

"Yes," he said flatly.

Opening my eyes, I looked down at my bare feet. I didn't think I'd spoken loud enough for anyone to hear. I looked up at him, not hiding the falling tears.

"How do you know it was her?" I coughed, trying to clear the rasp in my voice.

Drawing in a deep breath, he began to pace in a circle like a predator waiting to pounce. "I know things. Things that I don't always want to know. Things that are hard to know. That's what my life is."

I scratched my head in wonder. *He knows things*? Not sure if I could handle that burden.

"I'm glad it's you who knows the things you do. For that, I'm truly sorry," I said sincerely.

He smiled a weak smile. "The ball is in your court now. What would you like to do, Jasinda?"

"Excuse me?"

"Miranda. What do you want to do about her?"

My eyes darted around looking for Miranda, but I wasn't able to find her through the crowd of people pressed against the walls and overturned tables. So many different emotions coursed through me that I couldn't speak.

"Would you like for me to bring her to you?" he asked.

Without thinking it through, I spoke, "Yes, please."

With a fast lash of his whip across the room, Miranda was flung into the air and dropped on her ass a few feet before me. The landing wasn't soft. It was a hard thump, eliciting a yelp of pain from her. If she had just been Elier's bitch-fiancé, I might have felt bad, but she wasn't. This woman had cost me my child, and I had no sympathy for her.

Chapter Nine

Jace

"No," Elier growled in a whisper

Like me, he was pressed against a wall, held there by a strong magic.

"Elier, what the hell is going on?"

"Sorry, Jace. I'm a little preoccupied trying to hold these Dracolupus back from attacking. I need to concentrate on my hold." He strained as he gripped the beasts by their collars.

"Attacking who?"

"Miranda. They want her blood, and I'm almost ready to give it to them."

Miranda yelled in pain, drawing my attention back to the center of the room.

I wasn't sure who I was angrier with, Miranda for harming Jasinda or Elier for creating the situation that led to it in the first place.

"Why the hell would you keep Miranda around after Jasinda was pregnant?" I growled in a low voice.

"I didn't know." The words came out strangled.

"You're a fucking shifter. You should've known."

"Well, I didn't. Not for sure anyway. A few times I sensed something different in Jasinda. But I couldn't figure out what. Then the night before Miranda outed me, Jasinda felt full of life in such a different way. I didn't understand until I asked my mother a few weeks later. Mom told me that I was sensing an unborn life. I tried to tell her that I thought she was pregnant, but she wouldn't give me the chance after Miranda."

"You put that psycho onto Jasinda's trail with your inability to commit."

"I never imagined Miranda would go so far as to hire someone to kill my unborn son."

"But she did," I squared my shoulders as much as I could in this damn hold, fists tightening at my sides in frustration at barely being able to move. "What are you going to do about it?"

"I will avenge my son's life. She'll get worse from me than she gets here."

I turned away from him. My disgust with Elier took a backseat to the overwhelming need to be with Jasinda.

Miranda writhed in agony in the middle of the floor. Torment danced across Jasinda's features, as if she wasn't sure if this is what she really wanted, but her anger was rising like a giant wave. A chorus of growls echoed, caught in their throats as the pack tried to unpin themselves from the wall. Especially the three brothers in uniform who had shown up before Jako's appearance.

"Why?" Jasinda asked.

Miranda said nothing as she tried to stand.

"WHY!?" Jasinda yelled.

Miranda flinched back. The first time I had ever seen her do so from a word.

She straightened herself and lifted her head, meeting Jasinda's glare. "You didn't deserve to have Elier's baby."

The venom in her voice made me clench my fists again.

"Is she fuckin' serious?" Elier asked in outrage. "I'm going to fuckin' enjoy killing her."

Jasinda stepped closer, her petite form shaking with rage. "And *you* do?"

That's it Jasinda. I was proud of the composure she was showing.

"That's my girl. You let her know she doesn't deserve to carry my child," Elier huffed out.

I snarled at his use of his girl. She isn't his anymore.

"You have *no* clue what you're in for," Miranda spat back.

Before I could ask Elier what Miranda was talking about, Jasinda balled her fists and spoke, "You have *no* right to speak to me about what I might be in for. I might not have understood before, but I'm beginning to understand more. But then again you *knew* that I didn't know about Elier's *dating traditions*."

"My dating traditions? How did she find out about that?" Elier muttered in an annoyed tone next to me.

I smirked.

"So, you sprung that *being engaged shit* on me to make sure he'd follow through with your wedding."

Whoa. Seeing this little spitfire putting that bitch in her place was such a turn on for me.

Jasinda continued, "That's probably what bothered you the most. Elier's interest in me. His four-year relationship with me. You knew that he'd probably call off your engagement once he found out I was pregnant."

The emotions pouring from her were so powerful that I was jolted back a little. Her agony was like hot coal over my skin. I wanted to cry and yell in anguish with her. Elier whimpered next to me. A glance around the room told me that everyone in attendance felt her suffering profoundly.

"I wasn't there for her. I wasn't there to protect her, or even console her in her grief," Elier whispered, distressed.

His shame was palpable. But I couldn't bring myself to feel sorry for him. I turned my attention back to where it belonged, my girl. My heart swelled at the thought.

She was silent and so was Miranda. They just stared at each other. Jasinda moved closer until they were a foot apart.

Jasinda pointed a trembling finger at Miranda. "You had *no* right to send someone after me. No right!" Miranda shivered from the menacing tone. "I *wish* that you could feel..." her voice broke, "all the pain that you caused me. I wish you could feel what losing a baby does to your body. I wish you could understand what losing my unborn son felt like."

'Let me out. I will rip Miranda's throat out. It's better than she deserves.' My beast begged for freedom from my ironclad control.

The misery pulsating from her was barely tolerable. The others around me were becoming uneasy and the longer they bathed in her pain, the more they too, wanted Miranda's death on their claws. All around me bodies trembled as they fought the change. A change that would not come due to the magic band that held us in place.

"I don't give a *shit* about your pain," Miranda replied coldly.

No heart. She had no heart whatsoever.

A smile played across Jasinda's lips as she spoke, "Have you ever been pregnant before?"

"No," a bare whisper was all Miranda could manage. An insecurity that hit home.

"So, how long have you been trying to get pregnant?" Jasinda asked.

Miranda stepped back as if physically wounded by the question. But Jasinda stepped forward, not letting her retreat.

Distress radiated from the both of them, agitating the overly perceptive senses of all the shifters in the room. Miranda's suffering was colored by want rather than need. She wanted to be like all the females surrounding her. Most of them had cubs and were mated. Her desire to be pregnant was for all the wrong reasons.

Jasinda stepped closer. Her balled up fists pounded her thighs, punctuating each word, "How long?!"

Miranda snapped her head up, surprise flashing in her eyes. I was surprised myself that Jasinda could roar with such a force.

"Too long," she answered weakly.

Miranda's annoyance and discomfort rolled towards me.

Elier moaned softly beside me. "I was so stupid to not pay attention to my inner wolf. He was telling me that she was pregnant and I just didn't listen."

If he had, she wouldn't be suffering so much. But then if he had listened, I wouldn't have a chance to make her mine.

It wasn't easy, feeling all these emotions, especially from the woman I yearned to claim.

"I was ready to leave Miranda months before. I'd planned a special date to make things permanent with Jasinda. That was the day Miranda confronted her." Elier confided as we both watched the ticking time bomb in the center of the room.

"You waited too long. You had four years with Jasinda to do right by her, and you didn't," I admonished.

"I know. But there are other things at play that you can't possibly understand. But I was ready to say fuck it to all those reasons. Then she called me to tell me she knew about Miranda. In that instant, my heart sank down into the pit of my stomach, and I haven't been able to put it back in place. I have so many regrets. All the lies and hurt I've caused Jasinda…" his voice trailed off as we both strained to hear the words rolling off Jasinda's lips.

Jasinda unfurled her fists and planted her hands on her hips. "Hmm. Then you really *don't* understand what you did to me, do you?"

She sounded like the smart-ass Jasinda that caught my eye when she'd first arrived, and I watched Jako smirk at her response. But I still sensed the rage concealed inside her.

Miranda started to speak, but Jasinda beat her to it, "Let me *tell* you all the ways you hurt me."

Fuck. It was killing me to hear her this way.

"You ordered the attack that made me to go into early labor with injuries and stress that then caused me to give birth" her voice cracked before she soldiered on, "to my dead son."

Jasinda took another step closer. They were now nose-to-nose. "Do you know what I had to do next, after giving birth to my *dead* son?"

Miranda cast her eyes towards the ceiling.

"Do you?" Jasinda screamed in her face. Miranda flinched but held herself in place.

When Miranda didn't respond, Jasinda enlightened us all further to the horrific ordeal she'd endured alone, "I had to name my son so that the hospital could produce a *death* certificate. A fucking death certificate instead of a birth certificate. All because you are a selfish, hateful bitch. You already had Elier. You didn't have to take my son away too."

Her anger roared through me, through us all. So much fury pulsed throughout the room that it was nearly visible. Everyone was looking at Elier, but his eyes were glued to Miranda. She wasn't looking at him though. Her guilt wafted off her, tainting the air. I glanced over at Jasinda.

She was looking at Elier with shock, not fear. Her eyes met mine briefly before returning to Elier's. That quick glance was enough for me to detect the red in them. All the tears that she'd been holding back, escaped one by one. The ache, the rage, and the anger all showed on her face. All my protective senses strained to rip through the fucking magic shield that was holding us all back.

Her eyes stayed locked on Elier's for what seemed like a lifetime. The tears were painful to watch as they tracked down her beautiful face, and I wanted to wipe them all away. I longed to take her away from here. Away from all the people here who had hurt her, and *never* bring her anywhere near these people again.

She opened her mouth and whispered to Elier, "I'm so sorry. I'm so sorry that I didn't tell you before. And then I didn't know how to after he died."

I hated being witness to what should have been a private conversation.

Then she turned back to Miranda and punched her right in the jaw. *Knockout!* At least it should have been one, but still...*Unbelievable.* Wolves weren't knocked out so easily. Miranda staggered back a few feet, her hand to her jaw in surprise at what had just happened. In that moment, Miranda's eyes glowed so brightly that I knew she was about to shift.

Fuck me. These damn magical shields were powerful.

Another blast of light jolted between Jasinda and Miranda, pushing them back a few feet from one another and making them land on their asses. Jasinda looked scared as Jako came into view. He transformed his paws into human hands and held one out to Jasinda. When she took it, he pulled her up to her feet, leaving Miranda to get up on her own.

He looked back to Miranda with death in his eyes. "If you even think of laying one hand or paw on her, I'll end your life right here, right now."

This beast was my kind of people. He knew how to handle someone like Miranda. I watched him look back at Jasinda, whose hand he still held.

His eyes glowed as he spoke, "Do you *truly* want Miranda to know what you went through with your loss?"

"Yes, I wish she could feel everything. But that's not possible," she spoke quickly.

From his question alone, I could guess what was coming next. I hated that I was standing here and not there with her.

"I can make it possible for you," he promised.

If he was a beast who knew things then he was magical in many ways, and Miranda was going to be fucked. He turned to Miranda and placed his free hand on her shoulder. At first, she flinched, but then I felt shock, profound joy, and utter sadness. Miranda gasped as did the rest of the crowd over what we all felt. We were sensing the emotions radiating from them both.

Then she cried out in scorching pain like she was being burned alive. "STOP, MAKE IT STOP. PLEASE!"

But he didn't. Her breathing was becoming labored. She let out a growl, "GRRR!" I sensed her physical pain and an intense pressure building up. "HEE, HEE, HOO, HEE. OOOOOH," she shouted in short bursts.

Was Miranda giving birth? Shit. She was going through the labor that Jasinda must have gone through. Words escaped me witnessing and feeling all these emotions. These emotions that were once Jasinda's.

The pain of it all sent chills throughout my body. Knowing that she'd done this *alone*. Knowing that she'd suffered with *no one* at her side. Knowing that there hadn't been anyone to take some of this pain away for her. I couldn't imagine the guilt that Elier had to be feeling watching the train wreck in live action, knowing that he'd set it on its collision course. I kept watching both women. Watching the surprised look on Jasinda's face. Watching the tears stream down her cheeks while she watched Miranda suffer the same fate she had.

After what felt like hours, but was only moments later, Miranda collapsed to the floor. Sweat drenched her face and plastered her hair to her forehead, as she panted and sobbed like a child.

Miranda managed to speak with anger in her voice as she turned her face up towards Jako, "Don't. Don't you *ever*…touch…me…again."

She was weak and fragile, which made me happy for the moment. A quick glance at Elier told me that he wasn't satisfied with her level of pain. He was anxious to deliver the punishment he deemed that she truly deserved.

Jako the wolf-lord let go of Miranda as he spoke, "The next time I touch you, it will be to kill you! But you're not mine to kill. I'll leave that for *him* to decide." He pointed at Elier.

Miranda's eyes crashed into Elier's and she went ghost-white. His wolf eyes were glowing. Everyone in the room was hyper-tuned to the emotional undercurrents, so we all felt Elier's rage and felt it was justified. My eyes tracked around the room and found everyone nodding in agreement, except for one person. His mother.

She was staring at Elier. She had experienced Jasinda's grief, just like the rest of us. The sadness and disappointment over the loss of her grandson was written all over her face. Mrs. Sky was a kind soul. She always compromised to keep the peace with everyone and other packs, only fighting when it came down to defending what was hers. Elier wouldn't look her way. I couldn't blame him. I knew she was torn between the grief she felt at the loss of her grandchild and the loss of the marriage she had hoped would blossom between Elier and Miranda.

"Jasinda?" Jako called out to her. She slowly looked away from Miranda and up at the beast. Something was wrong, I could feel it. "There's something I must do too. Please forgive me, but I must get you to remember."

What was he talking about?

Jasinda looked perplexed as well. "Wha…"

That was all that she could get out before he backhanded her across the face. Jasinda flew back with such force, landing on her side and skidding towards the stage.

"What the fuck, Jako?" Elier yelled at him.

The wolf-lord looked directly at Elier. "It's the only way to get her to remember. I *need* her to fight back. Fight to survive."

What the hell was going on? Elier had answers that I wanted to demand he give me, but I knew he wouldn't.

Jako turned towards her and pulled back his whip.

No, no fuckin' way was he going to whip her! No fuckin' way.

Elier and I both struggled against the hold on us. I was going to kill Jako if he hurt her.

Chapter Ten

Jasinda

Heat blossomed in my cheek. The burn from his smack was unbearable. Not to mention the pain in my hip from the landing. As I lay on the ground trying to get my wits about me, voices and growls filled the air around me.

What the hell was happening? My earlier curiosity was gone. I was terrified. From my position sprawled on the floor, I looked around, trying to locate the source of the growls. The Mitchell brothers. Eyes glowed brightly. Teeth and nails lengthened. Something was happening to their bodies, giving me a very different perspective of the brothers as I peered over at them.

Wolves? Were they werewolves? Maybe vampires? I've never seen one, so what would I know. Movies always seem to exaggerate. What did they call themselves? Through the split of hair that covered my face, I caught their predator gazes. I nearly gasped, sliding back a little to keep a safe distance. Breathing in through my nose and releasing a frightful breath, instead I swallowed hard. I am dreaming. I'm in a terrible nightmare. One that I wish I could wake up from.

Today I'd encountered four Dracolupus and a wolf-lord. And now I found out my childhood friends were…animals or possibly vampires? *Did vampires growl?* I needed a glass of wine…and a Tylenol. Would I be sent to the nut house if I spoke with a psychiatrist?

With shaky hands I cleared the hair partially blocking my vision and found the beast Jako turning towards me with his whip out ready to strike.

Shouts rang out from the crowd. My heart raced. I didn't want him to strike me with his whip. I didn't think I would survive it.

"I'm sorry, Princess," his voice full of remorse, "but I *must* make you remember. It's the only way. You *need* to fight back."

My mind raced over his words, trying to make sense of them before anything else happened.

"Wait, please don't do this." Panic struck me like lightening.

But my plea didn't matter. He drew back his whip and a gust of wind came through, followed by an explosion of red and white lights like firecrackers. My hands flew up, shielding my eyes. For some reason the ring finger on my left hand was getting warm and tingly.

A clank of metal on metal resounded in the air. After the light dimmed, I lowered my hands. A man and woman stood in front of me blocking me from the beast. They both had long, silver hair—silver like a shiny coin. The woman was gorgeous, with a model's figure and caramel mocha colored skin that looked great against her red leather bodysuit. He was handsome—tall and lean, with muscles that rippled through his red leather pants.

What a great ass. Shit! Get it together. This wasn't the time to admire his ass.

The couple appeared to be wearing some type of armor. A few of what looked like diamonds ran along both their backs in a wave type pattern. *But they couldn't be diamonds. No one would really have diamonds on their clothes, would they?*

The man stepped toward the wolf-lord. He must have intercepted the lash I was about to receive. Then he turned his attention to the woman.

I was immobilized and unable to speak. His beauty was alluring. I felt drawn to him, but I didn't understand why. His eyes captivated me. They were so unique—vibrant silver diamond shapes with red centers.

"Get Jasinda out of here. Now!"

The volume of his voice startled me.

The woman, who looked like his twin but with curves, nodded to him and fully turned towards me. She smiled at me and cautiously came closer. As she drew nearer, I saw that she was beautiful. Exquisite. Strong.

"Hey, are you ok?" she asked in a soft tone. But I couldn't speak. My heart twitched. But I felt calm and safe. I didn't even know her, yet I felt connected to her. "Jasinda, are you hurt?"

Finally, I found my voice. "No, I'm not hurt. At least I don't think so. I…I just need help getting up."

She leaned down and held out her hand. I grabbed it, and she pulled me to my feet with ease. She was strong.

"It took you long enough to get here," the wolf-lord spoke.

The man that came with the woman moved something from his side to his front. *A sword?*

"This doesn't need to happen, Jako. You know we cannot interfere with her memories. You *just* put her at risk," the man with the sword said.

My memories? What the hell was the issue with my memories?

"I need to get you out of here," the woman said to me.

"Get me out of here? I'm not leaving with you. I don't even *know* you."

She looked at me as pain quickly flashed across her face before she shuttered her expression.

She glanced over her shoulder, then back at me. "Look, I don't have time to explain. But I need to get you to safety. Now!"

Safety? From who? I wasn't sure whose side she was on, but I needed to get to the brothers. I trusted them, even if they might be wolves.

"I'm sorry, but I can't go with you," I said, spinning in a circle, scanning the crowd. "I get that your intentions are good, but you need to understand that I don't know what the hell is going on here. I'm not about to walk off with someone I don't know."

But, hadn't I done that with Jace? Hadn't I walked off with him and into a cave alone? And I even kissed him. But that didn't count, because he knew Anthony, right?

"Silva! Get her out of here," the silver-haired man yelled.

"She isn't comfortable leaving with me. She doesn't trust me, and I won't force her," she yelled back, her eyes locked on mine.

I liked her already.

"Silva, we don't have time for this bullshit. Just get her out of here!"

"Who the hell nominated you to be in charge?" I yelled back at him.

Shock flashed in his intense stare briefly before anger filled them. I glanced at Silva and saw she was smiling at me. When I looked back at him, I found his eyes were completely red now. I took an involuntary step back just as he waved the sword in front of him, connecting with the wolf-lord's whip without taking them off me.

"Holy waters! This is insane!

"Dammit, Jasinda, I don't have time to argue with you. You need to leave with Silva," he snapped impatiently.

"*No*, I'm not leaving without them." I pointed to the Mitchell brothers, who were still trying to claw their way out of the force field holding everyone in place. "And I won't leave until I know for sure that no one else will get hurt, and that everyone is released." I pointed over to Jako and he smiled at me. I dropped my hands and shuffled my feet. *What the hell? Did this guy have moods swings or something?* One minute he was angry, and the next he was freaking smiling at me.

"Spoken like a true princess." He bowed his head at me.

What? He needed to stop calling me princess. Only my father and the Mitchell brothers called me that. It was an endearment that meant something to me. But coming from Jako, it was just irritating.

"Don't call me that! You don't get to call me that," I shouted at him.

He cocked his head and looked at the man standing between us. "I'd thought she'd remember once you came. But it seems as though her mother took extra precautions." He took a step closer, putting his whip away.

Thank goodness. Maybe I won't die tonight.

"Silvo, I *need* her to remember. My world will crumble without her mother. She's the *only* one who can help me."

So, the guy's name was Silvo. Silva and Silvo must be like fraternal twins or something.

"This isn't the way. We must find her using a different method. I will devote my time to locating her. Just leave Jasinda out of it," Silvo pleaded.

Silvo knew something. *Did he know where my mother was? Why should they leave me out of it? Didn't they realize that I should've been left out of it in the first place?* I still didn't understand what was going on, yet they talked about it like I did.

Jako walked over to Silvo. "How can you be *here* with her and not want her to remember you?"

What did Jako mean by that? Remember him how? I didn't know any of them. What was he talking about?

"I can see it in your eyes. How much you still love her."

"What does he *mean*?" I managed softly.

Silvo turned completely towards me. His eyes burned into mine. They changed back to the silver-red color. His stare paralyzed me. He was beautiful—caramel-mocha skin tone, lean with muscles, no facial hair at all. He was a sight to behold, and I'm sure I'd be melting in my panties right now if I wasn't freaked out.

"He means nothing by that. Nothing that's important anyway." His eyes spoke in contrast to his words, but I didn't have time to examine this stranger's facial expressions. He continued softly, "But I do need for you to listen to me. *Carefully*." Silvo closed the short distance between us.

For some reason, I continued to stare quietly at him. My ring finger warmed up again as he got closer. Absentmindedly, I rubbed at it.

"Jasinda, I know you don't know me or my sister," his voice broke as he spoke. "But it's *very* important that you leave here now. I'd prefer for you to leave with my sister, so she can protect you while I look for your mother. But I know you'll say no."

Yeah, he was right about that. After he put his sword away, he reached in his pocket and took out a bracelet. It was the most beautiful piece of jewelry I'd ever seen, and I was immediately magnetized.

"Where did you get that?" I asked in awe.

He smiled down at the bracelet, then looked back at me with a tender expression making his handsome face even more breathtaking. "Someone I love wanted one of these for a very long time. They are very rare and *must* be given as a gift. It can't be found in your local store."

I leaned forward to get a better look. "I love butterflies. They're the most beautiful creations that we have. I feel a connection to them."

His eyes softened, and something that I didn't understand flashed in them. Something very much like affection. He stepped towards Jako then looked back at me.

"If I get Jako to release the force field, will you promise me that you'll leave here immediately?"

Staring at him, I wanted to say no. I wanted to know more about that bracelet. Something about it drew me in and made me feel like it belonged to me. Plus, I wanted to know more about how he was planning to find my mother. Even so, I knew when to take a step back.

"Yes," I finally agreed.

He nodded his head in approval and gave me a dazzling smile before turning towards Jako. They spoke softly to one another. Even with my ears straining, I couldn't hear what they said.

Finally, Dayne's voice cut the quiet, "Are you ok?" The force field was released as promised.

Chapter Eleven

Jasinda

"Yes, I'm fine. How about you and your brothers?"

He nodded his head and took a step toward me cautiously. Worry colored his eyes. In an instant, I closed the distance and hugged him.

"I'm scared, Dayne. I don't know what's going on," I whispered, holding him tightly.

As he squeezed me back, his claws lightly scraped my back.

"What's happening?" I grilled him, as I pulled back to look at him.

He opened his mouth but couldn't speak. "Why didn't you *tell* me you're a wolf, shapeshifter, supernatural, or whatever it is that you are?"

He looked puzzled. "You're not afraid of me?"

"Seriously? Is that a joke?" I retorted.

"No," he whispered.

"Dayne, you're family to me. No matter *what* you are. I see *you*, and I've always seen you. You and your brothers. This doesn't change anything. At least not for me." I confessed, hurt tinging my tone over the thought he had that I could possibly fear him. "Do you plan to hurt me?"

He reared his head back with anger in his eyes. "Are you crazy? I could *never* hurt you. Except for today." Pain replaced the anger in his eyes. "I never meant to lie to you about what we are. We've wanted to tell you for so long. But we couldn't, and I truly can't remember why," he finished as he stuffed both hands in his pockets.

"Well, you're lucky I forgive you. Maybe later we can talk more about it?" I asked him with a sheepish smile.

Continuing to focus on me he, softly spoke. "You can ask me *anything*, and I'll do my best to give you an honest answer."

I stuck my hand out for him to shake. "Deal."

"Deal," he agreed and shook my hand as he laughed.

I turned towards Silvo and caught him smiling at the sight of me.

Wow, did he have a beautiful smile.

Pearl white, straight teeth. *Sharp*, straight teeth—two on top and two on the bottom.

Was he a vampire?

"Your smile... it's beautiful," the words fell out of their own accord. I immediately clamped my hand over my mouth. His smile widened as he took a step closer.

"Thank you. You've always told me that."

"Really?"

He nodded. Dropping Dayne's hand, I stepped closer to him. For some reason I was caught up in him. Mesmerized. Drawn like metal filings to a magnet. Without thought, I ran my hand down his braid.

"I love your braids."

What is wrong with me? Why do words keep tumbling out of my mouth without permission?

His smile grew even brighter. "I know," he whispered intimately to me. "I've been wearing my hair like this since the first time you braided it." His voice was nearly a purr.

Surprised by his words, I dropped my hands. He had to be messing with me. *I'd braided his hair before? How was that possible?* I just met him, and we hadn't even been properly introduced.

"Do we know each other?"

His lips parted as he drew in a deep breath. He seemed to be working on a response. Pain and something else were visible in his eyes.

"This is so hard," he mumbled more to himself than to me. With another deep breath he said, "We made vows, promising *never* to lie to one another. Even if the lie was to keep the other from danger."

Oh, gods. We must know each other. Lying has always been one of my biggest pet peeves.

"What do you mean by that?" I asked confused by a truth I didn't know, but somehow felt.

He wrapped my hand in his, and it felt so natural to have my fingers entwined with his. Like we'd held hands for years. We walked towards Silva.

He looked deeply at me. "I'm so sorry, but I can't tell you more. All I can say is that we did *know* each another, and so did you and my sister."

It made sense why she looked so pained when I wouldn't leave with her earlier.

"I'm sorry, but I don't remember either of you. How is this possible?" My heart filled with grief over the loss of these relationships that I didn't even remember having.

"Your mother wiped away all of your memories and replaced them with fabrications," Silva confessed.

"Is that really possible?" I asked, unable to keep the doubt from my voice. *No way was this real. I had to be dreaming.*

"With your mother, almost anything's possible." She gave me a tentative smile.

Walking towards Jako, I asked "Do you still plan to hurt me in order to get what you're looking for?" He winced at my words and lowered his head. I took another step closer. "Well, do you?"

He finally looked up at me, his eyes filled with unshed tears. "I don't want to hurt you, but I also don't want to lose my people. Your mother is my only hope in saving my kingdom."

"Jasinda…" He closed the distance between us and took my hand into his gently. "I was wrong for what I did to you and everyone here tonight. No matter what my people may be going through, I shouldn't have taken it this far. I should've found another way to find your mother. For that I'm truly sorry." He sounded so sincere. "I've interfered with what your mother did to keep you safe. She went through great lengths just to make sure that he never found you both." He caressed his thumb over my hand.

"Who is us? And who's looking for us, Jako?" Nervousness crept into my voice.

"I'm not sure it's safe to tell you."

Couldn't one person tell me what the hell was going on? Why did everyone know except me? Wait, did my father know?

"Jako, can I ask you something?"

He squeezed my hand lightly and nodded yes. "I'll try to answer any question you ask. But if I'm unable to answer, I'll tell you so."

I prayed his answer was no to my question. If he knew my mother, then he had to know my father too.

"Do you know my father too?"

"Yes."

"Does my father know about my memories being altered?" I asked hesitantly. Something shifted in his eyes, and I knew I'd asked the wrong question. *Crap!* He dropped my hand and rubbed his eyes as if they were hurting. He paced for a few seconds.

"As much as I don't *want* to answer that question, I feel as though you need the answer." Stopping, he faced me. My heart raced so fast that I thought it would run away from my body while I stood there frozen in place. "Yes, your father knows about what your mother did to your memories."

I staggered back, appalled by his response. I'd hoped he'd say no, that his memories were altered like mine. My hand pressed over my heart to stifle the pain. My father had been lying to me for *years*. I was twenty-four, the last time I saw my mother. *Or was that a fake memory she' given me?*

How could my father have done this to me? All those times when I'd asked him where my mother was, and why she'd left, he'd always said that he didn't know. Told me she'd disappeared without a word, and he'd been searching for her ever since to get answers himself. After I'd pestered him a bunch, he'd told me that they'd fought all the time about her wanting to move to Spaino, an island that could only be reached by boat or helicopter. An island I'd never heard of and couldn't find on the internet. Since his work was here, he'd needed to stay. But maybe they were all lies. He'd been telling me lies for a long time apparently. Lies upon lies about my mother's disappearance. All this time he'd *known* about my memories, which meant that he'd known what was going on. The pain of his betrayal cut deeply. I closed my eyes to keep my tears at bay.

"Jasinda?" Silvo called out, concern lacing his voice.

His voice flowed through me, like a gentle caress. I didn't move. He was near. I stayed rooted in place with my eyes pressed tightly closed and my fists balled at my sides. My ring finger tingled again. Though I tried, I couldn't seem to open my eyes or even move. My pain was paralyzing.

"*Amare*?" Silvo called out again.

At that my lids popped open and were filled with his silver red eyes staring right into mine. *He called me love. Amare meant love. How did I know that?*

"What are you thinking?" he whispered as he stepped even closer. He reached a hand towards my cheek and stroked it once before dropping it back to his side.

"About how my father has been lying to me for *years*. And I'm wondering if the Mitchell brothers knew about it all too. And I want nothing more than to find my mother myself and ask her *why* she did this to me," I answered in a rush. The warmth intensified around my ring finger. Our eyes bored into one another. After an eternity of silence, I broke the stare and turned to Jako.

He spoke up, "The Mitchell brothers are as clueless as you are."

"How so?" Dayne asked with a little hostility in his tone.

Jako walked over to Dayne, who seemed ready for a fight.

"Relax, Daynard. I mean no harm," Jako calmly said.

Daynard? Why call him Daynard?

Jako looked back at me and spoke, "Your mother altered their memories as well. She made sure that they didn't know about your memories being altered, and she synced theirs with yours."

What the hell? How crazy but cool was that? How can it even be done? Why was I impressed by this?

"So, this whole time we've been living a lie? In a bubble of my own world? Is that right, Jako?" I asked bitterly.

"Yes and no."

He dropped his hand to Dayne's shoulder and closed his eyes. After a few seconds he opened them, and a flash of royal blue shone in his gaze.

"His memories were all altered for *your* safety, so he couldn't cave in and tell you anything. Your mother knew how close you and the brothers were. She *knew* they wouldn't be able to keep this from you." He looked back and forth between the brothers. "They know about themselves, but any memories concerning you were altered to fit what your new memories dictated."

That made me feel a little better.

"Why did you call me Daynard?" Dayne spoke.

Jako's body tensed briefly before he schooled his features. If I hadn't been watching Jako I would've missed it.

"Because that's your birth name. You were named after your father, grandfather, great-grandfather, and great-great grandfather. Your parents called you Dayne for short."

Dayne glanced at me, then back at Jako. "How do you know that, and how am I supposed to know if you're telling me the truth?"

Silvo stepped forward, bringing himself back into my line of sight. I'd somehow forgotten that he was next to, but slightly behind me.

Silvo turned toward Dayne. "Dayne, Jako *knows* things. Things that are hard for some of us to believe. But when he tells you something he knows about you, he *never* lies about it. He may keep information from you, but he doesn't lie. Not when it comes to stuff like this." The seriousness in Silvo's voice made me believe him, and I hoped that Dayne did too. "We're all connected, and until the memories are restored, you truly won't understand."

"This is fucked up," Darrell yelled from behind me. I hadn't even heard him approach.

Jako spoke, glancing back and forth between Darrell and me, "Yes, it would seem so. But I assure you, I speak the truth in this matter. I'll also have you know that your parents were great friends to me and my people."

Small world or did we all know one another?

Silvo walked over to Jako. "Jako, we need to leave. We must get them out of here and back to living their lives again."

How could we go back to living our lives? Were we just supposed to forget all of this?

"No," Jako and Silvo shouted simultaneously, turning their heads towards me.

"What?" I said, as Silva came towards me.

She took my hand into hers and studied me for a minute before speaking, "No, you're not supposed to forget about all of this. But we do want you to go back and resume your life."

Shit, had I spoken my thoughts out loud?

Might as well finish them now. "But how are we supposed to go back to normal? How am I supposed to go on with my life, knowing that my memories aren't really my memories? Knowing that there are people out there that I should remember but can't?"

Jako opened his mouth to speak, but Silva stepped right in front of me blocking him from my view.

She gave me an easy smile. "I know this isn't easy for you, and for that I'm truly sorry. But you must go on with your life, Jasinda." Taking my hand, she walked me over to Dayne. "All I can suggest is that you need to try to process this as best as you can. Your safety is what's important right now. So, please try and live the best of your life." She put my hand into Dayne's. "You'll have questions, many questions to ask. But right now, we're not allowed to answer them as much as we may want to. I promise that I'll try to visit you and answer the questions that I'm able to, without triggering your memory."

How could I argue with that?

"How will you find me?"

She smiled at me, revealing her teeth. Hers was a beautiful smile, one that reached her eyes, just like Silvo's. "I'll always find you. Just like I did today."

That was all she said before she began to walk away. I looked over at Silvo and found him staring at me. Something in his eyes worried me. I couldn't stop staring back at him. He had me in a trance. Next thing I knew, he was walking off after his sister.

He looked back and spoke, "Jako, let's go. It's time to find another way."

Jako looked at me, then at Dayne. "Keep her safe. Be well, you all."

Jako walked over to the twins. Silvo was still looking my way. He looked so tormented for an instant before he reined in his emotions and said, "Jasinda, stay safe. Don't go to work for the next few days. Actually, maybe you shouldn't go in for a few weeks. That's an easy place to find you."

Before I could ask him why, they all disappeared.

"Dayne?" I whispered.

"Yes."

"Now what?"

He squeezed my hands and turned me towards him.

"Now we leave. We take you home to get some of your things, and you'll be staying with Jace."

Jace? Oh crap! I'd forgotten about him.

"Why am I staying with Jace?"

He sighed, then answered. "Your father's orders. He wants us back at the base, so we can run through everything that happened tonight. He said that he knows you'll be safe with Jace." He lowered his voice and said, "I'm not sure if I should update your father about *everything* that happened tonight. All he knows is about the Dracolupus. We were texting him when we thought they were going to attack us. I have to update him within the next hour."

"I'd rather you not tell him anything yet. And you might want to relay that to Jace as well," I said.

He nodded in agreement. "I've already told my brothers to keep this quiet until I spoke with you," he assured me.

But there was something else on my mind. *How in the world did he know Jace? And was Jace planning on telling my father the rest of tonight's events?*

"Are you telling me that my father knows Jace?"

He whispered, "We all know Jace. He's one of the best trackers around and good at being invisible when needed. Your father uses him often."

Hmmm, that was interesting. It seemed my world was much smaller than I thought.

"Do you think Jace will keep this quiet for now?"

Dayne smiled a wicked smile. "Of course, he will. He's loyal to us, and we trust him. Besides, Jace knows when to stay quiet."

Good to know. Where was Jace anyways? I began looking around but stopped the moment I saw him. He was with Anthony and they were both looking at me. My eyes stayed on Jace. For some odd reason, I wanted his comfort. But then I felt guilty about that desire because I'd wanted Silvo to stay and comfort me too. *What the hell was wrong with me? I didn't even know these men.*

My eyes traveled the room looking for Elier. I figured I should apologize about the baby and ask him how he managed to control those creatures. But he was nowhere to be found. Miranda wasn't in sight either. *Where had they gone?*

"Who are you looking for?" My heart skipped a beat as I turned abruptly to face Jace. Anthony was right behind him, looking a bit pale.

"I...I don't see Elier or Miranda. Where did they go?"

He looked back at Anthony and nodded. Anthony turned and walked away without a word to me.

What the hell?

"Elier took Miranda home. She was still feeling the aftereffects from you."

Good. She deserved to know what I'd gone through. I didn't feel bad about that. But it stung to know that he left with her knowing what she did to me. A little loyalty isn't asking for much.

"Where's Anthony going?"

"To get the car. We'll take you to a secure hotel tonight. Then go to your home tomorrow to gather your things."

"I need to go by my office tomorrow before I can just disappear," I demanded, straightening my spine a little.

He nodded in agreement as he shifted nervously from foot to foot before speaking again, "So, you're Manny's daughter." He swallowed hard. "He doesn't talk much about you. Only to the brothers. I've overheard some of the things he's said about you." He cleared his throat. "Nothing bad of course."

I couldn't help but smile. "I'd hope my father wouldn't speak poorly of me. I mean what kind of parent does that?"

A bit of anger flashed in his eyes when he answered me, "You'd be surprised what kind of parents are out there." He was right about that. "Jasinda?"

I pulled in a breath as he said my name. "Yes?"

He closed the distance between us. "You'll be safe with me. I promise. I'll protect you at all costs, but I need you to do as I say if trouble comes our way. Can you do that for me?"

At all costs, huh? How could I say no to that? "Yes," I whispered.

"Good. Let's get ready to go. You must be tired. I bet a nice warm bath would feel great. Besides, we need to ice your face before it starts to bruise."

"Oh gods, my face. How bad is it?" My own panic took me by surprise.

"Red like a tomato." He pulled out his cell and swiped his hand across it. Then he handed me the phone. Looking at the screen I was met with my red face. The shock in my eyes was embarrassing. *How in the world wasn't I bruised already?* A hit like that should've done the trick by now.

Chapter Twelve

Jasinda

I don't remember falling asleep last night. Jace had given me some tea shortly after we arrived. I must have passed out. We'd spent the day at my office first since I needed a few things. Thankfully no one was in since it was Sunday. I'd hate to have to explain the presence of four men plus Anthony watching my every move. I packed up all the items I'd need to be able to work from home, well, Jace's home. Then I made lists for Anthony and Angie of the things I wouldn't be able to do while hidden away. Once everything was taken care of, they escorted me to my house, where Angie was waiting for me.

After spending an hour trying to explain to Angie that I needed to disappear for a few days, maybe even weeks, I managed to get her to understand that I couldn't tell her anything about my whereabouts. She wasn't happy, but when she saw the brothers were in my house gathering my things, she knew it was serious.

She looked at me with tormented eyes. "How long will you be gone?" The worry in her voice made me wince a little. I didn't know how to explain it to her.

So, I went with no details at all. "How about I make you a promise? After I get word that it's safe for me to be out and about, I'll make sure we get together for details."

She stretched out her hand with her pinky wiggling at me. "Pinky promise me, girl!"

She always made me pinky promise, so I wouldn't back out of things. "Ugh…fine." I hooked her pinky onto mine. "I promise."

She smiled. "Ok, you can leave now. But you'd better at least send me a text within two days. Just to let me know you're good."

"Sure, I think that's doable," I said, without knowing for sure.

Leaving my house wasn't as easy as I thought it would be. It had been my home since I was twenty-four. At least that's the way I remembered it. I'd always felt safe here with all the security measures my father and I'd created. Now I had to leave, and I didn't know for how long. I told Angie she could stay for as long as she wanted, since she was always spending the night anyway. I'd feel more comfortable knowing that she was here.

The brothers walked me to Jace's car and ushered me into the backseat. Anthony sat up front. He didn't even look back at me. *What was his problem? Had I'd done something? Weren't friends supposed to tell each other when they'd messed up?* I thought *we* had that kind of relationship. Jace talked with Dayne and Devon outside the car.

Darrell leaned in through the passenger side window. "Yo, you good?" he asked Anthony. Anthony drew in a breath as he nodded yes. He had a haunted look on his face.

"You don't seem good, bro," Darrell pressed.

"Just not in the mood to talk. Too much shit to process right now."

He wasn't lying about that. *So, it wasn't me? Was he trying to figure all this shit out too?* Before I could tell him everything would be ok, Jace climbed in.

"Time to go. We'll keep in touch, Dayne," Jace said.

I looked over at the driver's window and stared at Dayne. He blocked my view of Devon. I wondered what they could've been talking about privately

Dayne nodded and pinned his eyes to mine. He gave me a tentative smile, and then winked. I smiled and winked back. With that, he walked away, leaving Devon in plain sight. His gaze was on mine, not leaving it until Jace drove off. He seemed to be trying to tell me something with his look.

We sat in silence for about ten minutes. I kept my focus on Jace the whole time as he drove. His white-knuckled grip had me worried. He seemed angry or annoyed. Something wasn't being shared with me, and I didn't like it. Tonight had been crazy and scary, but after all that had happened, I'd thought things would be cleared up. But they were more confusing. Especially with Anthony. He was acting differently towards me.

We'd always been able to hash things out in the past. Now I was in the backseat, uncomfortable as hell, trying to figure out what I could've done to him. So many emotions rolled through me. Sadness because my best friend wasn't himself, not even with me around. Hurt because he hadn't even looked at me since we'd left the charity event. Anger at everything that took place tonight. My door opened, and Jace unbuckled my seatbelt. It all happened so fast, that I didn't even realize we'd stopped.

"Come with me," he said.

Grabbing my hand, he gently tugged me out of the car. Then he turned towards Anthony and commanded, "Stay." With that, we walked down the side of the road, stopping at a tree.

"Jace, what's going on?"

He gently caressed my cheek with his knuckles, as he gazed at me. His stare was intense and hot, but also nerve racking.

"I *cannot* take the intensity of yours and Anthony's emotions in such a confined space!"

"What are you talking about?" I asked.

"I'm talking about the sadness, anger and pain you're feeling. Heaped on top of the guilt Anthony feels for keeping things from you. Sensing all these emotions has been exhausting." He ran his hand down his weary face. "Jasinda, I can sense *all* of your emotions right now… and the residual from last night. The ripple effects of what you went through are still in the air. We're all having a hard time right now."

Whoa wait, was he serious?

He kept going. "Anthony is hurt because you didn't tell him about…you know." He gestured towards my belly. "But he got over it, once it seemed like you hadn't told anyone else. He didn't feel so left out. Then things got worse when he'd felt everything you'd gone through and realized that you'd gone through it alone." He took a step back to look at me. "Feeling the way he felt, the way we all felt, wasn't easy on any of us last night.

Every man in that room understands how bad a pregnancy loss can be on a woman. The worst part was feeling it through Miranda and you together."

Holy waters! "Are you telling me that every man in there felt my loss? My pain and heartache?" I questioned in disbelief. "No *way* that's possible."

"Yes, Jasinda. We *all* felt it. Every person."

Whoa. That was some crazy stuff right there. "How?" I demanded.

He looked me over again and straightened his whole body, making him look even taller. Oh hell, I wasn't going to like this by the seriousness in his features.

"Everyone at the charity event last night is supernatural, including me." He kept his focus on me. "You were the *only* human there."

I gasped and closed my eyes, because I felt so stupid. *How had I not known?* "That's why Frank acted that way when you first arrived."

That made sense. So, supernaturals don't really like us humans. Awesome. "What are you?" I muttered.

He tilted his head up towards the darkening sky. He stayed like that for a few seconds, then captured my attention. His eyes glowed green. Just like at the charity event.

"I'm a werewolf."

Chapter Thirteen

Jasinda

*D*id he just say werewolf? He meant wolf, right? Like a shapeshifter? *He couldn't be a werewolf. They were scary beasts. Ferocious killers.* But for the life of me, I couldn't picture him as a werewolf. He was so, so, so handsome, but more than that he was kind and very protective.

I'd heard about supernatural beings from my father. He would mention that he was off chasing some beast. I'd picked up a few conversations between him and the Mitchell brothers but I'd been almost compelled not to ever question my father. He never talked about his work in detail. However, he always made sure I knew the protocol. It was odd now that I thought about it, especially concerning the supernatural codes.

Could it be that I just didn't remember the supernatural? Did my mother take those memories from me too?

My stomach churned with the thought. I squeezed my lids together tightly. My world was filled with extraordinary people and possibly extraordinary things. To be unable to experience any of it with my right mind was sickening to me. I needed to find my mother and get my memories back.

"Jasinda?"

My eyes snapped opened.

"Are you ok?" Jace asked, worry and concern colored his tone. Frown lines wrinkled his brow.

"Am I *ok*?" I scoffed. Shaking my head, I balled my hands into fists. "No, I'm not ok. Not with being left in the dark. Not with discovering all of this, *this* way. Most of all, I'm not ok with learning that my *mother* tampered with my memories. None of this is *ok*. Not at all."

Jace looked stunned by my outburst. "If you want me to speak with your father about getting someone…"

"No!" I cut him off. "Don't call my father. I'm…I'm just not cool with being in the dark." I paced around the tree to keep myself from smashing my fits into it. "It bothers me that I didn't know I was the only human last night. I'm upset because I don't know what my memories are *supposed* to be." I breathed deeply and stopped right in front of him. With a whisper I said, "I'm not fine, because my father has been lying to me for God knows how long."

Pacing again, I tried to gather my thoughts and wrangle my emotions. Tears that I refused to cry blurred my vision. The desire to call my father and curse him out was strong. But more than *anything,* I wanted to find my mother and get my memories back.

Jace stepped in my path, forcing me to stop. "I can't even begin to imagine what you're going through. But know this, I'll be here for you Jasinda, whenever you need me. I'll help you in any way I can." He placed a comforting hand on my belly. At his touch, I gasped. Warmth generated from his palm. Flutters ran through me like the wind.

What was it about him that had me feeling giddy and brimming over with warmth as if from the sun?

"Jasinda?"

"Mmhmm." I managed.

"I'll answer any questions you have. Anything you want to know."

"Even if it's personal?" I had to know how far I could go with my questions.

"I said *anything,* Jasinda. I mean what I say."

Laying my hand over his, I smiled. "Do you still work for my father?"

He smiled and answered immediately, "Yes, I'll probably work for him until he dies."

"Why?"

"He's a good man. No matter what he's done to you, he's always done right by me. He's risked his life to keep all of our secrets. He even risked his life for yours."

"What do you mean, *mine*?"

"Apparently, your memories are a big secret. A *really* big secret."

Well, Jace was loyal. That was a good thing. "Do you know *why* my memories were altered?"

"Now that's the secret I *want* to know," he confessed.

My shoulders sagged. It was worth a shot.

"But I'll set up a meeting with your father. He said we needed to discuss more about you anyway. It's why he wants you to stay with me." He smiled at me and grabbed my hand, tugging gently. "Let's go."

When we got back to the car, he spoke, "When Anthony's ready, he'll talk to you. Don't worry. He's just trying to deal with all that just happened."

I nodded in understanding. His intimate knowledge of people who were close to me was a tad unnerving.

Back in the car, Anthony rested his head on the back of the seat with his eyes closed, his hurt and pain obvious to me now that I was looking. I'd never really thought about how he might feel about all this mess. Finding out about my loss wasn't easy for him. I hadn't told anyone except for Angie. She was the *only* one who knew. She was the one who stayed with me and had cared for me while I'd been on bedrest. I suppose Elier wasn't the only person I needed to apologize to.

Anthony deserved an apology, served alongside an *American Horror Story* marathon, popcorn, and M&M's.

"Jace?"

"What's wrong?"

"Nothing. Could we stop at a grocery store?"

He smiled, clearly relieved that it was something small. "That depends. Are you planning to buy the whole store?"

The corner of his mouth curled into a smirk. He was teasing me. Nice to know that he could tease when the tension was so high.

"Well, that depends on what's on sale," I teased back.

He rolled his eyes. "First stop, the grocery store. Any other places Miss Daisy?"

I grinned from the backseat. "No, Hoke. The grocery store is fine."

Five minutes later, we pulled into a parking spot. I unbuckled my seatbelt and opened my door.

"I'll stay in the car, if you don't mind," Anthony said to Jace.

Not sure if I wanted to hear the conversation between them, I closed the door and leaned against it. A moment later, Jace got out and took my hand.

"Is he mad about me wanting to stop at the grocery store?"

"No, he's actually relieved we stopped. He wanted a minute alone before we all are under one roof."

Thank goodness.

"He's being a bit hard on himself, don't you think?" I shivered from the night breeze. It was refreshing, but still chilly.

He stopped walking. Something changed in the air between us. *Oh, that felt so good.* After we'd left the event last night, it had gotten cool swiftly. But right now, I felt warm all over. It was almost like the air knew I was cold, so it wrapped a blanket around me. A warm one. Weird.

"Yes, he's being too hard on himself. But right now, he needs to see reason. Maybe being alone will help."

We walked into the store, and he immediately grabbed a cart. I gathered the popcorn, M&M's, Raisinets, and a bottle of Pepsi. As I walked past the cookie aisle, I had an idea. Anthony loved my homemade, oatmeal chocolate chip cookies. *Why not make him some as well?* I gathered the ingredients and vanilla ice cream too. Then, I grabbed my tea and lemon. As I strolled the aisles, I became lost in my thoughts. When Jace's arm brushed mine, it startled me.

"Are you done?"

"Yes."

Back at the car, he loaded all the groceries into the trunk, while I watched, admiring his backside. "Thank you."

He looked at me with his vibrant green orbs. They glittered brighter than an emerald gem. "Maybe your lips can thank mine."

We've already gotten the first kiss out of the way, so why not a second kiss? My whole body grew warm again. Stepping closer, I leaned into him. It was as if I was under a spell. The torch of our kiss ignited a blanket of flames around us. He opened for me, allowing my tongue to slip into the warmth of his mouth in a dance. A growl reverberated from his chest, causing me to moan. He pulled me in closer. *Goodness.* He felt good against me. Breaking our kiss, he slowly pulled away a little, but kept us connected.

I was disappointed. I wanted him to keep kissing me. We held on to each other for a while longer. His irises devoured me in a way that made me blush. I wanted him. I *truly* wanted him, and I couldn't figure it out. I'd never felt like this before, not even with Elier.

"We should leave," he said, his eyes still staring into mine.

I nodded, and he walked me to my door, opened it and buckled me in. Sinking into the seat, I felt oddly optimistic about where all this was going.

Chapter Fourteen

Jasinda

T he car slowed and turned. Wrought iron gates opened. We drove atop a pea-gravel driveway up to a beautiful stone mansion. Right in front of it was a beautiful water fountain. Jace pulled around it and stopped at the mansion's steps. The front of the home was nothing but interconnecting balconies.

I was so busy admiring the place that I didn't budge when my door was opened.

"Ready?" Jace asked as he held his hand out to me. I was frozen in awe over his house. "Is something wrong?"

"No, I'm sorry. Do you live here alone?" The question was out of my mouth before I could think on it.

"No, my family lives here most of the time. And friends like Anthony come for extended stays. The members of my pack like to be close."

Seriously? I looked over at Anthony. He avoided eye contact with me, but nodded at Jace, before disappearing into the house.

"Jasinda?" Jace spoke softly.

"Oh, right. Sorry." Grabbing his hand, I let him help me out of the car. I took a step and stumbled. Jace's free hand wrapped around me reflexively to keep me from falling.

"You all right?"

"Yes, thank you. Heels aren't really made for walking on these pebbles." I laughed a little.

He smiled back at me. "Heels are just the right thing to be walking in."

With a wink, he brought me closer to his side and walked me to the door. His grin made me want him in a new way. I wanted to wrap myself around him. He squeezed me tighter, bringing me even closer than I already was. A sizzle jolted in my belly. Then *it* happened as I hit the steps. A rumble went through my mind, body, and soul again. Just like at the charity event.

He stopped as we reached the door. "My enchantress, what's wrong?"

"Enchantress? Did you just call me enchantress?" I went to yank my hand out of his, but he held on tighter.

He looked flabbergasted, but quickly recovered as he cleared his throat to speak. "No, not a witch. Enchantress is a type of rose."

"Oh, right." Enchantress *was* a type of rose now that I thought about it. A beautiful one at that. They came in many different colors—blue, yellow, white, pink, and the very rare lavender.

"I'm sorry," I said shyly, coming closer, flattered that he compared me to such a beautiful flower. "I forgot about the enchantress *rose*."

"I like a woman who can apologize when she's wrong. But I shouldn't have assumed that you knew what I meant."

Wrapping my hand around his bicep, I tugged him gently towards the door. But he didn't budge.

"What is it?"

"I don't know. You tell me? You still haven't answered my question."

I couldn't put anything past him. "I honestly don't know. I felt a little strange for a moment, but I'm fine right now."

It was the truth, because I couldn't rightly say what I felt a moment ago.

"Good," he said and guided me through the open door.

The place was gorgeous. The foyer floor was a dark grey marble that complimented the dove grey walls. A large rectangle table stood at the center of two converging staircases that curved up to the second floor. My heels clicked as we approached the table, which had a huge vase in the middle filled with white enchantress roses. Little figurines surrounded the vase—tiny, wood carved wolves. They were grouped together in different colors. *Different packs?*

"Go upstairs and make a right. Scarlet will be waiting for you."

I turned to thank him, but he was gone. Slowly, I walked up admiring the photos along the walls. They looked centuries old. Some of them appeared to be hand painted. When I reached the top of the stairs, I turned to my right just like Jace had ordered me to do.

A beautiful, tall woman with ruby red hair and matching eyes stood there. She bowed and smiled. I stood there awkwardly, unsure if I should bow back.

"Jasinda, is it?"

"Uh, yes."

"Please follow me. I'll show you to your room."

I followed her down the long hallway, still admiring the décor as we walked. The walls were a dove grey just like downstairs. Black symbols adorned the wall by each door. We passed two doors before she stopped at a room with a beautiful, cherry wood door. It was the only cherry wood door in the hall. The rest were plain black, except for the door directly across from this one. That one was a dark grey.

"Your room is ready. I'll bring you some fresh towels. Is there anything you need?" she asked.

"Tea. I bought some tea and would like to make a cup if that's all right?" It felt strange having someone serve me this way.

She smiled at me and gave me a nod. "Of course."

After I walked through the door, I turned to give my thanks, but she was gone. Just like Jace. Gone without a sound.

The room was just as beautiful as the rest of the house. As I spun around, I decided this was less of a bedroom and more like a small apartment. To my left was a fully loaded kitchenette with a fridge, a small stove, microwave and marble countertops. Directly in front of me was a king-sized bed, covered in dark grey covers. Four pillows formed a mountain at the head of the bed. Plunging my hands under the duvet, I discovered that the sheets were silk. Sighing, I appreciated Jace's impeccable taste.

Near the bed was a small couch and what looked like my luggage. Gathering my things for a shower, I headed to the door to the left of the bed.

The moment the hot water hit my back, I allowed my overwhelming emotions to surface. I wanted to fall to my knees and cry my heart out. The events that had happened last night hit me like a wrecking ball. Pressing both hands to my mouth, I attempted to mute the sobs escaping me. I hoped the noise of the shower drowned out my cries.

Chapter Fifteen

Jace

Being around horses when my wolf was this anxious probably wasn't the best idea, but I needed some distance from Jasinda and Anthony. The stables had always been where I could find peace. The horses stomped and bowed as I passed by on the way to Gravis's stall. He was dark grey all over and had been with me for the past twenty years. His wings were always hidden within his skin, never to be seen by the enemy. He was a royal horse himself, and loyal 'til death. Born from two full-blooded Searin horses, he was a strong runner that I could count on to keep up with me on the trails.

Gravis's impatient tone invaded my mind, *'It took you long enough. Tell me what's going on? I sense the uneasiness in you.'*

It was as if he was inside me too. Bonding with my horse allowed me to speak with him via my thoughts. But my bond with Gravis was stronger than the typical bond due to my telepathic and empathic abilities.

'Too much to explain. Just stay linked and you'll know what things have been like since last night.' I replied, as I took him from the stall. Together, we embraced the night.

Just as I was starting to settle down, my beast awoke again. He was on high alert as if danger was near. My steps paused, and Gravis' did too. I checked my surroundings. But nothing was there. I patted him reassuringly.

My beast spoke up, "She cries. She fears. She aches. She's angry."

Even from this distance, my beast was tapped into her. It was exhausting, but I knew why. He wanted her as much as I did. This bothered him too. Not to mention we couldn't just *take* her the same way we would if she was a female of our kind. We couldn't console her in the way we wanted to. Couldn't truly assure her of her safety.

"What do you expect me to do? I can't tell her that my beast is sensing all her emotions. I can't tell her how much we want her. I can't go up there and conquer her the way we want to!" I yelled in frustration, forgetting to answer him in my mind.

Gravis pawed the ground and shifted nervously.

"Shhh…" I said, smoothing a hand along his neck.

My beast was so agitated by my inaction that he channeled her feelings to me. I knew what she had been feeling earlier, but it had been mild. But this… this was a hit with a metal baseball bat.

"*She was holding back earlier. Waiting to be out of sight to let go. She downplayed how all of it was affecting her,*" I said, and I knew my beast knew it too.

"*Her control makes for a great mate. A great leader. A great queen. She's what we've been waiting for. She isn't like the others. We need a mate that can control her temper around us and keep her emotion at bay when needed,*" my beast explained.

He was right about that. Every wolf-woman I'd ever come across had been challenging. Female wolves were submissive to their mates or potential mates, but in human form their temperaments made most men struggle to keep the inner wolf from attacking them. Our females knew when to stand down, but they were also strong minded. As a prince of my kind, being challenged by a female wolf wouldn't go well. Especially if she challenged me in front of my people.

"*She'll challenge you, but in different ways. Ways that would change the way we do things. Ways that would bring our pack into the modern era. She's the change we need.'* He howled. *'She wants you. Us. You could have taken her when we got home. Claimed her right then. You felt the same rumbling she did. Our soul reaching for hers. She just didn't know what it was. We do.*"

I knew he was right, but there was one thing she wouldn't be able to give me. *Give us.* She could not bear us strong children. Strong males who could take the throne. *Wolves.* Our young wouldn't be wolves. Just supernaturals with super senses and strength.

Could I be ok with that? Could my wolf be ok with it?

My beast and I were one and the same in nearly every way, but I knew this was one thing he wanted more than me. As long as I had children, I didn't care too much about them being shifters. Strong, healthy children were fine with me. I hoped like hell he wanted her more than having wolflins. Because I did.

"I want her. I did from the instant I saw her. But I want wolflins too. We can mate with more than one. Jasinda can be our mate, our wife, our souls combined and our queen. We can choose a female wolf to give us wolflins. Even if that's all she is to us, a mother." The beast suggested.

I balked at the idea, but I knew that he was serious about her to have a solution so readily available. After learning about her run in with Miranda, I was sure she wouldn't understand *that* part of our lives. That was if she even fell in love with us.

"She must fall in love with us. And she must be willing to accept it all. She's the missing piece. I know it." He explained.

"Let's hope she's willing to accept our way of life. And if she is willing to accept us, then we can talk with her about the wolflins issue. You saw her heartbreak over the loss of her child, and you saw her pain over Elier's unfaithfulness, even though it was in keeping with our ways. I will not *be the cause of that kind of pain for her. And I won't make those kinds of decisions without her. If it comes down to it, we may have to choose her or wolflins. We both need to consider that."* I told him.

He snorted in my mind. *"I don't want to cause her pain either. Her pain becomes our pain. One can hope that there is a way to have both."* He was a stubborn beast.

"Well, we can always use human technology to obtain wolflins in a way that won't break our love's heart," I offered.

"What technology?"

"Artificial insemination into the chosen female wolf. Or even obtaining a donor wolf egg and implanting it into Jasinda so she could still carry and bear our wolflins."

"Yes, yes. I like the sound of that." I could feel his pleasure at the possibility of a solution we'd all be able to accept.

"There may even be a magical solution out there."

"Let's look." His excitement evident.

"But none of it matters if we don't get her to fall in love with me. With us."

"That's a foregone conclusion. She's already falling. We just need to catch her."

Gravis and I finally made it deeper into the trails. My beast's uneasiness trembled beneath my skin. He was afraid to lose her. I was too. The connection brewing between us felt so deep, that it would be heartbreaking to lose her because of our traditions and beliefs. It was a chance we had to take. I'd do everything in my power to make her mine. It didn't matter how long I needed to wait. I'd wait, and I'd do it with patience. She was mine, and I didn't care how selfish that made me.

"Made us," my beast reminded me.

Of course, he would. *He* had awoken the moment we'd met her. She was ours without any of us even knowing it. As I made my way further along the trails, I felt Scarlet's approach. Slowly, I turned toward her.

"My lord, forgive me for interrupting your run, but I wanted to update you on Jasinda."

I nodded giving her the ok to continue. Afraid of what she was going to say, I held my breath.

"She isn't doing well. I went back to her room to make her tea and found her on the shower floor crying," she spoke quickly, so I wouldn't interrupt. "It wasn't a pretty scene. I realize this is something she needs to release, but I'm worried about her being alone. With your permission, I'd like to be her servant for the remainder of her stay." She drew in a deep breath when she'd finished.

I *hated* the word servant. It's what we'd normally use while in the presence of humans, but that wasn't the case right now. Jasinda has to at least be half supernatural. That was the only way to explain the strength of the connection between us that my beast and I were sensing.

"You have my permission to be her *lago*," I said finally. "She knows what I am, so it's no secret. You don't need to hide that from her." I *needed* her to trust me. I *needed* her to feel welcome here. "If she asks you questions, I want you to tell her as much as you'd tell any of my people."

Scarlet was visibly excited. She'd been a *lago* to my guests, but never for a guest's entire stay. I had a habit of rotating her, utilizing her where needed.

"I'll take good care of her, my lord." She bowed, waiting for me to dismiss her. I also hated doing that, and she knew it. I always felt like she loved doing this because it bothered me.

"Dismissed."

With a smirk on her face, she turned around and started to walk off.

"I want her spoiled while she's here," I called out to her back. "Make her as comfortable as you can."

I gave her all the authority I could manage. The heat rose within me and I knew I needed to change soon. "I want to see her smile and laugh. Please make sure you do that. I don't like what happened to her last night or the breakdown tonight. I especially hate that I'm not able to be the one to take care of her when she needs it the most. She doesn't know me well enough. Yet."

I stepped closer to Scarlet, as she slowed her steps, her back still to me.

"You should go attend to her. Pick her up from the floor and bathe her. Give her the royal bath."

Scarlet's annoyance with me rippled off her. She wanted to say more, I could tell. But I didn't want to listen. I was already upset about last night and how it had affected my enchantress. I couldn't be more pissed about it all. It really enraged me that there was nothing *I* could do for her myself. Shifting into my wolf form, I ran. I ran hard through the woods. Gravis was right beside me running just as hard. His companionship was comforting.

"Follow me," he urged as he ran through the woods. A few seconds later he made a left—straight for the training course. The good thing about the training course was all the animals we hunted for training were virtual. The prey was limitless.

It was the only place I could run and kill for release. He knew me well. He knew I needed to dispense with all this anger. Within minutes, I was jumping logs and chasing cheetahs throughout the woods. They were fast, but I was faster.

A female cheetah was running fast and dodging me at every turn possible. She picked up her speed, and so did I. As she was about to make her next turn, I leapt with all my might and landed right on her. My jaws clamped down into her neck. We skidded a few feet before her body went limp. Panting, I stood over her and howled, feeling more like myself.

"Feel better?" Gravis asked.

"Yes, much better."

"Feel up to trying to take down an elephant?" he asked with excitement in his voice.

Gravis huffed and took off as an elephant entered the course in the distance. I licked my chops and launched after him.

Chapter Sixteen

Jasinda

S carlet stepped silently into the bathroom. "Let me help you," she offered in a soft voice, filled with tenderness.

My eyes had closed from the moment my tears had begun and stayed that way, even with Scarlet's presence. After I'd stopped crying, I still hadn't seemed able to open them. While the water ran over me, I sat in silence, riding the waves of emotions. I was so distraught anyone could have taken care of me and I wouldn't have protested. Her skilled fingers massaged my scalp and shoulders, which had me relaxed within seconds. Scarlet bathed me, washed my hair, dried me off and dressed me without uttering a word or demanding words from me.

Feeling more like myself, I sat down with a cup of hot tea and rollers in my hair that Scarlet managed to do up with ease. The heat seeped into me, causing me to slowly close my eyes and sigh. "Mmmm, this is good. I mean really good. Thank you," I whispered after taking a sip.

"You're welcome. I figured you liked it sweet. I mean you had a lot of candy in your grocery bags." She grinned at me, and I couldn't help but smile back at her.

"So, do you feel up to talking about it or would you rather leave it be?" she asked.

Color flooded my cheeks at the thought of dumping my emotional baggage on this stranger. Though, she had just bathed me. She deserved to know why I was such a mess.

I took in a deep breath and began to tell her everything. "Last night, I found out that my memories have been tampered with. I've been living a false life. My name seems to be the only thing I really know about myself." I paused, still stunned by how strange that felt. "I never thought it possible to actually be around the supernatural." Sipping more tea to stall, I looked at her.

Scarlet stared at me, waiting for me to finish.

"Those closest to me are werewolves, and I didn't even *know*." I shook my head. "I mean, how long have I been in the dark? That's the real question. I'm afraid that I've missed out on my *real* life."

Fresh tears formed at the corner of my lids. "I want to know what life I had *before* my memory was tampered with." I paused for a moment, trying to gather myself. "The worst part of all this is my own *mother* did this to me. And I don't know why or even where to find her to get answers."

Scarlet's gaze was filled with sympathy over my pain. She didn't think I was nuts, so I continued, "But it seems others are looking for her too, and not for answers. For something much more dangerous," I said softly. "I'm scared. But I'm angry too. I just want to… *break* something. It's frustrating as hell." My fingers balled into tight fists.

Scarlet stood and moved to sit right in front of me. Without a word, she took my left hand in hers, flipped it over and uncurled my fingers to study my palm. She shut her lids, and a smile formed on her lips.

"Your memories are the only thing that have been tampered with. The life you've lived is truly yours," Scarlet said when she finally opened her eyes. "Once this magic is broken, you'll remember. The only thing that changed is that you now…you now live *here*. Your new memories are here, in this town."

Her voice sounded almost disembodied. I didn't dare move my hand from hers, nor did I lose her stare. She was observing me, but also seemed to be looking *through* me. I wanted to know what else she saw or felt. Knowing something was better than nothing. So I waited for her to continue.

"It seems as though anything related to the supernatural or magic has been removed from your memory. You were brought here because the supernatural roams around in plain sight, but still discretely from human eyes. You're strong and special. Gifted in ways that I can't even begin to understand." Giving my hand a reassuring squeeze, she placed it back on my lap. "Don't upset yourself just yet. Save your energy until the time comes for you know the truth of it all."

"Ha…easy for you to say. This isn't happening to you."

She strode over to the kitchenette and poured herself a cup of tea.

"How do you know all this, Scarlet?"

"I used to be in love with a man. He was… extraordinary," she said with a wistful sigh. "Well, at least to me." She laughed and took a sip of tea. Her gaze met mine over the rim of her cup. "He introduced me to a syrkin. She was beautiful and powerful. At that time, I was going down a dangerous path, chasing the men who raped and killed my sister." Her eyes glistened as she took another sip of her tea.

"I'm so sorry. We don't have to talk about this if it's too painful for you."

"No, it's fine. Anyway, my love hated that I was searching for revenge and wanted me to see what would happen if I pursued that path. The syrkin told me I'd die a horrible death if I continued with my search. She gave me many signs of danger. Blinded by my own rage, I didn't believe her." She paused, gathering her thoughts. "So, a few days later, I continued searching. I found one of the men who raped her and I killed him. The following night, three men followed me home. I didn't notice until I pulled down my street. I was still too obsessed with revenge, so I wasn't thinking. When I got out of my car, I attacked them first." She began to pace the room.

My throat tightened while tears clung to my lashes. Retelling her story was so hard on her. I admired her for trusting me and having the courage to relive this moment just for me.

"What is a syrkin?" I prodded.

She paused in her step and cautiously examined me. She placed her hands on her hips, unsure about telling me. The struggle was there with the biting of her lower lip and the creases she caused on her forehead.

To my surprise her mouth slowly opened to speak.

"They are mythical creatures who can see into the future. Your future." She stated.

Intrigued by her response, I leveled my back. I wondered what kind of creature. *Was it like the one at the charity event?* Before I could ask, she continued with her story all the while pacing again.

"They overpowered me and stabbed me several times. I passed out from blood loss. They must have thought they'd killed me." She stopped pacing and looked back at me. "When I awoke, I was in a cave with the syrkin lady. Her eyes were sad and filled with worry for me. She never said *I told you so,* but she showed me another vision that finally scared me into leaving my need for vengeance behind."

Though she was facing me, Scarlet was looking through me, into the past, into that vision.

"She showed me my death. If I tried again to seek those men out, the man I loved would die right by my side."

"Shit," I cursed softly.

"So, I packed up my things and moved away from temptation." She settled back in front of me.

Giving her another moment, I took a sip of my tea. "What happened to the man you fell in love with?

I really wanted her to keep telling her story. But I wanted to know if she was still with her lover.

"Sadly, we are no longer together. Finish up your tea." She said briskly.

"Ok," I tried to disguise my disappointment. I brought the cup up to my lips and sipped on the now perfectly cooled tea. I wasn't going to push it. I could tell I hit a sore spot.

"Jace wanted to come up tonight and check on you," she said softly. "But he wasn't sure if you wanted his company." I looked over for a clock and found one by the nightstand stating it was nearly eight. Well, time flew faster than I'd thought.

"What would make him think I didn't want his company?"

"Maybe he knew that you were feeling…well…emotional and thought you wanted to be alone. Rather than ask you, he stayed outside." She laughed. "It's almost like he was a lost puppy."

I couldn't help but laugh too. "Wouldn't he be a cub, not a puppy?"

She nudged me playfully. "Ha...that's right. He *would* be a cub and not a puppy."

Tipping up my cup, I drained the last drops of my tea. Scarlet took my cup and her own back into the kitchenette and began to clean up.

"Something tells me I'm going to enjoy your company."

"Me too," I agreed.

She seemed nice, and I wanted to get to know her better. I wanted to know if she was a wolf like Jace. Or was it a werewolf? But tonight wasn't the night to ask her.

"You should get some rest. I left my number by the phone. Call me when you're up, and we'll have breakfast together."

What if I woke up too late? She'd be waiting for me. No, I couldn't let her do that. Lunch would be better.

"I think—" I began, but she interrupted me.

"If I've eaten by the time you've woken, then I'll have some tea while you eat." She winked and headed for the door.

"Scarlet?"

"Yes?"

"Thank you for tonight. I apologize if I was a burden to you." I chuckled a little, still feeling embarrassed about it.

"Don't you dare apologize for releasing your emotions." There was a stern look on her now. "Last night was a difficult night for you. You're handling things better than many people would." She opened the door and turned back to me one more time.

"Goodnight, Jasinda." She whispered.

"Goodnight, Scarlet."

I walked to the door ready to lock up. Then I realized, I needed her to do something for me. Opening the door as quickly as possible, I looked out. But she was gone.

"Scarlet?"

Nothing. The hall was absolutely empty. No trace of her. She must be a wolf. Stepping back into my room, I turned to close the door.

I nearly jumped right out of my skin. She was right there waiting. "Did you need me?"

I gathered myself and calmly spoke, "Yes. Could you please give Jace a message for me?"

"Of course," she said with a knowing smile.

"Will you tell him that I'd like to say goodnight to him?"

"I think he'd like that."

"Thank you."

After I closed the door, I ran straight to the bathroom. I looked in the mirror to make sure I looked presentable.

Damn, the hair rollers.

With quick fingers, I got them all out then smoothed my thick locks. My lavender silk pajamas were cute and sexy. My eyes were a little puffy, but there was nothing I could do about that. Satisfied, I went out into the bedroom to wait.

The bed was extremely comfortable. My body relaxed into the down pillows and the soft mattress immediately. The sheets felt luxurious against my skin. Jace certainly knew how to treat his guests. I decided to watch TV while I waited for his knock at the door.

Chapter Seventeen

Jace

After running and hunting with Gravis, I decided to head back and shower. I was relieved that I'd let loose on the course. I didn't want Jasinda to see that side of me yet. She'd had a lot thrown at her already. The woman was tough, though.

Closing my eyes, I could still recall the punch she'd given Miranda. The power behind it stunned me and had turned me on at the same time. Most of the men there had felt the same way too. Her confidence had radiated from her. Her righteous anger demanding retribution from the one who'd done her wrong. And she'd been willing to handle it herself. But what shocked me most was that her punch had affected Miranda. There's no way a normal human could punch our kind and do any damage. Our females were *nothing* like her.

Perhaps that was the problem. Is it possible that was why I'd had a hard time mating? The wolf craved a strong-hearted woman who knew where she stood in this world and in my life, but who also knew not to control me. I needed a woman who could handle being alone a few nights and make decisions in my absence. I required a mate who could protect those who weren't able to protect themselves. A mate who could help guide my pack. That mate was Jasinda. I knew it, and so did my beast.

A knock sounded at the door, and I knew it was Scarlet. Nerves had me fidgeting about what she might tell me from her time with Jasinda. I didn't know what to expect. Did Jasinda feel safe and secure here? Would she understand that I was giving her space and not trying to suffocate her? She needed that release, even though I wanted nothing more than to console her. But I wasn't sure she wanted me around. She seemed different right before she came inside the house. Something had happened, and I wanted to know what it was. It seemed like she wanted to tell me but didn't know how.

"Come in." I sat on my couch.

Scarlet entered with a big grin on her face. Good. I'd thought she might be annoyed with me. She'd served my family for the past two hundred years, the past twenty of which were with me. I loved her dearly, and I valued her more than that. From time to time, she'd take on my asshole-ness, and I'd let her, but not tonight. She sat beside me, folded her hands on her lap and let her head fall. My heart thundered as I waited for what she had to say.

"I like her, Jace. I truly *like* her. I can see her as queen and as a suitable mate for you."

Relief washed over me. I already knew that she was my queen, but it felt reassuring to have Scarlet feel it too. "She seems to be doing much better after a good cry. She's a bit embarrassed about it, but that's normal for a human. We talked for a bit, and she was comfortable telling me about her feelings." She lifted her head and looked at me. Joy shone in her eyes. "It's about time you had an interest in someone."

"I know." I nodded at her. "My beast awoke the moment I saw her. I've *never* felt him this strongly before. It's as if she powers him in some way." I sighed.

Scarlet looked amused but kept quiet.

My fingers nervously ran through my hair. "Scarlet, it's odd that she is going along with all this and not arguing about being here."

"That does seem odd. Did Manny tell you anything?" She poked.

"He's not telling me everything." I assured her, taking my cell out of my pocket and dialing his number.

The phone only rang once before he answered. "Jace? Is something wrong with Jasinda?" Manny Santana worriedly asked.

"I know there are some things you aren't telling me here. But she came home with me just a little too easy. Why?"

"Jace, she has been oblivious to anything supernatural." He stated.

Scarlet's eyebrows shot up and I knew we were both wondering why the hell that was.

"What the fuck is going on, Manny? She should at least know something about the supernatural."

"She does. From what she hears here and there. But she never gets suspicious of the unknown or the oddest things."

"You're not making sense." I told him, tightening my grip on the phone.

"I trained her with real wolf shifters and non-wolf shifters. Jasinda asked if they had been steroids and the Mitchell brothers told her that they were just greedy fuckers who couldn't stop eating." Manny had amusement in his tone. "She believed it."

"Since you work with shifter wolves and the Mitchell brothers are wolves themselves, why not tell her?" I pointed out for him.

"Because I was instructed to not say anything about the supernatural to her directly. Leave it at that Jace. I am not able to say anything else. Be mindful when sharing things with her. Introduce her slowly, if possible."

He cut the line before I could try and ask him anything else.

"Why would anyone leave her clueless like that?" Scarlet questioned angrily.

"I don't know." I said walking over to my table and tossing my phone onto it.

Casting my eyes up at the ceiling, I remembered the last time the beast rose from within. It was a painful memory. One I didn't like to recall, but sometimes I needed the reminder. It was when Lina, my brother's mate, died. We all transformed the night of her burial. It took me three days to change back.

Scarlet had never seen my werewolf. My true beast. Much more dangerous than my wolf. She knew my family and a few others had the werewolf within. Our inner beasts. My family line was the strongest line known to carry the werewolf beast. I could transform into a wolf and a werewolf that was stronger than my wolf, but as the werewolf beast I didn't always have control. I turned around to face Scarlet as I heard her approaching me.

"She asked for you tonight and wants to see you before she goes to bed."

"And you're just now telling me this?" I scolded her.

Scarlet smirked, then turned to leave the room. "Her door is unlocked. Knock before entering."

"Scarlet?"

"Yes?"

"When do you leave for your assignment for the other king?" Scarlet had a secret assignment from a king in another realm.

"Soon. Why?"

"I just want to make sure I didn't disturb your mission. Can you make sure to add it to my schedule?"

"Already did before I came here. Goodnight," she called over her shoulder as she closed the door behind her.

She'd asked for me? That was a good thing. It was what I'd been wanting. Her wanting me.

"Oh, do you need to…you know…to change? I mean… shift?"

"No, I already went for a run earlier. This is different."

"Are you sure? You look like you're about to pass out on me." She chewed her bottom lip, trying to stifle a smile.

"What's so funny?"

"Nothing. I mean, you can pass out on me all you want. It's fine with me," she said with a wink. I knew she was trying to lighten the mood, and just when I thought it wouldn't work, my beast took a step back.

"Passing out isn't my style, especially not while I want to have my way with you," I expressed in a deep voice as another blush escaped across her cheeks.

She covered her mouth as a yawn escaped. "You should rest. Maybe you're stressed and working yourself up."

With a chuckle, I said, "Looks like someone else may need some rest as well."

"Yes, I do."

Jasinda snuggled into me, while I gently caressed her hair. She was asleep within moments, and I was grateful for it, because I'd almost lost it earlier. It was getting harder and harder to resist her, especially since I knew she wanted me too. Looking up at the ceiling, I willed the lights off and prayed sleep would find me.

Chapter Eighteen

Jace

When I arrived at her room, I knew she was sleeping. *Dare I knock?* Seeing her would ease me. She'd told Scarlet she'd wanted to see me before going to bed. Scarlet mentioned she'd left her door unlocked. I knocked and waited a few seconds to see if that might wake her. Nothing. Slowly, I opened her door and peered in. She'd fallen asleep with the TV on. It was muted. *Dammit, I'd left her waiting too long.* Quietly, I closed the door behind me and made my way over to her bed.

Her hair fanned out loosely over her shoulders and pillow. Her silk pajama bottoms hugged her thighs so perfectly, and her breasts were free inside her tee. Her hard nipples begged to be touched beneath the fabric. I wanted to explore every part of her. The thought made hard. I adjusted myself and sat beside her. Drawing in a deep breath, I took in her scent—lavender, roses and something else that was just Jasinda.

With gentle fingers, I caressed her face, tucking her hair behind her ears. She was achingly beautiful. Her soft, plump lips parted on a sigh and I longed to kiss her. I wanted to taste her sweetness again, but I wouldn't steal a kiss while she was asleep. As I looked her over, I smelled the tears she'd shed earlier. The saltiness still in the air. My heart ached knowing she'd cried. I always hated seeing a woman cry. The feeling of helplessness bothered me to the fullest. With her, that feeling was much sharper. I closed my eyes and inhaled her scent again.

"Jace?" she whispered.

My lids flew open, and I couldn't help but smile at the sweetness of her sleepy face. "I'm sorry. I didn't mean to wake you."

"You came," she sounded surprised.

"I wanted to say goodnight."

Relief flashed over her. "I'm glad you did. I wanted to say goodnight and to thank you for letting me stay with you."

If you only knew it was my idea. "I'm glad you agreed. I'm not sure if I would've been ok with you going somewhere else," I admitted to her.

"Lie down with me?" she asked shyly, patting the bed next to her.

My heart leapt with joy at her request. My beast and I feel the urge to always be near her. "Are you sure?"

The look that she gave me sent a bolt of electricity to my groin.

"I'm sure, Jace. I want you to stay for a little while at least."

Words escaped me at the moment, so I answered her without them. I closed the distance between us, kissing her softly. She opened her lips to welcome me. Our tongues collided as she moaned into my mouth. *Shit, this woman.* I rolled over onto her, spreading her legs apart so that I could fit between them. I pressed my hardness against her core. She tilted her hips up, pushing against me. A growl escaped my throat and she shivered. *Damn, she was aroused and she wanted me.*

I slowed the tempo of the kiss and pulled back. Jasinda bit her bottom lip as a blush darkened her cheeks. My heart lifted knowing I affected her as much as she affected me. Her eyes finally met mine as she lifted her head and pecked my lips. This woman would drive me insane. My beast lurched within me, determined to make his presence known. The urge to give in was so strong that my whole body tensed.

"Jace, what's wrong?"

I couldn't answer right away, which made the panic start to roll off her. But I couldn't seem to form any words. Slowly, I eased off her, rolling onto my back.

"Stop!," I shouted in my mind.

"I want her!" The beast yelled in return.

"Control yourself. You don't want to scare her."

"Jace, are you ok?"

"Yes. Sorry. I'm just struggling with my inner beast."

Chapter Nineteen

Jasinda

*M*mmmm, *bacon. Was I dreaming?*
It smelled likes eggs too, but everything was pitch black. My body was cocooned in softness. Relishing it, I remembered I wasn't in my bed, but in a guest bed at Jace's mansion. Involuntarily my arm reached for him, but only found sheets. Every morning for the past week, I'd woken up not recalling where I was initially.

It was hard to believe that much time had flown by already. Without my phone and laptop, I'd spent my days party planning the old-fashioned way —by hand; sketching themes, color schemes, setups—all while Jace worked at whatever it was he did. Every night, he came to my room for make out sessions and mindless TV watching. I felt like a teenager with a new crush. Each night we kissed a little longer and he left me wanting a little more. I was going to spontaneously combust soon. Normally, he had breakfast with me before leaving for work. He must have had to leave earlier than normal.

With a frown, I opened my eyes and looked at the spot where his body had been.

Why had he left without waking me?

With a leisurely stretch, I rolled toward the edge of the bed. Turning the bedside lamp on, I saw a cart with covered trays and pitchers of orange juice and water. Oooo, and a coffee thermos. A note was propped up against the front tray. The handwriting was neat and slanted.

Jasinda,

I have a few meetings this morning, but I should be back by mid-afternoon. I made breakfast for you. It's a bit of everything I like. Last night was amazing. Sorry for falling asleep on you this time but I'll make it up to you soon. Horseback riding under the stars. Not sure if you've ever been on a horse, but Scarlet will take you for a lesson today. So, no work today. Eat up, you'll need your energy. Call Scarlet when you're ready.

JACE

I bit my lip, cheesing at his note like some high school chick.

He thought it was amazing that we laid in bed most of the night talking. So, did I. I was the one who always fell asleep first, but not this time.

Even though we still hadn't done anything but kiss, which still didn't last long enough, everything seemed fine. I felt how excited he was and thought we might go further, but then he tensed up all of a sudden just like my first night here.

Was his beast that much in control?

The delicious smells halted my musings. Removing the lids, I found that he'd prepared omelets, scrambled eggs, and eggs over medium. Removing the remaining silver tops, I found pancakes, waffles, and fresh fruit.

Wow.

There was no way I could eat all this.

I made a plate with the eggs over medium and waffles. Then I opened the last dish and discovered sausage and crispy bacon. I helped myself to some and poured a cup of orange juice.

When I finished, I called Scarlet.

"Good morning, Scarlet. I just finished breakfast."

"Wonderful. I'll be up in about five minutes to clean everything up."

"I hate that all the uneaten food is going to go to waste," I said with regret coloring my tone.

"It won't be wasted. I promise."

Where does she take the leftovers?

"That's good. What should I wear?"

"I have the perfect outfit ready for you."

"Ok. I'll see you soon."

After hanging up, I decided to take a quick shower with that wonderful lavender rosemary stuff she'd used on me.

When I was done, I came and found clothes on my bed. All the food was gone. I pulled on the jeans and knee-high boots first. Once they were zipped up, I tugged on the orange t-shirt, which was nice and snug on me. It was bright as hell, but I guess she needed to make sure she could find me if I got lost during the riding lesson.

I made my way down the beautiful stairs. The minute I hit the bottom step, Scarlet came around the corner.

"Ready?" she asked excitedly.

"Yup. As ready as I can be."

"Good. Have you ever been horseback riding before?

"Yes, I actually love horses."

It was something my dad and I had done together. It has been almost two years since I'd been horseback riding, and I was stupidly enthusiastic about it. Brownie points for Jace. Three brownies stacked already. Two more and I'd drop my panties and say, *Yes, master. Do as you please with me.*

Damn, when had I started tracking brownie points?

"I'll take you around the land instead, since you know how to ride."

Scarlet led the way to the stable. The large red building was visible as soon as we stepped outside. A quick golf cart ride soon had us in front of the stables. Fenced in pastures stretched beyond the barn. Horses grazed, dotting the green landscape.

My eyes widened as I took everything in. "This is huge, Scarlet. How many horses does he have?"

With a slight twinkle in her eyes, she said, "Sixteen and one on the way." She opened the entrance while I followed behind her.

"Whoa. How long before the mare gives birth?"

Please be soon, please be soon. I'd always wanted to see a baby horse born.

"Any day now. I'd say by tonight or first thing in the morning, but you never know. This one is hard to tell."

"Is it ok if I watch the birthing?" I crossed my fingers like a kid.

She laughed. "Of course. Have you ever seen a foal born before?"

"No, I'm happy she's due any day. I'll get the chance to experience the birth."

The stable was even bigger than it looked on the outside. There were more than sixteen stalls. There was even a shower area for the horses. The walkway was big enough to host a party in.

But where were the horses? They were nowhere to be seen. Horses tended to be curious animals, hanging their heads out of their stalls to see what was going on. But none were. It seemed very strange.

Chapter Twenty

Jasinda

"Where are the horses?" I asked curiously. Scarlet stopped mid-step and tilted her head as if she was listening for something. She looked around as if she just realized they were missing. "That's strange. They normally hear me coming and are always waiting for me to attend to them."

"What's different today?" I asked quietly.

"*You.*"

"Me?"

"Yes, you." She peered into the first stall to her left. "Oh, dear goddesses!"

Her gasp made the hair on the back of my neck rise. She quickly ran to the stall on her right and gasped again. Fear had me rooted in place. I didn't know what to make of this. *Were they alive? Sick or something?* I was too afraid to look for myself. It didn't smell like death or disease. Scarlet had made it to the end of the walkway. A shell-shocked expression covered her face.

"What!?" I shrieked.

A small smile formed on her lips. *What the hell was going on? Why was she smiling?* One minute she seemed freaked out and shocked, then she was smiling.

Since the charity event things had been strange. Unbelievable and unimaginable things had happened to me in less than twenty-four hours. I should be running far, far away from all the magical things intruding in my life, but something in me wanted to learn more.

For some odd reason, I had an urge to hum a melody. A melody I'd never heard but was suddenly in my head. Closing my eyes, I took a few deep breaths. *What was happening to me?* When I opened my eyes, Scarlet was a few feet away, staring at me with a worried look on her face.

"You ok?" she asked.

"Yes, I just felt a little funny, that's all."

"You should see what the horses are doing," her voice was awe-filled.

"Is it bad? Are they hurt?" I was concerned.

She shook her head no. "Just peek into each stall. You'll see what I'm talking about."

Taking in another deep breath, I walked to the first stall. Lifting up on my tiptoes, I peeked in. The horse was... *bowing.* Right leg forward, left leg bent, and his head was tipped down.

I looked back at Scarlet.

"Bronze is his name," she answered.

"Great name. Fits him like a glove." I smiled, admiring his honey golden color. His mane was braided, causing gold highlights to appear woven into them.

"This is Ash." She nodded towards the next stall.

Ash was a light grey, like ashes. His mane was grey as well and fell over his face as he too bowed. *What in the world was up with the bowing?*

I kept moving down the line and around the other side, finding the same thing with each of the other horses. They were all bowing. Except for one, the pregnant mare. Her head was bent down, but she wasn't kneeling. I was in awe of her. Her belly bulged with the body of her baby. But the most astonishing thing was her massive size. They were all massive, much larger than normal horses, but she was the biggest of them all. I'd never seen a horse that big.

Or maybe I had and just couldn't remember.

The mare was a pearl white with a grey, braided mane. I don't know what came over me, but I opened her stall and walked right up to her. Gently, I put my hand on her forehead, and she slowly lifted her head. When our eyes met, it almost looked like she smiled at me. Her eyes were a midnight blue with specs of silver in them.

Before I could think about it, words were rolling off my tongue, "Blessings to you and yours." Bowing my head slightly to her, I ran my hand down her neck and stopped right before her belly.

"May I?" I asked softly.

She nickered at me as if she understood.

I smoothed my hand over her belly. The baby stirred. How amazing this was. I knew the foal was ready to come into the world, but the mare was anxious about her birth. I knew that feeling all too well. Hoping to ease her a bit, I closed my eyes and began to hum, as I rubbed circles over her belly. She relaxed. *How did I know to do this?* Shaking my head in confusion, I decided she should be lying down. So, I gently continued my humming and rubbing her belly, hoping to calm her enough so she would lie down. "It will ease you," I whispered.

Chapter Twenty-One

Jace

"So, how is she?" Elier asked as he paced his office.

I hadn't wanted to return his call, let alone actually sit down with him. He had some nerve asking how she was doing, when *he* was the reason for her suffering in the first place. His inability to just be honest with her and his cowardice in not breaking things off completely with Miranda wouldn't earn him much sympathy from me. It was on the tip of my tongue to tell him to mind his own damn business when I noticed the tortured expression in his eyes. Regardless of how poorly he'd treated her, he did truly care about her. I decided to throw him a bone.

"Better than I'd expected honestly. She's an amazing woman. And you're an idiot," I couldn't help the jab.

"I know. How's she handling the change in her living arrangements? She's always been pretty independent."

I hated the reminder of his familiarity with her and her mannerisms. My beast didn't like it either. Before he could even growl, I answered, "She seemed pretty comfortable when I tucked her in last night. And she's befriended Scarlet."

His eyes flashed anger at my initial comment, but he let it go. "I locked Miranda in a cell in the basement."

"What? Why?" I was astounded by the news. She should be dead, not in a cell.

"To punish her," he stated matter-of-factly.

"I figured you would've killed her by now." I said furiously.

"Believe me, I wanted to initially. But I decided that a quick death would be too easy of a punishment for her. She needs to suffer for what she did to Jasinda. For what she cost her. Cost *us*."

I didn't have anything to say to that. I agreed death was too kind, but I loathed the reminder that she'd caused Jasinda to lose the baby and that she still lived. My fists clenched at my side, and I gritted my teeth. My beast wanted out. He trembled in anger and the need to exact revenge.

"Do you have any ideas?"

"How about putting her on a leash? That way she can't shift at all. You could even zap her with one of those shock collars every hour." Although, to be honest, I preferred he end her.

"I like the way you think." He chuckled. "On a different note, are we still meeting on the next Tri Moon?"

The Tri Feast was a tradition to celebrate our ancestors. We only ever cancelled when there was an emergency. "As of right now, things will continue as planned. I'll let you know if things change."

With that I shook his hand and headed back home, thankful that my morning meetings ended much sooner than I'd expected.

I'd barely been in the house a few minutes before my phone started ringing. With a heavy sigh, I pulled it from my pocket. Had it been anyone else, I would've sent it to voicemail. But Scarlet was with Jasinda, so I answered.

"Yes?"

"You need to come to the stables right away," she whispered excitedly.

"What is it? Did something happen to Jasinda? Is she all right?" I pivoted and headed toward the stables.

"She's fine. Nothing's wrong, but you need to *see* this. You need to *see* her with Zosia."

I hung up, not caring if she had more to say. In minutes, I reached the stable doors where Scarlet waited for me.

"Look." Scarlet pointed.

With quiet steps, I made my way towards her stall and stopped. Jasinda was rubbing her belly in soothing, circular motions and humming a melody. With both hands in my pockets, I watched her in disbelief. In all my years, I couldn't ever remember seeing anything like it. Zosia didn't let anyone near her except me, my mother or Scarlet. She'd become even more ornery since she was foaling. Most times she didn't even like anyone looking into her stall. But here was Jasinda, in her stall, soothing her and her unborn baby. It was extraordinary to see. I quietly stepped back and turned to Scarlet.

Keeping my hands in my pockets, I moved near the stall. I really wanted to be in there with them. But I knew better. I could sense Zosia, and I knew whatever Jasinda was doing was easing her in her final stage of pregnancy. Gratitude kept me from interrupting.

"Jace?" Scarlet whispered just enough for my ears when she returned.

I looked at her. She was smiling from ear to ear like a little kid. "Yes?"

"Another thing you should know. Every horse in here bowed to her when she first walked in. Do you know what that means?"

"I have no idea. I'd have to ask Gravis. He might know."

She huffed, "I can't explain it, but this is something beyond amazing. She's truly special. I know I've said it before, but I'm telling you there's more to Jasinda. Please don't let her go."

Was she insane? "Why would I do something so foolish?"

"I don't know. Like you, I'm concerned she won't find some of the ways of supernatural beings very acceptable. It's a lot to take in, even when you're raised witnessing them. I can't imagine what it would be like asking her to just accept all these new things she's never dealt with before. But even more than that, I worry about the things you keep under lock and key, your secrets. If she is who we think she is, she will love *every* part of you. But if you keep things from her, you don't give her a chance to really know you. And eventually she'll learn more and more about you on her own. I'm afraid it might be a little too much for her if she discovers things without your guidance. I don't want her scared away. That's all."

She too was worried that my beast might be the cause of Jasinda never accepting me. But I wasn't about to let her go without a fight. I'd show her that she could trust me. Trust my pack.

"I know," I said gently. "I don't want to scare her either. I promise you, if I'm ever fortunate enough to win her love, I'll make her my priority.

She'll know me. All of me. And I'll protect her with all that I am and from all that may harm her. Even if that means protecting her from myself."

"Ok. Now go keep yourself occupied while I take her around the trails."

I took once last glance into the stall and smiled at the sight of them all wrapped up in one another, as I walked away.

Chapter Twenty-Two

Jasinda

Once I soothed the mare, I left her stall to find Scarlet standing there staring at me. Our eyes were locked and she seemed to be amused.

"What?" I asked her.

"Nothing. Are you done soothing Zosia?"

"Zosia?"

"Yes, Zosia the mare. The stall you just came out of."

"Oh, right. Zosia is her name, huh. It's beautiful."

I looked back and the horse met my eyes. It felt almost like she was thanking me or something. I shook my head at my crazy thoughts and the idea of reading messages in a horse's eyes. The possibility of understanding animals was nuts.

Then again, how had I known what to do?

Maybe my mother had the answers.

"What's going on in that head of yours?" Scarlet interrupted.

"I was just thinking," I said, waving my hand in the air.

"About what?"

"Well, I was wondering how in the world had I known *how* to soothe Zosia? I mean I just walked in her stall and relieved her of her pain and worries."

"You, my dear, are gifted," Scarlet offered.

"What does that mean?" I asked.

"It means that some people have abilities they aren't aware of. You have the ability to sense someone's worries or fears, then ease them." She said it like it's no big deal.

Was she serious?

"Abilities? Abilities I'm not aware of," I echoed with a laugh.

"I believe you *were* aware of them. You just don't remember." She opened Bronze's stall. Just as quickly as she went in, she came out with Bronze following behind her. "Your gift is part of you. It will always be within you. Even if you don't remember, it remains your gift. It comes to you naturally when needed."

She disappeared around the corner and returned with two saddles. After handing one to me, she put the other on Bronze. The weight of the saddle nearly caused me to fall and I had to grip it with both hands to prevent it from dropping to the floor. *How was she able to hold it with just one hand?*

"When you first saw Zosia, you went right in to ease her pain and worries." She opened Ash's stall. "It just came to you naturally without you even realizing it. Your gift came to life. It needed to be used, so you used it."

"But how can I use something when I don't even know what I'm using?"

Scarlet came out with Ash and took the saddle from me. "Like I said, it's a natural gift. Even if you don't consciously know what you're doing, your heart and your soul knows... Those things help us when we need them most."

"So, you think my subconscious reacted on its own?"

"Yes, your memories are in there, Jasinda. Just not front and center."

"This is all so strange to me. I don't know what to do with it."

Scarlet studied me for a moment before leading Ash and Bronze out of the stables. I followed, still deep in thought.

The grounds behind the stables were beautiful. Bright green grass rolled out as far as the tree line. To my right was a fire pit with a few chairs gathered around it. Straight ahead was a trail leading into the woods.

"Ready?"

I slowly nodded. "This is beautiful. Please tell me there's a waterfall out there somewhere?"

"Yes, we'll take the trail that leads to it."

"I would've never guessed all this was back here."

"That's because magic cloaks it. We don't want outsiders to know too much about us," she said sternly. "Don't want to draw attention to people who may be looking to do our kind harm."

"Our kind?"

"Yes, people like Jace, me and… others we care about," she said softly. "If the wrong people knew of our existence, they'd do everything in their power to capture us."

"Oh, ok. Got it." *Would it be rude to ask her what she was?* Maybe she wasn't ready to tell me.

She helped me mount Ash, then climbed up onto Bronze. "The trail ride takes about two hours, but it's fairly easy terrain." She nudged the horse with her heels, and I followed suit. Thankfully it was like riding a bike.

Chapter Twenty-Three

Jasinda

After trotting through the woods for a few minutes, we came upon a stream. The fresh water hit all my senses, causing me to inhale deeply. To yearn for a taste or a swim. The crystal blue color was unlike any water I'd ever seen before. The gentle sound it made as it flowed over rocks and brushed the edges of the bank was like a lullaby to my ears. It smelled amazing. Something told me it would be refreshing to my skin. It called to me, drawing me nearer. My horse wasn't too fond of getting closer to the stream, but he cautiously moved closer when I encouraged him. As he neared the edge, I noticed it wasn't a shallow stream.

It was deep, so deep I couldn't see the bottom. Only a few scattered rocks and a handful of fish were visible beneath the surface at the edge. Towards the middle there was nothing but the blue-green shadows and I didn't know what caused them. I felt the urge to swim. It was as if the stream was talking to me through its currents.

"Do you see something?" Scarlet's voice interrupted my thoughts.

"No, only a few fish. It's beautiful though."

"It's calming for me. I like riding through here," she admitted.

"I think I'm going to like it too. Actually, I think I like everything so far. It's pretty amazing."

She smiled pleasantly. "Good. You can come grab a horse whenever you like."

"But don't ride Gravis," she said in a stern tone. "He's probably the only horse who won't leave his stall for you. He's Jace's horse and doesn't like anyone else riding him."

I stiffened. "Why?"

"To be honest, I think it's about loyalty to Jace. And as strange as it may sound, I believe Gravis feels no one else is *worthy* of riding him."

"I guess that's understandable," I said with a nod.

"Horses are special creatures. They tend to bond with their primary riders and normally don't care for anyone else to ride them. All the horses in the stable haven't really bonded with anyone, yet. They're picky, if you ask me." She laughed playfully. "But they're loyal to Jace and those who are deserving. Bronze here just bonded with me a year ago." She gently caressed his neck.

"How long have you been riding him?"

"About five years. He's stubborn and knows it."

Bronze nickered at her response.

"See. He agrees that he's stubborn."

I laughed, because for some reason that's exactly what I understood from Bronze. Scarlet grinned at me and moved us along the trail.

Ash and I rode well together through the trails. He wanted to run but seemed hesitant because of me. It'd been a while since I had a good run with a horse. *What the heck. What fun was life without taking chances?* A thrill of excitement went through me. I kicked my heels and yelled, "Heeyah!"

Ash took off like he had turbo power running through his veins. It was magnificent how he could instantly reach such speed. I held on tightly, not telling him where to go. He was in control.

"Woohoo!" I could tell he liked it and approved of my excitement. It was so odd being able to read an animal, but I didn't care at that moment. The thrill of the ride made me forget everything that had happened the night of the charity event. Happiness flowed through me, and it was as if I belonged on Ash.

He ran faster and faster, jumping over logs and rocks that were in our way. If I hadn't known better, I'd have thought he was showing off.

After a few minutes he slowed to a trot. We were going down a path that led us straight to a pool of water. *Does the stream run through here?* Ash stepped into the water a little to drink. I wanted to get down so he didn't have to worry about my weight while he drank. He must have understood that's what I wanted, because he bent his front legs. I hopped off, stretched my back and went to the water's edge. Stooping down, I ran my fingers through it. It was cool, but not cold. Refreshing in my hands. I scooped up some water and drank it.

"Whoa. I see why you ran straight here. This is amazing water," I told Ash.

That small drink made me feel hydrated and rejuvenated. I thought I would have wanted more, but I was sated. Ash moved closer to me. He leaned in, sniffing my face, hair, and side. He was so gentle it tickled, and I couldn't help but laugh. *Was he smelling me?*

"Stop," I said, still giggling.

He whinnied as if enjoying it. Both my hands finally settled on each side of his muzzle, and he stopped. His ears swiveled around, and that's when I heard another horse.

"Jasinda?" Scarlet yelled.

"Hey, I'm over by the pool."

"Are you all right? You guys took off so quickly. I wasn't sure if you were ok with Ash's speed." She looked worried.

"Are you kidding me? It was incredible!" I patted Ash on his neck. "He is exceptional."

Scarlet chuckled at me and hopped off Bronze. She went over to the water and scooped up some for a drink.

"I really like you. You delight in the simple things. You make the best of things, even when the situation isn't ideal."

"Is that an odd thing?" I laughed.

"Yes, not many can do that. But you manage to. You have great strength within you." She turned back towards Bronze and hopped on. No way could I jump up on Ash like her.

"Ready?"

"Yes."

When I walked over to Ash's side, he knelt down so I could mount him. Scarlet was already trotting away. Just before I hooked my foot in, a branch cracked in the woods.

Chapter Twenty-Four

Jasinda

I turned toward the noise but didn't see anything out of the ordinary. Must have been a deer or something in the bush. I mounted Ash and made sure my other foot was securely in the stirrup. As I made a clicking sound signaling Ash to move, a growl pierced the stillness. Ash jumped, pivoting toward the growl. It was a good thing I'd had a good grip when I got on. He turned again, kicking his back legs as if something was coming. Laying my hand on his neck, I tried to calm him down. Instead, he started running. Hanging on tightly, I did nothing to stop him. The growl came again, closer than before. I finally glanced back.

What the hell was that? It was huge. Some sort of animal. *A bear maybe? Shit!* My heart was pounding faster than Ash's thudding hooves. I leaned forward, flattened my body against his and gave him full control. He sped up even more. But whatever that thing was, it kept up with us.

Oh no. Did it want to eat us? My curiosity was killing me. I *had* to know what it was, or at least try to figure it out. When I turned back again, I saw a wolf-like face. It had teeth sharp as hell, and drool dripped from its jowls.

Werewolf? Was that what Jace was talking about? Was a werewolf chasing us? Was it Jace? I shook my head. *No*, it couldn't be, he wouldn't chase me. *Would he?*

Ash was in complete control, because I sure as hell didn't know how to get back. I closed my eyes, trying to control my horror. Take in some calming breaths, my body relaxed, the terror subsided. The next thing I knew, I was unhooking my feet from the stirrups and leaping into the air, leaving Ash to continue his run on his own. I somersaulted and landed on the ground with a light thud. I glanced up, just in time to see the beast dig its claws into the ground and stop a few feet from me. A pair of yellow-green irises were glowing in my direction.

Crouching, I readied myself for a fight. The beast glared at me, and I glowered back it. It growled and I straightened my back, giving it my full height. Which really wasn't much, but I wanted it to see me as someone strong.

With a huff, it began circling me. I turned with it not wanting to give it my back.

Finally, it stopped and stalked toward me. Every movement was slow and deliberate. It huffed again and shook its head like a wet dog. I backed up, and immediately realized my foot was dangling in empty air. I tried hard to keep my remaining foot on the ground, but I lost the fight just as the beast pounced.

I tucked into a ball and hit the water hard and sank deep. My body unfurled and relaxed against the water, waiting to surface on my own. The current was too strong, pressing me down longer than expected, but I knew better than to fight against it. That was how most people drowned. When my lungs felt as if they'd burst from holding my breath, the current shifted and I swam up, bursting through the surface. I pulled in air, gasping as my lungs burned.

The current swirled around me, but I paddled with it, letting it carry me downstream. The trees changed color, shifting from green to a deep purple. Despite my predicament, I couldn't help but stare at them in awe.

How was that color possible, and how far was I from Jace's house?

They shifted again, fading into a shimmering sapphire blue. Before I could think about it too much, something brushed against my legs. Not knowing what it was, I tried to swim away, but something wrapped around my leg and I was pulled under.

Chapter Twenty-Five

Jasinda

Whatever had wrapped around my ankle pulled me through the water with unimaginable force. Bubbles streamed by me as I kicked and thrashed, trying to fight my way to the surface. Just as I broke through, I sucked in a breath of air before being pulled under again. Panic seeped through me, and it took everything not to struggle and lose air. Closing my eyes, I kept my body relaxed, letting whatever had me continue to pull me through the water. Fighting would just waste my energy and air. No way was I getting out of this. I was going to drown.

The bubbles had receded revealing a long, silver tail waving back and forth. It had thick scales and glowed like a fluorescent light.

What could it be?

It was skinny and very scaly. Little by little I blew out some of my remaining air to last a little longer before the burning of my lungs took over. Fear kept me from looking towards my ankle to see what had a hold of me. I didn't want whatever it was to know I was scared. We finally stopped just as I blew out the remaining air. I was lifted out of the water like a fish on a fisherman's hook. As I gasped for air, I was gently tossed out onto the ground, my body rolling in the process. I laid flat on my stomach sucking air into my lungs. My hair served as a curtain, shielding me from seeing who my captor was. I was grateful I didn't swallow any water.

Then I heard Jace's terrified voice shouting, "Jasinda! Are you ok?"

He sounded as if he'd been running from some distance. I slowly pushed up on my knees and looked towards the water.

"What the hell?" I muttered. What stared back at me was incredible.

A dragon. A real dragon. A beautiful, silver dragon. Holy waters! I was looking into the eyes of a dragon.

"Jasinda!" Jace drew closer.

The dragon roared, its breath going right through me

Jace broke through the tree line and stopped in his tracks.

Terror gripped me (cause ya know, Dragon).

"Jasinda?" The despair in his tone reached my heart.

"Don't move. Everything's going to be ok." He took a step closer, and the dragon roared again.

I nodded towards the dragon. "Don't move, Jace. He doesn't want you to move."

"She. The dragon's a she, Jasinda," he corrected me.

"*She* doesn't want you any closer than you already are. So, let's not piss off the pretty dragon," I said sternly.

Frowning, Jace tilted his head to the side a little and stayed put. Taking a deep breath, I turned back towards the dragon. A white glow cascaded around her. She had long lashes framing eyes with silver irises and white diamond-shaped pupils.

"Is it normal for you to have a dragon here?" I asked Jace. The calmness in my tone surprised me.

"Yes and no."

"Yes and no?" I mimicked, my heart racing uncontrollably.

"Yes, I have dragons that visit me occasionally, but she's not *my* dragon," he said through gritted teeth.

"I don't know what to do here, Jace." I was wet, on my knees, and biting on my lower lip to keep from screaming. I trembled inside, still too afraid to move.

"She doesn't want to harm us, especially you. She would've killed us by now if that's what she wanted," he stated.

His confidence made me relax some more. But I couldn't stop shaking—from the cold or adrenaline, I didn't know which. My teeth chattered, and I brought my hands to my mouth to blow warm breath on my palms. Jace took another step closer to me, concern etched into his features. I shook my head indicating for him not to move, he frowned again.

"We just need to find out what she wants," he said.

So many thoughts swam through my head. As much as I wanted to know more about her, I needed to get dry. Once my hands were nice and warm from my hot breath, I rubbed them up and down my arms. But it wasn't working. I sighed.

"Jasinda, we need to get you inside."

"How do you suppose we do that when she's staring at us?" I asked through clenched teeth.

"It's simple. We swap places," he suggested. "I'm fast. I can move you out the way and take your place to see what she wants. In the meantime, you head back."

He said it like it was no big deal. I looked back at the dragon, who was still staring at us. Well, staring at me. She stretched out her muzzle and blew on me through her nose. I tensed up thinking she was about to incinerate me with her dragon breath, but relaxed once I found myself getting warm and dry. *Did she just warm me up and dry me off at the same time?* Looking down at myself, I noticed that I wasn't drenched anymore. I was dry, even my hair, which I ran my fingers through to make sure of.

I looked back to find Jace smiling with his arms folded. *What was so funny?* I wanted to ask, but felt it was better to save it for later. Looking back at the dragon, I smiled and bowed my head. *Why did I just bow at her?* Lifting my head up, I was surprised to see she bowed her head in return. *What in the name of all goddesses was going on?*

"Thank you," I blurted out.

I wanted to stand but didn't know if it would antagonize her.

"You are more than welcome, *princeps*," She said.

Princess.

Holy waters! She can speak! I rubbed my hands together with excitement that a dragon spoke to me and I understood her. Clapping my thighs together, I rocked back and forth with an urge to shoot up to my feet and bombard her with many questions.

Chapter Twenty-Six

Jace

"**W**hy are you here?' I asked the dragon telepathically. I caught Jasinda staring back and forth between the dragon and I with a frown on her face.

"*I needed your waters to heal my injuries. My apologies for not seeking permission, but my injuries would not permit it.*"

"*Apology accepted. You can stay as long as you want, so long as you don't harm anyone here,*" I said firmly.

"*Of course. I am well aware of your rules.*"

"*Good.*"

"*Is she your mate?*"

"*I'm hoping one day she will be. But right now, she's not.*" I was sure the perceptive creature could hear the disappointment in my voice.

"*You'll be lucky to have her.*"

"*I would be. But I'm still trying to figure her out,*" I admitted.

"You're beautiful," Jasinda spoke in a reverent tone.

When I stepped closer to Jasinda, she grinned at me. She was excited but surprised by the dragon who was nearly 9 ft tall. Curiosity more than fear flowed from her. It was odd but it gave me joy knowing that although this was all new to her and might be scary, she'd decided not to shy away from the experience.

"Thank you," the dragon said.

"Can I…can I come closer…you know…to get a better look at you? I've never seen a dragon before," Jasinda asked in a soft timid voice that made me smile.

In answer, the dragon blew out smoke from her mouth towards Jasinda. It cloaked her at first, and then formed a cloud beneath her, lifting her in the air.

Jasinda gasped, as she steadied herself. It moved up slowly, higher and higher until the dragon was satisfied with her stature. Once the cloud stopped, the dragon stood to her full height. She wasn't a full-grown dragon, but she would be one in the next year or two.

"Do you have a name?" Jasinda asked.

"Skyla."

"That's a beautiful name. I love it," Jasinda said.

Skyla? She must be Sariya and Rave's daughter. They announced that name when they had their dragon years ago. How had I missed that? She was the same color as her mother, and they had the same eyes. Sariya was bigger and had gold weaving through her silver skin. I stepped closer to get a better look myself.

"Skyla, are your parents Sariya and Rave?" I asked.

She hesitated for a long moment before she answered, "Yes...they are."

"I wasn't sure. I never got the chance to meet you."

"Wait, you *know* her parents?" Jasinda gave me a puzzled look.

"Yes, they're my dragons. When Sariya was pregnant with Skyla, they went to a secure island to give birth."

"You *own* dragons?" She looked at me with disbelief.

"You don't truly *own* dragons unless they give themselves to you. Owning is probably not the right word. But having a dragon of your own is to have a true bond with it," I explained.

"Never in all my years would I have ever imagined a dragon would be in front of me. I thought they were extinct... Until now," she finished softly.

"You believed in dragons?" Skyla asked.

Jasinda tilted her head, her gaze going far away. "I guess I did. An older woman...my grandmother maybe? She used to tell me stories. That dragons were once the protectors of the universe, keeping the worst kind of evils at bay." She blushed and looked down in embarrassment as she explained.

"That *is* true. Dragons are known as the protectors of this universe. Each realm has its own dragons to ensure the realm doesn't disappear. If that happened, all those who lived there would die," Skyla informed her.

"Wait. So, other realms exist? I thought that was a myth too." Jasinda asked.

What the fuck had her mother done to her memories?

"Yes, we have many realms. You are…" Skyla stopped speaking and turned her head to the left, sensing a new being.

I already knew who it was and hoped to gods I could stop him from coming any closer. As I walked past Skyla and Jasinda, I looked directly into Skyla's eyes.

"Do *not* let her down until it's safe."

Walking away, Jasinda's soft fragile voice, tore at my heart, "Jace, what's going—" her voice stopped abruptly as she gasped. "Shit, it's back!"

Her fear called to me, but I also sensed her inquisitiveness.

When Ash had come running home faster than I'd ever seen before, he'd told me Dorik had chased them for no reason. Without waiting for more details, I'd immediately run towards the trail and had called for eyes in the sky to tell me where to find her. The dragon had been pulling her out of the water when I'd arrived. The appearance of the unfamiliar dragon had distracted me. I'd forgotten about Dorik. Now I faced off with him, standing with my legs apart and my arms folded to my chest.

Chapter Twenty-Seven

Jace

"**D**orik! What the hell are you doing?" I yelled, using every ounce of authority I could muster.

He stared me down, shoulders bristling as if uncertain whether to change back or continue on his hunt. He paced in a circle. Anger rippled through his wolf, but confusion filled his eyes. He was in between his wolf and werewolf forms. Trying to change from werewolf to wolf. His legs were his wolf's, while his shoulders and torso represent a hairy beast. Dorik had been angry for the past few years, and I wasn't sure if he'd ever be the brother he'd once been to me.

"*Who is she, Jace, and what's she doing here?*" he asked me in a strained voice.

I looked back at Jasinda. The dragon stood beside her, stance fierce and protective. Jasinda's racing heart echoed in my ears. But her gaze was locked on Dorik. This woman was truly unique. Most humans would've freaked out at the sight of all this monstrosity. *How odd was it that I'd found someone who could take things in stride and experience them with ease? Maybe I shouldn't jinx myself.*

I smiled at Dorik. "*She's my guest until it's safe for her to return to her normal life. Or should I say return to her life with a touch of supernatural?*"

"*Safe from what?*" Anger vibrated from him as he asked this question.

"*What the fuck? Are you serious? Why are you even asking me that?*" I spat, giving him back the same anger he was giving me. Why was he suddenly angry? As if he actually cared. He's been distant and secluded from the pack. Now he suddenly wanted to be involved?

He didn't answer at first. But of course, he couldn't help it. *"Her curiosity is refreshing and has me curious about her."* He shrugged sheepishly.

Watching him shrug almost made me laugh. Note to self, don't shrug while between beast and wolf mode. *"If you were curious about her, then why were you fuckin' chasing her while she was riding Ash?"*

"Her scent was driving me crazy. I just wanted to play with her. I wasn't going to hurt her. At first, I thought she was one of us."

"You had Ash running fast as lightning to get her to safety. You spooked them." I kept my arms folded to my chest, because if I didn't, I'd try to snap his neck with both my hands. *"Care to explain that a little better?"*

"I don't know. She's odd, Jace. She was scared one minute, but within seconds the fear was gone." He looked at me intensely. *"She flipped off of Ash and landed with such a grace that it surprised the hell out of me. It was a skilled flip, nothing easy. Something I've only seen in martial arts fighters."*

Unfolding my arms, I stepped closer to him. She knew how to handle herself with Miranda at the event. Maybe she'd been trained in martial arts.

"Are you sure, Dorik?"

"Yes, I was shocked myself. It was unexpected and impressive. Sexy too, if you ask me," he said with a chuckle.

I growled at him, *"I didn't ask you about the rest, did I?"*

"Relax bro. Nothing to lose your wolf over."

"Next time, don't chase a female on one of my horses."

"Whatever, Jace. You know I don't like newcomers. But there's also something different about her."

"What the hell are you talking about?"

Dorik sighed, *"I can smell it, Jace. It's not like you and me. She's so much more. She has so much power in her."*

He stood from all fours to his full height on two legs, deciding to transform into his werewolf. The new stance was less threatening because he no longer looked like a wolf ready to pounce. At his full beast height, he was eight feet tall.

Being a wolf and a werewolf was complicated at times. Werewolves were believed to be evil beasts. But that wasn't true. Wolves looked like your typical wolves, but larger than what they are supposed to be. We become both. We can change into our wolves at will but the werewolf comes with increased anger or at every Tri Moon that occurs each month.

A gasp came from behind me.

"That's a werewolf?" she spoke ever so softly.

Bringing my head down, I pinched the bridge of my nose. This was what I was afraid of. I put my senses out and felt a spike of fear coming from her. *Dammit!* If she only knew my brother and I looked alike in werewolf form. The only differences between us were our eyes and one of my legs was a shade of light grey, indicating I'm the prince. My fur as a werewolf was black, and Dorik's was jet black. But the colors were so close no one noticed. When in my normal wolf form, I was just a shade of grey, while Dorik's was a darker grey. We had enough similarities that sometimes we were mistaken for the other.

"I didn't want her to see this yet. I wanted her to see me change first, so she'd know I wasn't a danger to her. And you had to go fuck that up!"

"You should've warned me you were bringing her here, and I would've been in my wolf form instead!" He yelled back.

Without thinking I shouted, "I don't have to tell you shit! I don't owe you anything. You've excluded yourself from the pack and our family. You isolated yourself in your room, and you don't give two shits about anyone else.

"Except for today. Had I known, I would have stayed in my damn room," he said and ran off.

I stood there seething and defeated. I'd tried to get my brother more involved with the pack, but he'd kept himself locked up in his damn suite of rooms and would only come out alone for periodic runs. He'd withdrawn from us. I knew he was heartbroken, but he wouldn't let us help. It bothered me that he refused to join us on Tuesday and Thursday nights, when the whole pack got together as a family. We ate and bonded. Something my mother had taught us to embrace.

"Are you all right?" her voice, a bit shaky, sounded much closer than before.

Still lost in my thoughts, I turned, glanced down and met with a beautiful face. A slight smile trembled on her lips. Even without my full focus on her, I could read her. She wasn't sure what to do. I inhaled and smelled her fear, her worries and her nervousness. *Was I ok? What should I tell her?* Part of me wanted to lie so I wouldn't freak her out even more. But the other part of me wanted to tell her the truth. She'd said before she didn't like being in the dark. That's what I'd be doing if I lied. But I wasn't sure I was ready to tell her everything.

Chapter Twenty-Eight

Jasinda

Werewolf. *That was a werewolf. I think it was the same one that was chasing me.*

Now that I wasn't running for my life, I was not as freaked out. I was actually more curious than anything else.

"Please say something. I'm the one who should be speechless here," I pleaded while staring up at him. In his eyes, I could see he was trying to figure out what to say. His stare was crushing mine. "Was...that an actual werewolf?"

Pride filled me that I'd managed to ask that in a steady voice. Closing his eyes, he took in a deep breath. His shoulders drooped. Once he opened his eyes, those beautiful emerald that I loved to look into, were glowing.

"Yes, that was a werewolf," his confession was soft and defeated.

"Is that what you look like when you turn into one? Is that reason why your eyes glow?" I asked.

"Yes."

"Who is he or she?" I asked, careful not to assume like I did with Skyla.

"That was my brother, Dorik."

"Oh. Then why did he chase me?"

He paused to think about it. Pacing a little, he ran his hand through his long hair. He was nervous.

How could I ease his nerves? Without further thought, I stepped closer and grabbed his hand, pulling him to a stop. He faced me with concern in his eyes.

"It's ok. Just tell me. If he wants to eat me, then I'll run. But if he doesn't, there will be no running in my future," I said jokingly, my thumb tracing circles on the back of his hand.

He laughed while shaking his head. "You are truly *remarkable*." His hand tightened on mine. "He said that he wasn't going to hurt you. That *your* curiosity got him excited."

"That's all?"

"Yes, that's why I yelled at him."

I closed the space between us. As I looked up at him, all coherent thoughts fled my brain. *God, he was so tall and handsome.* A shy grin formed on his lips, and I couldn't help but grin back at him. Heat radiated from him, cloaking me like a warm blanket. Biting my lower lip, I gently rubbed the tip of my nose along his and pulled back enough to study him. His nostrils flared, like he'd read my mind. He closed his eyes.

"Jasinda, right now I want nothing more than to take you, claim you, mark you as mine. Can you please control your needs?" he growled.

"Mmmmm. I could go for that." *Oh god, what did I just say?* I trembled at my own words and bit my bottom lip again to keep me from speaking.

"Damn!" He pressed his forehead to mine and drew several deep breaths. "Do you still feel up to going horseback riding under the stars tonight?"

Hell yeah, if it means I'll be spending time with you. I wanted to shout my thoughts, but instead I kept them to myself.

"Yes, I'd love that," I said calmly, suppressing my excitement at getting him alone.

He smiled, his gaze penetrating mine. With my hand still in his, he stepped back, and we walked back to Skyla. I stifled my whine when he put space between us. I reminded myself we were still getting to know each other. It was strange that I felt as if I'd known him so much longer than the short time we'd really known each other. It was like some part of me had always known some part of him.

After everything I'd seen and experienced today, I wanted more. Needed more. *Who knew these unique creatures were not as bad as the books made them up to be?* The need to know what had been hidden and taken from me, was now exciting. It seemed like I'd find the answers right here with Jace.

"You ready to head back?" his voice cut through my thoughts.

"Do we have to?" I whined. "I'd love to spend a little more time with Skyla."

He smiled at me. "That would be nice. Let's take a walk towards the campsite." He tugged my hand, causing our shoulders to bump.

"Campsite?"

"Yes, it's where we hang around during the Tri Moons every month."

"Tri Moons?"

"One night every month the skies of other realms align with this one, making the moons from the Syrkin and Drakin realms light the night sky alongside the Lupkin moon. It's a really spectacular sight and a magical time."

"Realms?"

"The other realms where other creatures like myself live in. Lupkin is the native land of the wolves."

"Oh. And the Drakin?" I urged.

"That would be the realm where I live." Skyla chimed in.

My head swung her way. She was beaming at me. Pride was evident in her smile. I was lost to her.

"The campsite is just up ahead." Jace informed me, breaking the spell.

"So, what happens at the campsite?" I asked, immediately remembering that I didn't ask about the Syrkin realm. How quickly I was to want to know things but forget to finish asking about the current thing I come to learn about.

"That's when all the packs get together and have fun. It's like a party, but for the supernatural only. We have a big feast with plenty of food and drinks," he explained with tremendous pride. "We tell stories and tease one another about the stupid things we did in our past. Then we shift into our wolf forms and our ancestors' spirits join us. It's the one time we all put our differences away. Us celebrating in harmony as a big group helps to keep the souls of our ancestors alive. They feed off our combined energies."

"That sounds magical." I told him, rubbing my free hand on my thigh to tamper down my amazement and disbelief at what he revealed.

This was unbelievable! I wanted more than anything to prod him for more details, but I didn't want to sound too desperate.

"It is. I'd love for you to join us at the next one in a few weeks." He said, cutting through my thoughts.

"Really?"

"Yes, please come with me."

"As your date?" I asked, lowering my gaze at my sudden boldness.

What is wrong with me? I'm throwing myself at him like I've been craving a man for years.

His gaze fell on me. For a moment everything around us stopped, and we were the only ones there. His mouth tipped into a slow sexy smile.

"Yes, I wouldn't want it any other way."

My stomach did backflips as I beamed up at him. How was it that I was already captivated by this man? "I'm happy to be your date."

With another heart-stopping grin aimed at me, the world started moving again. Before too long we arrived at the campsite. It was a huge setup with tables and fire pits. Lounge chairs were scattered everywhere. Fat logs perfect for sitting were mixed in too. A few trees had tire swings and hammocks. There was a pool behind the trees with a path that led to it.

How much land did he own? Or was it his pack's? His place didn't look this big from the outside, but then I remembered what Scarlet had said. It was made this way to not draw attention. Now I understood what she meant.

"This is beautiful."

"Thank you."

He led me to a lounge chair, and I collapsed in it, folding my hands behind my head. He sat in the one next to me, while Skyla carefully lay down on the ground between us. She suddenly seemed smaller.

"Um…Skyla, did you shrink yourself?"

"Yes, it's how some of us have stayed alive for centuries. It helps us hide ourselves in places no one would think to look."

"That's frackin' remarkable." I said.

A husky laugh drew my attention to Jace. He coughed, trying to hide it. "What?" he asked, his eyes still smiling.

"Something funny?" I asked with a raised brow.

"Frackin'? So instead of saying fuckin' you say frackin'?"

"So. Is that bad?"

"No, not at all. It's cute. And I like seeing you get excited."

The teasing tone behind his words made me blush. A soft caress brushed against my skin. "So, do you live in water?" I asked Skyla, trying to distract myself from the heat building between me and Jace.

"I *can* live in water, if I chose to. But I mostly live on land," she said shrinking to the size of a small dog.

"Whoa. How cool!"

She jumped onto my lap and excitement shot through me at holding a real live dragon. Touching her tentatively, I paused to make sure it was ok before I proceeded. She leaned into my touch, and I was amazed by how she felt—smooth and hard, not unlike a bowling ball. I expected her scales to be rough, but they weren't. They were cool to the touch.

Holy waters! I was holding a miniature dragon on my lap. Could this get any better?

"Do you breathe fire or ice? I know it's a silly question, but…"

"Not silly at all, Jasinda. I breathe fire *and* ice," she said with confidence.

"Wow, now that's impressive!"

"My fire isn't just regular fire, and my ice isn't just regular ice."

"How so?"

"If I want to burn things, then I breathe fire. If I'm looking for something much stronger, my fire can become like lava."

"Lava fire?" I questioned.

"Precisely my, *princeps*."

It was odd that she called me princess again, but her endearment was touching.

"What about ice?" I pushed.

"When breathing ice, I can breathe sharp icicles meant to kill. I can also breathe a liquid slush that freezes almost anything or anyone."

"So, it's lava ice?"

"Yes, exactly."

"Show me," I squealed, leaping from the chair with her in my arms. "I mean…"

She laughed and jumped out of my arms, floating away enough so I wouldn't get hit. She opened her mouth and shot out icicles. Then she turned towards an empty chair and slush poured out of her mouth, freezing the chair.

"How frackin' amazing." I walked over to the chair, now a solid ice block. I ran my fingers along the solid cold block.

This was so amazing and wonderful. Pain washed over me when I considered I could've been a part of this world in some way. Then, anger rushed in on the heels of the pain.

Why had my mother chosen to leave us? How could my father have kept this from me?

So many different feelings flowed through me that I didn't know how to begin to interpret them. My body vibrated with more anger, and my hands began to tremble. I was still touching the ice chair when the unthinkable happened.

Chapter Twenty-Nine

Jasinda

The ice shattered beneath my hands and I jumped back as thousands of tiny shards trickled on the ground by my feet.

Jace took a step toward me, his expression troubled.

"Did I just do that?" I asked, the shakiness evident in my voice. I felt very unsure of myself at that moment.

"I think so," he answered quietly.

"Yes," Skyla said with certainty from above.

"Yes?"

"Yes," Jace said in a more determined voice.

Chills ran down my spine. Skyla landed a few feet away from me. She'd grown a few feet bigger than before, and her scales were glowing.

"It looked as if you knew what you were doing. I thought you wanted to smash the ice on purpose." She summed up the past few minutes for me with a faint smile on her face.

I didn't like the uneasy look on Jace's face.

"I don't remember doing that." *Which was true. I didn't remember.* My hand had vibrated, but not once had I raised my hand to smash the ice.

Cautiously, Jace stepped closer and ran his fingers through his hair nervously. "I wasn't sure of what I saw either. It was as if you were in a trance," he softly told me. "I called out your name, but you didn't respond. Somehow, I knew better than to stop you. I just hoped you wouldn't hurt yourself. Part of me figured you knew what you were doing, even though I wanted nothing more than to stop you."

"I don't understand." I massaged my eyebrows trying to remember. Bringing my hands in front of me I examined them for any injury. Nothing. Only trembling hands could be seen, but how is this possible? How was I able to shatter the ice without feeling any pain or sustaining any wounds?

"It's ok. Maybe it'll come back to you when you need it the most," Skyla said, sounding less concerned.

Jace closed the distance between us again. But I stepped back maintaining my space. Pain flashed in his eyes, but he hid it quickly.

"I'm sorry. I just need a minute to get my head on straight." I walked past him and sat back on the chair.

"It's so much to deal with, you know?" I looked up at him.

His face softened, as he came over to my side. He stuffed his hands into his pockets, but I could tell he was debating getting closer. With his eyes on me, he finally knelt before me, putting his hands on his knees. He opened his mouth to say something, but I cut him off.

"I'm hurt, Jace. Hurt that I've been left out of *this* world." I wave my hands around me. "The *real* world, not the fake world from my memories. I'm so… angry at my father for not telling me about any of this. For him *knowing* what my mother had done, while making up story after story to keep me in the dark," I spat out through gritted teeth.

I ran my hands up and down my cheeks.

"All of this amazes me. I want to know more. I feel left out. At first, I was confused about staying with you instead of the Mitchell brothers. They're all the protection I've ever known. Like big brothers." I turned fully towards him and ran my fingers over his cheeks.

Looking deeply into his eyes, I said, "Now… I just want more. I want to know everything. I even want to see you in your werewolf form and your wolf form."

His eyebrows shot up, stunned by my words. But even his surprised look didn't stop the words from flowing out of me. I needed to say them and I was pretty sure he needed to hear them. "I want to know *everything* about you, Jace. Everything. The good and the bad. Even some of your secrets if you're willing. However, if you want to tell me all of them, I won't stop you." I gave him a soft smile.

His features morphed into something I didn't understand. Was it incredulity, apprehension, desire, or possibly wonder? All of the above seem to fit. Heat ran through my body and I felt as if I was coming down from a high.

No, not again. The rumbling. My stomach heaved and churned like weights were being tossed around inside. I closed my eyes and waited for the cramps to come.

"Jasinda, what's wrong?" he asked with concern.

Taking in a few deep breaths, I finally opened my lids. The torment he held melted the cramps away. Hesitantly, he brought his hand to my face and caressed my cheek. I relaxed, enjoying his touch.

"Talk to me, please," he pleaded.

"Nothing. It passed."

"What passed?"

"Some weird rumbling inside me. Kind of like cramps, but not painful. I don't know how to explain it."

He blinked, and then recognition hit his face. "Let's get you back to your room."

"No, I want to hang with Skyla a bit longer," I said.

"It's best that you rest, my *princeps*. Don't worry, I'll come back to visit you. I've truly enjoyed your company." She bowed her head.

"Are you kidding me? I'm the one who has enjoyed your company. Thank you." I bowed my head in return.

"Until next time," Skyla said, as she flew off into the blue-grey sky.

Looking down at Jace who was still kneeling before me, my vision blurred, and flashes of white came into view.

His panicked voice pounded in my ears, "Jasinda! Jasinda! Jasinda, what's happening?"

I could hear him, but he sounded far away. His voice was fading and muffled, until I no longer heard him. Everything around me washed-out to nothing...

A sunlight came into view, while light blue smoke covered the air. No ground was to be seen around me. Only the sky with its sun. Then I saw them. Dragons in the clouds. No, they were flying *through* the clouds, leaving dragon prints behind. The tinkle of familiar laughter met my ears. *Was this a dream?*

Confusion filled me as I listened. The laugh was too close to home. It almost sounded like *me* laughing. My eyes dropped down, and I found my hands clutched around spikes. *This was a dream! Did I fall asleep? Could this be a possible memory of my past life?*

Wait…

Then it hit me. I was riding a dragon and…jumping from one dragon to another like an acrobat. It was a game between us. They were having fun with me because I liked it. The dragon beneath me leaned to its right, and I jumped into the air again doing a somersault. Screams of joy erupted from my mouth. Completely free in the air and trusting of these dragons. My body turned and landed on the next dragon. But his body tilted too much to the right, and I lost my grip and slid off.

I quickly turned my body over, so I could look up. I screamed, "SLATE!"

He roared and circled back, diving straight for me. At that point, I closed my eyes and hoped he caught me before I splattered on the ground. My heart raced faster than I ever thought possible. I screamed for Slate again. A shadow covered my form, and claws grabbed me with such force that I jerked in its grip. A pain shot through my neck, but I easily ignored it. I was too relieved by being caught instead. But it wasn't Slate. I *knew* this grip and the anger radiating from the dragon. I opened my lids and saw Slate hovering above us.

"Now, do you understand why I don't like when you guys play this game?" my captor scolded me in a firm tone.

"Yes, but I'm not sorry for doing it." I tried smiling, hoping he'd forgive me.

"Jasinda!" he yelled.

The image began to grow hazy. Sounds that didn't fit began filtering into my ears. My mind tried to process everything.

It was me in the images. Just when I was hoping to see more, cold creeped into me, and I awoke in water. My body trembled, and I looked around frantically to see where I was. But there was nothing. I couldn't see anything. Just a blur of white. A shadow approached my face.

"Jasinda?" Jace's frightened voice jolted me.

"What happened? Where am I? I can't see. It's all a blur." Panic invaded me like a tidal wave.

"Enchantress, calm down. We are back in your room and you're in the bath. I've already called for a doctor," he said.

I closed my eyes, trying to relax. However, I was in full panic mode and I wasn't sure what to do. *What happened to my sight?* The water began to warm, and I settled into it.

"Jace?"

"I'm still here. Just keep relaxing."

The sound of his voice soothed me. The water lapped around my limbs. His body settled behind mine, and he pulled me to his bare chest. The connection of his skin on mine zapped me. Though I couldn't see, I began to assess my surroundings. I was in water. Snuggled in Jace's arms. Wearing... my bra and... panties. His legs were bare against mine. He wore...shorts or perhaps boxers.

Blowing out a breath, I turned my head to the side. His hands dragged up and down my arms in a comforting motion as tears fell from my eyes.

"What's happening to me?" I faintly murmured.

Chapter Thirty

Jace

After bathing her and getting her as relaxed as I could, I stepped out to give them privacy while the doctor examined her. While he was with her, I dashed to my room to change clothes.

God, that woman was good at holding herself together when things were falling apart around her. She'd shed a few tears. But I was surprised it wasn't more. It broke me to see her this way. *How could she be so strong?* The females in my pack weren't as strong. And they were shifters. Maybe that was why I was so attracted to her.

My mother had always said I was different. That I was a king like her father had been. A fearless leader who protected those who couldn't protect themselves. She'd once told me I needed to find someone who could closely mirror my status if needed. Now I knew what she'd meant.

While I waited for word from the doctor, I wandered, ending up at Scarlet's door. When I knocked the door flew open and she moved aside to let me in. My eyes met her gaze. Creases marred her brow and the skin around her eyes. She was worried.

"How is she?" she asked in a rush.

"She's strong, that's for sure. And she's good for now, I think. Dr. Brown is with her."

"Jace, what happened?"

"I honestly don't know. All I know is her eyes rolled back, and she was gasping. Next thing I knew she screamed Slate."

"Who's Slate?"

"I don't know. I want to. But I didn't want to trigger another episode, so, I thought it best not to ask."

"Wow. Patient Jace has arisen," she teased.

"Shut it, Scarlet," I growled, annoyed at her comment while she laughed at mine.

"How are you doing?"

"Truthfully, I'm not sure. I hated seeing her like that." I sat in the chair beside her kitchen counter. "Putting her in the water seemed to relax her better. We sat like that for almost an hour before I took her out. After I got her dressed, Dr. Brown came up to see her." My fingers restlessly combed through my hair, then gathered it up into a ponytail. "I didn't want to leave her, but I thought it might be best for her to be alone with the doctor."

"Jace, I'm sure she'll be fine. Don't worry."

"I told the doctor to meet me here. I hope that's all right?"

"Of course it is. How long has it been?"

"Thirty minutes or so."

"Waiting sucks," Scarlet reminded me.

She was right about that. We sat there in silence, occasionally glancing at one another. The waiting was fuckin' killing me. But I couldn't think of a better place to wait. Scarlet poured me a glass of whisky.

"Drink. You need it to settle you."

When I met her gaze, pity colored her eyes. I wanted to tell her to shove her pity elsewhere.

Rising to my feet, I just stood there, lost. Shaking myself to gather my wits, I started towards the door so I could see what the hell was taking the doctor so long. A knock at the door halted me. Scarlet beat me there and threw it open, revealing Dr. Brown. I gestured for him to enter while Scarlet politely showed him where to sit.

"Scarlet, how are you?" he asked her.

My teeth clamped down on my tongue to keep me from telling him to toss the polite shit and get on with what could be wrong with my enchantress.

"Good, thanks. I like the haircut," she complimented the Doc.

My girl was sick and they were making small talk. Screw the compliments and let's just get straight to the point.

"Thanks. I thought I'd try something new," he returned.

"What's wrong with Jasinda?" I interrupted, my patience running thin.

"She's suffering from memorist," he replied.

"What does that mean?"

"It means she's having episodes of her memories. Reliving them," his tone was terse.

"I know what memorist is." My temper started to flare. He didn't react. He'd known me for years, so he was used to my temper.

Finally, I took a seat and inhaled a few quieting breaths. With my eyes fixed on him, I calmly asked him to explain, "Can you elaborate?"

"She had a memory of riding a dragon when she was younger. Playing games with them while in the air. The dragons used to toss her back and forth, until Slate accidentally dropped her."

"She's been around dragons before?" Scarlet's voice was surprised.

"Yes, in the memory she was reliving, Slate never caught her as she fell. That's why she yelled out his name—in the memory and out loud. She explained to me, Slate dove down to get her, but another dragon caught her instead." He crossed his legs, getting more comfortable. "The dragon who caught her was Rave. Isn't he one of yours?"

The revelation sent a jolt of surprise through me. Scarlet's eyes went wide. She was just as shocked as I was. "How do you know it was him?"

"Because I made her retell me the story. During her retelling, I invaded her mind seeing flashes of the dragons and recognized him. What I *don't* understand is why you didn't enter her mind when this all went down to see for yourself?"

"Because I don't think it's fair to enter her mind without her permission. And we haven't had time to talk about the fact that I can read her memories and her thoughts. Did you explain what you were going to do?

"Yes of course. That's the first thing I did," he said matter-of-factly.

I nodded my approval, but still wondered how she knew these dragons.

"He's yours, right? Rave? You two have a bond, no?" he asked me.

It wasn't possible. How could that be? I needed to pay Rave a visit. "Yes, he is one of mine. But how do you *know* it was him?"

"The scar on his leg I stitched up long ago. Visible to only me. That's how I remember my surgeries. It tells me the story behind the scar and gives me the memory of what I did."

"This is a mistake. It has to be," I told him, disbelief coloring my words.

"You won't know until you ask Rave." With that he stood and grabbed his medical bag from the floor.

"But other than that, she's all right?" I sputtered. Completely thrown off by what he'd told me.

"Yes, she's as healthy as can be." He walked towards the door and looked back at me. "By the way, she's a few days away from going through menstrus."

"*What?* How is that possible? She's not a wolf," I asked astonished.

"The hormones of the pack and the magic swirling in your cloaked world have apparently created a potent cocktail to make her experience the effects of menstrus rather than her normal period. Her body, for some reason, is adapting to the biology of her surroundings. I don't understand it, but you need to be aware of it and keep her safe. She won't understand what's going on," the doctor explained.

"Will it be a regular cycle or the Calling?"

"I don't know. I would assume if she's found her true mate at any point in her life, then that would affect the cycle and create a Calling. It will be an intensifying heat for her that she will be too sensitive to. And if that's the case, you need to be extra diligent in keeping her away from the other men." Opening the door, he disappeared.

"Not good, Jace," the worry in Scarlet's voice was apparent. It echoed my own.

"No shit!" I agreed.

Dropping my head into my hands, I groaned. *What the hell was I going to do?* She was possibly about to experience a Calling. That was why she'd been feeling off. It explained *everything*. And complicated everything. I needed to keep her locked in her room for three days. *Shit. Shit. Shit. Shit. How the hell was I going to do that?* I was too busy being too caught up in her that I didn't pay attention to the signs. Although I didn't think it possible for a human.

Getting up from my seat, I paced around Scarlet's room. "This isn't good. Scarlet, I'm not sure if I'll be able to resist her. I'm trying to take things slow. Make her fall in love with me first." *My beast was sure to rise over this. I'd have to get a few females involved to help me take care of her in case I had to disappear if I couldn't resist her. Fuck!*

I stopped in front of Scarlet. "I'm going to need your help on this," the desperation and worry in my tone surprised me.

"How else would you manage?" she said sarcastically. "I'll figure something out. Now go check on her. I know you're dying to."

Spinning on my heel, I nearly ran from her room and straight to Jasinda's. As I was about to knock, I inhaled a familiar scent.

Anthony. What was he doing here? I thought he wasn't ready to see her yet. He must have found out what had happened earlier today. The scent of his concern filled the air with an acrid smell. I tapped softly on the door and opened it.

He was in her bed, and her head was on his chest. Reflexively, a growl rumbled up my throat. The acrid scent of concern turned into the bitter aroma of fear. His whimper in my head cooled down my rising temper.

"It's not what you think, Jace," he pleaded. *"I came in to check on her, and she was asleep already. So, I climbed into bed and adjusted to hold her this way. I wanted to feel close to her. Needed to feel close to her. I wanted to sense she was all right,"* he explained carefully.

"I have to keep in mind that you guys are friends," I said begrudgingly. *"It's hard though."* That was the closest to an apology he'd get. And it was a begrudging one at that.

"I didn't mean to overstep. I know taking care of her is your duty." He frowned. *"Anyway, what happened to her?"*

"What have you heard?"

"Nothing. No one has told me anything."

"Then why are you here? Why do you think something happened?"

"Dammit, Jace! I'm not stupid!" he yelled, immediately realizing his mistake at shouting at his alpha. He cringed. *"Sorry. I saw you run in here*

with her in your arms. I saw the anguish in your eyes. Felt it from where I was. Please just tell me."

"Not in here. In your room. I'll explain everything to you. But not a word to anyone else. The only one in this house who knows anything other than me is Scarlet. Am I understood?"

"Jace, I trust you with my life. That's why I gave her to you. I've never brought her around, because she's not like us. She's different. But that event meant so much to me and I wanted her to be proud of me. She's the reason I got these clients. She believed in me. So you don't have to worry about me being a gossiper." Pain echoed his voice.

"I trust you, Anthony, but I needed to be sure you understand I'm not telling anyone else. So, if someone tries to fish information from you, I want you to shut it down immediately," I growled.

"Done," he said, bowing his head as much as he could in his position.

"Thank you. I'll meet you in your room in fifteen," I commanded. It left no room for argument.

He gently eased her off him and planted a kiss on her forehead. He loved her, and I knew he was loyal to her too. He'd do anything for her. As much as I tried not to show weakness, I liked that he cared for her in a platonic way. It showed me another side of him. One he didn't show much of to others. I stopped him just as he passed by me. Turning around I couldn't help but ask, *"Why did you give her to me the night of the charity event? Why did you trust me to be with her?"*

'Because I knew you would do just as I asked and I wanted her to have a good time. She deserved that too. Before this event I had been thinking about how I could Introduce my alpha to my best friend. One I lived with too. You always respected my privacy outside the pack, but one day I knew our worlds would collide. I'd been dying to tell her the truth about me, but with your permission of course. I thought that if you met her, you'd be more inclined to let me tell her everything. I felt as though you needed her, just as much as she needed you. I knew she'd intrigue you."

"Intrigue me how?"

"She's not like us, Jace. She is your strength. Your keeper of good and bad. She's someone different from us. You need a woman like her to be your

queen. Our queen. You haven't mated. All these females who want you, and you haven't mated. That's because none of our females are well suited to match you and understand the status of your role. She's the one, Jace. I feel it." With that he walked out the door.

He was right, I hadn't mated yet. Priscilla had been an option just to bring our packs together and bring strength between us, since she herself was a princess. But I'd never chosen her as a mate. She'd always wanted it, and yet I could not bring myself to say those words when we'd had sex.

Infinitely mine.

Those two words that would have bonded and mated us.

Chapter Thirty-One

Jace

Pulling a chair closer to her bed, I sat. Peace graced her face while she napped. She still wore my shirt from earlier. I hadn't taken the time to look through her stuff and dress her. I'd been in a hurry to get her skin covered up. Lathering her body with soap hadn't been easy. The feel of her breasts against my hands still sizzled through me when I thought about it. *God, she'd even let out a small moan when I'd touched her.* As I sat behind her in the tub, I was sure she could feel my hardness through my boxer briefs. I'd begun wearing them since her arrival. Made it easier to hide my erection. Feeling her pressed against my chest earlier had stirred my emotions. My cravings for her body grew even more.

Watching her now, I gently ran my fingers down her face. "What are you? You're definitely not human. You're so much more," I whispered to her.

What could she be? I couldn't make out anything from her scent.

And how did she know Rave?

I'd soon find out.

I softly planted a kiss on her lips and stood to put the chair back.

"Jace?" her voice was too soft.

"Yes?"

"Are we still on for tonight?"

"What?"

"Horseback riding under the stars. Remember? You said you were going to make it up to me." Her eyes drifted closed.

"Maybe we should save it for another night, don't you think?

"Nope. I think tonight is good. I still want to go… unless you don't?" She sounded disappointed.

"Of course I want to go. I just want to be sure you're feeling well."

"Nothing's going to stop me from going riding under the stars. Unless it's you."

This woman. "Then I guess I shouldn't stop you then." I couldn't keep the smile from stretching my lips.

"Good answer," she teased.

"Rest. When you're ready to eat, call Scarlet."

"Ok. Thanks"

"My pleasure. See you later."

After quietly leaving her room, I headed straight to Anthony. I wasn't sure how to tell him everything that had happened earlier this morning. Talking about it was just too hard. Before I could knock, he opened the door wide enough to let me in. His sadness and uneasiness hit me like a freight train. The smell of fresh tears was strong in the air. *Shit.* He really must have been scared for her.

"Anthony, she's fine."

"What's wrong with her eyes? Why can't she see?" Anger seeped out of his voice.

"How do you know she can't see?"

"I was by the door when she told the doctor."

Eavesdropper.

"Anthony, it's hard to explain everything. It's best to let you see for yourself."

He followed me to the balcony, and we sat side by side.

"Are you sure? You rarely let anyone inside your mind." He was nervous, yet excited at the prospect.

"Yes, it'll ease your mind."

"If that's what you want, then let's do this," he said eagerly.

Closing my eyes, I relaxed and felt him seep into my thoughts. When he saw Skyla, he jerked in his chair, causing the legs to scrape. He gasped at Dorik coming into view in my memory. And then seeing Jasinda use supernatural abilities left him reeling. His presence in my mind made his feelings very strong. He was beyond stunned by it all.

Turning his head towards me, his eyes were wide. I nodded at him, letting him know that I knew what he's thinking. He opened his mouth, then closed it. He was in disbelief, but he wanted to know more.

"She's fascinating, isn't she?" I asked.

"Yes, but I don't understand." He shook his head. "She should've been terrified of Dorik *and* the dragon."

"Yes, I know, and she was for a moment."

"Who knew there was this side to her?" he said in amazement.

"Yes, and can you believe she still wants me to take her horseback riding tonight?"

"Really?"

"She insisted."

"Why horseback riding?"

"Earlier today I had to leave for a while so I told her I'd make it up to her and horseback riding is a way to get to know her better."

"You mean get closer to her?"

"Same thing isn't it?"

"No, it's not."

I smiled, showing off my teeth. *Yes, I wanted to be closer to her.* I wanted to feel her, and Anthony knew it too. He grinned at me knowingly.

I returned to her room and set up watch in case she woke and needed something. I couldn't imagine how afraid she'd be if she was still blind when she awakened.

Chapter Thirty-Two

Jasinda

W hen I woke, Scarlet was there. She was sitting by my bedside and I could see her clearly. Blinking rapidly, I moved my gaze around to catch the shadow of the sun through the window. Apparently, I'd slept all night and half the morning away. Jace had recently left to take care of a phone call, Scarlet had explained. My stomach growled, so Scarlet quickly fixed me a plate. I ate while she watched. When I was done, I told her all that had happened after we got separated yesterday. Shock and relief flew across her face. It felt good to know in the short time I'd been there, Scarlet cared about what happened to me. I have yet to understand why my vision was temporarily lost.

Tired of being in my room, I asked if we could go downstairs.

We headed to the kitchen, and Scarlet navigated the wood cabinets and marble-topped countertops, gathering ingredients to make cookies. We'd just finished the oatmeal chocolate chip batter and were dispensing them onto three cookie trays. I hoped three dozen cookies were enough. All three trays fit into his triple oven. *Yes, he had a triple oven.* And he had two stovetops—one by the ovens and one on top of the huge island in the middle of his kitchen. The stove by the oven was gas powered, and the one on the island was glass electric. Everything was silver and black. The fridge was huge and had a touch screen on it. He even had a separate freezer. I could spend all day in his kitchen.

"I'll be back. Need to grab a few things," Scarlet told me.

As I cleaned up the kitchen, I hummed a tune. The melody was soothing and relaxing, but it was also unfamiliar, and I wondered where I'd heard it.

Suddenly, I felt a tingle through the hairs on my head. I spun around to find a man standing inches away from me. The heat from him was maddening. Anger haunted his yellow-green eyes.

"Stop fuckin' humming," he roared.

His fury pressed me back against the counter and the humming deflated. Fear rose in my throat, but no sound came from me. I was immobilized for a moment, until I realized who he probably was. He must be Dorik since he resembled Jace. I must say I preferred his human form over his scary-ass, horse-chasing wolf form.

"Did you hear me?" he barked.

Anger took over and I straightened myself. "I heard you." My strong and confident voice surprised me. "But who made you the humming police?"

His eyes glowed, the same glow as in his werewolf form. He advanced on me so quickly I didn't have time to move out of the way. He pinned me to the counter. His hard body against mine. I rose on my tiptoes and grabbed at his hard hand where it gripped my hips. He squeezed me and brought his face so close to me that our noses were touching.

"Because I told you to stop. I don't like your humming."

Closing my eyes, I swallowed my fear. Rage engulfed me, and I pushed him off me as he staggered back a little. While he was distracted, I slapped him. He stiffened and started to step towards me again, but this time I advanced first.

I pointed my finger in his face. "Don't you *dare* touch me again. If you don't like my humming, then...then plug your ears up. I wasn't made to be your punching bag. Besides, I wasn't even humming loud enough to bother anyone. So, go blow off some steam and stress on someone else. You don't even know me to act like such an ass!" I folded my arms across my chest.

As the adrenaline faded from me, I realized I was stupid for talking to him like that. But I didn't like being bullied by anyone.

"I could easily snap your neck. Or maybe I should chase you again and take a bite," he snarled.

"Seriously? You're trying to scare me with the werewolf? I'd rather face the werewolf, than face the asshole in front of me. At least the werewolf's nature is to bite. What's your excuse?"

He flinched at my words, a dark shadow appearing on his face.

"The song you were humming triggered some bad memories for me. I don't want to hear it." Pain filled his words. The type of pain that told me this really bothered him. His shoulders slumped and he teetered back and forth on his heels. Lost in those memories.

Stashing my anger in her closet, I tried to reason with him. "You know, there's a nice way to ask someone if they could stop humming? Or didn't they teach you manners? All you had to do was ask, rather than bark orders and manhandle me," I stated.

"He was taught manners, but it seems as though he'd rather get his head bitten off instead," Jace growled from behind him.

Dorik slowly smiled at me, before turning to face his brother. Jace's hands hung by his sides, but they weren't normal hands. They were long fingers covered with fur and claws as his nails.

"Brother," Dorik sneered.

"Dorik," Jace growled.

"Did you even hear what she was humming?" he asked Jace.

Something inside of my stomach flipped. I didn't know what was wrong with the melody. To me, it had been beautiful, but to them, it obviously meant something more.

"Yes, I heard it." he said ever so softly. Pain colored his words too. Before I could ask what was going on, he stepped toward Dorik. His claws had retracted back to human hands.

"Handling it this way is wrong. No matter how much it upset you. She's not like us. Jasinda doesn't know what happened."

The alarm for the cookies went off, so I quickly went to the oven and opened it thankful for some distraction. Cooked to perfection, I took them out. Silence filled the air. Turning off the oven, I focused on the cookies. They looked delightful, bringing a smile to my face. Even though they were piping hot, I had to try one. I always tried one. Taking the spatula, I scooped one out, blew on it a bit to cool it down and took a bite.

"Mmmm. That's yummy," I murmured to myself. "I did good."

Turning back to the room, I found both the brothers staring at me with hungry eyes. I froze in mid bite.

Both their eyes were glowing, which did nothing to settle my nerves. Jace's eyes glowed differently than Dorik's eyes. It was the same look Jace had given me that night in the water fountain. The fire in his eyes turned me on right then. I wanted him to take me right here on the kitchen floor.

A growl filled the room and like a rocket, I was pinned against the stove. *Again.* Cookie still in hand, Dorik's body pressed into me. A moan of yearning escaped my lips.

Oh, dear gods, what was I doing?

Pulling his head back, he looked at me with a devilish grin. He tried to bite the cookie that was still in my hand, but I was too fast and put the remaining piece in my mouth.

His smiled widened. "You want me, don't you?"

"No," I whispered, hoping I sounded convincing.

"Oh, I think you do. You *like* it. Me on you."

"Liking it and wanting it are two very different things. Sure, I like that a man is hot for me and trying to dry hump me here in the kitchen. But wanting *you* to do it, is different than what I imagined."

A growl came from behind him, but I couldn't see anything over Dorik's hulking form.

"How so?"

"How so? *Really?* Are you sure you want to know?" I blush at what I was about to tell him.

"Yes," he bit out.

"Ok. I like all this *being on me thing,* but Jace is the one I want all over me. *Not* you." Heat crept up my neck and back.

He pulled back from me completely. The grin stayed on his face. He reached for a cookie, but I slapped his hand like a little kid being scolded.

"Um…that's not for you. They're for Anthony. He gets first dibs," I kept my tone as firm as I could manage.

"Well, he's not here so first come—"

I cut him off, not wanting him to finish that sentence, "Oh, hell no. Not with me buddy. You back off, or I'll leash you." I pointed a scolding finger at him. I was going to have my head bitten off for that.

"You're joking?"

"Why wouldn't I be?"

He turned back to the audience behind him. Standing there was Scarlet with her arms wrapped around Jace in a bear hug hold, Anthony with his arms folded across his chest and two other females I didn't know.

"She's joking, right?" he asked them.

"Hellooooo! Of course, I'm not. Why are you asking them? I'm the one who baked the cookies." Now I was annoyed.

"Not a joke, Dorik," Scarlet said. "She baked them for Anthony because they're his favorite. She's going to share them with the rest of us in the house, but her number one reason was Anthony."

"Thank you, Scarlet." I smiled. Then I remembered how Dorik was just on me a few seconds ago. And how I moaned.

Another burning sensation began at the nape of my neck as I wondered what they would think of me. Thousands of dolphins jumped inside my belly from the way Jace drank me in with his stare alone, causing me to nearly whimper. The warmth and weight of Dorik's body had felt good against me, and I'd responded for a split second. But in the end, I truly wanted it to be Jace. No one else would be enough. I had to smooth things over.

"I'm sorry. I know I shouldn't have let him…" *What should I say? Hump me?*

"Don't apologize. It was all my fault. You don't know our ways." Dorik paused and took a labored breath. "And you really don't understand how you smell right now."

"Dorik," Jace said sternly.

"What? I'm just trying to explain myself."

"Not now, Dorik. Right now, you might want to go for a run."

Maybe the energy in the air shifted? I imagine Jace is feeling pretty hostile right now. Eyes still locked on me, Dorik smiled. "You all suck."

"Run, Dorik, before I chase you out of here," Jace retorted.

"Dorik," one of the females said with great authority. Both women seemed older, yet they still looked young.

Spinning, he growled at the group. Only Anthony and the woman who hadn't spoken flinched. Casting a look over his shoulder at me, he growled again.

I stood my ground. I wasn't afraid in the way he wanted me to be. He remained in the kitchen, brooding.

"Dorik, I'm Jasinda Santana." I held out my hand to him.

He looked at me oddly, then took my hand and pulled me into a hug. He inhaled deeply.

"You're squishing me. Remember I'm smaller than you," I croaked, causing him to step back.

He laughed. The lightness of the sound made him handsome. I smiled back at him and stepped out of his hug. He let me go, and without a word to anyone he walked out the backdoor.

What the hell just happened?

Chapter Thirty-Three

Jace

Scarlet's arms continued to squeeze me for several moments after Dorik disappeared. I wanted to rip my brother's heart out and eat it.

What the fuck was he thinking approaching her that way? He knew not to mess with her, yet he just couldn't help himself. I knew he smelled her after he pinned her the first time. I knew it hit him hard. Her scent crazed him just as it crazed me. She was going into menstrus and potentially a Calling and soon wouldn't be able to control her needs. I needed to get her to stay in her room for a few days. Away from *all* the males. It wouldn't go well for me if she had multiple sex partners. My brother wanted her. Her impending cycle had driven him to act the way he had today. But I'd hurt him if he touched her again.

Her nervousness overwhelmed the scent of her desire. Confusion and uncertainty marred her features. She needed me. The tension left my body, causing Scarlet to slowly let go of me. I walked over to Jasinda and gave her a sheepish smile. She smiled in return, but there was a nervous twitch to it.

"Are you all right?" I asked.

Her mouth dropped open. "Am *I* ok? I was going to ask you the same thing. Being that you walked in here and saw your brother pin me not once, but twice, I'd say you shouldn't be ok, or should you?" she asked and looked disappointed.

Her sadness twisted my heart. I longed to erase her doubts about my feelings for her. I also had to find a way to explain what she was doing to the men in the house. She didn't know how badly her Calling was going to affect us all. Even if she didn't experience a true cycle. Luckily, Anthony wouldn't be as affected because he has been avoiding her as much as he can. He viewed her as family and wouldn't make a move on her. But he would have to find someone to release all his arousal on from the exposure to the increased hormones that are caused by her Calling.

Grabbing her hand, I pulled her closer. The motion stirred up her scent again, making me suck in a sharp breath. "Honestly, I'm not fine with what he did at all. *But* I do understand why he did it. I'm not angry with the way you reacted to him. Maybe a little bothered by it happening, but not angry with you."

"Ok..." She frowned in confusion. "Not the reaction I was expecting. I *am* sorry though. I didn't mean to react to him...that way. I mean..." She was adorable when flustered. "I mean, I was already turned on when I looked into your glowing eyes. The heat and desire in them... Anyway, next thing I knew, your brother was pinning me, and I was liking it. But I didn't want to," her voice sounded a bit shameful and her eyes seemed to be memorizing the patterns on my kitchen floor. "I thought you know... that you might... be angry with me," her voice dropped with the last part.

Oh, I was angry. I was angry with Dorik.

She was turned on? I knew I'd smelled it. But I wasn't sure if it had been toward me or my brother. When a female entered menstrus, if she wasn't mated and with the one she was destined to be with, the influx of hormones would drive her to have sex with any man who attracted her. If her mind was weak, then she'd have any man in her bed. The fact that Jasinda had been able to resist Dorik and tell him she didn't want him, suggested she might not be as weak minded as most of our females who were in the Calling. The possibility brought me immense joy. My heart lightened, and some of the worries I'd had since I'd started considering the possibility of her being mine began to ease.

Anthony cleared his throat behind me. "You think I can cut in and give her a hug?"

I grinned at her, and she rolled her eyes playfully. She sidestepped me and hugged him. They stayed like that for a moment. Her breath hitched, and the smell of saltwater filled my nose as her first tear dropped. She was crying softly and so was he.

"Please don't be mad at me. I'm so, so, so, so, so, so, sorry that I didn't tell you about my pregnancy and the stillbirth. I just couldn't bear telling anyone else. But the way you found out wasn't fair," she rushed through her tears, blowing out a relieved breath.

Anthony pulled back to look at her. "Don't apologize. What you went through was…was…it was a lot, Jasinda. I hate that you went through that. I don't *ever* want to experience that again. Feeling that you were alone when it happened was the worst part for me. I hope next time you go through something that you can count on me to be there for you no matter what."

Anthony cast his eyes in my direction, seeking permission to be there for her in the future. She laughed as she sniffled.

Taking her hand in mine, I lightly tugged her toward my mother. "Come on, I need to introduce you to two of the four important females in my life."

My mother and aunt observed her closely, taking her all in. Their excitement was palpable.

"Jasinda, this is my mother, Sheraphina and my aunt, Lizbeth."

Shock filled her eyes instantly. She lowered her chin nearly to her chest with embarrassment. It made me want to laugh.

"Uh…uh…hi," she said nervously.

My mother stepped closer and drew her in for a hug. "It's so wonderful to meet you." My mother spoke gently, trying not to make Jasinda feel any more uncomfortable than she already was. Especially after we'd all witnessed what Dorik had done and how she had reacted to him.

"Sorry you had to see all that. I'm not sure what came over me."

She turned fully towards my Aunt Lizbeth. "Hello."

Lizbeth stayed quiet as she approached. She gently grabbed Jasinda's cheeks and they both lowered their gazes. A gasp escaped them, and a moment later my aunt lifted her gaze. Her eyes widened, and soon after a smile formed on her lips. Jasinda's lids fluttered, squinting in some sort of understanding.

"Hi," my aunt signed.

I watched in amazement as Jasinda signed back, *"It's a pleasure to meet you."*

"You know sign language?" I asked in awe.

"Yes, I've had to use it several times. Especially for parties for We Can Help." She signed as she spoke.

"You're the one who does those events?" I couldn't keep the surprise out of my voice.

"Yes."

I had donated every year to that facility. They specialized in finding solutions for those who couldn't hear, see or speak. They'd begun branching out to seeking answers to help those who couldn't walk or had lost mobility function in their hands. It was a great facility. They catered more to children than adults.

"How often do you do their events?" I couldn't help but ask, seeing as my aunt loved attending them. She had always been amazed by the themes.

"All the time. Anytime they need me, I work my schedule around to fit them in."

I approved and I saw that my aunt did too. She was beaming over meeting the person who was behind the event planning.

"Interesting," Anthony said. "You know, Jace is the top donor."

"You are?" she asked.

"Yes, I am. My aunt started going there to see if they could figure out a treatment for her."

A jab of pain hit my gut at the lack of progress so far. She'd once had a voice, a beautiful voice that used to sing to me when I was little. Now I sing to her, because she loves it.

Jasinda gave my aunt a beautiful smile.

"They're amazing. I'm sure they'll find a solution that's best for her. I've seen some pretty amazing things happen." Her confidence was reassuring.

"That's good to know," my mother replied, relief evident in her tone. "I see you're using the lavender rosemary products in your bathroom. How do you like them?"

"I love them. Lavender is one of my favorite plants. And I love the way it smells when it's mixed with the rosemary. I hope you made a perfume out of it, because you'll have a customer for life." Jasinda pointed to her heart.

My mother clapped with her excitement. "Actually, I just finished it. I was looking for someone to test it. Would you like to be the first?"

"Yes, please." Jasinda joyfully responded, rubbing her hands together.

Was that all it took to make other females happy?

"The gift set in the bathroom, do you actually sell it?"

"Yes, but it's not going quite as I expected."

"Really? May I ask why?"

"The females among us don't really care for it. They prefer name brands."

"Hmm. I did notice there wasn't a name on your stuff. It just says *Rosemary-Lavender Shampoo* and lists the ingredients. Maybe you need to give it a name." She bit her lip and put both hands on her hips as she thought. "Like Shera Natural Collections or Sheraphina's Natural Collections. You can do something like that. It's just a thought."

"I like that. I didn't think about putting a name on it. I just make the products and try to sell them in our market."

"You'll sell more if you give it a name. Trust me. Especially when it's all natural. I'd love to buy some gift baskets from you and include them in my event packages."

"That would be lovely. But only under one condition."

"Shoot," she said.

My mother looked at me puzzled. *"What does shoot mean?"* she asked me mentally.

"Just tell her your condition and I'll explain later."

"I'd like to come see the place where you work. To see how you plan your parties and events. Does that suit you?"

"Of course. That would be great, but it might be boring too."

"Good. I'll start getting baskets ready for you."

"Thank you."

My mother squeezed her hand and said, "See you later," as she and my aunt walked away.

The excitement from meeting Jasinda danced between my mother and aunt's features. They kept passing glances and smiles back and forth. A quick look from my mother reminded me that I needed to explain our ways sooner rather than later to Jasinda. I just needed to pay Rave a little visit first. Something told me I'd find my grandmother with him. I hadn't seen her all day.

Chapter Thirty-Four

Jasinda

"Jasinda?"

"Huh?" I jumped and turned towards Anthony. I'd been lost in thoughts of all that's occurred in the past few days, trying to make sense of it.

"I said that I need to take care of a few things. Can we hang out maybe tomorrow?"

"Yes, of course. That's fine. I just wanted to make you some forgive-me cookies and hopefully have a Netflix-and-chill night."

He busted out laughing and I couldn't help but join him. We used to tell others that we were going to make it a Netflix-and-chill night just to make them think there was something between us. Elier never minded. He thought it was funny. Scarlet gave Jace a puzzled look and I stopped laughing, pointing a finger at them.

"I'm not explaining this to them, you are," I expressed.

"Oh, it would be my pleasure." Anthony smirked at me.

"Are you going anywhere near the office?" I asked.

"Yes, why?"

"Can you do me a huge favor?"

"Yeah, what's up?"

"Would you check in and make sure that Angie isn't going too crazy without me and I'll check in soon?"

"You got it. That'll be my first stop."

"Thank you."

He hugged me goodbye and left. Scarlet followed him with a grin. *What was funny?* I looked at Jace and found him beaming too.

"What?" I shrieked.

"I get the Netflix-and-chill thing you guys got going on. It's pretty funny," he said with a smile dancing on his lips.

"You do?"

"Yes, I do. So does Scarlet."

"How? We didn't explain it."

"You didn't have to. Anthony did." He pointed to his head.

"Ahhh. So, telepathy huh?"

"Yes, you could say that. I can also see someone's memories and thoughts."

"*Really?* Can you see mine?"

"No, I mean I *could*. But I'm not trying to. I really don't pry unless I need to," his voice was clipped.

How embarrassing if he'd been reading my crazy sex thoughts about him. Worry must have flashed across my face because he reached out to brush my cheek and said, "I promise not to read your mind or your memories without your permission."

"Sorry. I wasn't really accusing you of doing it. Just curious to know how you go about it"

He studied me for a moment and relaxed. He put his hand in his pocket and pulled out my iPhone, staring at it.

"I pick up your brainwaves using my magic. That's how I know when you are thinking or possibly day dreaming." Stretching out his hand slowly, he finally handed it to me.

"It's fully charged and safe to make calls now. No one can trace you. I'd still like for you not to tell anyone your location."

"That's all right by me."

He nodded and those emerald eyes burned right through me. *Was he in my head?* I wanted to ask him so many questions, but I didn't know where to start. To distract myself, I opened my phone and saw 102 new emails.

"Shit! Can I email as well? You know… do more of my work from here?"

"Yes, all is clear. I also made sure your laptop was cleared as well. A chip has been implanted so you can email and video chat if you like."

"Wow. You went all out, didn't you?"

"I had to take safety precautions to keep you and this place safe. The Mitchell brothers helped." My heart leaped at the mention of the brothers helping. I miss them.

"Thank you."

"I need to get back to my office. I have a conference call to make. I'll see you at eight." He kissed my cheek and walked off.

So many emotions rolled through me at his quick retreat. I felt like I was on a seesaw. *Was Jace pissed at me for reacting to Dorik?* He said he wasn't, but he had every right to be. But then again, we weren't a couple. We hadn't even defined our relationship. I felt the overwhelming urge to connect with him more and hoped to do just that tonight. He had awakened something in me that I couldn't explain. I wasn't sure what had come over me since I'd been here.

Leaning against the counter, I began reading my recent emails. I replied to the ones from today and noticed that Angie had replied to all the ones prior to that. On my phone were a few text messages from Elier and missed calls from Angie. Other than that, no one else texted me. *Strange.*

Elier: please call or text me and tell me how you're doing. I just need peace of mind.

Elier: just one text telling me you are all right. Nothing more.

Elier: I spoke with Jace today and he said you're doing well. Can we talk? Maybe do lunch?

I owed him lunch and an explanation. He needed to know why

Me: Hi. I just got my phone back. Are you available for lunch tomorrow?

My phone chimed immediately, as if he'd been waiting for my text.

Elier: Yes. What time?

Me: How does 12:30 sound?

Elier: 12:30 it is. I'll pick you up.

Me: Ok.

Elier: Jasinda?

Me: Yes?

Elier: How are you feeling?

Me: Good for now. Thank you.

Elier: Ok. See you tomorrow.

A nervous feeling settled over me. *Would Jace be upset about my lunch with Elier?*

I wished I could engross myself in work so I wouldn't think about tomorrow. Speaking of work… my fingers quickly tapped on the screen.

It rang once and she answered. "Girrrrrl! How are you? Are you back home? When are you coming back to work?"

I laughed. "I miss you too, Angie. Can you take a breath?"

"Are you kidding me? I've been worried about you. Even though Jace called to give me updates, that doesn't mean I still don't worry."

"Jace called you to give you updates on me?"

"Yes," she whispered. "I kinda blew up your phone after you left. I wanted to make sure that everything you told me was true. He called me back that same night on another line and explained why you didn't have your phone. He said it was best that you didn't communicate with anyone until he fixed your phone and laptop." She sighed. She wasn't kidding about blowing up my phone. I think I had over a hundred calls and text messages. "He even came to your office and fixed all the phone lines. Well, actually he sent someone to do it. So I didn't get to see him. He had my cell phone fixed too."

Whatever was going on must be extremely serious for him to go through all that trouble just for me. Maybe it was orders from my father. My father could be a little overprotective.

"Jasinda, are you there?"

"Yes, sorry. I'm just baffled by all he did. He said I can start video chatting, so on our next call I'll FaceTime you."

"You better. He said within the next week or so you might be able to come to work for a few hours during the day. He wasn't sure yet. He's waiting for more info from your father."

"He didn't mention it to me."

"He said he wasn't going to because he didn't want to get your hopes up if it didn't happen." She cleared her throat. "He sounds handsome. Please tell me he's handsome. You deserve it. Because that man speaks of you as if you're a treasure." Excitement filled her voice.

"Well…he is more than handsome. He's scrumptious girl!" I blurted.

She squealed loudly in my ear. "I *knew* it! There was something in his voice that told me he was."

I laughed, because I couldn't help it. I owed her an explanation. Sighing dreamily and taking a deep breath, I gave her the condensed, non-magical version of what had happened the night of the charity event, from meeting Jace up to the Mitchell brothers appearing.

"Shit, that's crazy."

"Yeah, I know," I agreed. "And you know how overprotective my father is. He knows Jace, so he asked him to look out for me. Jace's place is off the beaten path and his family is around."

"At least you've already gotten the awkward meeting of the parents out of the way before you even start dating." She laughed.

"Speaking of his family, I need to ask you for a huge favor. Can you work on some logos for me and get them printed within the hour?"

"Is a client coming by?"

"No, Anthony is stopping by to check in on you and the biz. He was going to give you an update too, but now you don't need that."

"You need logos for labeling?"

"Yes, I'll send you an email in a minute with what I am looking for."

"Great. Send it when you're ready."

"Perfect. And I'll try and stop by tomorrow. I'm supposed to have lunch with Elier."

"Wait. What? Elier?"

"Yes, he now knows about me losing the baby and I need to apologize to him." I explained.

"Right. How did he react?"

"He wasn't too happy about it. He was more hurt than angry. So, I decided to have lunch with him and try to explain why I didn't tell him."

"Are you ready for that?"

"No, but can I truly be ready?"

"You got me there."

We talked for a few more minutes. She told me about how the days have been without me at work. "You really need to get back here and do your work."

I laughed and told her, "What if I give you a raise?"

"I guess that would be good."

"Talk to you soon," I said.

"Bye."

When I disconnected, I sent a quick text to Anthony then booted up my laptop to get to work on the logo.

Chapter Thirty-Five

Jasinda

"We're going to need a lot of cookies to feed the crowd around here," Scarlet informed me.

"How many people are we talking about?"

She paused and mentally counted. "There are twenty bedrooms in the mansion. Each is built like an apartment, giving each person complete independence and privacy. Eighteen of the rooms are occupied, including yours."

"Wow. I'd have never guessed there were so many suites from looking at the outside."

"And that's not even counting all the cottages spread across the property. Most of the pack lives on the property or in the main house. Some don't stay here all the time, but everyone has a place when they need it."

"That's awesome. Has it always been like that, with everyone living here?"

"For about the last twenty years or so. That's about how long Jace has been protecting his pack by moving everyone close."

"So how many little cottages are there?"

"Fifteen at last count. The pack members who are mated like their privacy, so they take the cottages. Jace has new ones built whenever new couples form."

"I can't believe I didn't notice fifteen cottages on the grounds in all the times I've been outside the past week or so."

"Oh, you wouldn't notice them unless they were pointed out to you. They're cleverly hidden with the pack's magic. If you are not a pack member you are not able to see it until it's disclosed to you. It's an extra precaution to keep the pack safe and away from prying eyes."

She knew a lot about things around here. "How long have you been here?"

"I've been with Jace for about twenty years now. I love him as if he was my brother, and I want the best for him. He's a good leader and takes care of everyone under his charge."

"Since you've been around so long, I guess you know his brother pretty well too."

"Yes, he's not as bad as he seems. He's been kind of lost ever since Lina, his mate, died."

I gasped. "Oh no. I had no idea. That must have been terrible for him."

"It has been. And to make the tragedy even worse, Lina was two months pregnant when she died."

Tears filled my eyes as my heart identified with Dorik's loss. "What happened?" I whispered.

"They were ambushed one night while they were camping out with a few other packs. They fought together, side-by-side, trying to protect each other. Dorik tried to get her to safety. But... she was beheaded before he cleared a safe path for her to take."

My body jolted in place, placing a hand over my now pain-filled heart. "That's horrible."

"Dorik carries a huge amount of guilt over what he sees as his failure to protect her. Adding that to the unbearable grief of losing both his mate and his unborn child, and he's been a pretty miserable person to be around," Scarlet explained in a pain-filled voice.

"I can understand that."

"Anyway, I've worked for Jace's family for a long time. But my time working for the prince has been my most enjoyable."

"Prince?" I asked in confusion.

"I guess you didn't know. Jace is actually a prince."

I cocked my head to the side considering this strange new piece of information. "Really? Jace is shifter royalty? I bet that complicates things for him."

"What do you mean?"

"In the human world, there are certain expectations for those of royal blood. What they can do, who they can befriend, hell, who they marry."

"Yeah, I guess some of that is true of shifter royalty as well. Jace's parents actually wanted him to mate with Priscilla because she's a princess. They figured it would be a great fit that would bind two packs together."

"Priscilla, you said? Angry looking, woman about this tall," I asked with my hand indicating the height of the woman who had approached us the night of the charity event.

"Sounds like you met her."

"You could say that." I refrained from commenting on how ill-suited I thought that bitch was for Jace. Scarlet continued to talk about Priscilla, but I zoned out. When she mentioned his mother and aunt, I started to pay attention again. It seemed Scarlet was quite the talker when she was comfortable around a person. I continued to listen without interrupting her as she explained all of the family dynamics. I wanted to know *everything* about wolves, werewolves and whatever else I could.

Finally, I asked the one question that was playing in the back of mind the whole time she spoke, "What are *you*? Are you a wolf and a werewolf?"

"Oh, no. I'm neither."

"Supernatural though?"

"Yes, this world has many supernatural beings. Almost all the ones you can think of really exist." Opening the oven, she took the cookies out and placed them on the counter. "I'm different. Ancient. My kind is in hiding. We do our best to stay invisible to the human world."

"Really? Is it so much of a secret that you can't tell me?" I urged.

"Yes and no. I can tell, but I'm very careful who I tell. I only tell those I trust," she said with a hint of a smile.

"Oh, right. I'm sure that must be hard. I understand why you won't tell me." I wasn't bothered by it at all. It was hard trusting people with a secret like that.

"Do you truly understand?" she asked.

"Yes, I mean…I may not be in your shoes, but I understand keeping something like that a secret is important to you and probably your kind. It's a risk you take *every* time you divulge who and what you are. That's something worth keeping safe. So, yeah, I understand."

She studied me for what felt like forever. I was frozen in place, held by her stare. Quietly, she took the cookies off the pans and placed them on the plate. Then she scooped more cookie dough and plopped it on the cookie sheets. When the pans were full, she popped them in the oven.

She then turned back to me and looked me straight in the eyes. "I'm a dragon. Some of the pack think I'm a vampire. But I'm truly a dragon."

"Whoa! Are you serious or are you messing with me just to see my reaction?"

She burst out laughing, and my excitement depleted for a second. Knowing another dragon excited me. If she was telling the truth, it meant I'd met different shape shifters!!! Not just wolves. *Was Skyla a shape shifter?* If so, I wondered what her human form looked like.

"Yes, I'm serious. I've just never heard anyone talk like that before," she confessed.

"Holy waters! You *are* serious. Can I see what you look like as a dragon? Wait, no sorry. That just came out. Of course, you can't show me. It's a secret."

"One day I'll show you. I promise."

"You don't have to. I get it. It's fine. But if you're serious, just know I'll be super excited and I might pass out." I was acting like a child in a toy store. "Oh, and I promise to take this to my grave."

"Thank you. That helps to know," she said with a smile.

"So, why are you guys in hiding?"

"There are men killing dragons for sport, out of fear and for the dragon's skin. Others want to study us. Now there are so few of us left. Our numbers have been in a steady decline for a long time now. I worry that we will go extinct."

"That's awful."

"Extremely. There aren't enough of us left to mate and get our numbers back up. Some of my kind have tried breeding with other shifters or even humans. But there's been no luck producing any dragon offspring. The babies born of the mixed unions produce half-breeds who are immortal, but they can't shift."

Tears shimmered in her eyes as she talked. I decided to change the subject. I hoped I could ask Skyla more questions since she was an offspring herself. Did Scarlet know about her?

"So, I'm a little nervous about having lunch with Elier tomorrow."

She gasped and dropped the spoons she was holding.

Shit! I tried to change the subject again. "Does Jace know you're a dragon?"

"Yes, but he's the only one here who knows." She cleared her throat. "Did he say it was ok for you to go out? I mean, to leave without him or a guard with you on your lunch with Elier?"

"He didn't say I *couldn't* leave. Besides, this is Elier we're talking about. He wouldn't let anything happen to me."

"Yes, I know that, hun. But Jace and Elier aren't really on the best terms right now. I'm not sure if Jace trusts him."

"Well, *I* trust him to keep me safe. That's all that matters."

Why couldn't I have a say in who I thought could be trusted? Sure, Elier had lied to me and had kept things from me. But he'd never physically harm me or let anyone else do so. I knew he still cared for me. Jace would just have to understand that I trusted Elier. For some reason, I think I'll always trust Elier.

Chapter Thirty-Six

Jasinda

After heading back to my room, I got ready for my date with Jace. Shuffling through my clothes, I finally decided on jeans and a sleeveless purple shirt that said, "Make it rain," in white letters. It was one of my favorite shirts, which was why I ended up with a few of them in different colors. I pulled on the same boots Scarlet had given me for my horseback riding lessons. My hair fell in loose, wavy curls. Deciding to go light on the makeup, I applied black eyeliner and put on a plum matte lipstick.

Anthony came back while I was getting ready and gave me what Angie had put together. She'd boxed it up like a present. I set it aside for Jace's mother. I hoped she liked it. The artwork was just how I envisioned her logo in my mind. Hopefully, she'd agree.

"You mind if I hang out for a few minutes and keep you company?"

"Like you ever have to ask that. Please sit."

I waved my hand at the many sitting areas he could place himself.

He sank onto the couch. "I'm so glad that you know that I am a wolf now."

I smiled. "Me, too."

He ran a hand through his hair. "You have no idea how hard it was keeping it from you all this time. To have to be so careful about what I said."

"I guess we both kept secrets. But we don't have to anymore," I confirmed, taking a seat next to him.

Over the next hour, I peppered him with questions about the part of his life he'd kept hidden from me. We laughed about stupid stuff and caught up, letting me know that things were back to normal between us.

"Well, I should let you finish up so you won't be late." He stood to leave, causing me to stand with him.

"Thanks for keeping me company. I've missed you the past several days. Don't ever get so mad at me that we don't talk again." I swatted him on the arm.

"Yes, ma'am." He bowed playfully.

"So, we're good for our slumber party tomorrow night?"

"Yep." He pecked my lips. "See you later."

That gesture restored something in my heart. It let me know that we were truly fine. He'd always said goodbye with a kiss and a see-you-later.

It was a quarter till eight. I had just enough time to deal with the labels. Picking up the phone, I called Scarlet and asked her to give Jace's mother the gift I had for her. I scribbled a note telling her if she didn't like it, we could always change it.

Within moments, Scarlet was at my door. "These are some labels I had designed for her natural beauty products. When you give them to her, can you please stay and make sure she approves."

"Absolutely. This is really sweet of you."

"Please reassure her that it's no big deal if she doesn't like them. We can work on the artwork and logo together until she's happy."

Scarlet smiled at my gesture. "I promise. I'll take care of this for you."

Nervous and excited, I made my way to the back of the house where I was supposed to meet Jace. He stood there, looking up at the sky. Blue jeans and a black V-neck shirt worked well for him. I admired his backside as I approached. He turned then, his eyes already showing a light spark in them. I tried not to trip over the last few steps. *Why did I feel so stupid and clumsy around this man?* His intense look made me feel like I was dessert, and he couldn't wait to taste me. I was dying to taste him. My fingers itched to run through his long hair and tug at it.

Closing the small gap between us, he touched his lips against mine. Without thinking, I put my hand at the side of his neck and wrapped my fingers around the back of it, keeping our lips connected. A rumble sounded in his throat, and I slowly tilted my head back to look at him. The glow in his eyes was luminous, and *that* did something to my insides. Heat rushed through my veins like liquid fire. My belly dipped and twirled like a ballerina.

He grinned at me. "Hi."

His husky voice was so sexy.

"Hey," I barely heard myself say.

A flash of confusion and anger crossed his face. "Who's been on your lips?"

"Um…Anthony kissed me today. But it's not what you think," I said hastily.

"Then what *should* I think?"

"It's how we've always greeted each other. A quick peck on the lips. Nothing more," I said.

A smirk lit up his face. "I'd rather he not kiss you there. But I can't deny that he truly cares for you as if you were his own flesh and blood, so I won't let that bother me or change what you two have together."

Relief splashed through me. "Thank you."

He kissed me again. "By the way, I like this shirt. Ready to ride?" He waggled his brows at me.

Multiple meanings to his question and so many ways I could answer him. One of which was a resounding yes. *I'm ready to ride you all night and all day.* Clearing my throat and watching his grin spread, I nodded. He *knew* what he was asking me. Probably knew my silent answer too. He grabbed my hand and held it tightly—almost as if he was trying to tell me he'd never let go. I smiled to myself, because I loved how his hands felt on me. Rough, working hands that shifted into claws when he became his wolf or beast. Hands that I wished would touch me everywhere.

We walked through the stable and straight to the biggest stall. He opened the door and tried to grab a horse, but the horse was bowing. This had to be Gravis. I didn't get the chance to really see him when I came with Scarlet. My body walked in on its own accord. Gently, I placed one hand on his cheek and the other on his muzzle.

"*Joyed*," I said.

The horse finally looked up and gave me his attention. He knelt again, then lifted his head back up. Slowly I backed out of the stall, and Gravis followed me.

Jace was grinning at me. "What did you *do*?"

"I don't know," I said with a shrug. "I just acknowledged him."

"What does *joyed* mean?"

"Um…I don't know. I think it means at ease, and it's a pleasure all in one."

"Do you *know* that for a fact?"

"No, it's what came in my head."

"That's strange. It sounded like you knew what you were talking about."

"I do know what I am talking about." I winked.

Once Gravis was completely out, I gasped at how huge he was. He was the biggest of them all. Gravis kept his eyes on me the whole time I stared at him. He was a beauty and there was a sense of peace in his presence. I walked up to him again and he bent his head, putting his cheek against mine.

"Nice to meet you too. I'm Jasinda, and you must be Gravis." He blew out a breath acknowledging me.

"Did Scarlet tell you about him?" Jace asked in awe.

"A little. She said no one rides Gravis but you. So, am I taking Ash?"

"No, you're riding with me on Gravis."

I smiled. Uncertainty warred with excitement within me. I wasn't sure how it was going to go, but I was thrilled about riding on the same horse. It was intimate and I liked the idea of it. Gravis was certainly big enough to carry us both with no problem. With a speed I couldn't fathom, Jace got Gravis all saddled up and ready to go. Grabbing my hand, he pulled me towards his horse and helped me get on. With skilled grace, he lifted himself up behind me. God, his body felt rock hard pressed against mine, and he smelled so good. An impulse to lick him ran through me. He tugged me closer and I obliged nervously.

"Are you comfortable?" he asked.

"More than you know."

A satisfied growl rippled from his throat at my words.

He pulled the reins and leaned into me. "Hold on."

I tightened my legs and held on to the horn of the saddle. Without a word or sound, Gravis began walking out of the stable.

Chapter Thirty-Seven

Jace

'*Take us through the trails that are open to the sky. I promised her a night of stars.*'

Gravis did just as I asked. He walked us down the trail while the stars illuminated the night. I still couldn't believe that she wanted to go for a ride after what had happened yesterday. Then to see her in my kitchen today baking away like nothing had ever happened. It tugged at my heart. I wanted her in my kitchen, baking as many cookies as her little heart desired. It's as if she belonged here and my kitchen was built to please her.

As we rode through the trails, wind swirled between us. I felt as though this was exactly what we needed. Gravis walked rather than trotted, knowing I wanted to make it special for her. Her nerves sparked and bubbled with enthusiasm, and I liked that I made her feel that way. Smiling to myself, I knew my beast was satisfied as well. He hadn't really interfered too much after that first night here when it came to her. Thank the wolves for that.

She leaned further back into me, and her body relaxed immediately. It was as if she needed my touch just as much as I needed hers. I was glad her experiences in the woods yesterday hadn't deterred her from coming with me tonight. This just showed me what kind of woman she was. Strong.

We were supposed to be stargazing, but she hadn't looked up at the sky yet. *Wonder why?* Slowly, I reached around and placed my fingers on her chin and tilted it up towards the sky, making her head rest against my chest. She gasped at the sky's splendor, and I let my hand fall to her thigh. I watched her profile, as in awe of her as she was in awe of the sky. She turned her head from side-to-side, watching the luster in the stars. Then she slowly looked down at my hand on her thigh. The smile that lit up her face rivaled the beauty of the stars. Heat and desire filled her irises. *God, did this woman not know how much she turned me on with just her smile?* She *wanted* me to touch her. She liked it when I touched her. That just made this night even better.

"What do you think?" I asked in her ear.

"I think...I think it's magical. I can't remember ever seeing stars that shine this brightly. The sparkle in them is breathtaking."

"I wanted it to be special. They kind of remind me of diamonds. What do you think?"

"They do! How amazing?"

A grin lifted my lips at her reaction. Her wonder pleased me, and I couldn't wait for us to get to the sparkling waterfalls. I was pretty sure she'd go crazy for them. I'd arranged for us to eat inside the cave behind the waterfall. I'd also lined up for a few wolflins to pay us a visit. I wanted to see how she'd interact with a few teenaged wolves. There were a few wolflins under my charge that had been abandoned by their mothers when their mates died. It was a rare thing, but sometimes female wolves became weak after their mates' deaths, and thus unable to care for their children.

"So, you're an alpha prince?" she asked.

Damn you, Scarlet. I should've known she'd tell her eventually.

Clearing my throat, I answered her, "Yes, I'm the alpha prince of my people."

"Of your people?"

"My pack. My father's pack, my grandfather's pack and my uncle's pack."

She turned back to study me. Curiosity sparkled in her eyes. Thousands of questions had to be running through her mind, and I found myself wanting to answer them all. It was odd, this wanting to share everything with someone.

"Do you have a big pack? How do you manage them all?"

"First, I really only have one pack. It's the one I manage for right now. My father, grandfather and uncle have their own packs. To my pack, I'm their king, their leader. To the other packs, I'm just a prince. Being an alpha prince means if the alpha in the other packs should die without a challenge, then I automatically become their alpha. If they should die by challenge, and I feel the challenger isn't alpha material, then I can ask him to step down. I'd become alpha or he could challenge me as well. If I was the king, no challenge could be made unless everyone is in agreement."

"Wow. That's a lot, don't you think? I mean for you to pick up a pack from another alpha?"

Her asking me this question made me giddy inside. It showed an understanding of the job few within the packs even comprehended. Everyone thought it was easy to do.

"Yes, it can be. It can get pretty tricky. Some males may feel like they're ready to be alpha but being alpha is a big responsibility. One can easily let it consume their minds. Some males let the power of being an alpha corrupt them. That's when I come in."

"How do you decide if they'll be alpha?"

Another good question. None of the other females ever cared to know any of this. They just wanted to be my queen and have my status.

"It's something I do with my father. I ask him for his advice, and I tend to talk to the pack as well. I try to see how they feel about the challenger."

"That seems fair."

She turned her eyes back to where we were heading, but before she did, I saw approval in her eyes. I wanted so badly to see what she was thinking, but I'd promised I wouldn't do that without her permission. Her head fell back against me, so she could gaze up again towards the diamond sky. My eyes followed hers. We rode silently for about five minutes, then she turned her face around again. But instead of just looking at me or asking me questions, she grabbed my arm that rested across her thighs and lifted it off her. Then she carefully lifted herself into a crouching position. Before I could ask her what's she doing, she spun herself around to face me. The move was graceful, and if I hadn't seen it myself, I would've said impossible to do in a shared saddle on a moving horse. She bit her lower lip and grinned at me. Then she eased herself back down facing me.

"Were you uncomfortable?" I asked, though I approved of this change in seating.

"No, not at all, but this is much better. Now I can see you without craning my neck."

My smile widened. "Oh, I think I like you this way better too."

"Oh, *do* you?"

"Yes."

"Good. Because I have another question."

"Shoot," I said, mimicking her tone from earlier.

She smirked. "How do you become king besides your father dying? Is that even possible?"

She was on a roll with her perceptive questions. I had to give her credit for being genuinely interested in me.

"Yes, it's possible. It can happen two ways aside from my father dying. One would be me getting either mated or married. Or my father can announce me as king and step down."

"Are you ready to be king?"

Was I ready to be king? I'd been asking myself that question for the past ten years. That's when my father had first approached me about it. He'd asked me to mate with Priscilla. I told him no then. If mating with Priscilla was what would make me king sooner, then I'd rather not. I knew I'd disappointed my father with my decision. He'd been wanting to step down as king and hoped he'd have grandchildren to teach instead.

"Only if it chooses me."

She frowned in confusion. I knew my answer was a riddle. But it was the only way I could answer honestly. She stared at me with her bewildered expression. I refused to elaborate any further and hoped she didn't ask me to explain.

"Ok. Not the answer I expected, but I'll accept it." She winked.

I let out a breath of air, grateful that she wasn't pressing the subject.

"So, this land of yours is pretty impressive. I like how the seen is unseen. What else is hiding here?" She seductively asked.

Did she realize how sexy she was? She wasn't even consumed by her beauty. It was one of the reasons I wanted her so badly.

"Look to your right. Tell me what you see?"

She scrunched her nose and leaned over a little to get a better look. Then she quickly peered back at me, then back again. When surprise registered on her features, I knew she'd finally seen what was out there.

"How did I not see this before?" she whispered more to herself than to me. "That's what Scarlet was talking about. Hidden before your eyes are things you aren't looking for. Awesome."

Her eyes stayed focused on the cottages, unable to peel them away.

Chapter Thirty-Eight

Jasinda

I couldn't believe there were miniature homes right before my eyes. They looked like little cottages with chimneys on them. *Who would've thought?* They were hidden behind the trees, and fog surrounded them like a cloak. Shadows moved inside the windows. There were three cottages in this area. But only one was completely lit up, and smoke flowed from the chimney. That's the one I saw someone moving in.

"Who lives in that one?" I pointed.

"That would be Dalo's cabin. He's my beta wolf, and one of the most loyal."

"What about your brother? Since you're a prince, does that make him one?"

"Yes, but what about him?" he asked dryly.

Did I hit a nerve there? "I thought he'd be second in command. You know, your beta?"

"It doesn't always work that way. If I should die before I stepped down, and there was no one in the position, then he'd become king. And he'd be responsible for caring for my mate."

"What if he wants a mate of his own?"

"When I'm mated, she becomes my queen. Which means she also becomes an alpha. The pack must respect and abide by whatever she says, unless I overrule her. She must very careful in her decisions and always consider the packs wellbeing. The two are supposed to make a good team." He smiled as he took in a breath. "The pack must protect their queen at all times. She's the important one in the pack once she's mated to her alpha, her king. They'll kill for her and die protecting her. No ifs, ands, or buts."

Wow. That was deep. Did it bother the pack to do those things for their alphas? I wasn't sure I wanted to know the answer.

So, I asked another question instead. "So, you automatically become king once you're mated?"

Shock filled his eyes before he quickly hid it. "That is correct. In a perfect scenario, the overall leader of the packs is a mated pair. A king and queen ruling and nurturing the pack together. A mated pair provides everything the pack needs. So, when I enter into that kind of relationship, it automatically makes me king."

"What does it mean when you say mated? Is that like married for wolves? Or is it just about sex and procreating?"

"It's more than a physical connection. It's partnering with a person for life. It's a bond even stronger than marriage because it isn't easily dissolved by something like a divorce. It's the joining of hearts, minds and bodies. It's being so connected with your partner that you always think of them first. And in the case of soul mates, the souls are bonded irreversibly."

"That sounds pretty amazing. Maybe the supernatural world has figured out a better way."

"My parents say it's pretty amazing. They're soulmates. If anything were to ever happen to one of them, I know the other would be devastated. They don't like to be away from each other for even a day."

If only humans could be so devoted to their spouses, then my mother wouldn't have left us. I needed to change the direction of this conversation before it made me sad and ruined our night.

"And your brother isn't your beta because you chose Dalo?"

"Yes and no."

"I'm confused."

He smiled a little and explained, "Dorik doesn't want to be my beta. He doesn't want to be a prince king. He said the only way he'll become king is if I'm dead. So that he can keep the royal line going in our family."

"Why doesn't he want to be king or your beta?" I asked and regretted it right away. Pain darkened his eyes before he closed them. When he reopened them, I could see tears forming, but not falling. "Sorry. Forget I asked. I overstepped."

"It's all good. The apology isn't necessary. You'll find out eventually, and it'll explain my brother's behavior." His sadness was evident. "Ever since his mate, Lina, died, he's been shut off from the world and from the pack. He barely talks to our parents."

I recalled what Scarlet had mentioned about it. "I'm an ass for asking. I'm truly sorry for your loss."

No one wants to lose the person they love. I was sure this was hard on him.

"It's fine. It's been five years since her death, but it still hurts when we think of her. She was a great wolf, and I truly can say I loved her very much. We got along so well, I was shocked by it."

"Why?"

"She was a fireball!" He laughed. "She spoke her mind and didn't care how it came out. At times, she'd tell me I needed to let loose and have some fun. She said I should date more and be more open to different females rather than just wolf ones." He laughed again. His eyes showed how much he loved her. "She also was the one who controlled what went on in the kitchen, and the dinners we had every week. She pretty much took over the Tri Feasts when she started dating Dorik."

She sounded like a woman who likes to be in control. That wasn't a bad thing. She must have been a good woman to win his affection.

"She sounded nice. I wish I could've met her," I said softly.

"I think she would've liked you and would've never let you leave."

I smiled at him. "Well, let's hope it's you who gets me to stay." *Oh crap! Did I just admit that out loud?* I couldn't believe I'd just said that.

"You'd better be careful what you say, because *that* my enchantress, is something I'm aiming for."

His voice had a sensual tone and I felt heat between my legs. A lopsided grin appeared on his face as his eyes bored into mine. Without thinking, I quickly grabbed him by his shirt and pulled him to me. I put my arms around his neck and shifted so I was sitting in his lap rather than the saddle.

He was shocked by my advance, but his grin widened. His grip on me tightened, and Gravis kept walking along the trail.

Chest to chest and nose to nose, I slowly put my lips to his. He immediately opened his mouth and slipped his tongue into mine. I moaned as our tongues became familiar with one another. I straddled him, the rhythm of Gravis's gait making me go up and down. His hardness beneath me had me gasping between breaths. I wanted nothing more than to tear his clothes off and feel him deep inside me. Gripping my ass with one hand, I moaned even louder as he squeezed it. He pulled away slowly and rested his head against my forehead.

"I want you, Jasinda. But the first time I take you will be in my bed, not here in the open. Not like this. Not on a horse." He chuckled.

"Ok," I hoarsely whispered.

I was a little disappointed because I didn't care if he took me right here. But then I remembered there were cottages scattered out here, and I was happy he didn't let me get carried away. He tightened his grip on my ass and kept me on his lap. Still facing him, I bit my lower lip and turned to face the trees.

Were the trees changing color? I turned back to him to ask but stopped when I saw he was still staring at me. His eyes were glowing, and heat surged behind them. His scent was like linen or something. Leaning in, I inhaled him and felt a bit lightheaded. He made me feel so erotic when I was with him. I just wanted to jump him whenever I saw him.

"What are you thinking about?" he asked me with suspicion in his voice.

"Nothing. I was just wondering if the trees were changing colors?"

"Yes, they change colors based on the mood surrounding them."

"Really?"

"Yes."

"Wow, that's amazing. I thought I was seeing things and felt a bit lightheaded."

His grin widened. "Light headed?"

He knew something. "Did you do something to me?" I accused, teasingly.

"Me? You think I did something to you?"

"I don't know. I'm asking so I don't look stupid here."

"You don't look stupid, enchantress. And no, I didn't do anything to you." He kissed the tip of my nose.

My eyes flickered close, and I felt this rush of electricity hit my entire bloodstream. I moaned and let it engulf me. I welcomed it and didn't fight it. The feeling was incredible, and my body felt light. Free. Like I was floating in midair, and warm hands were caressing me. Jace's moans sounded in my ear, but I kept my eyes closed, enjoying what was happening to me. My back arched as a mountain of sensation hit me. These feather-light, butterfly kisses peppered my back. I didn't stop to wonder what it could be, but rather I relished every kiss. The kisses moved from my back to my shoulders and down to my breast. Another gasp escaped my lips, and a rumble vibrated in my ear. But I didn't care, I was enjoying whatever it was.

Heat seared between my legs, and I jumped a little as a zap of electricity hit me again. Jace was still gripping my ass. I only knew that because he ended up giving it a gentle squeeze. Goddesses, it felt good. Kisses rained down my bare arms and on the skin of my legs even though I was wearing jeans.

How could this encounter with all of my clothes on feel better and more amazing than any actual sexual experience I'd ever had?

It felt as though I was on the verge of orgasming right here, fully clothed. I was perched right there on the edge about to tip over, but I knew I wasn't going to. It was as if I was high on some type of drug that made me feel everything around me. I sucked in a breath as I felt a tongue go across my lips. Moaning at the sensation, he moved to my neck, then my ear, down my chest and between my breasts. *Oh god, please lick my nipples I need him to lick my nipples. I have no idea how Jace is doing this, it must be some super power of his. Whatever it is, I don't want it to stop.*

As if he's read my thoughts, he sucked my nipple into his mouth swirling his tongue lazily in circles. I whimpered as the prickling hit me right in the center. In an instant, it all slowly faded away. Each touch, each sensation and each kiss leaving me gradually.

Chapter Thirty-Nine

Jace

I couldn't believe that just happened. I'd never experienced it before and was taken aback by it. I'd heard stories of it happening, but it was a better feeling than they'd explained. My grip tightened on her, as my heart rate slowed. I was doing my best to keep us upright on Gravis. We were both panting. Her lids were still closed, and her grip around my neck tightened.

"She's going to ask what that *was. What am I going to tell her?"* I asked Gravis.

"Just explain to her that your souls merged. That's the truth," Gravis said to me.

"Sorry, you had to witness that..."

"Don't apologize for something so rare and incredible. How many people can say they've had their souls merged with the *one? However, humans can't withstand their souls merging..."*

She was more than human. That experience proved it. But what was she?

"Jace?"

Shit. I was too busy speaking with Gravis that I hadn't realized she was even calling my name. Her brown eyes were filled with concern.

"Sorry. Still feeling the effects of what just happened."

"Yeah, me too. Speaking of, what did just happen?" Her sexy voice sent soft caresses to my skin.

"This is going to sound crazy, but it's the truth." I let out a breath and squeezed her hip with one hand for courage. "Our souls just merged and had foreplay with each other."

Silence and a confused expression were her initial responses. Slowly, she released her grip around my shoulders. It took all my willpower not to bark at her to put them back.

She tilted her head slightly. "Okaaaay. Is that truly possible? Because I honestly want to ask you if you're being serious."

"It *is* possible. And it's the first time it's ever happened to me. I've *known* of it happening. I just didn't know it would feel so good... so right."

"Well, it definitely felt good. But I think it was more astounding than that," she purred. "It felt...it felt true to my soul."

"It did, huh?" I smirked in amusement.

"Yes."

"That's good to know."

"*Why* did it happen though? Did you do it on purpose?"

"I don't know why it happened, and no I didn't do it on purpose. I mean, I have an idea as to why it happened. But until I confirm it, I'm not a hundred percent sure."

"What's your theory then?"

I didn't want her to feel pressured into moving too fast with me. I wanted us to take things as slowly as possible, so she'd be my mate. My *true* mate.

"It means that our souls want each other. I *could* be wrong, but I'll make sure to find out more about it."

"Our souls, huh? Are you sure?"

"Yes."

"Not that I didn't like it. I *really* enjoyed it. But it was also weird in a way." She paused for a second and closed her eyes. "It was like my soul was...I don't know...awakened?" She bit her bottom lip as she opened her eyes. "Does that sound crazy?"

She had a better reaction than I thought. "No, not at all. I think there could be many reasons why it happened."

"Somehow I knew it. I knew it was you even though you weren't actually touching me."

I brushed a strand of hair from her face and smiled at her.

Gravis stopped at the waterfall. Jasinda looked over her shoulder and....what was her reaction?

"Are you freaking kidding me? It's beautiful. Wow."

"Good to know you like it."

"I don't like it," she whispered.

"Come again?"

"I love it, Jace. How could anyone not?" Her eyes met mine, and it was a struggle to not take her right here.

"Not everyone feels that way about the waterfall. Especially the younger females. They think it's boring. I don't know why they can't see its beauty."

"Oh, so you've brought a lot of females here, huh?"

It sounded more like a statement than a question. Maybe more like a tease? But I answered her anyways.

"I've never brought anyone here myself. You're the first. Some of the females who stay around here always seem to pass this spot. They stop for a drink of water and move along. They don't stop and admire it. My mother and aunt are the main ones who love coming here. They don't need me for that."

"Really? No one really comes here? How sad."

"Nope. Like I said, it's not something they care for."

"Well, they suck. I care for it. You can bring me here anytime you want." She shrugged one shoulder and tilted her head towards the waterfall. "Maybe you can show me how to get back here, and I'll come visit this beautiful spot all the time."

Her grin was intoxicating.

"I'll bring you anytime you want. But if I'm not here, all you have to do is take one of the horses and tell them to take you to the waterfall magic. They'll bring you right here."

"Waterfall magic?" She raised both eyebrows.

"You'll see soon. Come on, Jasinda I'll help you down."

She blushed and winked before she stood up and steadied herself with both hands on my shoulders. She was a daring woman, and I liked it. I gripped her hips and eased her down. Then I dismounted and sent Gravis off. Taking her hand in mine, we walked to the trail.

Chapter Forty

Jasinda

The waterfall was huge, with a drop as high as a building. Leaning back to peer up, it seemed as though it touched the sky. The clear water sparkled with life. Rocks leaned and stacked on either side, as if trying to climb to the top. A cave sat, hidden behind the water, like a long shadow someone might not notice. The pool had shallow areas, but I sensed it was deep in the middle. The water looked alluring.

A light tug stopped me from moving forward. Still mesmerized by the water, I tightened my grip in his hand. I wanted to take it all in—beautiful rose bushes scattered about, rocks for jumping off into the water and a hot spring in the corner. Steam billowed from it. It was all breathtaking, and I could almost imagine never wanting to leave. Looking back at Jace, I found him gazing at me. Our eyes locked, and he had a slight grin on his face.

"What's so funny?" I questioned.

"Nothing. It's nice to see someone appreciate its beauty like a little kid would a big bowl of chocolate fudge ice cream."

"Chocolate fudge ice cream?" I repeated.

"Yes, chocolate fudge ice cream. Who doesn't like that?"

"For one, I prefer vanilla ice cream with caramel sauce and chocolate chip cookies on top."

"Wait." His hand waving in front of him and then pointing at me. "You don't like fudge? Every woman likes fudge." He dropped his hand to his side.

"Not me. I mean fudge is good, but I prefer caramel. That's my favorite and number one choice. Of course, chocolate and caramel make a *great* couple," I defended, as I went up a hill that led us into the cave behind the fall and tugged him along.

"Wow!"

The inside of the cave was set up like a picnic with baskets and wine bottles on a blanket. As I spun around, I noticed the walls sparkled. Upon closer inspection, I saw that real diamonds were embedded into the walls. They lit up the cave like a flashlight. Butterflies swished through my stomach from the romantic gesture. When I looked out into the waterfall, I could make out the shapes of trees and bushes. Stepping closer to the edge, I couldn't resist putting my hand out to touch the water. It was cold, but not freezing. It felt nice on my skin. I wanted to swim in the pool and let the water surround me.

"We'll go in later. But first let's eat a little. I'm hungry," he told me.

"I ate already. I mean, it was a few hours ago, so I guess I can eat a little more," I explained, as I walked back over to him.

"Good."

We sat down on the blanket, and he opened one of the baskets, removing a few containers. There was steak in one container and bread in the other, surprisingly still warm. The noticeable steam and smells filled my nostrils, causing my stomach to growl.

"Mmmm...that smells good. What kind of bread is that?"

He looked a bit worried. "Potato bread. It goes good with skirt steak. Is that ok?"

"Yes, this is all perfect."

"Good. I made the steak and my mother made the bread from scratch. She loves to bake. I'll ask her to make a loaf just for you. I'm sure she'll love that."

"Do you think she'd teach me how to make it?"

"I don't see why not."

"Does she know how to make coconut bread?"

"It's her all-time favorite. I'll have her bake you that instead."

Wasn't I lucky? I'd always wanted to learn how to make fresh bread. While we were talking, he put pieces of steak on flattened potato bread, then rolled it up. Potato steak rolls. After that, he took out two wine glasses and set them between us. He filled them with red wine and handed me a glass. His efforts to take care of me made me feel all warm and gooey inside.

This was nice and different from when I dated Elier. Elier always took me *out* to fancy restaurants for dinner. I'd get dressed up, and we'd spend hours dining. I preferred this. This was nice, sweet, yet simple. I swirled my wine, sniffed and took a sip. It was good.

"So, you cook?" I asked.

He eyed me with a slight smile. *How long had he been looking at me?* I lowered my eyes and drank a bit more. *Please say something.*

"Yes, I can cook. But I leave the baking to my lovely mother and sister"

"Does your sister live in the mansion too?"

"Sometimes. She comes and goes. She likes to be in her wolf form more than her human one."

"Will I meet her?"

"Trust me, *you'll* meet her."

What did he mean by that?

I took a bite of my rolled-up steak. "Mmmm. This is so good. And the wine is delish! What type of wine is it?" I asked, taking another sip.

I picked up the bottle to see the name. But there was no label.

"It's my family's wine. We have our own vineyard."

"Seriously?"

"Yes."

"Can I see it sometime? If that's good with you?" I hoped he said yes though.

He laughed. "I like how you're interested in knowing things, especially when it has to do with me."

Heat sliced through my cheeks. His eyes began to glow, which set off the butterflies in my belly. He pushed the plate towards me so I could eat more.

I took a potato steak roll and bit into it. "Mmmm. You really *can* cook."

He shook his head and began eating, all the while his stare remained glued on me.

By our third glass, we were laughing and talking about everything.

"I still can't believe all of this is out here and no one ever sees it," I said in disbelief.

"Magic. Unless I want someone to see something, the magic I used keeps it all hidden. From the outside, only my house is visible. Anyone wandering around the property, only sees nature."

"That's amazing. And pretty handy for protecting everyone."

"All the horses know the area, so if you ask them to take you somewhere, like Waterfall Magic, they'll know the way."

"Tell me about dragons," I requested.

"Dragons were the first supernatural beings in this world. They're the ancient ones. They made the werewolves, shifters and every other supernatural being from here. They're my first ancestors."

"Why did they make the other supernatural beings?"

"Dragons were the protectors of the sky. And they needed protectors on the land."

"How rare are dragons now?"

"Very. There was a time when the skies were full of them. But they've been in hiding for some time now because they've been hunted for their power and skin."

"That's so sad. Why their skin?"

"Dragons are the best protectors in the universe because they are very hard to kill. A lot of that is because their skin is like armor."

"Oh. Why are they here?"

"They came to Earth to hide and to protect humans from the dark dragons who wish to rule the world. Those dragons enslaved humans and forced them to mate with them."

"Oh, God. That's horrible." Scarlet had filled me in on some of this, but Jace's added information made my heart hurt for the humans who were forced into unions with evil dragons.

"Their experiments breeding with humans failed though. The children born from those pairings could never shift into dragons.

"So, they're just humans?"

"No, they're immortals. Very strong immortals. But they have very little supernatural ability. Some of the dragons killed their young when they were unable to shift."

"That's just awful. How could someone kill a *child*, much less their own?"

"That was the mindset of some of these dragons. It's frowned upon by the supernatural community as a whole. Humans are no match for a dragon. Some of the females were smart enough to realize what would happen, so they ran away with the child and sought shelter."

"Well, that just sucks."

"Yes, it does. It's why I have people out there searching for the females who have these children. So, we can keep them safe. Keep them alive. Even if they don't shift into dragons."

"But if they know they won't have a dragon child with a human, then why do they continue mating with humans?"

"Some dragons mate with them because they *do* fall for humans. Some are hoping for a miracle. You see, legend says there's someone out there who *can* bear a dragon child. The dragon just has to find him or her. But the person has yet to be found."

"Do *you* believe that he or she is out there?"

"Yes. I believe the legend."

"What about you? Do you have to mate with a wolf in order to have shifters as well?"

He looked at me and smiled. His eye glanced over my entire body. He inhaled deeply, and his front canine teeth came out. I gasped softly, shocked I could see them.

He grinned at me and gave me an apologetic look. "No, we can mate with humans or any other supernatural beside wolves. Children from those unions won't be full-blooded shifters, so they'll shift only during the Tri Moons which is our full moon. Not during the day. If we mate with another wolf, then those children will be full-blooded shifters and will be able to shift at will."

So, much information, and I still wanted more.

Chapter Forty-One

Jasinda

I s this common knowledge?"

"Yes and no. It is taught in schools as folklore. Most do not believe, and those that do know about our existence, keep our secrets. Just like witches, no one believes in them. Yet according to your history, during the 16th and 17th centuries those that were believed to be witches were hanged." He explained.

It all seemed so... bizarre. But then again, I don't remember much about the supernatural world. I wish I could *remember*, but I needed time to process all I'd learned so far. So, I had to change the subject. *Work.* That was a safe topic that wouldn't set my heart racing or my body tingling.

"So, you're a tracker?"

"I guess we're tabling the mating conversation for later," he said with a wink.

I couldn't stop the blush that crept over my features.

"Yes, I'm a tracker." His answer saved me from spontaneously combusting over imagining mating with this man.

"How did you come to work for my father?"

"One day I was tracking a werewolf. In our circles, we knew him only as 'the Demon Beast'. Anyway, he was a disgrace to our kind. He'd made a deal with a demon and had become possessed. He was killing other wolves, even newborn wolves."

I jerked at his response. "Why kill newborns? They're innocent." *Talk of harming babies always did something to me, like a punch to the gut.*

"Werewolves have the ability, through dark magic, to steal the life force or soul from whoever they kill, thus adding it to his own and making them more powerful. Newborns have the purest souls, completely untainted by the world."

"That's awful. But how does my father fit into this?"

"He was tracking the Beast too. I closed in on him while he had your father pinned to the ground, about to kill him. I saved your dad, and the Beast got away. We've been working together ever since to find him."

Even though I was angry with my father for lying to me, my heart ached knowing he'd nearly died. "Wow. I guess I owe you a thank you."

"If the roles had been reversed, I have no doubt your father would've saved me."

"Tracking must pay well to afford you all of this," I swept my arm around. "I'm sorry. That sounded so nosy."

He chuckled. "Don't be silly. Tracking does pay well. But that's not my soul source of income. I'm a proprietor. I buy abandoned properties, like warehouses and commercial properties. Then I fix them up and either flip them or lease out the space."

"That sounds like fun. Taking something that everyone has given up on and breathing new life into it."

"I never thought about it that way, but I guess you're right. Many of my packmates help with the business."

"Don't you guys get tired of each other? Living near each other, socializing with each other and working together?"

"It can be challenging at times. But we're really like a big family. And there's no one I trust more than my packmates. Having them on board, means extra security. So, how did you come to start JNS Events?"

"I helped a friend's mother plan a baby shower one day. I wound up pretty much taking over the event's planning. Or should I say, they handed it over to me, because they liked my ideas. I ran with it, and the couple expecting loved how it all came out. The husband was a wealthy man and offered me a loan to start my own business, which I did."

"That sounds great. Did he give you a good interest rate on the loan?"

"He wouldn't let me pay interest. I rented the building he suggested, and six months later I had his money." I took a sip of my wine and laughed, more to myself remembering it like it was yesterday. "He said he and his wife wanted to do it for me. They booked me to handle their daughter's first birthday and all the birthdays afterwards until she can't have any more birthdays or until I can't do them anymore."

I chugged the remaining of the wine in my glass. It really was delish! I needed to remember to ask him where I could buy a few bottles.

Jace remained quiet so, I continued, "I agreed, of course. That was six years ago. So, I've done five birthdays for them, and last year I did another baby shower. And I'll be doing a first birthday sometime next year for their son."

"That was nice of him. You must have gone all out for the baby shower and made quite an impression." His voice was filled with pride, for some reason.

"Oh, I made an impression all right. He's all about his wife. What she wants and what makes her happy. He said she was very picky and had a hard time picking things out. Most people had a hard time working with her. That's what he told me. He said I was the first event planner who didn't roll my eyes or looked annoyed with her. She was ecstatic to have me as her event planner. I pretty much made her decide what she wanted, because I gave her only a few choices. He said no one seemed to get his wife but me."

He laughed. "She must have really been an indecisive woman."

"The minute I met her I saw how indecisive she was. That's the first day we were all in her living room, and she couldn't decide on a theme. I swooped right in and gave her three choices. She was going back to the second one the most, but she still couldn't decide. So, I told her to trust me, and she did. When she showed up to her baby shower, she was almost in tears from the joy of it all. She was truly impressed with me."

"A true event planner gives the people what they want," he acknowledged, as he tilted his head forward a little.

I smiled at him. "I could see her husband stealing glances my way and nodding in approval every time our eyes locked. I knew how much he loved his wife, and I knew how grateful he was for my planning and executing the shower. He was just happy. I mean, really happy that I made his wife's day. I knew then that was what I wanted to do."

Remembering it all was a little nerve-racking. I'd never told anyone the story. Not even Angie. Even now, she thinks that I rented the building and paid it all off outright. The Landers were grateful I didn't say anything to anyone about it. I never realized how wealthy the Landers were until after their daughter was born.

"Mrs. Landers pulled me aside and told me that her husband held me in high regard. That he respected me and what I did. That's how they became my clients. My best clients. They call me for all their events."

Jace was looking at me funny. I couldn't read his expression. *Had I said something wrong? Crap. Maybe I was talking too much. Maybe he thought I was a blabber mouth.* I knew I was nervous, but I also felt comfortable talking to him. He made it so.

"The Landers, huh?" he questioned.

"Yes, do you know them?"

"I know them."

I stared at him waiting for him to explain. I raised my eyebrows.

"The Landers are part of our pack family."

"Holy waters!" I screeched as I waved my hand around, nearly knocking the empty wine glass over.

He burst out laughing as I said that. *How in the world was all this possible?* That meant the Landers were wolves. I'd been working with wolves this whole time.

"Were you at the baby shower and the birthdays?" I curiously asked.

"Yes, I was at all the events."

"I didn't see you. But then again, I never stayed long."

"I didn't see you either, but now it all makes sense."

"What makes sense?"

"Your scent. I knew I'd smelled it before. That first night I saw you at the entrance of the charity event. I was trying to figure out where I'd smelled it before."

"You can remember my *scent*?"

"Once a wolf picks up a scent, it stays with them forever. They'll recognize it again, even if it's faint."

"Interesting."

"You know, they come to every Tri Moon Feast. You'll see them soon."

"Really?" The Landers were truly amazing people.

"Yes."

"That's nice to know. I really like them."

"So, do we. They've been great allies to us for many years."

This was going to be interesting. They were going to know that I *knew* what they were. *How would they react to that?* I was excited about seeing them sooner than I'd planned. Especially their daughter.

Chapter Forty-Two

Jace

I couldn't believe everything felt so… connected. She knew the Landers. *What a coincidence.* I couldn't stop staring at her. She was fascinating to watch and listen to. She was a mystery to solve. Green flecks sparked in her eyes from time to time. And her hair seemed darker today than when I first met her. I could sense her Calling now and smell her sex. The infusion of hormones surging in her body was definitely greater than a normal cycle. She was definitely going to experience a full-blown Calling. *My God, it was getting stronger.* She was going to lose herself soon, and she didn't even know it. I needed to make sure my brother didn't get near her after today. He'd lose control of himself. It was all I could do to control *myself* right now. And oddly enough, it seemed my beast was the one keeping me in check.

"Yes, I'm helping you stay calm. I've realized she means too much to us for me to just jump her the way I want to. I want her to be ours. Forever! So, I'll do what it takes. Even if it means going slow."

"Even if it means no wolflins?" I asked hesitantly to be sure because it had been such a sticking point with him initially.

"Yes, if it means having her and her love forever, I could be happy with just her and no wolflins," he whispered. *"Or I'll at least try not to let the no wolfins cloud me."*

His answer floored me. I had expected to have to fight with him on the wolflins front. And shit, he *had been* listening when I said I wanted to take it slow with her. She wasn't one of our kind where we could just pick her as our mate and that was it. We had to treat her like a human, even if we didn't want to. By the Gods, I wanted this woman. I knew she was *the one* I'd been waiting for, even if I hadn't believed in that sort of thing before. I'd never cared to mate with anyone. Until now. Knowing that both my parents and Priscilla's were trying to mate *us*, had me annoyed. I already knew, I'd *never* mate with Priscilla. She was too high maintenance and wanted everything for herself. Selfishness consumed her and caring wasn't part of her life, even less for the pups around here.

I'd brought Jasinda here to see how she'd react to the pups. They suffered from abandonment issues. I needed a caring woman who would be understanding toward them. They needed a bit of motherly love. A few of them were troubled. If my instincts were right, Jasinda would be the one to help me get these pups to grow into stable adult wolves.

"Want to go for a swim?" I asked her.

From the way she'd been eyeing the water, I knew she'd been thinking about it. She kept gazing at it, like it was calling her. Standing up, I stretched my hand out to her. Slowly taking my hand, she stood. I lead her to the mouth of the cave and stopped us right in front of the waterfall.

"What an amazing view," she breathed out. "Especially since I only expected to exit from where we entered.

"It's great, and a perfect place to jump from."

"*Seriously?* You've jumped from here before?"

She looked excited and curious at the same time. Cute.

"Yes, and it's fun."

"Can we...um...jump?" she hesitantly asked.

"I was hoping we would. I packed us some swimsuits."

"You thought of everything, didn't you?" she asked, sounding impressed.

I gave her a seductive smile and a wink. "Can't have you wet and cold. I prefer you wet and warm."

She blushed at my words and her scent filled the air even more. *Shit what the fuck was I doing?*

I motioned her to sit at the ledge, while I went and got her a bathing suit. In the darkest corner, I changed into swim shorts. Then I headed back towards her with a swimsuit in hand. Stopping right behind her, I watched her fingers playing in the waterfall in front of her. She'd already taken off her boots. With her toes out, she was playing peek-a-boo with the water. In amazement, I observed how the water flowed with her as she touched it. It seemed different when she touched it. Like she was influencing it somehow. Like it was more in tune with her. I couldn't explain it.

"Here. Scarlet picked this out for you."

She reached one hand out without looking at me, and I placed it in her hands.

"Thank you," she whispered.

Turning my back, I let her get dressed. My ears stayed tuned to her movements, so I'd know when she was done changing. Closing my eyes, I sensed her. And in my mind, I *knew* she'd turned back to look at me. She stood, and as quickly as she undressed, she put on the pale green Brazilian bikini just as fast. In slow motion, I turned around. Once I was facing her again, I could see her eyes had turned a pale green. It was as if they'd changed to match her swimsuit. I shook my head. She smiled at me seductively and dove off the edge into the water below. I watched stunned at how smooth her dive was. I followed right behind her, smiling the whole time.

"Nice dive," She said, as I popped up.

"*Me?* Yours was great."

"Thanks. I've always loved the water. It's soothing to me. I've never been afraid of it."

"That's a good thing. There are plenty of pools around here for you to swim in."

"I've seen three so far. I'm excited to explore them, but I think I'll stay away from the streams. Not sure if I want to be pulled under again." She laughed slightly.

"You don't have to worry about that. Skyla thought she was helping you. She thought you were one of us. She won't make that mistake again."

"Good to know." Relief showed in her eyes.

She went back under and swam around. She seemed so happy to be here, and I was happy I'd picked this spot to show her. I knew she'd been sad and worried for days. So, I wanted her to have some fun. When she popped back up again, she made her way back to me, stopping just before she got to me. She gave me a hesitant look, then closed the space between us, wrapping her arms around my neck. Then followed that by wrapping her legs around my waist. I closed my eyes and wrapped my hands around her lower back. I wanted to put them on her ass but felt it might be too forward. Inhaling her scent, I reveled in the heat of her body against mine.

When I opened my eyes, I saw a flaming heat in hers. Her pulse beat erratically against my belly. *Damn, she wanted me. Right now. Shit.* She had *that* look in her eyes. The same look she'd had her first night here when I'd gone to her room to say goodnight. She was ready for me to take her now. She ran her fingers through my wet hair and rested them at the back of my head. Then she tugged me to her and kissed me. At first it was a soft tap, but then she licked my lips, tilted her head to the side and kissed me again.

This time I opened my mouth, letting her tongue slide in and collide with mine. Our tongues swam together in a sea of honey. The movements were slow but inviting. Soft moans vibrated in her throat. The pulse between her legs played a beat against my belly like a drum.

I didn't want our first time to be *here.* I wanted it to be in my bed. My brain said I should stop her, but I couldn't. My need for her matched hers for me. She felt so good against my skin, and her lips were magic on mine. They were a perfect fit, as if they'd been made just for me. Only me. I didn't want anyone else tasting her lips ever again, and I'd make sure of it. My hands caressed her back, pressing her closer to me. When my hands reached her neck. I tugged on her hair.

When I finally pulled her back from my lips, she whimpered. *Oh yeah, this was perfect.* I too, loved kissing. It was such an important part of making love or even casual sex. Good kissing woke up all the body parts that needed to be awakened. Her eyes fluttered open, revealing wide pupils and darkened irises. *Damn this woman.* She was fuckin' hot when she was horny. With a gentle tug, I tilted her neck to the side, and she willingly let me.

"You're so beautiful," I whispered against her neck.

She shivered and small goosebumps rose over her skin. I pressed soft kisses up and down her neck. A gasp escaped her throat. With my hands on her hips, I lowered her, so she could feel my hardness against her center. The movement elicited a moan from her. It was permission to continue. So, I licked her neck in one long stroke up to her ear. She tightened her grip at the back of my neck.

"Jace," she panted.

Damn! If that was how she was going to say my name over a hot kiss, how would she say it with me inside her?

I continued kissing her neck with hot, open-mouthed kisses moving down towards her shoulder. She giggled and moaned. With deft fingers, I unhooked the top of her swimsuit, then pulled at her bottoms. Her wordless pleas encouraged me. Impatient to remove all barriers, I tapped into my shifter magic and willed my shorts away. I moved us into more shallow waters, for better balance.

Putting one hand between us, I ran my fingers down her stomach until they reached her warmth. With a gentle touch, I stroked her clit. Another moan escaped her, and her head fell forward against my forehead. We gazed into each other's eyes. My finger still stroked her, increasing my speed and pressure, while she struggled to keep her eyes open. I was challenging her. I wanted to see how long she could keep her eyes on mine. When I slowly inserted one finger inside of her, she cried out and closed her eyes. Internally, I pumped my fists in victory. *Yes! I'd won!*

She bit her lower lip and opened her eyes. *Damn!* So much heat and passion in them. I was trying hard not to lose control. Removing my fingers, I grabbed myself. I stroked myself a few times, creating waves between us and making her sweat a little. She grinned and licked her lips. She knew what I was doing and liked it. I positioned myself between her thighs and watched as her eyes took on a light glow. Closing the distance between our mouths, she kissed me. Her tongue dueled with mine and was winning the fight.

I eased the tip of my cock in just a bit, and she gasped in my mouth, keeping the kiss going. *Hell on wheels was coming for me.* This woman was incredible. I removed my hand from myself and grabbed her ass, pushing her onto me a little more. A moan escaped her, and I froze.

She broke our kiss and looked me in the eyes. "I'm all about this, Jace. I've wanted you inside me ever since I laid eyes on you. So please, tease me later. After you're inside me. Penetrate me," she panted.

"Penetrate you?"

"Fuck me, impale me, screw me. Whatever you want to call it! Just get inside me already!"

She was nervous and desperate to feel our connection completed. I chuckled at her impatient words and hauled her right onto me, penetrating her to the hilt. She cried out and stilled. I figured I'd have to wait a bit, so she could get used to my size. But she began moving up and down, up and down. *Shit, she was even more amazing than I'd imagined.* Her legs tightened around my hips, and she squeezed my dick with her pussy muscles every time she pulled back. *Shit, it felt so fuckin' good.* She threw her head back, enjoying the ride. No way was she getting away with not having her lips on mine.

Keeping one hand on her ass to make sure she didn't stop her rhythm, I grabbed her hair with my other hand and forced her head forward. *God, she was sexy when she was in The Calling.* She was fucked now, because we'd be fuckin' all night tonight and in the morning. Crushing her lips against mine, I muffled her cries. I growled with pleasure at her orgasm. The ripples of another one started before her first could end. I quickened our pace, and when she cried out again, I spilled myself inside her while howling along with her.

Her rhythm didn't slow. She kept riding me and squeezing me with her pussy. Suddenly, I came again, emptying more of myself into her as she cried out once again. *What the fuck was that?* No woman had ever made me come back to back. *Thank heavens she wasn't ovulating yet.* Finally, she slowed her pace and bit my lower lip.

God, this was fuckin' great. She was fuckin' great! My mind was incapable of deep thoughts.

She planted soft kisses on my lips. "Mmmmm. You feel so good inside me." Her body snuggled up even closer to me.

"You're warm and tight. Just right."

She kissed me again, this time slowly. We made out like a couple of high school teenagers. I'd never felt anything like this. I never wanted it to end. With one arm, I gently swam backwards towards the waterfall, while keeping the other hand on her ass. We passed through the waterfall, never breaking our kiss. When my back hit the rock wall, I pulled back from her lips.

"The pups will be arriving soon. We need to get dressed."

"Pups? What pups?" She was fidgety, as I felt her legs tighten and loosen around my waist.

"Just some wolflins I've kind of taken under my wing since they don't have parents to watch out for them."

Her eyes grew wide with compassion. "Those poor things."

I chuckled. *The pups were a lot of things, I wasn't sure poor was one of them. Excitable, untrained, loud—yes. Poor? I wasn't so sure.*

"What happened to their parents?"

"Their fathers died for various reasons. Upon the deaths of their mates, the mothers became weak. Too weak to take care of their children. As alpha prince, I took it upon myself to care for them and try to train these essentially orphaned pups."

"So, you're like a father figure to them?"

"That's right."

"But they have no maternal influence in their lives?"

"Sadly, not anymore. My mom and aunt help out a little. But they're too old to really keep up with these energetic creatures. Anyway, they'll be here soon. So get dressed, you sex beast."

"Sex beast, huh?" she playfully returned, staying tangled up in my arms.

"Yes, sex beast."

"Do those really exist?"

"As of today, yes. You've become the sex beast. What we did tonight, and you seducing me, that all stems from a sex beast."

"*Excuse* me, but I did *not* seduce you. I just made the first move," she scoffed, pretending to be offended.

"Ok. In my book, that's seducing me. Enchantress, can't you learn some control?"

"Only if you can unlearn some control."

"That's possible," I chuckled.

"Then it's possible for me too." She faked another pout. She was too sexy right then to pout.

"I'll be back. I'm going to get your bikini."

I never imagined she could be this way sexually. Out in the open, she let me take her, just like that. I'd wanted our first time to be in my bed, but she'd changed the game around. Secretly, I was glad about it. Now that I'd gotten a taste of her, I wasn't letting her near any other males right now. Not when her Calling was about to kick in within the next few hours. That was how close she was to losing control of herself. And she could, but only with *me*.

I *needed* her with me more than anyone else. I needed to see if her enthusiasm towards me was of her own accord. Not due to the magic that laid within my pack.

"*Don't forget that your souls have chosen one another. She wants you just as much as her soul does,* my beast interrupted my thoughts."

"*How can you be sure of this? How can you* not *wonder if it's the magic causing her to feel these feelings?*" I questioned my beast.

"*Because, her soul chose yours when yours chose hers. You can feel a connection with her. You claimed her that first night without her knowing. Your heart and soul staked their claim.*"

Chapter Forty-Three

Jasinda

While I caught my breath, Jace back stroked in the water to catch my floating bikini. I didn't see his trunks. Hopefully, they hadn't gotten lost. Watching his muscles ripple and the water droplets flowing off his body made something inside me coil tighter with need. *Again.* I admired the shape of his jaw, the sparkle in his reflective orbs, and the hint of a smile on those kissable lips.

As he stalked back towards me, the small scraps of material dangled from his fingertips. His eyes flashed with desire. The next thing I knew, my lips were plastered to his in a clash of tongues and teeth. Five minutes ago, I was fully sated. Now I couldn't get enough of him again. My ache was so great that I'd made the first move, which I'd never done before. What the hell kind of spell had he cast over me?

There had been this attraction sizzling between us from the moment we'd first locked eyes on each other. I hadn't understood it then and I still didn't now, even after experiencing him fully. But Jace brought out something daring in me, and I liked it.

I peeked up at him through my lashes. The lust and hunger in his gaze, surprised me. I didn't expect him to be ready for more so quickly. It hadn't even been five minutes. Must be a wolf thing. Whatever it was, I could certainly get used to it. *Thank heavens for birth control.*

When we were done, he helped me slip back into my swimsuit. And somehow, magically his swimming trunks were back. My mind was too fuzzy from orgasms to question how *that* had happened.

"Is there a trail that'll take us back to the top where we left our stuff?"

"There is, but I know a shortcut." He grinned mischievously at me.

Scooping me up in his arms, he waded back out into the pool. His muscles tensed as he crouched down and I clung to his shoulders. And then like a shot, he flung us up towards the top of the cliff. I closed my eyes, squealing from the surprising ride. Experiencing his strength like that was such a rush. Another squeal escaped me when he landed with a soft thump.

"That was amazing." I told him, winded by his jump.

Jace grinned, handed me a towel, and we both dried off. He nodded towards my pile of clothes. "Might want to get dressed before the pups arrive."

"No funny business, mister. Or your pups might get an eyeful."

He growled and turned his back, so I could dress in private. I was only teasing him but loved how he respected that I may want some privacy.

When I turned back around, he was fully dressed and cleaning up the remnants of our picnic.

Now we were ready to see these pups he'd told me about. A giddy feeling filled me, and I couldn't stop stealing glances at him.

"Tonight was about getting to know each other better. Do you feel like we accomplished that??" Jace asked as he tucked the food back into the bag.

"Oh, yes, I know you *really* well. I'd like to learn more, though," I answered him in a seductive tone.

He waggled his eyebrows at me. "And what else would you like to know?"

Keep it PG. The pups are on their way, I reminded myself.

"What's your favorite..." I licked my lips, causing heat to flare in his eyes as they zeroed in on my tongue. "Color?" I finished with a giggle.

He let out a husky laugh. "Black and grey. Though sometimes, I'm partial to red. What's yours?"

"Green is my absolute favorite color, but lavender comes in second."

"After seeing you in that bikini, I think green may be climbing up my favorite's list."

I pressed a kiss to his lips.

"So, what do you say after we're done hanging out with the pups, we spend some more quality time getting to know each other better in my room?" he asked with a seductive grin.

"Why, Jace, I think you're trying to seduce me. And to that I say, seduce away."

I sashayed over to a fallen log and plopped down. Jace sank down next to me. As the sky got darker and the moon rose higher, I looked out over the beauty spread before me. Gravis stood by the water's edge, drinking. And all was quiet and peaceful.

"Keep quiet now and see if you can hear the pups coming," Jace whispered.

My ears strained, trying to capture little puppy sounds. At first, I just heard the whip of the wind in the trees. Then the rain-like sounds of the waterfall. And then the pounding of something on the ground. The earth danced beneath my feet, and I knew it was them. The howls of the pups reached my ears, making me smile. They sounded so cute. Nothing like I expected. Nothing like that night at the charity event.

"They're coming," I announced excitedly.

"That's them all right."

"I'm a bit nervous about meeting them. Any advice?" These were like surrogate children to Jace. I wanted them to like me.

"Just try to stay calm. If you get scared, try to control it. They'll sense it and react to it. We don't want them getting all riled up, especially Edwin. He's a bit of a challenge."

"Why not Ed…" was all I managed to say before I was stunned into silence.

They darted out of the woods and on to the trail, running towards us. They were running into one another nearly tripping amongst themselves with their tongues hanging out to the sides of their mouths. My eyes nearly bugged out of my head. They looked like regular-sized wolves, not pups. They looked excited and were coming straight for us, without stopping. I braced myself and took in a breath. I wasn't scared, because Jace was right next to me. He'd protect me if anything went wrong.

The first pup to arrive was a nice chocolate brown and slammed itself right into Jace. Thankfully, he stood up right before impact. The rest of them went around to his side and back to lick and nip at him. Well, except for one wolf. The black one. That pup studied me and approached slowly, stopping a few feet away—close enough to attack, but not close enough to touch. It sniffed at me while I met its eyes. With my head held high and my back straight, I managed to keep its stare. It was like time stood still for us. I couldn't hear anything going on around me. The black wolf pup sniffed some more and came a bit closer.

I waited, hoping I'd be able to tell when it was done sniffing me. It kept cocking its wolf shaped head from one side to the other. Slowly, I held my hand out to it, palm up. The pup, keeping eye contact with me the whole time, crept closer and sniffed my hand. Sniffed and sniffed, then he licked my hand. I pulled my hand back, and a growl escaped the pup.

Giving it back my hand, I cleared my throat. "I'm sure you can understand me. So, I'll only say this once. It's rude to growl and show your teeth to someone who isn't threatening you." I took my hand back and slowly stood from where I was seated, never breaking our gaze. "Especially someone who's defenseless."

The pup lowered its head, while it walked away from me and approached Jace.

"*Excuse* me? I wasn't finished" I spoke softly.

The pup stopped before Jace's hand could touch him.

"Come here, please," I commanded in a velvety voice.

The black pup looked at Jace, then back at me. Gradually it made its way back and stopped right in front of me.

"Hi. I'm Jasinda. Who might you be?"

"His name is Edwin," Jace said.

I'd figured this had to be Edwin by the way he'd acted. No wonder Jace had said he was trouble. I'd sensed his attitude from the moment we'd locked eyes. I put my hand out again for him to sniff, and he did. Hesitantly, I moved my hand and stroked his muzzle. I was kind of surprised he let me.

"You know, where I come from, we greet with kisses on the cheek." Leaning forward, I tapped a quick kiss to his.

He stood still. His eyes were closed when I pulled back. Then without a sound, he moved forward, planted both front paws on my thighs and licked my cheek.

I laughed at his efforts to kiss me. "It's nice to meet you too. I'm hoping you can show me around the woods one day. You know, show me what you guys do for fun."

He yelped and jumped down, heading over towards Jace. His demeanor wasn't anything like the others. The rest of the pups scattered when Edwin got close. The other three pups came to me and sat on their haunches. Holding my hand out again, I let each one sniff and lick me. Then one by one, I gave each a kiss on the cheek, which they returned with licks to my face.

"Samuel, Tony and Kat, meet Jasinda," Jace said. "Jasinda, these are the pups I was talking about. They haven't fully matured into wolves and haven't been able to change back into their human bodies."

"Wait. So, they're not *full-grown* wolves?" I conveyed.

"We're larger than that, enchantress."

"Really?"

"Yes."

"Can you show me?"

"Are you sure you want to see?"

"Yes, I'm sure," I said softly.

He walked a few feet away from where we were sitting. He looked at me and winked. Then, just like that, he shifted into his wolf form. No clothes to be found anywhere. *Could he will them on and off?* That was something I needed to know. But that could wait, because the wolf before me was huge. Breathtakingly massive. *Holy cannon balls!* They looked like babies compared to him.

He was getting closer, but his legs weren't moving. I blinked in confusion, then realized I was the one moving toward him. His fur was grey and he seemed to be the size of a small horse. I studied him as I kept walking and noticed his legs were a lighter grey than his body. The colors faded into each other so perfectly. He was beautiful. And those green eyes... Damn. They'd always been my weakness.

As I reached him, I put my hand out towards him. He sniffed it, then licked it. Then he proceeded to circle me, sniffing at me from all angles. In every area. Part of me wanted to protest, but I didn't because I enjoyed it. *How crazy was I to let a wolf sniff me there and like it?*

When he nipped at me through my jeans, I gasped. Then he rubbed his huge body against my legs, going around me in a circle. *What was he doing?*

When he finally came back in front of me, he lifted his two front paws and gently knocked me to my butt.

"Hey! What was that for?" I yelled in mock aggravation.

Pouncing on me gently, he licked me all over and put his muzzle all over my face. He nipped at my neck like an excited puppy who hadn't seen his mother in days. Giggles bubbled from my lips. My hands sunk in his fur as I petted him. It felt so soft, and he was nice and warm. I'd thought his fur would be brittle, but I was wrong. Closing my eyes, I inhaled his scent. He smelled like fresh linen, a faint trace of the woods, and a scent uniquely his.

"Yes," I whispered.

I didn't know why I was whispering, or what question I was actually answering. But *"yes"* felt right. A moan escaped me, and my eyes flew open.

What the hell was that? It felt like I was being pulled into another world or something. Kind of like the sensations I'd experienced while we rode Gravls earlier. *What was it Jace called it? Souls merging? Guess our souls were ready to play again.* But in a flash, Jace was off me and standing before me with an intense look on his face. His clothes were back on, and his hand was stretched out to me. Grabbing my hand, he lifted me up and hugged me to his chest.

He inhaled. "I'm sorry. I didn't mean to get carried away."

I wiggled my arms from where they were trapped against his chest and wrapped them around his waist. I nuzzled my face into his neck almost like he did with me. Then I licked his earlobe and bit it gently. He shivered, then went still when I cupped his butt with one hand.

"You might want to rethink that, enchantress. I'll take you right here, Jasinda. And I don't think you want the pups to be in on that action."

"Nope. An audience isn't necessary," I sighed.

He laughed and pulled back to study my face. His eyes were telling me something, but I didn't understand. I only knew that it was good stuff. He looked over at the pups and laughed. I looked over. All but one of the pups had their paws over their muzzles, trying to cover their eyes. I couldn't help but laugh too. Edwin was the only one who didn't have his eyes covered. Instead, his eyes were locked on me. I couldn't grasp what was going on in those brown eyes, but something was playing there.

Chapter Forty-Four

Jace

The shock of her asking to see me shift still clung to me. I was a bit nervous about it, because I wasn't sure if she'd fear me in my wolf form. I was way larger than the pups. They looked like regular dogs compared to me. But she was amazed. Her excitement about it was driving me crazy. So crazy that I marked her with my scent. A scent that told others to back off because she was taken by me.

When I'd nipped her neck, I was putting claiming marks on her neck just to confirm that she was mine. Those marks could only be seen by supernaturals, mostly by the wolves. Others would have to look closely to see those marks. She wouldn't be able to see them. *Ever.* They weren't meant for her eyes since she was human.

The pups knew what I was doing. And their reactions made me laugh. They were pretending to be disgusted by my actions with Jasinda, but I knew they were happy. They were teasing me. Edwin was the only one without a reaction. He was staring intensely at her, and I wasn't sure I liked it.

"Hey, it's not like we were having sex in front of you," I said teasing them back. Jasinda gave a slight chuckle.

"*Ewwwww! Please don't,*" Kat squealed.

"*Wait, it would be almost like a porn, but live!*" Tony expressed in disgust.

"Tony," I warned.

Jasinda looked back and forth between us. But he just laughed. He really laughed and rolled over on the ground. Kat followed suit with her laughter and began nipping at Tony. Edwin turned his head at them and growled.

"*Show some respect for her. Besides, she's left out of the conversation and doesn't know what's going on,*" he scolded.

"*We were just playing Ed. Besides, it was more towards Jace than her!*" Kat replied.

"*Man, what's with you today?*" Tony asked.

"*Nothing,*" he said with a bit of annoyance in his tone.

"*I think she's pretty. I mean more than pretty. Not beautiful or gorgeous, but more,*" Samuel said.

"What are you guys talking about?" Jasinda said with arched eyebrows.

"They're teasing me about what I did to you. That I treated you like one of us."

"Ah. So it was weird for them that you did that to a human?"

"Yes and no. It's something the wolves do with other wolves, either in wolf form or human form. As far as I know, you're the first human that it's been done to."

"Oh. So am I one of you?" she asked with a smirk on her face.

"I'm not sure, but it doesn't matter. You're now one of us." I winked at her.

She smiled, and the blush that filled her cheeks did something to me on the inside. I mean, my dick was having feelings too, but the warmth that ran through me was unexpected. Priscilla had *never* made me feel this way. Nor had any of the others I'd dated. Her eyes filled with relief at feeling accepted and wanted. I needed to make sure I kept her feeling that way.

I brought her back to the logs to sit and tapped a kiss on her lips. She looked at me confused and grabbed my hand before I could walk away.

"Where are you going?"

"I need to run, enchantress. My changing stirred the wolf in me."

"But how will I communicate with the pups?"

I smiled at the fact she was more focused on communicating with them. Not scared at all. That was my girl.

"You don't need to. You can just hang out here with them. They like the company."

"So, you just will your clothes on and off when you shift?"

"Yes, we're magical creatures," I retorted with a wink.

"Ha. That's pretty cool. I wish I could will on different outfits all the time."

I wished I could will her clothes off her now and have my way with her again.

"What's that wicked smile about?" she asked quizzically.

"Nothing. Edwin let's go."

Just like that, I shifted and ran off into the woods with Edwin.

"What are we doing?" Edwin asked me.

"I want to see how she'll react without communication. And I want to see what they'll do around her."

"And I'm here with you because?"

"Because, I wanted to ask you how the lessons are with Priscilla?"

"They suck."

"Come on, Edwin. Give me something." I laughed a bit.

"No really, the lessons suck. Priscilla is a royal pain in my..."

"Don't you say it," I commanded.

"Fine. Whatever. She's a bitch!"

"Edwin!!! Language!" I yelled firmly.

"Oh, come on, Jace. We both know she is. And why can't I say bitch?"

"I want you to go without cursing for a while. It seems like those are the only words in your vocabulary."

"True. But they're my favorite vocabulary words, and they're amazing to use."

"Yes, I know. Just stop calling her that."

"Fine."

"I was hoping you guys could hang with Jasinda one day. Show her around and make her feel safe with you all. What do you say?"

Cocking his head, he stared at me through those wolf brown eyes. He was nervous and excited at the same time. Then he looked back to where we'd left them. I too glanced back at them. Tony and Kat had their snouts on her thighs, and she was talking to them. Samuel was swimming, like always. He loved the damn water.

"I think they'll be fine with it, and so will I," he said.

"Good. I was hoping for that. Now, tell me why Priscilla is being a bitch?"

His laughter filled my mind. I knew *why* he was laughing, and I was happy for it. This pup rarely laughed, and he always kept to himself. I wanted more for him, for him to be happy for a change.

"She doesn't do anything but yell and boss us around all day. When we're out in the woods, she just sits and eats the fruit we find. Then she wanders off without us for hours at a time. And when she gets back, she just yells at us some more."

"I see." My ears slumped and my claws dug deep into the ground. It was distressing to hear this. *"Anything else?"*

"I just feel like she hates us and would rather not have anything to do with us."

"Why didn't you ever mention this to me before?"

"We didn't want to seem ungrateful for all you've done for us. This has been the best home we've had. So, we decided we were willing to put up with her, so long as we got to stay." Edwin hung his head and tucked in his ears.

I struggled to keep my rage in check so the young impressionable pup didn't pick up on it. Priscilla knew working with the pups was a sensitive assignment and that she needed to treat them with care. I'd have a talk with her tomorrow and make sure she truly understood what I expected of her.

"Why is she here?" Edwin asked, turning his attention back to Jasinda and the pups.

"I'm keeping her safe. She's in the middle of some trouble we're all trying to figure out. It has something to do with her mother."

"You mean someone's trying to kill her?"

"No, I think someone's trying to kidnap her. They want her mother, but she's nowhere to be found. From speaking with her father, if they don't find her mother, they'll come for Jasinda instead."

"Not fuc...not cool," he corrected himself.

"Not at all."

"I can help you," he offered eagerly.

"I'm counting on it."

If making him feel like he was a part of something would get him involved with the pack, then I'd make sure to tell him more about her. I needed these pups to change into their human forms soon or they'd stay this way forever.

Discreetly, we watched her with the pups. Twitching my ears, I listened as she told them a story and rubbed them behind their ears. They were fixated on her words. It lifted my heart to see this. I hoped this gave them a shot at showing others who they really were. They needed to come out of their shells with others, not just with me.

Chapter Forty-Five

Jace

Slowly, I began to walk around the bushes, staying hidden from her. The pups were too busy to even notice. But it was probably because they'd already figured I was close by watching. Edwin moved quietly alongside me. I knew he wanted to sit beside her with the other pups, but he was curious and knew I had something to ask of him.

"Do you think you can keep an eye on Jasinda when she ventures into the woods? She likes riding horses and loves the outdoors. If you sense her hitting the trails, I want you there watching and protecting her."

"I can do that. But this place is well secured. You really think anyone could find her here?"

"I'm not sure, but I'm being extra careful. Just make sure she's safe. That means from anyone *you think will do her harm. Even if it's me."*

"But you wouldn't hurt her."

"No, but you never know if someone or something might possess me to do her harm."

"Got it."

He longed to be a guard. This was the first step for him. I'd consider him if he did well with this assignment. His excitement made his body tremble.

I finally stopped and listened in on what Jasinda was saying to the pups.

"I'm serious. They *are* real, and I'm hoping to meet one eventually," she said with a small laugh.

"I *know* you both think I'm crazy to believe in unicorns, but I do. I mean we live in a supernatural world, right? Why *wouldn't* we have unicorns?" She was reassuring herself.

"You know, this kinda sucks. You can understand me, but I can't even figure out what you're thinking."

The pups whined in response. They too were annoyed they couldn't speak to her. I came out of the bushes. She looked at me and her hands in the pups' fur stopped. They whined again but stopped when they noticed me. She held out her right hand and I rubbed my face against it. Then she brought her left hand to the other side of my face and cradled it.

"You're so hot. Like you have a fever. But oddly, your warmth feels good."

She snuggled her face with mine. *Damn this woman.* She kept surprising me. I'd never known anyone but our kind to touch a wolf like this. *Could she be half wolf? If so, why was I not able to sense the wolf in her?* Even if she might half. I should sense it.

Most humans were terrified at first. But she acted as if she was one of us. No fear, just affection. There had to be something supernatural in her.

"Jace, I think the pups are tired."

I moved out of her grip to see that two of the pups had fallen asleep on her thighs. Samuel was curled up by Tony. Edwin curled himself next to her feet, waiting on me. I nudged him, and he got up waking the others.

"You guys go get some rest. It's late," I told them.

"But we wanted to hang out with you a little longer." Kat yawned.

"Tomorrow's another day, Katti. Get some rest. We're going hunting tomorrow afternoon."

Kat perked up at the same time Tony did. They loved to hunt with me and were always excited about it. They leaped off the log and trotted away. Edwin walked up to Jasinda and put his paw on her lap. She took her hand and placed it over his paw.

"It was nice meeting you," she said.

As soon as the words left her mouth, Edwin ran off. Just as quickly as he did, the others came back. Kat and Tony both put their paws on Jasinda's lap as well.

"Nice meeting you both too. Thank you for spending time with me. Oh, and if you see a unicorn, please come find me." She looked over at Samuel who hadn't moved from the log but was staring at her with his head tilted to the side. "Samuel, it was nice meeting you too." She scratched behind his ear.

Together the pups ran off and disappeared into the woods. They liked her. They'd never cared to get too close to anyone before, and they'd been with me for six years now. The closest they'd come to anyone was my mother, and even then, they didn't let her touch them. Mom always gave the pups space, because of what they'd been through. Jasinda just showed them affection.

I shifted back to human form and sat beside her. Taking her hand in mine, I looked over at her. She was still staring in the direction the pups disappeared. I sensed worry in her and a bit of unease. She still hadn't looked back at me. I squeezed her hand gently, and she looked at me then.

"What's on your mind?" I asked her.

"What's Edwin's story?" she inquired, getting straight to the point.

I inhaled a breath and pulled her onto my lap facing me. She looked down at me with tears settling in her eyes. She could sense there was a story that came along with him. "Hey. It's fine. He's better here with me, and he likes it here too," I said, rubbing her arms in hopes she wouldn't shed those tears. "His father left his mother once he knew she was pregnant. Since he didn't want to be with her anymore, she didn't want Edwin when he was born. His grandmother took him in for the first three years. Every time her daughter came to visit, she always ignored Edwin."

"Why even go visit?"

"Because that's how messed up his mother is."

"Has he seen her again, his mother?"

"No, he got put in a different home after he turned four. His grandmother died, and no other family knew about him. Every home he went into, he'd just close himself off. He finally learned how to shift when he was five. It was his third home by then. This couple couldn't have children; they were half-breeds." I brought my hands down to her waist. "They spoiled him and loved him with everything they had. They died when he was nine. They were murdered, and ever since he hasn't changed back into his human form."

"How did you come to adopt him?" she asked, as she ran her hands up and down my chest.

"Elier knew the couple and asked me to help him find the pup. He'd been missing for three days. I found him at his elementary school. At first, he didn't want to come out, so I stayed there waiting and waiting until he felt I wasn't a threat. Since I had a backpack filled with water and food, I was able to feed him and myself while I waited."

"That must have been horrible for him and for you."

"It was, but then again look at where it got me. He's safe here, and he actually likes being here. Besides, I didn't *adopt* him. At the age of ten, if he has no family to claim him, then he's considered an adult."

"Seriously?"

"Yes, by the age of five, wolves should already know the basics of hunting and finding shelter for themselves. I saw that he didn't have those skills, so I asked him if he'd like to live with me. I told him that he could wander in a big forest where no one would bother him. He agreed and ever since, I've taught him what he should've been taught."

"So if he wants to leave, could he?"

"Absolutely. I wouldn't want him to go. But I also wouldn't hold him back from doing something for himself." She smiled at me. "What's the smile for?"

"For not wanting him to go. It's sweet and a major turn on."

I slid my hands to her ass. "Careful," I warned.

Chapter Forty-Six

Jasinda

He kissed *me*. I straddled him and wrapped my arms around his neck. Within moments, I became lost. I didn't want to let him go. When he finally pulled back, he lifted us both and put me on my feet. My lips turned down in a pout, causing a grin to fill his face.

"Someone likes straddling me, huh?"

"Maybe," I said.

"Maybe?" he questioned with a raised eyebrow.

"Yes, maybe," I said in a nonchalant tone.

"Oh, it's like that?" he said playfully.

I began to walk backwards, holding my hands in front of me to defend myself. But he just kept stalking towards me, making sure he stayed close enough to touch me. Without a sound, he grabbed me and rolled us to the ground. He pinned me, my back to the ground and his hip between my thighs. The fire in his eyes said it all. *Damn could I handle another round with him?*

"Are you always this much of a tease?"

"No, at least that I can recall," I panted.

"Good." He smirked.

Was he hoping for that answer? I hope he didn't think he needed to compete with Elier. Elier and I were over and had been for a while. From the moment Miranda had shown up at my door, I was done with him. Speaking of Elier, I needed to tell Jace about lunch tomorrow.

"Ummm…Jace?"

"What is it?" He looked worried.

"I need to tell you something. It's about tomorrow."

"Tomorrow? Wait, is it about me leaving in the morning? Because if it is, I'll be back in time to take you out to lunch."

"I didn't know you were leaving in the morning. I…I…well…I made lunch plans tomorrow." I closed my eyes. "With Elier." I spat out quickly.

I slowly opened one eye to look at him, and he wasn't happy. Anger and a flick of worry flashed in his eyes.

"Say something, Jace."

"*Why?* Why are you having lunch with him?" he asked through gritted teeth.

"Well…when you gave me my phone back, I had all these missed calls and texts from him. I decided to answer his text and let him know I was doing all right."

"I already told him that!" He was still grinding his teeth.

"I know. He told me. He asked if we could talk, and I said we could have lunch. He needs closure, Jace. He needs to know why I didn't tell him about the pregnancy," I finished softly.

He closed his eyes and brought his head down to my chest. I automatically ran my hand through his hair, feeling the softness in my hands. He kept his head next to my heart and purred through his throat.

"I don't want you to have lunch with him. I don't like it."

"I am sure you don't. But this won't be the *only* thing you won't like about me," I said dryly. He looked up at me.

"No, I just don't like the *idea* of it. You, I like. I don't like the idea of you going to lunch with Elier. Alone."

"I'm a grown woman, and I do as I please with whom I please. Going to lunch with Elier doesn't *mean* anything. I just need to do this, not just for him. But for me too."

He stared at me with an intense look. *What the hell was going on in that brain of his?* He growled again and hid his face in my neck.

"What if I asked you not to go?" he said into my neck.

Damn him! His breath on my neck was intoxicating.

"I *need* to do this. It's important to me. I had been too afraid to face him before. I'm ready now," I pleaded.

I was ready. I wanted this over and done with. I owed this to Elier and myself.

Jace began kissing my neck from my shoulder to my ear. *Oh god! That was my second weakness.* He was doing a good job of distracting me. I on the other hand, just played with his hair as his teeth pulled at the skin on my neck. Before I could ask what the hell that was, he *bit* me. I mean he really bit into me. A sharp pain flashed through me for less than a second, and then pleasure exploded into my breasts.

I arched my body underneath his. *Oh my!* Pleasure moved from my breasts to the apex of my thighs. My body started trembling. Small cries filtered into my ears. Cries of pleasure. They were coming from me. Somehow, his bite was giving me an orgasm. *How ludicrous was that?*

Oh, but it felt so good. An out of body experience. A quick, cool breeze teased my skin for a moment, and then heat licked all over me. Next thing I knew, he was inside me, filling me and making me cry out again. *Where did our clothes go? I still wasn't used to the magic this man possessed.* The pleasure he was giving me erased all thoughts from my mind. He moved in and out. I tightened my thighs against him and moved, meeting his thrusts. His teeth were still attached to my neck as he thrust harder into me. Before I could fully get lost in the sensations, a voice sounded in my head, shocking me.

"Tell me! Please tell me."

"What? Jace, is that you?" I hesitantly asked back.

"Yes, now tell me!"

"How is this possible?" I asked in confusion.

"I wanted you to hear my thoughts. I'm able to connect with anyone I want."

Then he pulled back to look at me. His eyes were like emerald diamonds. *Holy shit!*

"Oh, this is awesome!" I said.

He shook his head while he chuckled.

"Tell me, Jasinda," he grunted.

"Tell you what?" I panted

"Tell me who you belong to?"

"I belong to you."

"You belong to me?"

"Yes!" I screamed out, eliciting more chuckles from him.

"Do I belong to you?" he asked earnestly.

"You'd better." I moaned.

"Then tell me that you want me to be yours infinitely."

"Infinitely mine. I want you to be infinitely mine, Jace."

"I, Jace, choose to be infinitely yours."

"Mmmmmm," was all I managed to say.

"What about you, do you feel the same?"

"Yes." His thrusts were getting faster and harder.

"Say it, Jasinda," he demanded.

"I, Jasinda, choose to be infinitely yours."

I screamed out his name as another orgasm hit me. This one harder than I'd ever experienced in my lifetime. His grunts and moans filled my ears as his rhythm changed. His frantic thrusting from a few moments ago had shifted into long and slow motions that filled me completely. After his release, the wind suddenly picked up and swirled around us. A vibration went through me, and somehow, I knew it was going through him too. Next thing I knew, I felt something like tickles on my fingers. With great effort, I lifted my hands from his back and brought them to my face to see what it was, but nothing was there.

As quickly as it began, the wind was gone, and so were the vibrations. Closing my eyes, I dropped my hands back down. *Shit, what the fuck kind of orgasm was that? I wanted another one! That was amazing. Was this how sex was with a shapeshifter? Did all the supernaturals give each other amazing orgasms like that?*

I opened my eyes, and he was looking at me. The emerald glimmer had faded.

"Are you ok?" he sounded concerned.

"Uh…I think so. I hope so." I laughed. "Jace, what *was* that? I mean what just happened?"

"It was an infused moment. Not sure I can really explain it."

"Try," I pleaded.

"Not now. I have too many things on my mind." His eyes searched my face as he hovered above me.

"Like?"

"Like how I'm not sure how I'm going to handle tomorrow."

"Is this how you'll be when all other men are around? Because if so, then you should be worried about Anthony and not Elier," I teased.

Anger flashed in his eyes, and then he laughed. It was as if he had just remembered Anthony was a big part of my life. He tapped a kissed on my lips, then nuzzled my neck again. *What was he doing to me?*

"No, I won't *always* be like this. Elier isn't on my good list, and you have a history with him. Romantic history. Anthony on the other hand is on my good list, and he hasn't seen you naked. So, no worries there." He pulled back and winked at me.

Biting my lip, I thought it best to not tell him that Anthony had seen me naked before. I wanted to ask again about what just happened, but our clothes magically reappeared and I was a bit relieved. It was so odd to have him just will my clothes off without notice. But it was also exciting. I frowned internally. *Was I really this thrilled over disappearing clothes? Maybe things made me happy too easily. I might need to raise my standards.* Jace lifted us both to our feet, and Gravis was already waiting for us.

Before he helped me onto the horse's back, he stroked my cheek. "An infused moment happens when a couple allows themselves to ascend to the next level of pleasure. It also means we're in a relationship. What do you think about that?"

How the hell had he known I wanted to press for answers? Was I that easy to read? "Being in a relationship with you?" He nodded. "I like the sound of that. Is it exclusive?"

"Hell yes! One thing you should know about me is that I don't share."

"Good, because neither do I." I pressed my mouth to his.

He stepped back and said, "Everyone will see us as an infused couple."

"Ok. You're my wolfie boyfriend now."

"Something like that." He chuckled. "It's late. We should head back."

"Sounds good."

He lifted me onto Gravis, then settled gracefully behind me. I leaned back on him and just enjoyed the ride back. He was silent, and probably because of my upcoming lunch with Elier. He had nothing to worry about. It was just lunch. I hoped.

Chapter Forty-Seven

Jace

I panicked and reacted in a way I shouldn't have. What we'd done moments ago had been amazing. Beyond amazing. She didn't realize how remarkable it was because she didn't know the full effects of it all. *How could I tell her what I'd just done? How could I tell her that I'd fucked up, but hadn't fucked up? How could I explain that me panicking over Elier and her had made me do the unthinkable? What would my mother say about this?*

I wished she wouldn't go tomorrow. A part of me feared he'd try to get her back, and she'd welcome it. Especially, with the state of her hormones at the moment. The risk to her well-being was big. But the risk to my heart was *huge*. Elier had always been a charmer, and he'd charmed his way *into* many females. He'd even charmed his way into Priscilla when we'd been dating. He'd *known* she wasn't to be touched until I unannounced my claim. I'd only dated her because our families had wanted us together. It had been their rule that no other man should touch her while I was courting her. But she'd been attracted to Elier as well. She'd wanted to have fun. And she had, thankfully.

He'd done me a favor. I probably would've mated with her, even though I'd detested the thought. Still, it had been a shitty thing for him to do. I didn't want him charming his way back to Jasinda. *No way!* I didn't want the temptation for her. *Fuck!*

We finally arrived, and I helped her off Gravis. Jumping off, I grabbed her hand and led her inside. I stopped us right before the stairs.

"Is there any way I can convince you *not* to go tomorrow?"

She glared at me and folded her arms across her chest. I could sense her anger now. *Shit!* I had pissed her off.

"Drop it, Jace. You'll just have to deal with it." She snapped.

"Let's get this straight, Jasinda, I really *don't* have to deal with it. I *truly* don't want to. It's hard for me because I want you. I may not be yours, but you are *MINE!*" I said with a growl, "I'm working on being yours, and I *want* to be yours. I want you to *want* me to be yours. I want you in my bed, I want you on my horse, and I want you as part of my pack." I stepped closer. "This lunch with Elier, doesn't make me happy. But you're right, he needs closure. He deserves to know what happened and why you kept it from him. That doesn't mean I have to like it, and I don't."

With that I walked off, disappearing under the stairs. I walked into my office and slammed the door behind me. *Fuck!* We'd had a good night and she'd had to ruin it by bringing up Elier and the lunch. I shouldn't be as upset as I was. She was mine. I knew that, but I still didn't want her near Elier.

The look in her eyes before I walked away was unsettling. She was angry, but also pained by my reaction. I could see that now. *Damn.* I needed to find a way to make it up to her. I needed her to forgive me.

Without another thought, I turned back around and walked out of my office, planning to find her in her room. Before I made it to the stairs, I halted. She was there sitting at the bottom step with both her elbows on her knees and cradling her chin in her hands. She seemed so far away yet so close. She seemed to be deep in thought, and I craved to read her mind, see what she was thinking. But I knew better than to try. Slowly, I walked over to her and sat. She turned her head in my direction. Relief filled her eyes at the sight of me, but regret swam in them as well.

I was an idiot. "I'm sorry. I overreacted and I shouldn't have just walked away the way I did."

"Are you feeling insecure about me, about us?" she rightfully asked.

"No, that's not it."

"Do you feel threatened by Elier?"

"Maybe. Yes," I admitted.

She closed her eyes for a few seconds then reopened them. Straightening herself, she placed one hand on mine. A warm current went through my veins. Her touch was caressing my entire body, and she didn't even know it.

"You have *nothing* to be worried about. It's just lunch and nothing more."

"You two have history, Jasinda. History I can't compete with. What if he wants you back?"

"Then that's just too bad for him. He'll have to deal with me not wanting him. That's what you don't get. I *don't* want him. I haven't wanted him in a while." She let out a breath. "Do you want to hear a confession?" she asked me.

"A confession from you? Please, confess it all."

She laughed and scooted closer to me. "After I found out about Miranda, I was hurt and angry. But I got over it quickly. *Too* quickly. And I think it was because I truly wasn't *in* love with him. Yes, I *loved* him, but, Jace, I didn't even *miss* him. I was angry about how I'd been played like a fool. Yes, we'd had some good times and I'd enjoyed myself with him. But now I truly know that I wasn't in *LOVE* with him." She took her free hand and ran it through my hair. "He's more of a friend and a protector to me."

She kept eye contact with me while smiling. I loved her smile, especially when it was directed at me.

She placed her palm on my cheek. "Jace, you said you're working on being mine. But you *are* already mine, and I *want* you to be mine. What we did earlier… the things I said, weren't just because of the great orgasm. They were because it was what I wanted and how I felt." She smiled. "Elier once asked me who I belonged to, and I told him myself. So, you see I *knew* what I was saying to you, even if I was high off an orgasm." She winked.

Her winks were seductive. If she only knew what those words *truly* meant. If she only knew what really happened earlier. How I panicked and made a decision I shouldn't have made for the both of us. She'd hate me. She'd be angry with me. She'd want to undo it all, and it would *kill* me. Us mating earlier was one ceremony that would go down in history. Our souls were meant for one another. We *were* true soulmates, and the mating ritual we'd performed just confirmed what I'd already known. I'd never felt drawn to anyone before her. There had never been a desire to mate. My beast had always sat quietly in the backseat, except that time with Priscilla when he'd gone ballistic. My soul had never merged with anyone else's. And I'd certainly never lost control during sex before and formed an unbreakable bond with my partner. Then the world around us had applauded through the wind with joy that we were now one. Too bad she didn't know it. And wouldn't understand it.

I took each of her hands in mine and pressed a kiss to the back of each hand near her ring fingers. We now had wedding bands tattooed on both of our ring fingers. Our left hands had two large bands each, and our right hands had two medium bands. In between those bands were our names. "Hunt" branded on her left hand, and "Jace" was on her right. She wasn't able to see them, but I could. My right hand said "Jasinda," and my left hand read "Hunt." The tattoos appeared on mated shifters, so when wolves shifted, their bands could still be seen. By tomorrow, everyone in the pack would know we were mated.

Everyone but her.

Chapter Forty-Eight

Jasinda

I was being completely honest with him when I said I belonged to him. Because that was how I felt. The look in his eyes as he held both my hands, worried me. He looked scared and pained for some reason. I wasn't sure what to do at this point. I didn't know how to reassure him that he had nothing to worry about. If I could erase whatever fear and pain he felt, I would. Seeing him this way pinched my heart.

"Please don't be upset with me. Try to understand what I'm doing here. What if it was you, Jace? What if you were in Elier's shoes right now?"

"*I* wouldn't have cheated on you. Knowing you weren't one of us would've made me play it incredibly safe with you. I wouldn't have given *any* other female a chance until I knew what I wanted from you. He was a fool to have let this happen, and I know he's regretting it. I would too. But it isn't in my nature to let what's *mine* be put out there like it's available for someone else to try and take." His nostrils flared and a growl escaped his lips, exposing his canines

As possessive as that sounded, I liked it. He didn't want anyone trying to take me. Somehow, I needed to try to understand where he was coming from. Women didn't always get the way men thought. But Jace was trying to give me a piece of what he was thinking. So, I figured maybe since I still didn't get it completely, and I probably wouldn't, then I'd give him something to ease his worries a bit.

"Would you like to accompany me to lunch tomorrow? He's supposed to pick me up, but maybe you'd prefer to take me instead."

He breathed out a sigh of relief. "Yes, I would prefer to take you."

"Great. Then it's settled. You'll take me tomorrow, and you'll behave?"

"That's hard to promise, enchantress." He grinned.

"Jace," I warned.

"He won't even *see* me. I promise. But he'll probably smell me, eventually." His grin turned into a wide smile.

"Is there a Goddess of help? Because I need one." I joked.

He laughed and stood with one of my hands still in his and walked me to my room. He opened my door and led me to the bed. Sinking into it, I figured he was going to sit with me, but he bypassed me and went into the bathroom. After a few minutes, he returned and stared at me. And I sat there watching him gaze at me.

"*You* need a bath. Someone let you play in the dirt way too late tonight," he teased.

"Oh, well I hope that someone lets me get dirty again. Soon."

He knelt before me and lifted my shirt over my head. With a quick jerk, he snapped my bra apart. It fell down my arms, spilling my breasts.

"Hey! Now why would you waste a perfectly good bra when you could just will it off?" I asked with confusion.

He shrugged with a smirk. "I've always wanted to do that. I've seen it a few times in movies."

"What else did you see in these movies?"

He pushed me softly to my back and unfastened my jeans. The sound of the zipper slowly going down was unnaturally loud in the quiet room. He tugged on the denim. Once the fabric slid down my thighs, he pulled back quickly, leaving me in my panties. Bracing myself on my elbows, I noticed he willed my boots off and socks off at the same time.

"Show off!" I murmured.

He laughed and got closer, planting himself between my thighs. I squeezed his shoulders lightly as he squeezed me at my hips. *Shit!* It felt good. Without warning, he ripped my panties off as if he'd done it a thousand times.

"Jace?" I said lazily.

"Shhhh. I want to taste you."

He was going to feast on me. Thank you, Goddess! He leaned in close and sniffed me. He closed his eyes like he was savoring the smell.

It was the biggest turn on. Moisture pooled between my legs.

"You smell so sweet." His breath brushed me lightly, making me shiver. "You're wet. So, so wet. I like it."

Oh god, could he really give me an orgasm by just talking to my pussy? Because I felt like I was ready to erupt. I fell back, unable to hold myself up anymore. I closed my eyes in anticipation of feeling his tongue on me. He was driving me bat shit crazy! Time seemed to stand still with just the caress of his hot breath against my folds.

"You're a huge tease," I blurted out and lifted myself back up to glare at him.

"I want you to watch," he seductively taunted.

When my eyes locked on his, he took one long lick of all my wetness, making me come instantly while crying out his name. He licked again and again, his tongue circling in my clit in slow motion. I moaned and fought to keep eye contact with him. My arms trembled, and I wasn't sure I'd be able to hold myself up much longer.

Damn he was good. Gripping the sheets in my hands, I cried out again and fell back. His tongue traced a path up my stomach to my breast, then he stopped at my neck. He placed soft kisses around my neck, casually nipping my ear here and there. I didn't want it to end.

"You like this, don't you?"

"Yes," I said breathlessly.

"You aren't sore down there?"

"I don't know, and I don't care."

He growled in my ear. *Was he happy with my answer?* I didn't get a chance to ask because he plunged into me at that moment. Another cry escaped my lips, but it sounded off for some reason. *What the hell was he doing to me?*

I felt a little sore, but he felt so good inside me that I couldn't bring myself to care. He thrusted in and out, in and out, going faster and faster until he splashed his release inside me.

Didn't he need to recharge? How was it possible that he was able to go like a lion in heat? He slowed his rhythm and kissed me deeply. Moaning into his mouth, I deepened the kiss. He growled back at me. *Oh yeah, this was amazing.* He slipped from inside me and lifted me with ease. I wrapped my arms around his neck as he walked us to the bathroom and sat us in the warm water.

"Ummmm. This feels so good. No soap?" I asked.

"No, it can irritate a sore spot." He slightly smiled.

"Ah. I see."

He gently lifted me and turned me around, so my back was pressed to his chest. Lavender and rosemary filled my nostrils. I closed my eyes and just relaxed in his arms. This felt good. He rubbed my body all over a few times, then he did the same to himself.

"What are you doing?"

"Bathing us with essential oils. It's better for the body."

"Are these the same ones you left me?"

"Yes, the ones my mother makes."

"Her products are wonderful. I love them."

"I know. I saw the gift you gave her.

I turned my head to look at him. His eyes were closed, but he opened them to look at me. He looked so sexy all wet.

"Thank you," he offered.

"For what?"

"For being so thoughtful to my mother. I'm sure she'll love them."

"I hope so."

He pulled me closer and kissed me. I pulled back quickly and grinned at him. Then he pulled me back for another kiss. I ran my hands through his loose hair. *Oh, I was going to wash his beautiful locks. And all the rest of him.*

Chapter Forty-Nine

Jace

Jasinda still slept soundly when I left the next morning. I needed to take care of a few things before I took her to her stupid lunch with Elier. Last night was one of the most incredible nights I'd ever had. Since Jasinda had come into my life, it had been interesting and entertaining having her around. Especially not knowing what to expect from her and her reactions to things. I called a meeting with the pack first thing this morning.

"I know it's not time for our normal meeting, but I'm sure most of you have heard that I'm protecting a woman in my home."

Murmurings floated among those gathered. The whole pack had responded to my request to meet. Except my brother. I'd find him later to give him a piece of my mind.

"Everybody quiet down and I'll tell you what I can." I waited for silence to prevail. "Her name is Jasinda, and she's in danger from the supernatural community. I can't share all the details with you. But know that her presence here doesn't put any of you in danger. Please try to act as normally as possible for her sake. Our world is *a lot* to take in when a person isn't accustomed to it."

"When can we meet her?" a voice called out.

"Yeah," several others chimed in.

"Soon. I promise."

They smiled at me, eager to meet the new person in their midst.

"You all will have plenty of time to get to know her and love her. Because… she and I are mated." I held up my hands, so they could see my ring fingers. "Since she's not like us, I'm still explaining things to her about our world, our pack and what our lives will be like. So, I'm asking you to please give us some time and space, so she can adjust. I'll let you know when the time is right to offer your congratulations and well-wishes. I know she's going to love you all."

They seemed shocked, probably because they'd figured I'd never find *the one*. But everyone gathered whooped and hollered in pure joy for me. They scampered about. My pack was a mixture of crazy goofballs. A few could be hot-headed, but for the most part, they were the best pack I'd had in years.

Elation spread over my face as I took in their happiness. Then my eyes collided with Priscilla's, the thorn in my side. My brother had been wanting to rip her head off ever since we'd become adults. The look on her face at hearing about what had transpired between me and Jasinda was filled with pure hatred. For me, or maybe for Jasinda.

"How could you mate with a human? How could you stoop so low and be such a selfish beast? Just because she's pretty and needy?"

I didn't bother to answer her. It was none of her business, and I really just wanted to see her sweat about her attitude. I'd had enough of her.

At least I had the pack's approval. Not that I needed it but being included made them feel important.

My mother had always told me that was what made a great king and alpha. She had to be right because my pack was fully beside me whenever the time came and I needed them. We'd grown so much over the years.

Anthony caught my eye from the back of the crowd. But with everyone clamoring around me to talk about the pups and Jasinda, a conversation with him would have to wait until later. *"We'll talk later, ok?"*

He nodded.

I turned to all the bodies crowding around me, each with questions on their lips.

"What's she like?"

"Do you think she's the best option as a mother figure for the pups?"

"Yeah, she's not like us."

"One at a time, guys," I laughed.

I appreciated their concern for the pups' well-being. "Jasinda doesn't know very much about us yet. But she's patient and understanding. She doesn't scare easily, so I think she'll do better than expected. And she'll certainly be better than having no mother figure at all."

They nodded their heads in agreement.

"She's actually spent a little time with the pups already. And even though she couldn't communicate with them, they responded well to her."

Giving them the details of her interactions with the wolf pups helped to set their minds at ease. Soon they were as hopeful as I was about the role she could play in the pups' lives.

This was why I loved my pack so much. They, too, hoped the pups would one day be able to shift into their human forms. The pack didn't know how to act around the pups, so they never really got involved when it came to them. They didn't want to risk scaring them away. I understood. Besides, they were my responsibility, not theirs. But as a pack we took on responsibility together.

I let Jasinda walk in first. My plan was to walk her to his table. But when I noticed he wasn't sitting anywhere in the front, I decided to let her have her privacy with Elier. I didn't like it, but I wanted to watch and see what unfolded between them.

He didn't see me at first. I sat at a table in the front of the restaurant, while they sat in the back. Running my hand over my face, I saw his eyes go dark when she sat with her hands on the table. He was a bit enraged by her being mated, but he didn't speak of it.

"I'm happy to see you, Jasinda. It's been a bit crazy for me, worrying about you. Not knowing if everything was good with you," Elier confessed.

"I'm sorry. But you need to remember you have no claim over me. So, technically, I'm none of your business. No offense," she firmly told him.

"I know. But that doesn't mean I'm not concerned about your safety."

She is safe with me. You know that, asshole. The anger was easy to tap into. But I continued to remain calm, so I wouldn't interrupt them.

"I appreciate that, Elier. My father gave specific instructions to Jace. As much as I want to be able to do my own thing, I need to follow those orders. I feel safe with him, Elier. And I'm learning so many amazing things. I mean who would've thought I'd find myself in the presence of a supernatural? An alpha at that," her voice sounded excited. "He's amazing. And Scarlet and I are getting close. She's becoming a good friend to me. His brother's a little scary and misguided, but I don't think he's a bad wolf," she whispered and looked around.

"Don't worry about secrecy. Every employee who works here is supernatural. You're the only human here," Elier said easing her worries.

"*Again?* Man, how am I supposed to tell them apart?"

"You're not. That's the whole point. We are supposed to blend in with the humans. If everyone could tell us apart, then most of us would be hunted and killed by those who are terrified of us."

"Right," she said with embarrassment.

I wanted to flick him in the nose for making her feel that way. "Sorry. I didn't think about that."

"Don't be sorry either. It's not your fault you're oblivious to us," he said with deep sorrow in his voice.

"Ok." She blew out a breath. "I am sorry about not letting you explain about Miranda. That was selfish and stupid of me. Irrational even." She looked down at her hands and back up at Elier. "I was angry and in pain. Plus, your fiancé showing up didn't make it any easier." He went to speak, but she put her hand up and continued, "Finding out that I was pregnant the same day that I find out that you have a fiancé wasn't easy on me. I was going to tell you after I calmed down and then, well you know what happened. I thought it best to not say anything."

Elier nodded. "I wish I would have done things differently. But I was afraid to lose you and in doing that, I did. For that I am sorry."

"Jace explained it all to me." She gave Elier a tentative smile.

"So…" he started, then looked at her finger again. "Jace and you, are what a couple now?" he pushed in a demanding voice.

"Maybe that's something we shouldn't talk about." She twisted her fingers together, clearly uncomfortable with his tone.

"I want you back, Jasinda. I've always wanted you back. Give me another chance to make things right. Now that you know the truth, I can tell you everything," he pleaded.

Son of a bitch. This was what I had been worried about. Him moving in on what was mine. I gripped the table to stay in my seat.

"Tell me the truth about what?" she asked curiously. *Dammit.*

"About Miranda and why I kept her around."

"Why *did* you keep her around?"

"Because I was supposed to mate with her. *Eventually.* Then I met you, and I enjoyed having you around. Miranda knew I was free to date whoever I wanted. It was no secret."

"Except to me," she coldly announced.

That was a good sign I hoped.

"I know. Well, I didn't want to scare you away or have you think I was trying to have my cake and eat it too."

"But you were. You *did* have your cake, and you ate it too," she mocked.

"Yes, I guess you're right. But for what it's worth, I didn't want her. The truth is we were *chosen* to be mates. Something parents do sometimes in our world. We don't always have to agree to it, but I agreed to go through with it if I didn't find *the one* I truly wanted to mate with," he said.

She didn't respond.

"I was being selfish and trying to keep you all to myself. I wanted you to fall so madly in love with me that when I finally told you *what* I was, you wouldn't fear me or be disgusted by me." *I could identify with his fears, but it was no excuse.*

"I can't believe you thought so little of me. What you are wouldn't have disgusted me. What you *did* disgusts me. No matter your fears, you should've tried to tell me or hint at it at least."

"I know. For that, I'm sorry. Truly sorry for screwing things up between us."

She nodded. "Ok. I forgive you."

Not a good sign for me. The panic seeped in and soaked me. I'd have to void our mating. My father would have to undo it by the next Tri Moon. A void that was difficult to do.

"Easy. Stop jumping to conclusions. They haven't even finished their talk," my beast chastised me.

"I could lose her to him. They have history, and we don't," I snapped back.

"But you have a bond. Soul merging. He doesn't have that. None of that. You have more of a chance than the idiot who lost her," he replied.

She reached for Elier's hand, and I bit down on my lip. I didn't like the contact between them. "Elier, I loved you once. I *did.* But I don't want to be with you. I'm interested in Jace. We *are* in a relationship. My feelings for Jace are my *main* focus right now. I want *him.* Like *really* want him." She let go of his hand. "And I'm not sorry for sharing that with you. The only thing I can offer you is my friendship. That's all, Elier." She was sincere about it.

Disappointment filled his eyes and the pain was palpable from where I sat.

"I had to try. But I deserved what I got. Friends it is."

"Friends," she repeated as the waitress brought their food to the table.

"We never got the chance to order," she stated surprised.

"I'd already put in our order and gave them instructions on when to bring it out. Shrimp pasta. Were you going to pass that up?" he teased.

"Ummm...no." She grinned.

He grinned at her as she dug in. Then he looked over my way. He finally spotted me in the restaurant and knew it was over for real between them. I sensed anger, defeat, and respect from him.

"My apologies for all that has come between us. I do hope we can work on being better with one another," he mentally told me.

"As long as you don't make any moves on my mate, we'll be fine," I stated.

"Ouch! I respect that. So, am I forgiven?" he questioned me.

"Yes, but that's more for her. She loves you still and it seems she's hoping for this friendship. Don't mess this up or you mess us both up."

He nodded in agreement. I wanted him to know that I was forgiving him for her more than for me. I needed him to know she was mine, and I was hers. Jasinda caught my eyes and I stood. Her lips pursed as she'd figured out that she wouldn't be finishing her pasta.

Chapter Fifty

Jasinda

When we arrived back at Jace's, Anthony was waiting for me. Jace pressed a kiss to my lips before disappearing in the direction of his office. I frowned when I looked at Anthony.

"Were we supposed to hang out today?" It wasn't like me to forget something like that.

"No, I'm going to be gone for a few days, so I wanted to stop by and see you before I had to jet."

"Oh, where are you going?"

"Nowhere. I'll just be in the city for the next few days taking care of some things."

He was being oddly evasive. "Anyway, how have you been? You've got this… glow about you today." He interrupted my thoughts with his keen observations.

"Come on. I need to get out of these shoes." I walked gingerly.

Anthony quirked a brow at me. "That walk isn't just from a couple of hours in uncomfortable shoes."

I swatted him in the chest but didn't speak until we were behind my shut bedroom door. "The walk is a result of lots of … physical activity the past twelve hours."

"Hmmm, *lots*?" he teased.

"More than I thought was humanly possible. But then again, Jace isn't exactly human so maybe it was a normal amount for him. Do all you wolf shifters have marathon sex back-to-back?"

He busted out laughing. "We wolf shifters do have more stamina than a human male. But back-to-back sessions isn't exactly normal for us. Maybe a couple rounds, then a few hours rest, and then maybe a quickie in the morning."

"That man is *not* normal then."

"Well, all the sex certainly agrees with you. Other than the walk that is. But your eyes have a new sparkle in them I've never seen. And you're just radiating happiness. No, that's too tame of a word. Bliss and contentment. And maybe even… love."

Normally, I would have argued with him for throwing out the *L word* when things were still so new between me and Jace. But as I turned the word over in my mind, I recognized the potential truth in it.

When I was silent for too long, Anthony asked, "Was the sex good?"

"Was it good? Good doesn't even describe a tenth of what it was. It was the most amazing, most satisfying experience of my life. It wasn't just sex. I don't have the right words to describe it. But every single part of me—my body, my mind, my spirit, my heart and my soul—was engaged with every part of him. If I had known it could be like *that*, I never would've wasted my time with any other man. *Ever.* If there was a way to freeze time and keep me connected to him in that state of euphoria, I'd live there happily."

"Wow. I don't think I've ever experienced what you're describing. I hope I do one day."

"I hope you do too, Ant. It's worth looking for and holding out until you find it. I don't know how I'm going to let it go."

"Why would you have to let it go?"

"He's going to be king of the packs. He's supposed to marry, I mean mate with a wolf shifter and produce pups to be heirs to the throne. I'm just me. A human."

He stepped up to me and drew me into his arms. "Yes, he's going to be king overall… someday. And there are some who say he *has* to mate with another wolf. But if that was what Jace wanted, he's had plenty of opportunities to do that. He's never been like *this*, like he is with you, with any other woman. I think 'just you', might be just enough to win his heart."

"Time will tell," I agreed.

"Now, I've got to get going. I'll catch up with you again next week, and we'll have an *American Horror Story* marathon, Ok?"

"Sounds good."

After Anthony left, I filled the tub in the bathroom and settled in for a long, leisurely soak. The hot water was just what my achy muscles needed. Sinking down so that only my head was visible above the frothy bubbles, I let out a satisfied sigh. My head leaned back against the edge of the tub and I closed my eyes. I must have dozed off because the next thing I became aware of was a knock on my bathroom door.

"Jasinda, it's me." Jace's voice was muffled by the wood.

Crap. My robe and towel were on the other side of the bathroom. *What the hell, he'd seen it all before.*

"Come in," I answered.

The door to the bathroom swung open moments later. "There you are."

"I think I fell asleep while I was soaking," I murmured in embarrassment.

"Not a safe thing to do," he teased. "You should nap on the bed."

"I wouldn't need a nap if someone had let me get some sleep last night." I winked at him.

"Touché. You're just so damn irresistible." His fingers cupped my cheek as his lips descended on mine.

Instantly, I was lost in his kiss. In him.

"You're doing it again," he mumbled against my lips.

"Doing what?" I asked breathlessly.

"Seducing me, you sex beast."

Laughter bubbled up from my chest. "You're a pretty sexy beast yourself. And do I need to remind you that it was *you* who came in here and kissed me?"

"True. It's like your lips are magnets, pulling mine to them whenever we're close together."

"I feel the same way about your lips."

He moved out of my reach and grabbed my towel. "Come on, the water's getting cold. We need to get you warm and dry."

I stood from the lukewarm water. When I met Jace's fiery green eyes, he swallowed hard. "I thought you liked me warm and wet."

"Oh, I do, enchantress. I do. But your body needs to rest. So, for the next few days I'm going to pamper you."

He wrapped me in the warm, fluffy towel and began rubbing the water droplets from my skin. His touch was a little distracting, so at first, I didn't really catch his words. But after he slipped my robe on me, I frowned.

"What do you mean you're going to pamper me for the next few days? What about your work? What about the pups?"

"Work and the pups can wait. You and I are going to lock ourselves away in your room or in mine for the next few days. We're going to forget the rest of the world. I'll go down and get food for us and bring it back. And you will be waited on hand and foot by me."

There was something he wasn't telling me. "As tempting as that sounds, I still don't understand how you can step away from all your duties and responsibilities to hide away with me."

He drew in a deep breath and led me to my bed. Without a word, he settled himself against the headboard and pulled me onto his lap. His fingers ran through my hair as his eyes searched mine. I could tell he was warring with himself. But I wasn't sure what over.

"There's something I need to explain to you. I know it's going to sound crazy. And it might even scare you. But I promise, I'll keep you safe and won't let anything bad happen to you."

I nodded. "I trust you, completely." A pained look flashed across his face. But he quickly schooled his features and the look was gone.

"I know you're going to be… God, how do I explain this? I've never had to have *this* conversation before."

"Just give it to me straight. I'm pretty tough. I can take it."

"Ok. I know you're going to be on your period soon," he mumbled, and his face heated with embarrassment.

"What? How could you know *that*?" I pushed back from him slightly. We hadn't been together long enough for him to have my frackin' cycle memorized.

He gently touched his finger to his nose. "Wolf sense of smell."

"Oh." Horror made my mouth drop open, my cheeks redden, and my eyes darken. *OH! How embarrassing. He could smell me. God, I hoped I didn't stink.* "I think I need another bath. Sorry."

My body vibrated with the laughter rumbling up from his chest. "Don't you dare. You smell delicious. Good enough to eat." He licked his lips like the big, bad wolf.

My heart thundered, and desire pooled between my thighs.

"Ok, so what does my coming period have to do with me needing pampering and you locking the world out for a few days? I don't turn into a raging bitch when I'm on my period. You can ask Anthony. I'm not a danger to myself or anyone else. Well, unless they get between me and my chocolate that is."

"I'm sure under normal circumstances you're perfectly safe. But there's been a slight complication with your … um… hormone levels since you've been here surrounded by pack magic. I should've let the doctor explain all of this to you the other day."

"I'd rather hear it from you."

"Female shifters don't go through menstruation like humans, and they don't go through estrus like wolves. They go through something called *menstrus*."

"So, kind of like a combination human and wolf. That makes sense."

"Right. Female shifter cycles run normally once they hit puberty, but without ovulation. Because unlike in animals, it isn't beneficial for a female shifter to get pregnant unless she's found her mate. Her mate would care for her and keep her safe. And then help her raise their pups. So *The Culling*, kind of like a superheat, doesn't kick in for our females until they've found their true mates. Shifter bonds are sacred."

"Got it. I'm with you so far." *What he was explaining was fascinating.* I still didn't understand his concerns for me. But I was intrigued by the differences in shifter biology and my own.

"Anyway, once a female has found her true mate, she's able to ovulate. And when she does, her body goes into overdrive producing an insane amount of hormones. The increase in hormones makes her desire to mate during that time exponentially high. Because at that point in her cycle, the odds of her getting pregnant are greater. The flood of hormones is very hard to resist."

"So, you're telling me that female shifters are extra horny when they're experiencing The Calling?"

"Not just extra. Like a thousand times hornier than you could imagine. That's why it's important that *her* true mate is around during her Calling, so that she doesn't mate with the wrong man and get pregnant by someone else."

"So, shifter biology is designed to make sure that wolflins aren't produced by accident, and that they have a mother and father who love each other to raise them?"

"Yes, shifter biology doesn't let females get pregnant easily until they find *THE ONE*. The extra hormones, once they have their proper mate, are to help ensure that wolflins will result from these perfect bonds of love. But the hormones are nearly *impossible* to resist for males and females, which creates problems when the bonded couple is apart from each other."

"Humans could learn a thing or two from wolf shifters."

He chuckled. "Anyway, the doctor told me after he examined you the other day that all the hormones in the pack and the magic in the air that we use to cloak our realm have worked with your own body chemistry to turn your normal period into a mimic of a shifter menstrus."

"And will my … menstrus be a normal one or a Calling?"

He thought long before he answered me, "The doctor wasn't sure. But from the hormone levels I'm sensing I would say probably not a normal one. But even if it isn't a Calling, the hormones that you'll put off, that you're *already* putting off, from a regular menstrus will be insane. I'm not sure how your body is going to react. And I want to keep you safe. Plus, the closer you get to even a normal menstrus, the harder you'll be to resist. So, I sent everyone away for the next few days. We have the whole house to ourselves. No males will be on the property until I give the all clear."

"That's why Anthony is going to be gone for a few days?"

"Yes, and your impending menstrus is why Dorik pinned you to the counter in the kitchen. He could sense it, and it made him nuts."

I couldn't resist the shudder of fear and anxiety that rolled through me. His hand stroked soothingly down my back. "So, my little bit of extra hormones the other day made him think he could be forward with me, and made him think I'd actually want him back?"

A smirk lifted Jace's lips. "Yes, and your reaction to him when he was pressed against you was *not* typical."

"Well, in case you haven't figured it out by now, Mr. Hunt, I'm *anything* but typical," I said with a huff.

He kissed my nose. "You're right about that. I've never seen a female of our kind who's unattached that is able to resist the advances of a male while under the influence of hormones. The fact that not only did you resist him, but you shot him down, astounded me."

"Who said I was unattached?" I teased.

Confusion and worry filled his eyes. "I thought you weren't seeing—"

I interrupted him by pressing a kiss to his lips. "I wasn't seeing anyone then. And I know we weren't an... infused couple then, but I was already growing pretty attached to you."

"The feeling is mutual, my enchantress."

The romantic moment was ruined by my growling stomach. I wrinkled my nose and said, "Sorry."

"It's time for me to feed you. Any requests?"

"Hmmm. Pasta. I didn't really get to enjoy my pasta at lunch."

"Pasta it is," he announced. "You stay here and find us something to watch." He shifted me out of his arms and kissed me deeply before climbing off the bed. "And put some clothes on so I won't be tempted to eat you instead of dinner when I get back." He winked and walked out.

Pressing my hand to my fluttering heart, I flopped back on my back. Even with the uncertainty I *should* be feeling about whatever craziness my body was going to dish out in the next few days, I couldn't wipe the smile off my face.

By the time Jace returned, I'd slipped into my favorite pajamas—a silky purple tank top and little matching boy shorts. Then I wrapped myself in the knee-length matching robe. A martial arts movie I'd been wanting to see was queued up on the TV, and I was nestled in a cocoon of covers and pillows.

The aroma of garlic and tomatoes filled my nostrils, making my stomach rejoice loudly. Jace rolled a cart in with a bowl of salad, a basket of garlic bread, two covered plates and wine. "Ready to eat?"

"Absolutely." I clapped my hands together as he set up everything on the little table in the corner. He moved efficiently around, and in no time the table was adorned with a vase of flowers, flickering candles, filled wine glasses and the most delicious looking spaghetti and meatballs I'd ever seen. It could've been because I still hadn't replaced all the calories I'd burned last night.

"That looks heavenly," I said as I climbed out of bed and made my way over to the table.

A growl reverberated in his throat. "Damn, you're going to be the death of me."

I shot him a confused look. *What had I done wrong?*

"You didn't do anything wrong. You're just so tempting."

"Are you reading my mind?"

"No, just your face. When your guard is down, everything you think and feel is written in your eyes. And I'm becoming quite fluent in *Jasinda* eye language."

How did he always know just the thing to make my heart swoon? My hand involuntarily clutched my heart.

Jace pulled out my seat for me and pressed a kiss to the top of my head when I sank down.

"You picked a martial arts movie for us to watch?" he asked incredulously.

"I love action movies, and I've been wanting to see this one. Besides, I thought it might be in poor taste to watch *Underworld* in the presence of a werewolf and all." I winked and took a sip of my wine.

He chuckled and said, "If you want to see a beast, I'm sure I can arrange for you to see one right now." His eyebrows shot up seductively.

"Maybe after dinner and a movie, the sex beast can come out to play," I teased back.

"Sadly, that's probably a bad idea," he said with regret.

"What? *Why?*" He'd just told me about an hour ago that I was going to be wild with lust, and I wasn't going to get no satisfaction? *Oh, hell no.*

"Well, because if your menstrus winds up being a Calling cycle, then you'll be ovulating. The whole point of The Calling is to ensure a pregnancy results from all the wild, crazy sex."

A light laugh erupted from my lips. It wasn't because he didn't want wild sex with me. He was trying to look out for me. Which was really sweet. No one had ever been so purposeful in taking care of me before.

"What's so funny?" He paused a few seconds but continued before I could stop my laughter to speak, "Honestly, the thought of your body swelling while growing my child is the hottest thing I can picture, I'm not ready to share you yet. Babies that we aren't ready for aren't a laughing matter, Jasinda. And it certainly won't be funny being locked away with you for days and having to resist you."

I laid a hand on his shoulder and composed myself. "I'm not laughing at the prospect of babies. I'm laughing because I'm relieved *that* was the reason you were planning to deny me pleasure when you say I'll be frantic for it. Because babies aren't something we have to worry about. I'm on birth control. I've been on birth control for years. According to my potentially faulty memories, as a teenager, my period was always irregular. Never coming every twenty-eight days like the perfect monthly visitor it was supposed to be. Sometimes it was three weeks, sometimes seven. I got sick of the irregularity, so I went to a doctor, and his magic pills made it come on a predictable twenty-eight-day schedule. The only reason I got pregnant before was because I was on other meds that made the pill not work properly. But you and I have nothing to worry about."

"Thank heavens," he breathed out on a huge sigh of relief. "You've just made me the happiest man in the whole damn world."

"So, fuel up mister, you're going to need your energy later."

"Yes, ma'am." He saluted and twirled a big serving of pasta around his fork.

We ate and watched the movie in companionable silence. When the closing credits rolled, Jace cleaned up the dishes. "You ready to work off all those carbs?" I asked when he bent over to tuck the empty wine bottle on the bottom shelf of the cart. His butt was mouth-watering. Watching his muscles ripple as he moved about, I realized I wasn't sore or tired anymore. And I was hungry. *For him.*

"You sure you aren't too sore?" he asked even though his eyes were already undressing me.

I stood and untied my robe and let it fall to the floor. "I'm sure."

He cast his eyes heavenward and whispered, "Thank the Gods for birth control."

Then he stalked towards me. I scampered around the table with a squeal and ran towards the bed. He caught me quickly and tossed me on my back. Giggles erupted as he lowered his frame over me and caged me in with his arms.

"So, when will this hormone influx really kick in?"

He buried his nose in my neck and took a deep breath. "Any moment now," he rasped out.

"Will you tell me when it hits?" I was a little bit nervous about the unknown and uncertainty of it.

"I won't have to tell you. You'll know it," he assured me.

"How?"

"Well, you'll get warm all over. Like your blood has rushed to the surface of your skin. And desire will flare higher than you can imagine. You'll be dripping with want. Literally and figuratively. And I'll barely be able to keep my hands off you when it happens."

"Oh. Will it feel different?" I was truly curious. Plus, the more I understood, the less nervous I'd be.

"Yes, but good different. Orgasms will come more quickly and last longer. You'll be floating for a long time."

"I like the sound of that. But how will I ever walk after days locked away with you if it's as intense as you say?"

"The amazing thing about the influx of hormones is that they also work to relax and loosen your muscles. Because it would be counter-productive for shifter biology to increase desire and intensity for sex during a Calling, if it just wound up making the female hurt as a result."

"So, three days of crazy monkey sex without any painful soreness afterwards?"

"Crazy wolf sex," he corrected with a wink.

"Bring it on," I challenged and pulled his mouth to mine.

A nd for the next three days, he did bring it. Morning, noon, and night. We were insatiable, only stopping to catch naps and refuel. There wasn't a surface in my room that wasn't utilized. There wasn't an inch of skin on either of us that was left untasted and not worshipped. No one had ever taken better care of me or made me feel more beautiful than Jace did during those three days. And he was right, the orgasms under the influence of a Calling were out of this world.

The last night of our sexual vacation, as I lay in his arms completely satisfied—for an hour at least—I closed my eyes and began to dream of the future. I could see a forever here. It was something I'd never been able to envision before. Even without all my memories intact, in my heart I knew without a doubt, that an image of *forever* with someone didn't exist before Jace. This man, this beast, was branded on my heart and soul. He was mine, and I was his. Of that, I had no doubt. Now I just had to make sure I didn't scare him away by telling him my *very* serious feelings too soon.

Chapter Fifty-One

Jasinda

S unlight danced beyond my closed lids. Lazily, I stretched my limbs
and felt for Jace. But his warmth was missing. I must have slept in.
Cracking an eyelid, I looked over at my phone on the nightstand and saw it
was already ten in the morning. *Holy waters!* I'd slept in. Yet I still didn't
want to get out of bed.

I was utterly spent from the way Jace had worn me out the past few
days. This calling crap was no joke. But I didn't care. I'd enjoyed every
moment Jace was inside me. Every single second, and I still wanted more. I
hoped my birth control held up. The door opened, and Jace sauntered in
wearing jeans and no shirt. He was barefooted and had a mug in his hand.
He smirked at me as he closed the door with his foot.

"Well, sleeping beauty is awake."

"I don't want to be. I'm still tired," I whined.

His smile widened, like he knew he was the cause of my fatigue. "If you
weren't such a sex beast, then you wouldn't be so tired."

I shot up from the bed into a sitting position. "*Me?* You were the one
who had me in every inch of this room. Geeze, if we didn't have the door
closed and the windows shut, you would've sexed me through them both!"
I teased.

He laughed, almost spilling his drink. "I brought you some green tea."
He handed me the warm mug. "Our food should be up soon. And after you
finish your breakfast, you need to get dressed."

"Are we going somewhere?"

"No, the Mitchell brothers will be here within the hour."

I nearly spilled the tea out of excitement. "Oh. Really?"

"Yes, they're also bringing you some things from your house."

"That's great!" I cheered.

He smirked at me. "I like seeing you happy, which is why I told them they're welcome to visit anytime. They don't need to ask."

"Thank you, Jace. That means a lot to me."

"I know how much you all mean to one another. Now drink your tea so we can take a shower," he said as he stood and willed his jeans off, leaving him naked and hard for me to see. *Damn him!* He winked at me and walked into the bathroom.

I took a few sips of my tea and placed it on the nightstand. No way was I going to miss out on having some shower fun with that hot wolf!

***

After our hot, wet shower sex, we dressed, ate a little, and then kissed some more before he left me with the Mitchell brothers to run some errands. My curiosity begged me to ask him what his errands were, but I didn't want to seem too nosy or untrusting. So, I let the question fade away.

As I entered the kitchen, I found the three brothers sitting at the table with mugs to their lips. I beamed at them, and they were elated at seeing me. They stood and I flung myself into Dayne's embrace.

"I've missed you guys," I softy mumbled into his chest.

"We fuckin' missed the shit out of you. It's not the same without you popping in on us or vice versa," Dayne muttered into my hair. He squeezed me just a bit tighter before I was gently pulled from his arms and turned to meet Devon's chest. I looked up into those hazel brown eyes. That was Devon, always gentle and careful with me, like I was porcelain. Emotion clouded his face as he gave me an uncertain smile, then hugged me. His hug was longer. I knew it was his way of telling me he loved me and was happy to see that I was ok.

"Guys, I mean you act like she was on death's door and is finally recovered or something. Let her go, so I can squeeze whatever life force is left in her," Darrell said jokingly.

I turned around with a knowing lopsided grin. Both his arms were stretched in front on him and he was opening and closing his palms. "Come to Darrell. Darrell missed you!" His attempt at a baby voice was a huge failure, since he had a deep voice. I laughed and walked into his arms. "How are you holding up, princess?"

"Good. All is good. I like being here, and so far, everyone has been great." I walked over to an empty chair and sat. "So. How's my so-called father doing?" My sarcasm was palpable.

"Jasinda, don't be mad at him. He was only doing what your mother asked him to," Darrell explained. "Besides, who can refuse your mother? Manny's words, not mine," he stated with his hands up.

"It still doesn't make it right," I told him.

"We know. Just let it go," Dayne added.

"Wrong thing to say to her," Devon chastised.

"Yeah, wrong thing to say to me," I mimicked. "Why do you want me to let this go?"

"So, we can figure this shit out without you getting in the way or hurt," Dayne responded.

"We want answers too, and we know your mother's the only one who can give them to us. Once you get your memories back, ours will be restored as well."

Ah. This was also about them, how horrible of me to forget that part. "I'm sorry guys. I forgot this affects you as well. But you just want me to do nothing?"

"Yes," they said all at once.

I looked at all three brothers, taking them in. They all had the same hazel brown eyes, beautiful black skin and dreads kept in a nice twist. They were gorgeous, sexy men. But I'd never wanted any of them in my bed. They were my family, and no matter what, I wouldn't change that for anyone. Jace understood they were mine, and I was theirs. And he was more than fine with it. He trusted them, and that meant *everything* to me.

"Jasinda, are you ok?" Dayne interrupted my thoughts.

"Yes, sorry. Um…I was just thinking." I grabbed Devon's mug since it was closest to me and took a sip. *Coffee.* "Hmmmm. Just the way I like it." I gave Devon a side look, and he grinned while shaking his head. He knew the coffee was no longer his.

"I guess I should make him another cup?" Sheraphina said. I snapped my head towards her voice in shock. She was standing beside the table with a mug dangling from her finger. I didn't even hear her come in. Or did I just not notice her, and she'd been here the whole time?

"Yes, *please*," Devon replied.

"Hey, Sheraphina. Sorry for being rude. I didn't even notice you were in the kitchen." I rose from my chair and hugged her as she beamed at me.

I sat back down just as she spoke, "Why would you? You were excited over seeing them, and I see why. They're hunks!" She grinned impishly.

Opening my mouth to explain, she cut me off, "I already know who they are to you. Jace explained everything to me. And no, I don't think you have the hots for them." With that she moved to make another cup of coffee. Relief washed over me that I didn't have to explain myself to the mother of the guy I had feelings for.

"Jasinda, I need to ask you to *not* look for your mother," Dayne said as he held a hand up to stop me from talking. "And before you protest, let me explain. We're already looking for her, and not by your father's orders."

"Why can't I help?"

"Because we want you to stay safe here with Jace," Devon added.

"We'll work more efficiently if we know we don't have to worry about you. And when you're with Jace, we don't. Tracking her isn't easy because we can't track her scent. So, we've been tracking Silvo instead. And he isn't easy to find."

"Yeah, one moment we're close. Then *poof*, nothing." Darrell said. "He disappears somewhere we can't track him."

"Then how will you find her?" I asked.

"Not sure, but we're not giving up. Silvo is the key, and so is Jako. If we find Silvo, then we'll find Jako. Then we'll get them to help us search," Dayne answered.

The Mitchell brothers were my family, just not by blood. After them making a rescue attempt that night at the charity event, they too agreed it was best I'd be safe here with Jace. Little did they know how well Jace was taking care of me. I had to find a way to tell them that Jace and I are an item now.

"*Fine*. I'll leave it up to you guys. But I hate not helping," I grumbled.

"You staying safe *is* helping us," Devon chimed in.

Picking up the mug again, I sipped on the coffee I'd stolen from Devon.

"What the fuck?" Dayne yelled as his angry eyes looked from me to my mug and then back at me again.

"What?" I asked.

Before they could answer, Jace's mom walked up to the table. "Are you guys hungry?" Sheraphina interrupted, fixing Dayne with a very stern look. No one answered and she pressed on. "Well?"

I glanced at the brothers and found they were all staring at the mug in my hand. They looked horrified or something. *What the hell? Was there a bug on it or something?* I turned the cup around and saw nothing to warrant their reactions. "Guys? What is it?"

"Nothing, Dayne just remembered something. Sheraphina, we're starving," Devon spoke in a controlled tone.

"Good. I have some pork leftovers and I thought I'd make sandwiches."

"That sounds good. Thanks," Davon replied.

"BBQ, spicy mustard, or no sauce at all?"

"BBQ for me, please," Darrell told her.

"I'll take Spicy mustard, and Dayne will take BBQ, please." Davon spoke for his brother.

"What about you, Jasinda?" Sheraphina asked me.

Something was going on here that I didn't understand. Dayne still looked horrified about something. "Sure, a small sandwich with spicy mustard would be great. I had a late breakfast and now this coffee." I jerked my head at the mug I held.

"Appetizer size coming up." She walked back to the counter where she already was prepping food.

Dayne kept his eyes on me now, no longer looking at my mug. But he wasn't looking at me directly in the eyes either. They were roaming my face and neck. *Seriously, what was going on?* "Dayne are you all right?"

"No, I'm not fuckin' all right. Where the hell is Jace?"

"He went to go see Rave. He had a meeting with him today," Sheraphina spoke without looking our way.

"Who's Rave?" I asked.

Chapter Fifty-Two

Jace

O nce I'd explained to Mom about who the Mitchell brothers were and hinted that she should run interference on any mention of the mating rings Jasinda was sporting, I decided to pay Rave a visit and find out if he really knew Jasinda. Normally, I'd have sent a hawk to see if he was available to receive me, but I didn't want him prepared for anything. I wanted to catch him off guard. But when I arrived, he was out on his own mission. Sariya was nowhere to be found either. She must have been with him. As his mate, she always fought by his side.

As I made my way back to the house, I pondered how I was going to break the news to Jasinda that we were *mated*. I didn't want to scare her away. *What if she didn't want a mated life with me, now or ever?* Unintentionally, I'd mated us. My father had embedded those sacred words in me when I was seven, but not once did I *ever* speak them out loud. *Until her.* With her it was instinctual. Like it was supposed to be.

I had to tell her and I had to ask her for forgiveness. If she was completely opposed, we could get my father to void it. That was the last thing I wanted to do. And I hoped like hell she agreed with me.

As I got closer to the kitchen door, I felt the tension from inside. Then my mother's voice sounded in my head. *"They know about the mating. The one called Dayne is the most upset. The others are just confused by it."*

I heaved a heavy sigh. *"I guess today's the day I tell her. I didn't want it like this. What did she say?"*

"She has no clue, my grey wolf. She doesn't suspect a thing. But you must find a way to tell her soon. Maybe not tonight, for she's filled with

happiness. It fills me with joy to see her like this. It's contagious." I could hear the smile in her voice.

"I love when she's happy. It makes me forget I'm an alpha prince. I get to live while she's around. I need to face the brothers and explain to them what happened. I can't let this get in our way. They are everything to her."

"You'll figure this out. Just be prepared for Dayne. He's ready to pounce."

I reached the back door and opened it. Just as I closed it behind me, I was pinned against it by Dayne. The angry blaze in his eyes stirred the beast in me.

"What the hell are you doing, Dayne? Let him go!" Jasinda protested.

"Did you *force* her?" Dayne shot out. I didn't answer. I couldn't. Keeping a tight grip on my beast was taking all my concentration. "Did you?" he shouted.

It infuriated me he thought I'd be capable of that. Claiming her against her will. Technically, she didn't know what was going on and I *had* been lost in the moment. But I'd *never* force myself on her in any way. He was fueling my beast and I needed to keep it under control. His unthinkable question was like a slash to my gut.

"Dayne, come on. Let him go," Devon spoke calmly.

"Yo, you can't just come into his house and pull this shit," Darrell tried.

"Dayne?" Jasinda softy spoke. "Dayne, he didn't force me to do anything. Now let him go."

She approached, and I growled at her with a warning to stop. My beast was looking to rip some tongues out and if I didn't keep the control he would. No way could I let her possibly be in the middle of it or see it.

"Stay back," I warned her. I didn't want to shift and accidently hurt her. "Please," I strained.

She nodded but kept speaking, "Dayne, he didn't force me. If anything, I'm the one who threw myself at him. How could he say no?" She shrugged. "He doesn't look so good, Dayne. I think he's fighting the beast within. Let him go, please."

Dayne released me and ran his hands over his face. "He didn't force you?" Dayne kept his eyes on me, as I fixed my clothing and straightened.

"No, no *way* did he force me. Dayne, what's gotten into you? Why do you think he forced—" she tried but was cut off by my mother.

"I think you boys need to take this outside. *Now*." My mother's voice was stern but filled with power.

I opened the door for the men to walk out. Devon and Darrell went right out. Dayne, of course, just kept his gaze on me. After a few more seconds, he walked by me, and then we were both standing outside. I flung the door shut just as I heard my mother say, "Don't worry, the brothers are being overly protective of you. As they should be. Now, let's not waste that pork sandwich I made you."

My mother was the best. The best of all mothers. My eyes drifted to the brothers. Inhaling a deep breath, I said, "Now, let's not put your hands on me again. I don't need my beast rising, going crazy and we risk hurting Jasinda."

"How the *hell* did you two *mate*?" Dayne asked.

"I didn't *mean* for it to happen. I mean, I do *want* her as my mate, my forever. But I didn't mean for it to happen *this* way. She doesn't know we're mated," I confessed.

"You've got to be shittin' me!" Darrell said.

"Hey. Let's not get on him too much. We all *know* Jace is someone we can trust," Devon added.

"You didn't just mate with her, but you *marked* her. You *claimed* her," Dayne yelled, his anger still tipping over.

My anger engulfed. "Yes, I've claimed her and that's no secret. She is *mine*, and I am hers. But she doesn't understand the ways of our world. I'm still explaining things to her. So, I'd really appreciate it if you didn't tell her about all of this. *I* need to be the one to tell her what I did. What I *accidentally* did to us." Defeat caused my shoulders to slump. "I'm in love with her, but I'm afraid of scaring her. I don't want to lose her over this. She needs to *not* learn all of this from you guys. She's *mine* and it's no secret to anyone, not to *her*. Not even to you."

Dayne's anger depleted.

"*How* did you manage to mate with her, and her *not* know it?" Darrell asked a good question.

"We were...well, and... we got carried away. Before that, we were talking about Elier, and her having lunch with him. The next thing I knew, I was mating us." I walked in a circle as I stammered out my explanation. Stopping, I looked back at the three brothers. Their lips were pressed into thin lines like they were on the verge of laughing. "What's so funny?"

"Oh, you got it bad for her. *Real* bad," Darrell pointed out.

Dayne shook his head and held his hand out for me to shake. Without thinking, I did. He pulled me in for a hug and patted me on the back as I did the same. "Sorry, Jace. I shouldn't have assumed you'd force this on her. I should've known better. Welcome to the family that does *anything* for her." He gave a short laugh. "We're very overprotective of her. She's been a great friend to us and will always be like our baby sister."

"I know, Dayne. I swear to you, I'll never do anything to intentionally hurt her."

"Well, your jealousy of Elier is what got your mating in gear," Devon explained. I quirked a brow at him in question. "When a male has found his soulmate, his soul tends to push him further than what he normally would *consciously* do. Which means, you guys are soulmates. Am I right?"

"Yes, we're soulmates. We shared an infused moment. But how did you know about this?"

"Infused moments are very rare. You guys *definitely* have something special. Anyway, we have an old wolf friend who works with us. He was mated to his soulmate. He told us the story of how the souls just takes over when it's the right time. Which means that *whatever* you guys were doing, was the right time and it was meant to be." Devon shrugged, then continued, "One good thing about Jasinda is that she doesn't scare easily. She fights, and she fights hard. So, you've been warned."

We all laughed.

"I think I can handle her. And I really like having her here."

"Good. We want her to stay while we search for her mother. We decided to hit the realms and see if anyone knows anything. *Someone* has to know something," Dayne huffed.

"Keep us posted on your progress. If that's ok?"

"We'll keep you posted. We think it's best not to tell her too much right now, or she'll persuade us to let her help."

Darrell looked at me and nodded. "We're suckers for her. Now, you'll be one too." His grin was haunting.

They *really* loved her.

"Thanks guys. I didn't mean for this shit to get this far, this fast. I was trying to court her slowly and help her understand my world, my beast. And accept everything. Because in such a short time, she's become vital to me."

"Yeah, well she's yours to deal with now," Darrell teased.

Dayne elbowed him, and Devon looked down nodding his head. The brothers exchanged looks, like they had some inside joke. "Care to share?" I asked.

"Oh, *now* you want to share her?" Darrell shirked and slapped his brother Dayne on the shoulder. "You see, it could've worked to our favor."

"Shut up with that shit, Darrell. I thought we let this go fifteen years ago?" Devon questioned.

"Let what go?" I prodded.

"It's nothing. We all used to have a crush on her when we were younger. Since we couldn't decide who she should be with, we joked about sharing her and her being mated to the three of us," Devon added.

The beast grumbled within me, and I shook my head. My eyes burned and I closed them instantly.

"Jace, you good?" Dayne inquired.

"Please, tell me you *don't* fantasize about her" I gritted the words out.

They all snickered and exchanged looks. They kept laughing for quite some time. My beast was getting antsy and so was I. It was taking considerable effort to keep him locked down. Shaking my head, I decided to listen to their thoughts.

"You should've never told him that. You know how mated males get, you goof. What the fuck were you thinking?" Dayne scolded.

"What? He's family now. He might as well know the truth and see the connection between us. Besides, he'll know it's not like that anymore. He'll appreciate our honesty," Darrell responded back.

"*Still, there's no need to tell a fuckin' werewolf that we used to crush on his new mate. He'll fuckin' eat us! I still want to live, and I want to get all our memories back,*" Devon said.

"*Ok. Ok. Geez. Hold on to your balls.*"

"*Shut up!*" Devon and Dayne yelped.

I pinched the bridge of my nose and sucked in some deep breaths. "We should go inside. The longer you guys talk about my mate, the more my beast wants a taste of the three of you. Especially you Darrell," I told him firmly and began walking to the door.

"He's joking, right?" Darrell questioned.

"Shut up and let's just go inside."

Life was certainly going to be interesting loving Jasinda and adding her people to my family.

Chapter Fifty-Three

Jace

Things had been pretty quiet the past few days. When I went down to the kitchen to fix Jasinda her favorite breakfast, I found Scarlet there. She'd been gone for almost two weeks on her assignment. I guessed she'd taken care of the things that had demanded her attention. As she moved towards me, a frown marred her face. From her expression, I knew what she wanted to ask me, so I waited for her to talk as she followed me to my office. She sat next to me and just stared for a moment. Normally, I would've initiated the conversation, and I wanted to this time. But the look on her face made me remain quiet. I respected her a lot and loved her like family. So, her opinions mattered to me.

"I haven't even been gone for a full two weeks and you two are already mated?" Her voice was filled with hurt and disappointment. "What type of ceremony did you guys have? How many people showed up?" she asked.

Here goes nothing. I had to confess the truth, and she was going to bite my head off.

Taking in a deep breath, I prepared myself for the worst. "It's not what you think," I said, putting my hand up to stop her from talking.

"*WHAT???*" she shrieked, jumping out of the chair.

I motioned for her to sit back down and told her my confession.

She gaped at me.

Then a slow smile spread across her face. "You finally claimed her for us all to know. For Elier to know." She stated the obvious. She knew me all too well.

"I needed him to know she's *MINE*!" I growled.

"Duh! I'd known that from the moment I saw her. I saw *selfish beast* written all over you. What about the pups? How are *they* with her?"

"Honestly, better than I expected them to be. They like hanging out with her. Every day she goes and spends time with them. Makes time for them. They explore the woods with her, and she plays tag with them. How crazy is that? When they play tag, sometimes they pretend they can't find her." I laughed. "It's pretty funny."

"You're different, Jace. Way different now that she's with you." She cleared her throat. "I mean that in a good way."

"I hope so. If I go bad, kill me!" I teased her.

She laughed along with me. "What about Dorik?" she asked me. "How does he feel about all this?"

"I had to get on him about not showing up to the pack meeting. But he didn't care when I told him. He pretty much was *blasé* about it. The funny thing is I've been catching him out of his room more than usual."

"Do you know why?"

"Sadly, yes, he's been following Jasinda when she's with the pups. Watching her from the bushes." I got up from my seat and walked around to my desk to check some papers. "I think he's protecting her. Making sure nothing happens. He's definitely curious about her."

"Well he was acting a bit crazy that day when we were baking cookies. He was ready to take her right there in the kitchen because she was going into The Calling soon. Which, by the way, how did *that* go?"

"We spent the three days in her room. I sent everyone away. She never left her room. And I took care of her."

"Did you explain it all to her?"

"Yes, she took it really well. Now, I just need to find a way to tell her we're mated."

"How do you plan to pull *that* off?"

"I don't know. Every time I try to tell her I get interrupted and then I'm not sure what to say to her."

"Explain to me what happened that night. Maybe I can help you."

That was Scarlet. Always willing to help me. So, while I continued shuffling through papers, I launched into a full explanation. By the time I was done recapping the events surrounding our union, without the actual details, I'd organized all my documents in the order they needed to be in.

"Jace, I'm worried that this will all be too much at once for Jasinda. What if once she finds out about the mating, she runs in the opposite direction? What will you do?" Scarlet asked in a concern filled tone.

"I know. Believe me, I'm worried too. But that was a chance I'd been willing to take."

"As long as you understand the risk and are prepared to do whatever it takes to bring her back should she run. You'd be broken without her at this point." She laid a soothing hand on my arm.

"I know. Now, tell me, did you make any progress on the missing person's case you're helping with?"

"No, it's really starting to stress me out. Every time I got close, my senses faded." Frown lines appeared on her forehead as her mouth turned down.

"You want me to see if I can help?"

She sighed. "Not yet. I need to do this myself for now. But thanks."

"If you change your mind, you know where to find me," I offered.

"Thanks. I'll see you later."

And with that she walked out.

Chapter Fifty-Four

Jasinda

J ace surprised me with breakfast in bed. I'd never been so pampered or
well cared for in all my life. Of course, by the time Jace was done
making me the main course, I was ravenous and needed all the food I could
get.

Once we'd filled our bellies and had sated our desire for each other, Jace
dressed to go take care of some pack business. He knew I'd be in good
hands hanging with Anthony and Scarlet.

I could barely contain my excitement, because Scarlet was back. I hadn't
seen her yet, because she'd been so busy and preoccupied since she'd
returned from her vacation. I wanted to tell her about me and Jace. I hoped
she'd be happy for us. And I needed her to give me some advice on what to
wear on Friday for the Tri Feast. It had been nearly three weeks already
that I'd been here. *How crazy was that?* There had been no hints of danger
since I'd been here. Jace had let me go to the office a few times to do some
work for a couple hours here and there. But I was quite content to return to
Jace's.

While I waited for Anthony, I decided to call my father. "Hey Daddy."

"Hello Jasinda. How are you?" he answered in his formal tone.

"How do you *think* I am, Daddy? These supernatural beings crashed my
charity event. They demanded to know where my mother is. They tell me
she stole my memories. Then the Mitchell brothers swoop in and whisk me
away."

I paused, waiting for him to speak up. When he didn't, I started pacing.
"The only word I get from you in all this is that I need to go stay with Jace.

Who at that point in time, I'd just met, and I was supposed to trust him to keep me safe?"

"Is he treating you well?" he sounded abashed.

"That's not the point, Daddy. But yes, Jace has been wonderful. I think a lot of him and his family."

"Good. Because I need for you to stay with him for at least a few more weeks," he said in a voice that brooked no arguments.

"That's fine. I'm comfortable here. They make me feel like family. And I'm helping them out." I was happy to stay. I *wanted* to stay. But I wanted something more from my father. Something besides treating me like an assignment.

"Glad that's settled. Now, I need to—"

"Dad. What you did? Keeping me in the dark? Lying to me? That wasn't right. I should be able to trust my parents. I want answers from you and from Mom."

"Jasinda, I'm not going to get into this with you. I did what I thought was best for your safety. And you are *not* to look for your mother. I have my best men on it. Leave it alone." His tone was very gruff.

My heart pinched. He sounded so uncaring. His dismissal of my feelings stung. But something in me tugged at me to let it go and do as I was told. To just go along with it.

Finally, I sighed and said, "Fine. I've got to go now anyway. Bye."

"Goodbye."

I resisted the urge to chuck my phone across the room and fisted it in the air instead. If he thought I'd stay hidden away and not look for my mother, then he had another thing coming.

I just had no idea where to start. Maybe I should reach out to Silvo. Or perhaps I'd ask Jace later if he knew how to contact him. Wait. The Mitchell brothers asked me to stay put. Maybe they could keep me posted on their search.

After hanging up with Dad, I started to evaluate things. He wanted me to stay for a few more weeks here with Jace. *But what would happen when the danger to me was over? Would I have to leave? Would I want to go? What if I wanted to stay?*

The past few weeks had been amazing. Each day better than the previous one. I'd been spending more time with Jace and the pups, especially Edwin. The sweet little guy had formed some sort of attachment to me. And I had to admit, I was pretty attached to him as well. Not just to him, but to all of them. I felt like they were mine. These poor motherless pups. Whenever I visited, Edwin stayed glued to my side, almost like he was watching over me or something. I also got this weird sensation whenever the pups and I were exploring that someone was watching me, us, from the bushes. But I never caught a glimpse of anyone, and the pups never seemed alarmed. It was probably just my paranoid mind playing tricks on me.

When I glanced at the clock, I scrambled up. I hadn't realized how the time had gotten away from me. Anthony would be here any minute for another *American Horror Story* marathon so I scurried to the theater room to meet him.

H ours later, I was still sitting next to Anthony. My gaze wandered the massive room. In addition to the large movie screen and real concession stand, there was a game room with pool and air hockey tables, four lanes for bowling, a bar, a stage for karaoke, and more. I couldn't believe Jace had all this in his house.

"Jasinda, did you hear me?" Anthony asked with annoyance.

"Wait, what?" I said clearing my thoughts.

"It's time for me to go. I have a few errands to run."

"What type of errands?" I asked.

"Personal ones, nosey posey"

"Really Anthony, what kind of errands?"

"Ones that I can't tell you about."

"*Oh.* That's all you had to say. No need to make it sound like I'd cut the info out of you," I said with a sarcastic tone.

He gave me a look of mock annoyance and turned the show-off.

"It's pack business. I can't share it with anyone but Jace. Well, until he tells me I can."

"Got it. So, since you cut our night short and are just leaving me hanging…want to stop by my office and bring me back a few things?"

"Of course. You know I'd do anything for you."

"Thanks. I have a few packages. Three to be exact. Angie didn't feel right opening them."

"Why?"

"The packages said *For Jasinda's eyes only.*"

"Well, there you go. Can I open them for you? I mean, you never know. I should inspect them first."

"Uh huh. *Sure*, but no thanks. I need to see what they're about alone."

"You suck!"

"I scratch and swallow too." I laughed.

Anthony burst out laughing. He loved my comebacks. He always said it was my alter ego talking. It had been an ongoing joke between us ever since the first time he said those words to me, and even Angie told me I sucked just to get me to say it. Anthony stopped laughing and really looked at me.

"Are you ok with how things have gone down here? You know being here and everything since the night of the charity?"

"Yes, I think I can honestly say that I'm fine. Not *great*, but I'm good. Besides, I wouldn't have met everyone here, including Jace, if everything hadn't happened. It's been a crazy and exciting experience. To be honest, this has been the most exciting thing that's ever happened to me. Being with Elier was a bit boring," I joked. "I like it here. And I really like Jace. Actually, I think it's more than like. As crazy as it sounds, I think I might be falling in love with him. I know it's too soon. And I have no idea how he really feels about me exactly."

"He's *really* into you, and he's finally happy."

"What do you mean, he's *finally* happy?"

"He's really never been with a woman for too long. Priscilla was the only one he dated for longer than two months. And she was already getting on his nerves by the second week. But he kept seeing her because of their parents."

"How long did they date?"

"Two years, or something like that."

"How long ago did they break up?"

Anthony gave her an inquisitive look. "It's been about six or seven years since they dated. The whole pack was relieved when it ended."

"Why?"

"Newsflash, Ja, she's a royal bitch, and we all hate her. She's always doing some stupid shit to Jace. It's like she's ten times more bitter since their breakup. She's been trying to get him back for a while now, but he just wasn't interested. Nothing like the way he is with you."

I smiled at that. He just confirmed all my suspicions about Priscilla. I'd seen her a few more times in passing, and she always looked at me with irritated eyes. She always murmured something along the lines of, *"You'll never be like us."* I didn't care. She eventually would have to get over whatever issues she had. I wasn't going anywhere anytime soon. Maybe ever.

"He never tried to… you know… to have kids with her?" I asked.

"You mean *breed*?"

I nodded as my face heated. Priscilla was his kind. And she was pretty. An alpha, especially a king, was supposed to have kids, continue the royal lineage.

"God no! Every time her menstrus cycle came around, he'd disappear for an entire week." He laughed. "It was pretty funny too. She'd get extremely pissed at him, and he didn't even care. Back then he told her flat out they weren't having children."

I sighed in relief. I wasn't sure how I would feel if Jace had tried to have kids with her.

"Then she did the unthinkable," Anthony continued, unaware of my inner relief.

"What?"

"I don't know if I should be telling you this." He leaned closer and whispered to me. "Maybe you should really be asking him these questions."

Why was he whispering? No one could hear him. We were alone. And no, I didn't want to ask him. I wanted the details from Anthony. They seemed more interesting coming from him. But he was right. I should be asking Jace these questions. I hated my inner voice of reason sometimes.

"Fine. Ruin my fun," I pouted.

"Hush, little baby, dry your eyes. You'll get over it and be fine," he teased me.

I threw a couch pillow at him. "Shut it!" I scolded with humor. But then I softly begged, "She cheated on him, didn't she?"

"Yeah, with Elier."

"Holy waters! Are you serious?" I shrieked.

"That's why they don't get along too well. Elier knew Jace was planning to court her. Or at least he was trying to. He wanted to shut his parents up and show them he *did* care about their opinions and his duties as alpha. It was more his dad's idea for them to mate. His mother encouraged him to choose wisely. That's it, I have no more to say. I can't say anything more." He clamped his lips shut and imitated locking them.

"It's fine. I don't need any more. It all makes sense now."

"What makes sense now?"

"Why Jace didn't want me going to lunch with Elier the other day. I just wanted to give him some closure. Jace got pissed off when I told him about my lunch date with Elier."

"I'm surprised he let you go alone."

"He *didn't*. He came with me," I chuckled. I could laugh about it now.

"*Wait*. You didn't tell me that!" He sounded wounded.

"Sorry. I was still foggy headed when I talked to you. Still feeling the effects of the evening before. And all night. And the next morning. I was overwhelmed," I admitted honestly.

"Yeah, you definitely were. You were pretty quiet when you told me what happened. So, tell me about lunch with Elier."

"Honestly? I spent the whole day after trying to process everything I was thinking and feeling. Seeing Elier just added more confusion. He was so upset when I sat down at the table. He kept staring at my hands. The weight of his eyes felt like stab wounds. It was weird. Then after a while his demeanor changed and he was fine. But he still seemed bothered by something. And I don't think it was the fact that I hid the pregnancy from him. He understood that. He seemed genuinely sorry about how everything ended between us." I shook my head. "His attitude just struck me as odd."

Worry filled his eyes as I finished my sentence. I knew that look. We'd been friends for a long time. He was hiding something from me. *What the heck?*

"What do you know, Ant?"

He regained control of his features and shifted a bit uncomfortably next to me.

"He could smell Jace all over you... and more."

"More?" I asked.

Ant just looked at me with knowing eyes, and it hit me. *Crap.* Because he was a wolf shifter his sense of smell was enhanced. He'd smelled all the *sex* on me. He smelled Jace all over me. *Oh, man.* That had to have sucked for Elier. It was as if I'd rubbed Jace in his face.

"Oh, God," I said, horrified by embarrassment as I put my face in my hands.

"The whole house could smell it," he pointed out.

"Seriously?" I screeched.

"Yes, babe. But there's no judgement from any of us."

How embarrassing! All part of being a wolf.

"Ant, can I ask you something?"

"Shoot."

"Elier seems...well he seems worried about something. It's as if he knows something but can't tell me."

"Did he tell you that?"

"No. I can't explain it, but it was all in his eyes."

"I don't know, babe. Maybe, it just hit him that he's lost you forever."

No, that wasn't it. Something in Elier's eyes unsettled me. I was worried about *him*. He knew something and wasn't sharing it with anyone.

"Don't trouble yourself too much about Elier. Things always have a way of working themselves out. You just concentrate on enjoying your new relationship."

"You're right. And I am enjoying everything about Jace."

"I bet you are, you horn dog."

Chapter Fifty-Five

Jace

I was impatiently, waiting on Dorik to arrive for our lunch meeting. Something was going on with him. I needed to know what it was and why he was really following Jasinda. On one hand, it bothered me that he followed her, but on the other hand, I was relieved that he was leaving his room more often. My eyes darted to the clock. He was late, and he *knew* I hated tardiness. The chair scraped on the tile as I stood to go look for him. Before I could take two steps, Jasinda's humming and Dorik's answering growl met my ears.

"Why are you fuckin' humming again?" Dorik barked.

"Why are you fuckin' rude again?" she bit back.

I froze at her response to him and smiled to myself for her boldness. "Because I hate that you hum those *lullabies*."

"Sorry, I forgot you're a humming critic. And I didn't realize I was humming a lullaby."

"They bring back bad memories for me." he growled.

Shit. I'd forgotten about that. But how did he know it was a lullaby that she was humming? It wasn't one I was familiar with.

"I'm sorry. I didn't realize it was a lullaby. It was just something in my head. But next time, rather than being an ass about it, just ask me nicely to stop and I will," she sassed him.

Silence. Dorik was silent and didn't give her a comeback. Normally, he won every argument with anyone he spoke with. Except for me. I always challenged him and only backed down when I was wrong. I gave him that much. But Jasinda gave him sass. As I was about to open the door, I heard him speak.

"Forgive me. I don't mean to be an ass," he apologized.

"Apology accepted. I'm also sorry that my lullabies bring you bad memories. I'll make sure to keep them to myself."

"*You* aren't the one who should be apologizing to me. I owe *you* an apology for chasing you in the woods that day. I was caught off guard by your scent. It won't happen again."

"It's all right. You didn't hurt me and I got over it."

"You shouldn't just get over it. You should be pissed with me or at least have my brother get on me about it."

Was he serious? Where the hell had my brother gone? This wasn't him.

"He already did, that day I think." She laughed lightly. "Dorik?"

"Yeah?"

I felt how nervous he was from behind the door. "Jace and I are having dinner tonight. I thought you and I could have dessert. But *not* like the one you tried to give me in the kitchen that day," she teased.

I stood here like a statue, my hand still on the door handle. My brother was just as shocked as I was. His emotions hit me like a brick. She was trying to reach out to him. My heart leapt with joy because she wanted to get to know the people I cared about. I frowned at the fact she was standing me up for my brother. Sneaky little thing. Her nerves spiked and slammed into me. *Shit, my brother was going to turn her down.*

"You like ice cream, right?" he asked.

"Yes," she replied with a little excitement in her voice.

"Then ice it is. We have a small ice cream bar in the basement."

"Is there *only* ice?" she asked, confused for a second.

He was being funny with her. "Yes, ice that makes the cream."

"No way! You're joking, right?"

I could picture her face right now. Her lips parted and eyes like saucers.

"No," my brother laughed lightly. He *actually* laughed.

"Ha, ha. It's a date then," she gushed.

That was when I decided to open the door. Looking directly at her, I put on my poker face, as if I hadn't heard anything and smiled at her. She blushed and smiled back.

"Are you done with your marathon of *American Horror* with Anthony?"

She looked at me and pouted. "Yes, it got cut short."

Shit. Just then I realized what I had done. I'd meant for Anthony to leave *after* they were done with their marathon. Walking over to her, I kissed her gently.

"I'm sorry. I'd meant for him to run the errands *after* you guys were done. I didn't mean to interrupt."

"No problem. I'm actually glad. I've been dying to see Scarlet. I was coming by to let you know that we can go see the pups earlier than we'd planned. I didn't realize you were busy."

"I wasn't busy. I was actually waiting for Dorik." He stepped into my office and took a seat.

"So, about dinner. I asked Dorik to have dessert with me. I hope you're fine with that."

"I'm cool with that."

"You *are*? I mean good. Either way I would've asked him even if you weren't ok with it. He'd have to be the one to turn me down," she joked.

I couldn't keep the smile off my face. "I know. Besides, I already figured out that you really don't like to be told what to do when it comes to certain things. I can respect that."

"Thank you. I'll do my best to consider your feelings when I make certain decisions."

She closed the space between us, got on her tiptoes, and kissed me. I pulled her in tighter, and she wrapped her arms around my neck, deepening the kiss between us. Her want and need for me was a sweet scent that filled my nostrils.

Apparently, so could my brother because he coughed and whispered quietly, so only I could hear, "There are so many rooms in this damn house. Pick one already. We can reschedule." His voice was filled with amusement, not sadness.

Breaking the kiss, I slowly pulled back, looking into her eyes. I thought I saw a hint of green in them, again. A little darker than when she had been in the water. *Strange.*

"I have to go. Call me when you're done with Scarlet."

I touched her lips with mine, lingering just a bit longer and walked back into my office. Dorik had a huge grin on his face. It'd been a while since I'd seen him that way. Since Lina's death, he rarely smiled. *My* mate did this to him. I walked around my desk and sat.

"You missed the last pack meeting."

"Did you need me for something?"

"Just to be with me for an announcement, I'm sure you're already aware of it by now." I held up my hand showing off Jasinda's name permanently on my finger.

"I saw hers. You're in love," he stated matter-of-factly, rather than asked.

"Yes," I admitted. "Is that a problem?"

"Not a problem at all. A step up from Priscilla, I see. I mean a *huge* step up."

"It doesn't bother you that she's not a wolf?"

"No, as much as we try to mate with our kind, that's not always important. You were trying to court Priscilla for all the wrong reasons. Jasinda is all the *right* reasons. Does it bother *you* that she's not a wolf?"

"No," I stated with total confidence.

"No part of you, human, wolf or beast is bothered by her humanness?"

"None. We're all in agreement that Jasinda is all sorts of right for me, every part of me, and for the pack. She's been spending a lot of time with the pups. They've gotten so used to her that when I go for a run with them they ask me why she isn't running with them too." I folded my hands together over my desk and got a bit serious. "Why have you been following her when she leaves the house?"

He became serious as well and straightened in his chair.

He shrugged. "Because she needs to be protected now that she's your mate. It's what we do as a pack. We protect the alpha's mate at all cost."

"Speaking of the pack. Why haven't you come to the meetings?"

"I just don't want to be around everyone. Don't need to feel how sorry they still are for me. Just because you don't see me, doesn't mean I don't come. I'm just not in a spot where anyone can see or sense me. I *always* attend your meetings."

"I thought you never came. My mistake. I'm sorry for doubting you," I admitted.

"Don't be sorry. I made you think that way. It's my fault. I'm sorry I made you doubt me."

"Forgiven. Always forgiven, you know that."

"I know," he whispered.

"I also wanted to speak with you because something's off with the pack. Do you sense it?" I asked, hoping he too sensed what I did.

"Yes," he growled. "It's had me in a bad mood. It's another reason why I've been following your mate."

"Then we need to get to the root of the problem."

"I agree," he snarled. His canines shot into view.

One of the reasons why I loved my brother. He and I were alike in many ways. He too felt something was off and he wanted to get to the bottom of it.

"Dorik, be good to Jasinda while on your dessert date."

"Don't you want me to be an ass so she doesn't fall in love with me instead?"

A snarl surfaced from my beast and with a quick flash I felt my eyes change into my beast and back to mine.

"Don't be a dick to the beast." I reminded him.

"Yeah, yeah, yeah. You have nothing to worry about. *Maybe*." He smirked.

I cleared my throat and gave him a look of reproach.

"All right, all right. I'll be good. Are we done?"

I maintained eye contact with him for a few moments, then we both smirked at one another. I nodded and he got up and walked away. He was getting there. Little by little he was starting to come back to us. This would make my parents happy, but I didn't want to give them hope just yet. Somehow, Jasinda was the cause of all this. My enchantress was healing a lot of hurts within my pack.

Chapter Fifty-Six

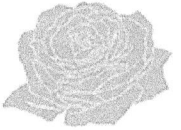

Jace

J asinda was anxious to see how the training was going with the pups. She had been uneasy when she'd asked me to show her earlier. I assumed Edwin must have spilled the beans about Priscilla. So, I promised her we would go today before dinner. And now that her TV marathon with Anthony had been cut short, we had a few hours to kill. The excitement rolled off her as she walked next to me on the trail in the woods but she remained quiet. For once, I was grateful for the silence. My mind reeled with trying to figure out how to tell her about our mating. Fixing this wasn't going to be easy, but it had to be done soon. We arrived at the pups' training facility, and I turned around to face her.

"I have to make a call. You all right just watching without me for five minutes?"

"Yeah, go make your call. I'm good. No worries." She leaned up on her tiptoes to press a kiss to my lips.

When she stepped back, I looked over her shoulder to see Priscilla was already in the middle of her lessons.

Edwin's thoughts filtered through. *'She came. She actually showed up to one of the lessons like she promised she would.'*

When Jasinda felt Edwin looking at her, she smiled and gave him a tiny wave. I hoped the pups couldn't sense her nerves. As I moved to the trees, I watched as she shifted a little closer. When she was a few feet away from Samuel, she stopped.

As I placed the call, I listened in. Priscilla was trying to teach them to go for the neck first when hunting. She'd brought in a few rabbits for them to try to kill, but apparently Samuel wasn't doing it to her liking.

"You're *useless* as a wolf! You'll remain a pup forever if you can't do this *one* simple thing!" she screamed.

I really was going to have to do something about her.

I cupped my hand around my phone and said urgently, "I think I'm going to have to call you back."

The answer on the other end was drowned out by more shouting from Priscilla. "Why are you even here?" Then a sharp yelp sounded. Before I could turn around, the air around me bristled with anger. *Edwin.* I had to stop the pup from losing his temper.

"Gotta go," I shouted and pocketed my phone as I spun around. The sight before me stunned me. It wasn't Edwin whose anger I sensed.

It was Jasinda. The sun was making me see things, but it looked like her eyes flashed green an instant before she lunged at Priscilla.

"Jace!" Edwin shouted in my mind.

She moved so fast. I didn't have time to stop her because I was taken by surprise by what she was about to do. Her fist was aimed at Priscilla's face. Startled by her actions, I stood frozen in place. To my shock and horror, Jasinda's fist actually connected with Priscilla's face, knocking her to the ground.

"What the hell was that for? You didn't have to put your hands on him!" shrieked Jasinda.

She straddled Priscilla's chest and started raining blow after blow.

"GET OFF OF ME!" Priscilla growled.

Priscilla bucked Jasinda off with her body and rolled her to her back, but couldn't keep her down, because Jasinda flipped her back with quickness. It then became a battle of who had the upper hand. Blow after blow, I stood here watching Jasinda serve Priscilla multiple hits. Priscilla struggled to even land one hit. It was amazing that Jasinda blocked and dodged *every* one of Priscilla's attempts. Finally, something miraculous happened. Edwin shifted into human form in midair and knocked Jasinda off Priscilla. Hastily, I willed clothes onto his body, then finally moved my feet to restrain Priscilla as she attempted to continue the fight.

"What the fuck, Jace!? You think it's acceptable for her to attack me first and me not defend myself!?" yelled Priscilla.

"You fuckin' fucked up. You broke a rule. My pups are *not* to be touched," I snarled at her.

She stiffened at my words. "I'm sorry, Jace. But Samuel wasn't getting it and I needed him to understand. Sometimes you have to get rough with the pups in order to keep them in line."

"It's not your fuckin' decision to make. Now leave before *I* rip your head off myself!" I roared.

She stood there trembling, fear consuming her body as her eyes never left mine.

Behind me, I could hear Jasinda rustling with Edwin, as if she was trying to get out of his hold. "You don't deserve to train these pups anymore. And if I catch you anywhere near them, I'll fuckin' kill you!" Jasinda spoke those words with a fierce and deadly tone.

When I looked towards her, her eyes blazed with anger while she was in Edwin's hold. She was serious and meant every word. With what I'd just witnessed, I'd put money on that she'd actually kill Priscilla.

"You're not even one of *us* and you don't deserve to be here. He shouldn't have picked you. You don't deserve to be his *mate*," Priscilla spat at her.

I flinched at her words.

Thankfully, Jasinda didn't seem to catch on exactly. "Why? Because *you* want to be his mate and he doesn't want you? Are you jealous that you can smell his scent all over me? That you can smell *our* sex all over us? Which one is it?" Jasinda strained against Edwin's hold. "Are you pissed at yourself for not making the move you should've made before I came? Well, guess what? I don't *care* how you feel. All I care about is *my* pups and their wellbeing. I won't let you or anyone else treat them the way you just did. So, yeah. You might want to leave because it won't be Jace ripping your head off. It will be me!" Jasinda shouted, with barely controlled rage.

I grinned. My enchantress was a gutsy woman and I liked it. I was even proud of it, but still shocked by it all.

Priscilla wrenched herself out of my grip. With one last look, she pointed at her and spoke with a threat, "This isn't over."

She shifted into her wolf form and ran off.

"Your pups?" I asked Jasinda with curiosity, forgetting Priscilla was even here.

I watched as the anger drained from her and a shy look came across her face. She blushed deeply.

"Umm...umm...well you see what happened was, it was in the heat of the moment. But that's also how I feel about them," she said, a bit embarrassed.

I smiled at her response. She'd protected them as if they *were* hers. And I wanted nothing more than for them to become her pups, just as much as they were mine. That was what they needed, a mother to protect them. And she'd reacted like any true mother would have. Any true wolf.

"Edwin," I said calmly. "You can let her go now."

"I don't want to. I don't want her going after Priscilla. I want her safe. With us," Edwin replied with panic in his voice.

Of course, he did. He'd never had anyone show him this much attention before. It was something he'd been craving for years and she's just given it to him.

"It's fine, Edwin. I won't go after her unless she touches one of you guys again," Jasinda confessed.

She calmly ran her hands through his hair, reassuring him that he could trust her words. Slowly, he pulled back and looked at her. I watched them closely and saw her give him a kind smile. Then she pulled him into a hug and glanced over at me. Emotion flickered on her face and her eyes shimmered with tears she was trying to not let escape. Then I watched Edwin's shoulders start to shake and realized he was crying and just like that, a tear escaped her.

"No one has ever defended us the way you did," Edwin sobbed.

"Well, then no one knows how special you all are," Jasinda told him.

I watched them in silence, rooted in place and speechless. This woman was mind blowing. I was glad I'd done what I had. I didn't regret mating with her. Maybe just the *way* I'd done it. *Damn, I needed to find a way to tell her. She was everything to me already. How had that happened so fast? And how, in such a short time, had she managed to change these pups?*

As I continued to watch them, Jasinda slowly took him down with her to the ground. She draped him over her lap like a baby and he went willingly. I was struck with an emotion I wasn't sure I could control. Tears streamed down my face. Sheer happiness filled me because she was able to get through to him. Now I knew there was hope for the remaining pups.

"Jace?" Kat called from behind me. Not in my mind.

I turned around slowly, not sure of what I was about to see. Sure enough, Kat and Tony were standing right behind me. My head dropped at seeing them in human form and I began to cry in earnest. I opened my arms wide to embrace them. Kat immediately ran into them and Tony followed closely behind. We were in a group hug when I felt Edwin hug me from behind.

These pups had become my children from the moment I had taken them in. I had been afraid they'd never shift into their human forms and be stuck as wolves forever. She had given me such a great gift. A gift that had so much power behind it. My mother was going to go nuts. Now she had grandchildren who knew their human forms. They would now be able to adapt to our world *and* the human one too. All because of my mate.

"Shhhh…it's ok. I won't let her touch you again," Jasinda spoke softly. "I promise. You have nothing to worry about. Lessons with Priscilla are *over* as of today."

Samuel whined. When I turned my head, I saw Samuel curled up in her lap, still in wolf form. *Damn*, I'd hoped he'd changed along with the others. But in time, I knew he would. I was grateful for three out of four. She'd accomplished so much in such a short time here, just a few weeks.

In two more days, it would be time for the Tri Feast. That was when I'd tell her, whether I knew how to or not. I'd just come out with it and accept the consequences. I just hoped she wouldn't leave me. Because without her completing me, I'd be a broken soul.

Chapter Fifty-Seven

Jasinda

I was nervous about meeting people at the Tri Feast. But I didn't know why. In my line of work, I was always meeting new people. It never made me anxious.

I sat quietly across from Jace as we ate in virtual silence. It wasn't an awkward silence. My mind was still reeling from what had happened earlier. The emotions that had rushed out of me, surprised me. And they had made me act in a way I never had before. Those pups meant everything to me, even though I'd only known them for a short time. To see them treated the way Priscilla was treating them had set me off in such an ugly way. Jace didn't mention my behavior during dinner.

Halfway through, he cleared his throat and took my hand. "Thank you for protecting them. They needed it."

I lifted his hand to my lips. "It was nothing. I love those pups."

"I know."

"You do?"

"Yes, I've known for a few days now."

I didn't respond, just smiled and continued eating. *Did he know I was in love with him too? No way I could say anything. It'd only been a few weeks. That was crazy, right?*

After dinner, he escorted me to my dessert date with his brother. As we walked hand in hand to the basement, I decided to share one of my concerns with him. "I'm worried about Samuel. Now, he's isolated."

He squeezed my hand. "Me too. And I'm not sure how to help. But I'm really hopeful. It was a huge deal that he let you touch him. He hasn't allowed anyone but me and the other pups to touch him in all the time he's been here."

"Really? Why?"

"Samuel was abused by his parents, so he doesn't like to be touched."

My heart soared at the thought that maybe I was helping him, even if I didn't think so.

When we got to the basement, Jace kissed me soundly. Right before he opened the door for me, he bent down and whispered in my ear, "When you enter, put on a sweater. It's a bit chilly in there. They're hanging to the left. I'll see you later." He smiled and I went inside.

When I entered the basement, I found an ice cream bar that was out of this world. To my left was the coat rack with sweaters. I snagged the black one up, since it looked like it would fit, and put it on. With wonder, I took in the details in front of me. The bar was an *actual* bar of ice cream. It was like going to an ice cream shop with a freezer showing tubs of all the flavors. Stools were positioned at the bar. On the walls were photos of Dorik and Jace as kids, sitting together eating ice cream.

Dorik grinned from ear to ear. "Well, what do you think?"

"I'm blown away. It's amazing. I can't believe you guys have this in your house."

"The smile on your face makes me feel like I've scored!"

I laughed. "You did, but don't tell Jace that."

"Are you insane? I'll definitely be rubbing it in his face."

I shook my head at him. "You *like* fighting with Jace?"

He sobered. "No, I actually *hate* fighting with my brother. I hate when he's upset with me too." He walked around the bar as I sat. "What's your flavor?"

"Vanilla with rainbow sprinkles. And do you have any chocolate chip cookies?"

"No caramel?" he asked.

"Nope. Just cookies."

"We have cookies." I watch him carefully take out a bowl and spoon. He scooped my ice cream, added the toppings and handed me my bowl. "I hope you don't mind the bowl, but those toppings won't stay on a cone."

"Bowls are great. They mean more ice cream. Although a sugar cone *is* crunchy and tasty." I wiggled in the chair and rubbed my hands together with excitement. "Thank you."

He chuckled. "Lina loved her ice cream in a bowl too. I had to fill it all the way up. Five to seven scoops."

"*What?* That's too much brain freeze for me."

"Not for Lina. I loved that about her. She didn't let anything stop her from enjoying what she wanted, even a brain freeze."

"She sounds like a good woman, Dorik. I wish I could've met her."

He pulled up a stool and sat on the opposite side of the bar, in front of me. "She would've loved you. Would've enjoyed the hell out of you, actually. Especially since she didn't hang around the other pack females very often."

"Really? Why?"

"She preferred to be alone. Pack females fall into two groups, single and mated. The single ones are more concerned with status- name brands, appearances, who they're dating. Lina joined the pack as my mate, so the single females definitely didn't accept her. Not that she cared about any of the stuff they cared about. And she didn't really fit in with the mated ones either. Lina liked to hang with men better. Less drama she said."

"Are the females in the pack *that* bad?" I tensely inquired. I hoped not. I needed to fit in with Jace's people. I wanted them to like me, because I wasn't planning on going anywhere.

"No, Priscilla is the only bad seed. The young ones are jealous of the mated ones. And the mated ones are wrapped up in their families and the freedom of nature."

"What do you mean 'the freedom of nature'?"

"Well, for one, they just like to have sex out in the woods and be free. They prefer the outdoors more than anything. It's why they live in the woods in the cottages. They like things simple when it comes to the way they live. Lina liked adventure and to explore different realms. It's how we met. She wasn't content to just hang out around our cottage while I was out doing things."

He was so happy talking about his memories. He was right. Lina sounded like someone I would've loved to have known too. I thought about what he'd said about the two groups of women in the pack. Status definitely didn't matter to me. I wasn't sure how I would fit in with the single females of the pack. But outdoor sex was pretty amazing. So maybe I'd just make friends with the mated ones. Though if I was going to make a future with Jace, perhaps I should try to figure out a way to bridge the gap between the two groups of females.

As we sat enjoying the cold treat, I decided that I owed him another apology. "I know I said it before, but I'm really sorry I upset you the other week and again earlier. The humming kind of came out on its own. Instinctive."

"I know you didn't mean anything by it. It's just when I heard it, I was transported back to a time I'd rather forget."

"Sometimes it helps to talk about it," I offered quietly. "I was pregnant. I lost my baby too. I didn't know I was pregnant for very long. I was already twenty weeks when I found out." I paused and took a bite of ice cream. "I loved my baby instantly. Then I was attacked, and... I lost my baby." I couldn't stop the tears from falling.

He cleared his throat. "I'm sorry for your loss."

"Thank you. For a long time, I tried to forget. It hurt to think about it. Memories can bring so much pain. But they're proof of how much we've loved. And they make us stronger. I know you don't *want* to remember. But you should embrace the pain and the rage. In time you'll find it easier to remember."

"Lina used to hum lullabies to her belly. She wanted our baby to love music. And she'd read that music stimulates their brains. She tried to get me to sing too. But I have a *terrible* singing voice." He chuckled. "I did hum with her a few times. But now... hearing the lullabies is like a stab to my heart."

"I'm so sorry. I'll try to be more aware of the sounds that slip from me."

"It's fine."

He was opening up to me. "So, I heard you guys fought side by side."

He puffed out a breath and a smile tipped up the corner of his lips. "It's what attracted me to her the first time I met her. Each time she fought at my side was such a huge turn on." Silence filled the room as he became lost in the memory.

I gave him the silence. I knew how valuable that gift could be. Moments pregnant with pain passed before he composed himself enough to continue. "It's how I lost her too. That was the hardest thing I've *ever* had to endure. I wouldn't wish that pain on my worst enemy. And I certainly don't want that for Jace."

His words stilled me. He was staring into his bowl, rather than at me. *What did he mean? Was he talking about me?* "Dorik...What—"

When his gaze met mine, there was sorrow in his eyes. "I wouldn't want that for you either, Jasinda. It's a feeling that doesn't *ever* go away... Until you find another mate. If you find another mate. The separation is like losing half of yourself." Stuffing a spoon of ice cream into his mouth bought him some time before he had to continue. He swallowed and kept his eyes on me. "I felt *so* empty without her, detached from everyone and the world. I felt like I'd never care again... Until I met you."

"Me?"

"Yes, *you*. You intrigued me in a way that woke me from my slumber. Your spirit and curiosity that day on the horse, the beast in me liked it and welcomed it. Then I got to know more about you. Even though you had been through so much, and lost so much, you still had this hope about you. I figured if you could find a way to live with optimism after losing your memories, your family, your baby, and yourself, then maybe so could I. I don't know, I'm just happy you're here and I'm overjoyed you're making my brother happy."

I couldn't stop the smile that lifted my face.

"I also feel like I need to apologize again for the way I approached you in the kitchen," he said sheepishly.

"Approached me in the kitchen? Are you *kidding* me?" I quirked a brow at him in disbelief. "That wasn't an *approach*. You threw yourself at me and pretty much tried to dry hump me in front of your brother, mother and aunt. *Then* you nearly attacked me for my cookie and tried to dry hump me again." My cheeks heated as I remembered that day.

"That sounds accurate," he admitted, with a knowing smile. "Did Jace explain to you about menstrus?"

"He explained it to me before he locked us away from the world for a few days." And though I had a pretty good grasp on things from Jace's description, something told me Dorik was going to go all in with more clarification.

"Sure, he did. In a textbook kinda way, I bet." He finished the last of his ice cream while I continued to eat mine.

"What other way is there to explain it?" I asked.

He drew in a deep breath. "Jasinda, you give off these pheromones when you're in your menstrus. In the days leading up to it, the pheromones increase. It drives *any* supernatural man crazy. Believe it or not, it also drives human men crazy, just not as noticeable as the supernatural ones. The supernaturals *know* what's going on. While a human would just think they were really horny."

Learning more was fascinating to me. But he wasn't done with his explanation. "It drives us fuckin' *crazy* and we lose all thought. That shit goes right out the window. Our dicks get hard and we want to fuck the shit out of you... or our mates if we're mated."

Holy waters! He was serious. "That's the real reason Jace wanted me locked away in the room?"

"Oh yeah, he wanted to make sure no one got a taste of you, including me." He winked at me and I giggled. "We just want to fuck. You know, stick it in a nice wet pussy." He shrugged while grinning.

"How unromantic. That was a little too much detailed info from my... boyfriend's brother." *Damn Calling cycles were some strong shit.*

"Hey, you can always count on me to give you the truth. The truth of the truth."

He seemed oddly proud to be teaching me things, like a big brother. Minus the wanting to screw me like a rabid animal a few days ago. I knew we'd formed a friendship tonight. A *real* one.

"I think your brother's version of the Calling cycle was a little watered down on the effects to those around me." I laughed.

"You think? Geez, we want to fuck, Jasinda... and connect. Don't get me wrong. It's not *all* about the sex, but it is still about the sex. The connection that's built *during* the sex is phenomenal. And it intensifies with the one you connected with. Your mate or even deeper with your soulmate. It's not just a casual fuck."

His wide eyes dragged up and down my form. "For example, I smell Jace all over you. And not from the sex, but just from the connection. Just like if anyone approaches him, they'll smell you all over him. Of course, they will still smell him, but *your* scent will be the dominant scent on him and his on you."

I sniffed my arm to see if I could smell him on me. He laughed at me, but I was pretty sure I detected a hint of that aroma that was uniquely Jace. The scent beneath his cologne and soap. That was incredible. "Whoa. That's fabulously magical. Awesomeness."

"*Finally*, she gets it," he teased. "I can't tell you how hard it was for me to control myself around you. *Very* hard, which is why I reacted the way I did that day and why you responded the way *you* did."

"Wait just a minute, buster. I *only* responded because Jace was there. I was turned on by *him*," I assured him.

"*Right*, can't you just give me this one? I mean, you didn't push me off you right away."

He had a point, but it was more like I'd been stunned at his boldness in front of his brother. However, I didn't want to damage the friendship we were building by crushing his ego. "Fine. Score for you," I gave in.

"Don't worry. Now that you're ma... Jace's and he's yours, your Calling won't call to every male like a siren's song demanding that we take you."

"That's a relief. For my sake, I hope you're right."

"For all of our sakes' too. Because if anyone were to approach you like I did, I know my brother and his beast would rip them limb from limb. Bonus tip for you since you let me score. If you see my nostrils flare and my eyes change, don't be afraid. It's my beast coming to the surface. Those same things apply with Jace. You don't need to fear either of our beasts.

They actually get more upset if you show fear. The beast will accept you as long as you acknowledge him. Always make sure you keep your temper under control when the beasts are near the surface. Our beasts are more instinctive, so less rational."

"Dorik are you trying to warn me?"

"I *am* warning you and preparing you to deal with our beasts." He pushed. "Jace as a man is incredibly disciplined. He learned restraint at a young age from our mother. I, on the other hand, haven't quite mastered his level of calmness as a man. My mother fought hard to teach us control and tranquility for our beasts. It is a lesson each of us only half mastered. Jace as a man, but not as a beast. And me as a beast, but not as a man. In time, maybe we'll both get it completely right."

He took my bowl and I realized my ice cream was gone. I'd been so enthralled with everything he was sharing that I hadn't even savored the last bites. "I can't imagine Jace lacking control in anything." He'd certainly exhibited all levels of restraint whenever I was begging him to make me cum this morning.

"One minor incident a few years ago has made Jace worried that someone might get hurt when he isn't fully in the driver's seat."

"Really? What happened?"

"His beast nearly ripped Priscilla's head off when she was twenty."

I was caught between horror and a sick sense of satisfaction. "I think his beast and I just might get along great."

He chuckled. "You see, my mom's reason for emphasizing peace and constraint for our beasts is so we don't become a demon werewolf."

"Demon werewolf?" I asked, my voice a mixture of fear and curiosity.

"That's what we call a werewolf who steals others' powers and tries to take over other packs."

"Wait…wait…*wait.* Do you mean it's like a teen wolf thing? You know, if a wolf kills another wolf, he gains its power?" I demanded. "Or if a wolf kills an alpha, he becomes an alpha?"

"Not exactly. A demon werewolf goes after newborn wolfins. If they kill a wolflin, then they get more power. Anyone who kills an alpha becomes the alpha only if challenged."

"Oh, ok. Not like Teen Wolf then. So, does the challenger become prince as well if they win the challenge or kill Jace?" In my mind Jace was indestructible. The thought of something out there being able to hurt him and then hurt his pack made my heart ache and worry.

"No, because I'm still alive and so is my father. They would just be alpha of Jace's pack. Let's say you're Jace's mate."

I watched as he looked beyond me. I wanted to turn and see what he was looking at, but I was too vested in his story.

"*You* as his mate, as the *alpha queen,* could challenge the wolf who killed Jace. And since you're a female, you'd be allowed two wolves to fight by your side."

"So, a mate can challenge an alpha if need be?"

"*Anyone* can challenge an alpha, even a woman. And if that ever happens, you as alpha queen could stand in your mate's place to fight the woman challenger instead."

The way he said *you* was a bit touchy. He must have read the thought on my face. "Hypothetically speaking, of course."

"There's so much to learn about you all."

With a chuckle, he walked around the bar. "Let's get you back to my brother before he assumes the worst of me."

"Dorik?"

He straightened and focused on me.

"Why does everyone hate Priscilla so much?"

He huffed. "Because she only cares for herself and only wants to gain status as an alpha queen. She's bitchy and moody because Jace won't take her back. Plus, she's just mean." He planted both hands on his hips. "She slept with Elier for attention and to try to hurt Jace. Who does that sick shit? She's spiteful and rubs me the wrong way. I wish Jace would let me rip her head off."

Okkie dokkie. I guess I shouldn't ask too many questions about her then.

Silently, he escorted me out of the basement. My time with Jace's brother had opened my eyes to things I'd never considered before. His blunt honesty was refreshing. No sugar coating anything from Dorik. I liked that about him and I hoped we had another ice cream date so I could learn more. When we arrived at Jace's room, Dorik pressed a goodnight kiss to my cheek. A blush stole across my cheeks from his sweet kiss.

Dorik had barely stepped away from my side before Jace opened the door. "Better watch how you put your lips on my girl," he teased his brother's retreating back.

Dorik just flipped him off over his shoulder.

Jace kissed my cheek and nuzzled me before capturing my lips with his. Without detaching himself from me, he moved us backward into his room.

When he finally let me come up for air he said, "You taste like ice cream and cookies. And now you smell like me."

"Did you kiss my cheek to cover your brother's kiss up?" I teased.

"What can I say? I've never shared well." Mischief sparkled in his eyes.

"That's a good thing, because neither do I."

I pushed him backwards until the backs of his knees hit the bed. And we proceeded to spend the rest of our night wrapped up in each other and communicating in the way we'd been perfecting—bodies, hearts and souls in sync.

The ringing phone roused me from slumber. Jace's sleep-thickened voice rumbled behind me. "Yeah, hang on."

He held the phone out to me with the mouthpiece covered. "It's Scarlet. She wants to have lunch with you." I stretched my achy muscles then accepted the phone.

"Hey, Scarlet."

"Good morning. Sorry to wake you. Normally, Jace is up at the crack of dawn, so I figured you guys would be moving about already."

"No worries. We were up late… talking and stuff. So, what's up?" I had to turn my back on Jace, who quirked an eyebrow at my up late talking comment.

"I feel like we didn't get enough time yesterday to fully catch up. I was hoping you'd be free for a picnic lunch."

"Umm…" Jace's finger tracing along the neckline of my nightgown was distracting me.

"If you aren't free, we can meet up another time," she hastily added.

"I am free. I'm just really tired. I think I need a lazy day today. Can we just do lunch in my room?"

"Sure, don't you worry about anything. I'll take care of it all and I'll see you at lunch."

After I hung up with Scarlet, Jace pounced, pinning me to the bed. "I'll give you a better reason to be tired than *talking all night*," he growled.

My giggles soon turned to moans as his lips devoured my neck and his hands began exploring the flesh beneath my nightgown. An incessant ringing coming from my cell phone had him mumbling curses against my skin.

"That's Angie's ring tone. I have to answer," I panted.

"Make it quick. I need you."

"Yes sir," I quipped and scampered to grab my phone.

Breathlessly, I answered, "Hello."

"Please tell me that whatever reason you sound like you're out of breath is a good one."

"Oh, it was, but the phone halted that."

"Sorry, girl. I'll make it quick. I haven't seen you outside of work in too long. From the little bit of info I've been able to twist out of Anthony, there's stuff you need to update me on. So I want to take you to dinner tonight."

I really wanted to see her. I'd really missed her. But worry over the unknown danger that had forced me into hiding kept me from jumping at the chance. "Ang, can I check a few things and then let you know?"

"Sure, text me if you can meet up."

"I will. Sorry I've been so absent lately."

"No worries. It's good to hear you happy. Now go back to whatever fun, breath stealing activities you were up to. I'll expect details later."

I laughed as I hung up. When I turned back to where Jace lounged naked on the bed, I couldn't hide the indecision on my face.

"What's wrong?"

"Angie wants to meet up for dinner. But I don't know if I should." I sat next to him on the bed.

"Are you worried your friend will be upset with you for moving too quickly with me?"

"Goodness, no. She'll be thrilled that I've completely moved on from Elier. No, I'm worried that I shouldn't leave the property. That whatever threat I'm here hiding from is out there, just waiting for me to show myself."

"I think it'll do you good to see your friend. What if I have two of my guys drive you and stay nearby in case something comes up? Would that make you feel better?"

"Actually, that would be perfect. How do you always seem to know exactly what I need?"

He picked up my hand and laid it against his chest. The steady rhythm of his heart pounded up into my palm. "Your heart speaks to mine."

This man slayed me with his sweetness. "What's my heart telling yours right now?" I asked teasingly.

Hours later, my lazy day was finally beginning as I enjoyed a cup of tea in my room. Scarlet would be here soon. And I'd worked up an appetite. If last night was any indication of how tonight would go, I'd need the extra fuel from dinner with Angie to help me stay alert.

The three small packages Anthony had brought back from my office were sitting on the counter and caught my eye. I'd been a little preoccupied with Jace and never got around to opening them. I sat on the stool, looking down at them lying before me. The rectangular boxes were about four inches tall and were wrapped in a soft lavender gift wrap. I picked one up and turned it over, examining it. The handwriting wasn't familiar, yet it was. The paper felt as though it was made of flowers.

"How creative," I mused.

As much I wanted to see what was inside, I didn't want to open it and ruin the wrapping. It was too beautiful to tear. My curiosity began to get the better of me. But I didn't see a flap or even a piece of tape to tell me *how* to open it.

"How do I open it?" I whispered.

The paper began to vibrate, and wings began to surface. I gasped. Fear clogged my throat for an instant. Amazement quickly replaced it as wings emerged from the surface. The wings were all facing up, like synchronized swimmers. Then they flew apart and butterflies lay before me, holding a bracelet. As I peered more closely, I realized I'd seen it before. It was like the one Silvo had taken out of his pocket the night of the charity event. The night my life had fallen apart. But it was also the night the pieces had started reassembling in a wonderful way at the hands of Jace.

"Holy waters!" *How frackin' cool was that?*

I couldn't believe it. It was too unique to be a replica of Silvo's. It had to be from him. The bracelet was white gold with diamond butterflies on it. Almost like the one on my ankle, but the whole bracelet was covered with them. When I reached a finger out to touch it, the butterflies dodged my attempt and placed the bracelet on my right wrist. They fastened it like they'd done it before. Silvo had given *me* the bracelet that had once belonged to someone he loved. *But why? And how could I complain when it felt like it belonged on my wrist?*

I looked at the other butterfly boxes.

"Open," I whispered.

They immediately obeyed and opened up just like the first one did. There was another bracelet similar to the butterfly one, but with dragons instead. It was exquisite. Fragile wings flapped as the magical butterflies placed the dragon bracelet alongside the butterfly one. *Odd.* I thought they'd fasten it on my left wrist.

I gasped when I saw the ring. It was white gold matching the bracelets. The band appeared to be formed from two tails of some sort. But what really stood out were the three pearls nestled in the middle. The winged creatures brought the ring to my right hand and slipped it on my middle finger. Now that I could see it up close, the tails looked like a dragon's tail and a fish tail intertwined together holding the pearls. The most distinguishing thing was that the pearls were nearly clear.

They had to have cost way more than I could even imagine. I really shouldn't accept a gift so expensive. I'd never owned anything this extravagant. *So why did it feel like these belonged with me?* I couldn't stop the smile that arose.

The butterflies fluttered nearby. "Thank you. Can you understand me?"

"Yes." The word was tiny and faint, but I heard them. I actually *heard* them.

"Can you thank him for me?"

"Yes," little voices chorused, like a beautiful song.

They disappeared through the open window. I watched until they faded from sight. Happiness and confusion rioted within me over it all. It was really thoughtful of Silvo to have sent such a unique gift to me just because I'd admired the butterfly bracelet before. But here I was all jeweled up with expensive gifts from a man I didn't even know. *What the hell was I going to tell Jace?*

A knock at the door halted my train of thought as Scarlet arrived with our lunch.

"It's open," I yelled.

"Hey, I brought Mexican burrito bowls for us," she announced, walking in with a cart in tow.

I smiled at her from my chair. When she reached me, she stopped dead in her tracks. Her mouth fell open, and her eyes went wide.

"Where did you get *those*?" she asked in disbelief.

"They were a gift," I said sheepishly.

"A gift? From who?"

"This guy who showed up at the charity event when my life started unraveling around me. Tall, handsome, silver hair. His name was Silvo."

"Silvo Agon?"

"I don't know his last name. Does he have a sister named Silva?"

"Yes," she whispered.

As she stared at me, she looked like she'd seen a ghost. I popped out of my chair and closed the distance between us.

"You know them?"

"Yes. Why would he give those to you?" Confusion filled her eyes.

"I have no idea. I'm just confused as you are. We only met that one time and barely talked then. But I did admire it when he showed it to me. Why do *you* ask?"

"Because those once belonged to his wife. His wife who was a princess."

I blinked at her, remembering what he'd said to me that night.

"He told me they once belonged to someone he loved," I softly said. "Is his wife dead?"

"No, at least, I don't think so. They're separated."

"Really? That's sad. He seemed like he still loves her."

"He *does* still love her, but she's gone away."

"To where?"

"No one knows."

Poor Silvo. He still was in love with her and she'd left him. Just left him behind. *How could someone do something like that? What was the whole point of marriage if you were just going to leave the person you'd vowed to be with forever?* But then again, I didn't know the whole story. Maybe she'd had her reasons. It wasn't any of my business anyway.

Chapter Fifty-Eight

Jasinda

"**W**hat did he *say* when he gave them to you?" Scarlet asked. We'd just finished eating in silence. Neither one of us spoke. Both of us were lost in thought and didn't know what to say. I was curious to find out how they knew each other. I wonder if she'd tell if I asked.

"He didn't say anything because he didn't hand them to me. The packages were delivered to my office and Anthony brought them to me."

"Oh, ok."

"Scarlet, how do you know Silvo and Silva?"

A pained look covered her face for a moment, then she gave me a small smile.

"I used to work for his father a *long* time ago. Back before Silvo was mated. His father used to be kind. I enjoyed working for him. Then something happened that made him different. Anyways, I left around the time when Silvo became of age to be king."

"He's a king?"

"He's a prince. I believe he's still a prince. At least until his father steps down."

"Cool."

"So, you and Jace got a lot closer while I was gone?"

I couldn't stop the dreamy sigh that escaped my lips at the mention of Jace. "We have. I know you might think I'm crazy, but I can see a future with us. I've never felt anything like this before. I know it's too soon to think like this. I'm only supposed to stay here until it's safe for me to go back to my life, which is in chaos. We're so different. But I can't help what my heart and soul feel."

"I don't think it's crazy at all. I need to ask something of you." The look in her eyes made me sober up.

"Of course."

"Promise me something, please," she pleaded.

"Making promises without knowing what they are is a bad idea," I teased.

"Promise me that if something goes wrong and you think the worst, you won't just run away and never look back. Promise me you'll stick around and at least listen and try to understand *why* things happened the way they happened."

Her words were vague and cautious. Like she was preparing me for a major backstabbing or fallout or something.

"I promise. But is everything all right?" Her worry was infecting my happiness from earlier.

"Honestly, I'm not sure. I think some things have happened but I'm not able to tell you about them. Someone else will want to tell you but they just don't know how to explain. They're afraid of how you'll react and afraid you'll leave."

"What are you getting at, Scarlet?" *Does Jace not feel that I am enough for him as a human? Has he found someone he wanted to be with and needed to end things with me? Did one of his pack members have a problem with me being human?*

"Just keep in mind that sometimes people do things by instinct and aren't always aware that they did it until it's done."

"Are you talking about Priscilla?"

"Oh, God *no*. She deserved what you did. Those pups are lucky to have you."

I laughed. I didn't feel bad for what happened between Priscilla and me.

"Is something about to happen, Scarlet?"

Her eyes searched mine for a long moment. "I'm afraid so, sweetie. I can't explain what exactly. My nose detects something odd in the air. A great danger coming soon."

"Danger? Do you know what kind?"

"No," she whispered. "And that's what I'm afraid of."

"Maybe we should tell Jace to cancel the Tri Feast."

"It won't matter. Tri Feast or not, something's going to happen."

A faraway look took over her features. A cold chill passed over my body suddenly.

"Scar, every time I venture out of the house and into the woods, it has felt like someone was watching me. I can't explain it, but it's what I felt. Could that be it?"

"No, not at all. That's just Dorik keeping watch. He's protecting you."

"Why? I thought Jace had this place hidden really well?"

"Yes, but sometimes things happen."

Fear started to grow in me. Before, I'd felt safe because I'd thought this place was hidden from any source of danger. But I should've known better. *What if it's the danger Jako mentioned? What if it's what my mother was trying to protect me from?* I stood abruptly and started pacing.

Calm down. Don't make assumptions. I closed my eyes and breathed in and out a few times. When I looked over at Scarlet, she was still in a daze.

Without stopping to consider what I was doing, I sat on Scarlet's lap like a little girl. It snapped her out of her daze. A smile played across my lips as I laid my head on her shoulder. Her fingers combed through my hair and she sighed.

"Don't leave him," she said softly.

"Jace. Don't leave him, please."

"I wasn't planning on it. I…I'm…I'm in love with him," I admitted.

"Thank the goddesses," she blew out.

I laughed. She was a bit too serious sometimes.

"Everything will be fine. We'll all be fine," I assured her.

"I hope so. I really am counting on it." Her voice sounded relieved by my words. "He *needs* you. We *all* need you."

"I don't understand what you mean by that."

"You don't need to."

And for some reason I accepted her words. I stayed on her lap, and we sat there in silence, looking through the open window. After a while, she rose and set me on my feet. She led me to the window. With a press of a button, a set of double doors opened onto the balcony.

We settled into chairs tucked away out there. I wished I'd known those were doors. I have spent a lot of time out here. My eyes darted around. A Jacuzzi was nestled in the far corner. I couldn't stop my thoughts from drifting to Jace and me in the hot, bubbling water later. I really needed to explore the whole house a little better. Find out what other treasures I'd been missing out on.

"Scar?"

"Yes?"

"I love you. You've been just the friend I've needed at this crazy time in my life. Thank you," I said looking over at her.

She was smiling while holding her tears at bay. *Crap. I'd made her cry.* I really didn't mean to. I wanted her to know that she meant something to me. Especially if something happened.

"I love you too. You've been the warmth I've been missing for many, many years. Thank you for giving it back," she said with sincerity in her voice.

Chapter Fifty-Nine

Jasinda

I felt as though Scarlet wanted to tell me more. It was like she was preparing me for something. Something *important* that she didn't want me to run from. My curiosity demanded that I ask her more about it but I felt it was best to lay off the subject. For now. After she left, I removed my new jewelry and got ready for dinner with Angie.

Dalo and Dorik drove me to the restaurant. When Jace had told me who my escorts would be, I was a bit excited because I hadn't met Dalo yet. I'd only heard about him from Jace. Dorik escorted me to the waiting Jaguar F-Pace Portfolio. Dalo was in the driver's seat. I couldn't believe I was getting into *this* car. *Angie was going to flip!*

Dorik opened the backdoor and I slid in. The interior was a light grey leather. It smelled brand new. Angie kept talking about how she's always wanted this kind of car and craved for us to go test drive a few. As far as I was concerned, my Acura RDX was just fine. As Dorik closed the door, I looked over myself, feeling underdressed for meeting Dalo. I wore a pair of faded blue jeans, a hunter green V-neck and brown wedges.

"Hello, Jasinda. Welcome to the Hunt family," a beautiful, bass voice greeted me.

I looked up into his striking cream-colored face—adorned with brown eyes and short, dark brown hair. "Uh…h…hi,' I stuttered and missed the connection with the seatbelt. Screw it, no seatbelt it is.

He smiled. "Buckle up. I don't need Jace ripping my head off if there's one scratch on you."

"Ok." I swallowed and tried again, successfully connecting the seatbelt this time.

The SUV shifted into gear and we were off. "So, Jasinda, I heard that Dorik here gave you quite a scare a little while back." The humor in his voice told me he was teasing Dorik.

"He did. I thought he was trying to eat me," I responded playfully.

"I wasn't going to *eat* you," he clipped.

Dalo laughed. "Good to know, brother." He looked at me in the rearview mirror. "How do you like staying here so far?"

"Oh, I love it. It's beautiful and peaceful. So much land to wander and enjoy. And of course, making new friends is always fun. Not to mention spending time with Jace."

"That's always good to hear." He made a few turns here and there while we sat in silence. "We can come in with you if you want."

I noticed we were pulling into the Cocoa Chocolate Restaurant valet. The building was brown and black, like chocolate. *Should they come in?* I wasn't sure what the *right* answer was, but I wanted them close. "That would be nice, if you don't mind."

"We don't mind. We'll get a table close enough to grab you if anything should happen," Dorik assured me.

Dalo pulled the SUV up. Dorik got out, then he helped me out. Dalo spoke to the valet, "The car stays out front. Keys at the ready."

"Yes, sir."

The two men escorted me inside. Angie was waiting just inside the doors as I entered. She squealed when her eyes met mine and I ran to her squeezing the life out of her. "I've missed you girl." She pulled back to take a better look at me. "Girl, even in those jeans and shirt, you still look sexy."

"Not as sexy as you. I'm loving the curls." My fingers gave them a little tug to see them spring back. "They're bouncier and curlier than before."

"Really? I'm using this new leave-in conditioner that works wonders. Come on. I got us a table already." She leaned in closer. "What's up with the bodyguards? I thought you were safe with Jace."

We walked over to our table and sat. The place was beautiful with paper lanterns hanging to give the right amount of light. A chocolate bar was always ready with a chocolate fountain as the centerpiece. "I am, but that's inside his home. With him. I wasn't sure about being away."

"Oh, right. Damn, I suck. I wanted to see you so bad that I didn't think how you coming out could potentially put you in danger."

"Don't worry about it. Jace was the one who told me I should come and suggested I take them with me so I'd feel safe."

"Did he now?"

"Shut up, Angie!"

The waitress came to our table. We were happy to see it was Faith. We'd had her a few times before. "Hey Ladies. It's been a while. Shirley Temples to start you off, and do you want the usual?" Her smile was warm and welcoming.

"Yes, the usual for me," I told her.

"Me too, Faith."

"Good. I'll be back with your drinks in a few." Faith walked away and I knew Angie was itching.

"So, spill woman!"

"Boy, someone is eager to get info."

"Uh…yeah! Now come on, spill the juice!"

"Well, you're not going to believe any of this. I lived through it all and *I* still can't believe it. I'll start at the beginning. The night of the charity event, the Mitchell brothers found out about this threat to my safety. I guess through my dad's connections."

Angie nodded and sipped her drink.

I told Angie everything and had to keep her calm when she wanted to kill Miranda. I was impressed with how well she seemed to be handling the information I'd dumped on her after the Miranda part. I hadn't given her enough credit to not lose her cool with all the weirdness that had encompassed my life the past few weeks.

Faith delivered our orders and we dug in for a few silent moments.

"So, have things calmed down since you've been at Jace's?" she asked as she swallowed her mouthful.

"No! Not long after I got there, this big-ass werewolf chased me through the woods." A snicker and a cough sounded from over my shoulder. I paid it no mind as I continued, "Then later I met a dragon named Skyla. It was scary, amazing, and for some reason, it felt normal. I can't explain it."

"Wow," Angie said as she kept eating.

I really expected the mention of a dragon to elicit some sort of reaction from her. Maybe she thought I was nuts and was just appeasing me until she could have me committed.

"Jace sounds like a good guy." She expressed with a mouthful.

I couldn't stop the dreamy sigh that escaped my lips. Just thinking of him made me hot. I lifted my hair from my neck to try to cool off a little. Angie's eyes zeroed in on my movement and my hands. An odd expression crossed her features.

"Jace is wonderful. So damn hot. And a wolf shifter." Not even a blink from Angie. She must be in shock from all the crazy information. "And I think he's into me. He's everything I never knew I needed and wanted. I know we haven't known each other for long… But it feels right. Like he's perfect for me in every way. I don't know how to explain it. But I'm crazy about him. Is it weird to be this crazy about him so soon?"

"No, I think when you feel something like what you are feeling for Jace, embrace it and let it take you where it needs to. Don't drive yourself crazy thinking it's weird to be crazy over him. Besides, crazy isn't always bad," Angie stated simply.

"When should I tell Jace how I feel? Do you think the intensity of my feelings will scare him off?" I worried.

"No, wolves don't scare easily."

"Oh *really*. And just how many wolves do you know?" I smirked at her.

She dropped her fork onto her empty plate. "A lot actually, since I'm a wolf myself," she huffed out. "Oh, it felt so good to finally say that out loud to you."

Her admission surprised me at first, but not for long, since everything in my life had felt supernatural from the night of the charity event. I was getting used to it by now. She was just like Anthony; she'd failed to mention *that* detail about herself.

"Why didn't you tell me?" I scolded.

"I don't know. I always wanted to, but you were so oblivious to the supernatural world that I just kept it to myself. I figured it was safer to not say anything." She shrugged.

"Ahhh…ok." *I'll wait to talk to her about not trusting me later.* "Let me sum up my past few weeks. I don't have my original memories or know who I am. I'm falling in love with a werewolf. I met a dragon. And my best friend is a wolf." I ticked the items off on my fingers.

"Pretty much."

"What pack are you in?"

"I don't have one. I'm considered a lone wolf. I haven't chosen a pack yet."

"Can't you just choose one?"

"Well, yes, I can. But they'd have to accept me first. Which means they'd make me go through a trust test."

"What's a trust test?"

"It's a hunting test to see how well I'll hunt with their pack. To make sure I follow well and don't try to dominate."

"Ugh. That sucks."

"No, not really. It's expected."

"Then why are you a lone wolf?"

She folded her hands together and placed them on the table. "Some alphas love the power they have. They use it as an excuse to treat people however they want and to get whatever they want. The rules aren't the same for them. For example, as an alpha, you can have any woman you want. It doesn't matter if you're mated. Which just rubs me wrong. Why commit if you're going to screw around?"

"So, some alphas are beyond assholes?" I asked.

"Some, but not all. You see, the ones I've been around were either assholes or they had mates who were intimidated by me. I didn't want that on me. I especially didn't need to always worry about what the mates thought of me. Some can be fuckin' cruel and evil. I'm not down with that shit."

"Jace seems pretty easy going. I mean, I don't think he's like the other alphas. At least, I hope he's not. I don't share well. Maybe you should come over one day and speak with him?"

"He *does* seem different. I'll think about it."

"Thinking about it is better than nothing," I expressed and watched her shake her head. "Now are you ready for molten chocolate lava cake with vanilla ice cream?"

"Yeah, but I am going to need them to add a few scoops of chocolate," she said with a chuckle.

"I figured," Faith said from behind me as she got closer with a plate in her hand. "Here's your molten chocolate lave cake with two scoops of vanilla and two scoops of chocolate, drizzled with chocolate syrup and caramel. Enjoy ladies. I'll bring your waters soon."

That was why we loved Faith. She always knew how to make us happy. Spending time with Angie was perfect. I was so glad I let Jace talk me into coming. Now I had another person I could share this crazy, magical ride with.

"By the way, I got to ride in a Jaguar F-Pace Portfolio." I blurted out.

Angie dropped her spoon, her eyes widened and her mouth fell open. I busted out laughing. I could already see the wheels turning in her head and I knew we'd be joy riding in it together.

As soon as I returned from dinner, Ash was saddled and waiting for me by the front steps. A note was fastened to the reins. *I need to see you* was scrawled in Jace's familiar handwriting but Jace was nowhere in sight. A smile spread across my lips as I figured he must be at the magic waterfall. Heat filled me as I recalled our last visit there. I was ready for another visit.

I just had to figure out how to climb up on the massive creature. My eyes darted around to make sure no one was watching. I ran and leapt, planting my foot in one of the stirrups and pulling myself onto Ash. It worked and I was quite pleased with myself. Just as I pulled on the reins, he ran straight to the trails. To my surprise, he took a different path this time. The trees changed color as we moved through the forest, like before. It was even more fascinating to watch this time because I was alone, and therefore not distracted by Jace. The colors vibrated in the wind with such radiance. It was such a sight to see. The blue lit up the trails the most.

Finally, Ash slowed and trotted towards a vine-covered wall. Jace stood in front of it. Being near him initially kept me from noticing the vines were filled with enchantress roses. They were stunning, opened wide and gorgeous. All the possible colors were before me, except for one, lavender. Disappointment filled me for a moment. It disappeared once Ash came to a full stop and Jace approached to help me down.

"Enchantress," his voice rumbled.

"Hey."

"How were your social calls?"

"They were both good. I've missed them."

"I know Scarlet feels the same way about you." His eyes crinkled as his lips turned up.

I smiled up at him, because I knew he was telling me the truth. Every other thought evaporated as he took that moment to kiss me. *Yes*, my mind cheered. That was what I was missing from him. The press of his lips on mine set everything right in my world. I hadn't realized that I was aching for something, missing something. Even in the moments before he married our mouths. His touch soothed me. And the fact we liked to make out like crazed teenagers was a definite plus. He pulled back just enough for our eyes to meet.

"I know it's late but I want to show you something. It's something special to me. I hope you like it."

"Since it means something to you, I already know I'll love it."

"I'm counting on it," he said, sounding optimistic.

Pulling the vine aside, he revealed a pathway. A gasp slipped past my lips at the cleverly hidden entrance. I stepped through the parted curtain of green. It was a bit dark, but I saw a flicker of light ahead of me. Once the vines dropped back into place, fireflies were lit up all over the grass before me. They flew low to the ground, illuminating the area with a green glow. I looked back at Jace. He was behind me and leaning against a rock wall, letting me soak it all in. The grin on his lips made the beat in my heart change its tune. I turned back and continued to walk along the stone path. I couldn't stop my smile as I took in everything. It was overwhelming. Tall trees with beautiful roses hanging from them upside down were scattered about.

I turned back towards Jace. "Roses don't grow upside down."

He winked at me. "They do here. This is how enchantress roses grow to their true perfection. The special ones," he clarified.

"Holy waters!" I said too excitedly and whirled around a few times before stopping to face Jace. "This is astonishing! How frackin' cool!" I turned back.

A lavender rose on one of the rose bushes caught my eye. It wasn't possible, was it? I walked closer towards the bush. As I approached, brightness appeared from both my left and right. The fireflies were coming closer to me. I stopped moving and waited for them to reach me. As they neared, they began to swirl all around me like a tornado. Almost as if they were performing a light show for me. They danced all around my body like they were cleansing me. I felt them throughout my hair and my skin. It was such a delight that I gasped and giggled.

It was then that I realized that I was five feet off the ground, floating in the air so gracefully. For a second, I was frightened. The wind softly blew through me, not at me. It was an extraordinary feeling. For some reason, it was as if the wind *liked* me. Like it was happy to see me. It was spectacular. In that moment, I knew I was getting higher because the roses were getting closer. There it was. The lavender rose! The rarest enchantress rose in the world was right before me, and I finally got the chance to behold it. It was stunning and it illuminated so lovely right before my eyes.

I looked down towards Jace. He was still in the same spot as before with his hands crossed over his chest. He looked puzzled or upset. I wasn't too sure. It was hard to read him. I didn't know him well enough yet. But one thing was certain, he didn't look happy. His mouth was tight, and his eyes took on a green glow. Before I could think about it too much, my head brushed against a few leaves. When I looked up, lavender roses illuminated even brighter.

My fingers plucked one out of the bush. There were no thorns to poke me. The bloom I picked was more beautiful than the others. Its petals were perfect and opened just right. And there was a shadow of a glow inside. I put my nose to it and inhaled the rich scent of rose-lavender.

"Incredible" I whispered to it.

Before I knew it, my feet settled gently on the ground and I steadied myself. I hadn't even realized I was coming down. Magically, Jace was right next to me with a confused look in his eyes. *So, he was confused not angry, but why?*

"What's wrong, Jace?"

He came closer and rested his forehead against mine. "I need to tell you something. Something important. And I'm not sure how upset you'll be. No, that's a lie. I think you'll be very upset. I don't want to upset you or hurt you. It makes my heart ache to think that I might distress you." With the words out, he leaned his head back, not meeting my gaze.

Based on his body language, I knew that whatever it was, it was bothering him. I wrapped my hands around his neck. Putting my hand into his hair, I gently tilted his head back down so he was forced to look at me.

I tapped a soft kiss to his lips. "Let's make a deal." I didn't want anything to ruin this precious moment. "Whatever it is that you want to tell me, tell me after the Tri Feast."

Hopefully, the smile on my face assured him that I trusted him. He'd never hurt me on purpose. Whatever had happened, we'd deal with together. So long as he wasn't going to tell me that he'd decided to mate with Priscilla or something along those lines. The broken woman I was a few weeks ago would've demanded answers now. Would've already been assuming the absolute worst. But the new me, or maybe the old me, was confident in what Jace and I shared. I knew that we'd get through it. *Together.*

He seemed shocked by my suggestion. And maybe it was crazy to delay dealing with an issue. But *this* right here, being in his secret garden, was such a great mix of pleasure. I wanted to enjoy it some more. "Today's a day I cannot begin to even conceive. I've always wanted to see an enchantress lavender rose. I never thought I'd get the opportunity, and today you gave me that. You didn't know of that secret wish in my heart. But somehow you made it come true. No way do I want to spoil the moment with bad news right now. From your body language alone, I can tell it isn't good. It can wait, Jace. It must wait. Tonight's about us. And magic."

He relaxed a little and planted a few kisses on my lips. I couldn't help the giggle that escaped me.

"You're full of surprises, my enchantress." He smiled, his face full of adoration.

"*Me?* What about you? What else are you hiding here on your land?"

"Many things." He winked. "This garden is special to me. I wanted to share it with you."

"Thank you. It's exquisite. I love it."

"Jasinda, how did you do that with the fireflies?"

"What do you mean? I didn't *do* anything."

"The fireflies are always in my garden. They light it up with such talent, and they're the ones who collect the roses for me. But I've *never* seen them interact that way with anyone before. Not even my mother and they adore her." His fingers stroked through my hair.

"Really?"

"Yes."

"I just figured that was what they did. Huh?" Lacing our fingers together, we began to stroll this magical world.

That was strange. I wasn't as frightened as I probably should've been. I just thought it was normal. He hadn't freaked out when I'd been airborne, so I hadn't either. I looked down at my rose and just stared at its beauty right in my hand. I saw a petal move and stopped walking.

"What is it, enchantress?"

"I thought I saw the petal move."

I looked up at him then and found a smirk upon his lips. *What was he hiding now?* Dropping my eyes back down, I watched the petal move again. A soft breath whooshed out. *Why were the petals moving?* Just when

I was about to ask him that very question, the petals flew apart. *Butterflies.* The petals were butterflies. Beautiful butterflies. I could see tiny faces with big eyes. Lavender eyes. They all had lavender eyes.

"Holy waters!" This day keeps getting better and better. "Hi."

They bowed their heads and spoke in unison, "Hi, princess."

What the heck? They called me princess. Their voices were so adorable and childlike. I looked back down and discovered that my rose was *way* smaller than before. It was like a closed rose and had no illumination at all. *Oh.* So, the butterflies were the reason why this rose was so rare.

"Are all enchantress lavender roses filled with butterflies?" I asked.

"Yes, we're the reason for the bloom and the illumination," they said, once again in unison.

"Is that why no one has really ever seen one?"

"Yes. We're hidden in magical places like these gardens."

"Ok. This is frackin' awesome. So, do I put you back, or do you fly away to be free?"

"You can keep us if you like and we'll always blossom for you."

"*Really?*"

"Yes."

"Holy waters!!! This is so cool!"

When I finally stopped staring at the wondrous creatures, Jace's lips were pressed into a tight line. He was trying not to laugh. He kept covering his mouth with his hand.

"What?" I huffed at him.

"You're like a kid in a toy store. I like it."

"It's your fault. You keep surprising me with amazing things."

"If amazing you with things looks and feels like this, then I want to spend my life amazing you... No, I want to amaze you beyond my existence. Because the joy and lightness in you every single time you find wonder in even the smallest of things… I feel too. The connection we have allows me to feel your emotions amplified by my own. It's like the best high in the world for your pleasure to infiltrate my heart and soul."

His words stunned me. They sounded like he might be just as crazy about me as I was about him. Before I could respond, his mouth claimed mine in an intense kiss that seemed to say everything the two of us were afraid to say out loud.

When his lips relinquished mine, he grabbed my free hand and tugged me along the stone path. We walked silently as the butterflies flitted alongside me. A waterfall appeared at the end of the path. Surprisingly, this one was even more beautiful than the magic one. Birds were singing from their perches on the rocks while butterflies flew around the water. Fireflies flew low enough to make the water ripple. Fog creeped along the edge of the cascading water. The sight stole my breath. I squeezed his hand, telling him that I loved it without speaking. Because right now he'd left me speechless. I wanted to dive into the water and never leave. This felt like home to me. As Jace gathered me in his arms and laid me down onto the soft grass, the magic of the moment amplified as he showed me without words how much he adored me. My mind, body, heart, and soul were at home in this place, with this man. I felt more complete than ever before.

Chapter Sixty

Jasinda

I woke up in Jace's California king bed. The sheets were dark grey and a luxurious silk. They felt so soft against my skin. Last night, when we'd returned from his garden, we'd made love without inhibitions. It was odd, in the garden when we were surrounded by the wilderness, Jace was slow, methodical and restrained in the tender way he took me. Here in the luxury of his room, he was wild and unhindered. And so was I. He'd had his way with me all night. *How the hell could this man last all night?* My pussy needed a rest, but then again, it came to life every single time he was near. *Traitor.*

He didn't even let me put my panties back on when we went to sleep last night. We went to bed naked and we woke up naked. At least I did, alone in this huge bed. I knew somewhere around here, he'd left me a note. I shifted around in the bed and found it. As always, he explained his day. When I sat up, I saw he'd already had breakfast brought up for me. He made me feel like a queen. His queen. Today was the Tri Feast and everyone would be arriving at 5 PM. My nerves were still fluttering but I sucked it up and got in the shower.

I dressed in jeans, a Green Lantern t-shirt, and boots, just in case I was riding to the Tri Feast on one of the horses. I ended the look with the jewelry Silvo gifted me and decided to find Anthony. As I made my way downstairs, I heard voices. That sounded like Angie. *What was Angie doing here?* When I made it into the hall going towards the kitchen, I saw them.

"Yes, I told her last night," Angie said to Ant.

"Good. I'm glad we're now all open with each other."

"So am I," I interrupted.

They both spun around with surprised, but happy, looks on their faces. Angie walked towards me to give me a hug. I embraced her and looked over her outfit. She too was wearing jeans, a t-shirt and boots.

"What are you doing here?" I asked, shocked to see her here.

"I'm attending the Tri Feast today. Jace called and invited me to come. He thought you might appreciate another friend in attendance while you meet everyone," she said smoothly, "Anyways, I also have a meeting with him. It's about joining his pack. He thinks I might be a good fit. I'll be the judge of that." She folded her arms across her chest.

"Really?" Anthony and I said in unison.

"Don't look so surprised." She shot daggers at Anthony. "You of all people know what I'm talking about."

"Yes, I do know. You should've listened when I asked you to meet with him before. But noooo, you said you'd do it on your own time. Look how that worked out for you. You met him anyways." Ant actually stuck his tongue out at her and folded his arms across his chest.

She tried to grab it with her fingers but he was too fast. I just laughed and walked past them to the kitchen. They followed me as I opened the fridge to get a glass of water.

"You're nervous about today, aren't you?" he asked me.

"Is it that noticeable?" I asked.

"Yes, you tend to go for a drink of water whenever you're nervous. Wait. What the hell are those?"

"What?" I asked.

"The damn sparkly jewelry on your right hand," Angie chimed in.

"Oh, that. It's what was in those gift boxes you picked up from Angie to bring to me."

"Who sent them?" he asked.

"Pretty nice," Angie said.

"Silvo," I timidly confessed.

Anthony stilled for a few seconds. He looked at the jewelry and then at me again. "Has Jace seen them?"

"No, not yet. I wasn't sure how to approach him about it. But it's not a big deal, right?"

"It's a big fuckin' deal!" he screeched.

"Why?" I asked in horror.

"Why…why? Because you're his…his…his…ma… his girlfriend," he finished with a stutter.

"So?"

"So?" He turned to Angie. "A little help here."

"Nah, I'm good. This one's all you. I don't know the story behind everything, and I don't care. The jewelry is fuckin' beautiful and it looks perfect on her."

"Goddesses all around, please help me with these two!" he bellowed.

"Hey, don't be calling the goddesses into this, they'd probably be on our side," Angie playfully scolded him.

"They mean something to me, Ant. I can't explain it, but I feel like these belong on me. They fit perfectly."

"He's probably trying to court you."

"He still loves his wife or ex-wife. She left him and he knew that I loved butterflies so he gave them to me," I said nonchalantly.

"Gave you what?" said the voice that always did something to my skin and my heart.

I straightened, looking past Ant and Angie to find Jace leaning against the table. *Oh shit.* He didn't look very happy.

Chapter Sixty-One

Jace

I watched as she straightened at my question. She stared at me with a shocked look on her face. I almost wanted to laugh but managed to keep it at bay. When I'd left my office to go check on her, I heard voices in the kitchen and overheard the whole story about Silvo giving her jewelry. *Why? Why would he give away his wife's jewelry? And why to* my *mate?* Especially rare pieces. From the moment I entered the kitchen, I eyed every piece on her right hand.

I had to admit the man had great taste and I also knew they were custom made. They weren't made in any jewelry store. Those stones and diamonds were from another realm. Just like the ones I'd used in my water fountain. They were way more valuable than what could be found in regular jewelry stores. What she wore was priceless because they're made of metal and stone purer than anything found on Earth. And that wasn't even considering the anklet, necklace and ring she already owned.

Silently, I leaned against the table and reached for an apple. I polished it with my shirt then bit into it, all while watching her. She snapped out of her daze and walked over to me. Standing in front of me, her face was filled with apology.

"Silvo gave me these and don't ask me why, because I truly don't know," she said without taking a breath. I remained quiet, because I knew there was more. "I *think* he gave them to me because I love butterflies. They seem like a matching set," she finished.

"You do?" I asked her.

"Yes, I think they're one of the most beautiful and peaceful creatures known to mankind."

"There are plenty of butterflies for you to love in the secret garden." I straightened, becoming serious. "What I don't understand is *why* he'd give you his wife's jewelry."

"Maybe he just wanted to get rid of them and thought it would be nice to give them to Jasinda," Angie said cheerily.

"Maybe, but it's still odd. Those pieces of jewelry once belonged to a princess," I stated. They all gasped at my words.

"Oh, that's right." Jasinda remembered.

"Yes, that's why I'm confused as to why he would give them up so easily. It's said that he truly loved her. Rumor has it that they were a great couple and then she left. Like nothing ever happened," I explained as I took another bite of my apple.

Sympathy reflected in her eyes. Her ability to empathize with others would make her a perfect queen. A whole new level of appreciation for my mate filled my heart. I couldn't help the small smirk that tipped my lips at calling her that in my mind.

She stepped closer to me and leaned up on her tiptoes as I went for another bite. Just as I bit down, she bit the opposite side of my apple. *Shit, that was sexy as hell.* She smiled as she chewed the piece in her mouth. My hormones raged. I wanted to grab her and flip her on her belly, then fuck her.

"If you want me to take them off, I will. I don't want to upset you or disrespect what we have. They're just bits of metal and stone. They don't mean anything to my heart, which is yours. But they do feel right on me, Jace. I can't explain it, but I feel like he chose the right person to give them to. If it bothers you, I'll remove them. But know this, I normally wouldn't care to do so. I'm only offering out of respect for you."

My heart jumped for joy at her consideration for my feelings. I'd spent enough time with her to know she was her own person and normally did whatever she wanted. Never caring what someone else thought unless it was out of respect. That right there proved to me that she felt our mating bond, whether she knew about it or not. I was pissed at first that he dared to give my mate jewelry. But then again, he'd sent them to her rather than hand them in person. He must not know that she's taken. And they represented something she loved. *How could I ask her to take them off?* Perhaps he and I needed to have a talk, so I could understand why he'd gifted her the jewelry. I wanted my mate happy, and happy she would be, even at the cost of me hating the jewelry.

"They look good on you. Keep them, they're rightfully yours."

I dove in for a soft taste of her lips and felt her body warm up. Moving back, I looked at her friends. Angie was smiling like The Joker and Anthony was shocked as shit at my response.

"I'm glad you could join us, Angie. Want to have your appointment moved up to now?"

"Heck yeah," she said as she walked up to me. "Lead the way."

I smiled at her. She'd make a great addition to my pack. And someone else who Jasinda already loved would be close by. I looked at my girl.

"What are you doing today?"

"You," she blurted out and quickly put her hand over her mouth.

Gods, I loved this woman. She was just as sex-crazed with me as I was with her.

"I mean…"

"Oh, you meant it girl. Don't take it back." Angie grinned.

"I'm going to see your mother. She asked me if I'd be willing to help today. I said yes."

"Good. Did she tell you about her body essentials being sold online?"

"It was all she talked about. She was extremely happy that she took both of our advice. More mine than yours." She winked at me.

My mother could take her advice over mine anytime.

"You can take the credit. She started listening when you arrived. Besides, this is what she likes to do. Now other pack communities are reaching out to her because you decided to send a package to the Landers. Now the Landers are recommending my mother to everyone they know," I informed her.

"Wait, so you're saying those labels you had me print were for his mother?" Angie asked with surprise in her voice.

"Yes, I told you that."

"No, you asked me for a favor and gave me the info. I just delivered like a good employee and friend would do."

"Ok. Regardless, that's great news. I'm so happy for your mother," Jasinda replied.

"Mr. Landers will be staying here for a few days with his family. He wants to have a meeting with my mother and me about marketing her product on a whole new level."

"Niiiice!" Jasinda and Angie said in harmony.

Oh boy. What have I gotten myself into?

"Jinx! You owe me a Pepsi," Jasinda said quickly, pointing a finger at Angie.

"Damn you, woman! You always win."

I cleared my throat at them both, amused by the playful arguing back and forth.

"Sorry," they both said.

"Let's start that appointment, shall we?" I urged.

Giving Jasinda one last kiss on her lips, I walked away with Angie by my side. I listened to see if Anthony would say anything. He'd been pretty quiet throughout the whole exchange.

"You see, nothing to worry about. He's not mad. Well, I hope he's not mad. I don't want to piss him off just yet. I'm enjoying him," Jasinda said to Anthony when she thought I was out of earshot.

Inwardly, I smiled at her comment. She was making it way too easy for me to not regret how we had mated.

"No, he's not mad. But then again, I think he'd do anything to make you happy. You should see your face when your happy, Ja," he replied. "It's worth it for someone who likes you. And it's more than like for him."

"Remember, I can't always look in the mirror when I'm happy. But he already does make me happy. All the time. So, let's try not to worry tonight, because I'm nervous enough as it is about meeting everyone."

"Why? They're going to love you. You'll see."

"I hope so. This is his pack and pack is family. I don't want to be booted out just yet."

"Don't worry. Jace wouldn't let that happen."

Anthony was right about that. I wouldn't let it happen. If I lost pack members over her, then they truly weren't pack. Tonight, I'd get to see if the pack really welcomed her.

Chapter Sixty-Two

Jasinda

After helping Jace's mother prepare the bread and cookies for the feast, she told me to make my way to the campsite. I hesitated, unsure where to go. She pointed in the direction for me to walk and gave me an encouraging smile. I nodded and left the hut where the pack prepared the food. Straining my ears, I could hear the crowd from here. Two huge sycamore trees framed a trail. Fireflies lit the pathway as I got closer. The night breeze was just right. Luminescent white butterflies flickered all around. It was like the white color of their wings was just bright enough for the dark night. "This is so heavenly. Just incredible," I whispered to no one and continued towards the trees. It was magical. I spun around completely enchanted. The butterflies followed me like little lanterns. Jace's realm was truly the most beautiful place I'd ever been.

Jace came from behind the tree, as if he'd been waiting for me. "What took you so long to walk the path?"

"I've never walked from this side before. It's breathtaking. And a bit distracting"

"Like you." He came closer, and his warmth wrapped itself around me. Without seeing or hearing him, I would've known it was him. I would've known it was his closeness that made me feel this way. "You'll have plenty of time to walk these woods. But now we have many guests to see, including ou—the pack."

Wrapping both arms around my waist, he lowered his head and kissed me. In return, I wound my hands around his neck and deepened the kiss. I was spellbound. In a good way, of course. He gently broke our kiss but stayed connected. "You ready?"

I slid both my hands from his neck up to cup his cheeks in a slow, affectionate way. "I'm extremely nervous. These are your people. I want them to like me. And I have no clue about what to expect tonight. It's all mystical and a bit eerie."

He smiled and gave me a tap on my lips with his. "You're feeling the magic that's here. Those few souls that still fight to stay. The magic is stronger than usual tonight. Their presence is more apparent. Maybe it's you. Maybe it's us. Whatever it is, don't brush the feeling away. It's special. Accept it and go with it. You think you can do that tonight?"

I guessed so. I wasn't sure what he was asking me. "You mean go with the flow of the night?"

"Exactly. Whatever you feel, I want you to act on it and not be afraid."

"So, join in and participate? I think I can do that."

"Good!" a voice rumbled, nearly sending me leaping into Jace's arms. "Now, can you two lovebirds take your hands off each other so I can have her?"

"Dalo!" Jace growled over me.

I smiled in satisfaction at Jace's reaction. I turned to look into Dalo's face. He was just a few feet away. Close enough for me to shake his hand.

"Hi. Nice to see you again," I blurted out, not knowing how I should greet his beta.

"I see you're enchanting our alpha king. It's nice to see him so enamored." He gave me googly eyes.

I laughed. "Thank you."

"No, thank you."

"Dalo, is there a reason you interrupted us?" Jace gritted the last part out.

"Yes, there is someone here who needs to speak with you. I figured while you speak with them, I'll entertain your...um...girlfriend and show her off to the pack."

I blushed at Dalo's words. "It's fine, Jace. It would be a pleasure to have Dalo introduce me to everyone."

Jace pressed a kiss on my forehead and gave Dalo his eyes. "I'll rip your throat out if you don't make this fun for her."

My jaw dropped at Jace's words, but Dalo laughed. Jace's lips twitched and relaxed.

"I wouldn't have it any other way." Dalo saluted, while Jace winked at me and walked off.

Now that we were alone, I didn't know what to say. I felt shy and unsure of myself. Dalo cleared his throat and gave me his arm to loop mine through. We began walking into the campsite. As soon as we crossed into the clearing, there were lots of eyes on me. They were all whispering and smiling. It made me a little more nervous. My eyes rapidly took in the scattered firepits, seating areas, and people everywhere.

Dalo was really enjoying showing me off as the alpha's girlfriend. His chest puffed out, and he had a protective, intimidating stare. I smiled broadly, but inside I giggled like crazy. After meeting several people, I searched around looking for the pups and Jace. Dalo turned me to my right. Right there where we'd once sat, where I'd first met Skyla the dragon, stood Jace and the rest of the pups. Edwin, Tony, and Kat were all circling Jace, and they were excited about something. Samuel was still in wolf form and I knew Jace was worried he wouldn't change into his human form. *So was I.*

I turned my head to face Dalo. "What are the pups so excited about?"

"The prophecy of the restoration of our ancestors. The story is passed down from generation to generation," he spoke hesitantly.

"What do you mean?" I asked.

He gently tugged me along and we walked towards the campfire where Jace and the pups were. "Listen. It's an interesting story," he said and placed me next to Jace.

"My enchantress," he softly said and planted a kiss on my lips.

"Dalo mentioned something about a prophecy?" I poked.

"You *see*, Jasinda doesn't know about it. Come on, tell the story," Edwin begged and gave Jace puppy eyes.

Jace burst out laughing and so did I. I couldn't help it. He really had puppy eyes.

Edwin folded his arms over his chest and growled. "Really, guys? Ganging up on me isn't cool. Besides, we need to hear the whole thing. How does it go....? Um...When wolf can dwell on water, he can reach the moon? No wait....um...when—"

"No, that's not how it goes. Sit. All of you." Jace's eyes landed on me and he pulled me against him. Then he sat down on the log with me on his lap.

"It is said that there will be souls that are soulmates of the Tri Moons. These souls together will bring power and add strength to one another. Packs will live longer, children will survive births and power will increase amongst these souls. Our ancestors' souls will no longer be lost to us." Jace squeezed my thigh as I listened intently. "Even though we have the Tri Feast every month to honor our ancestors, to keep as much of their souls alive, this union will bring them to join us and celebrate together."

"Wait, you mean like physically celebrate with them? Like see them, *see them*?"

"Yes, the Tri Feasts are for celebrating and embracing our ancestors. They're our guidance and teachers even if their bodies are no longer walking among us."

"Oh wow. That's pretty awesome. So, right now your ancestors are here?"

"Yes, you can't see them, but you can faintly *feel* their presence," Jace informed me.

Ha, well that was interesting. "So, if these souls were restored, does that mean I'd be able to see them too?"

"That I'm not sure, my enchantress. I hope so." He gave me an apologetic look and continued to speak, "Want to hear the way the prophecy was really told?" He looked me in the eyes.

"Yes," I whispered.

He cleared his throat, "When the beast's soul can dwell underwater, and the sea can howl at the moon... The love between souls will burn hotter than lava. Mating hearts will swoon as destined souls join... Binding the hearts into one's true mold... Ancestor's spirits will rise high again, restoring the order, uniting them again."

"Wow…I really had it wrong," Edwin purred.

Jace nodded. "Yes, you did, son. But not many remember as the hope has diminished."

"Why?" Edwin asked before I could.

"Because this prophecy was told centuries ago and the souls have yet to join," Jace told him.

I put both my hands on Jace's face and turned his head to face me completely. Heat radiated from his glowing embers and I loved every moment of his stare. "What about you, do you still have hope?" I inquired. While he searched my face, I linked my fingers with his in my lap.

He tilted his head, and then tipped it down to stare at my lap. He stayed like that for a few more seconds, then looked me dead in the eyes. His were illuminated and intense. "I didn't before, but since I met you, hope has risen within me like a force I can't control."

Ok. Not the answer I was expecting. "But why *me*?"

"I'd lost hope before because the prophecy has never been alive for me. No one has experienced it and no one believes it will ever happen since it's been centuries since this vision was foreseen." He stood us both up and I noticed a few others were now standing closer, listening. "Then you came along and I felt something I've never felt before. A spark. A spark that I've been yearning for. I thought I'd just have to pick a mate and move on. I should've mated by now. But somehow, it hadn't happened for me."

"So, you want to mate with me?"

How was it that a man like him had never found his mate? Was he considering me as a potential mate? Could I be enough for him, being that I'm just a human? As much as I'd love to entertain the idea of being mated to him, I was unsure.

A few coughs sounded behind me and pain flashed in his eyes. *Ouch. I guess that would be a no.* "Nope. Don't answer that. Forget I asked." I struggled to grasp the edges of my torn pride.

"My enchantress, I need to—"

"No, no, no. Just finish the story. I want to know more," I interrupted him and put on a bright face. I was too afraid he'd say something that might hurt me. I liked how things were going between us and I didn't want anything to ruin that right now. "*Please*. I'm curious."

Sighing, he continued, "The souls are a power source for our ancestors and the connection between the prophesized couple will bring balance back to them. All magic will return to our ancestors, making the supernatural grow with power. I don't know if you remember or not, but our original ancestors were dragons. So, restoring *our* ancestors will save the dragons."

My mind rewound to that magical night by the waterfall when Jace had told me the legend about saving the dragons. *So, then the ancestors would be able to save themselves from extinction.* I'd stared at him in complete shock. Once again, I'd known there was magic in this world. I'd *known* there were supernaturals amongst us, but I'd never known there was so much power out there. "That's pretty amazing, but how do *I* give you hope?"

"I believe those soulmates are nearby. I began sensing *something* the first night we met. I didn't understand it then, but I'm starting to wonder about this new change." He grabbed my hand and put it up to his heart. "*Everything* has changed since you came along. The pack has grown stronger. Their senses are on point. They seem more energetic than before. Charged. The water has more shimmer to it. The trees grow with more life and the animals are excited, especially the horses. Our ancestors are drawing closer to us."

"So, I came along and things started to change? Am I getting this right? Because it doesn't make sense to me." *I'm missing something for sure.*

He tipped his head towards Dalo and Dalo came straight to me as Jace continued, "I believe *you* are part of this. I think it begins with you. I'm not sure who it ends with, but I think your spirit is needed. Necessary. The ancestors are whispering about you, but we cannot understand what they're trying to tell us." He kissed me quickly then looked at Dalo. "Keep taking her around, I need to speak with Ulises."

"Understood. Come on, I have a few others to show you off to," Dalo told me softly.

Jace smiled and nodded for me to go along with Dalo, and I did.

The trees were swaying, and birds were chirping as we approached a couple. The Landers. The tension in my body fled as Mr. Lander brought me into a hug. "It's nice to see you again, Jasinda."

"Jasinda!" his pregnant wife squealed. "Oh, how nice to see you." She planted two kisses on each of my cheeks.

"Hi Mrs. Landers. How's the pregnancy treating you?"

"Oh, I've been a little sick, but thankfully nothing more."

After speaking with the Landers for a few more minutes, Dalo moved us along. I lost track of all the people I'd met from Jace's pack, not to mention members of neighboring packs. I hoped there wouldn't be a pop quiz later. Throughout all the introductions, I felt Jace's presence by my side. Every time I looked in his direction, his eyes beamed pride at me, melting my heart and calming my nerves.

Finally, Jace was done with official matters and Dalo escorted me back to him, but before I reached Jace, Elier stepped in our way. He smiled broadly.

"Hey. How are you liking the Tri Feast so far?"

"It's a lot. So much to feel, see and know. I was a little nervous, but since Dalo here," I said patting his arm, "made sure he showed me off, I think the nerves have been settled."

He chuckled, stepping closer. Dalo growled. "Relax. I was just going to hug her. Is that ok?"

"Of course, it is." I roughly pulled my hand from Dalo's arm since he had a death grip on it and accepted Elier's hug.

"I'm happy for you. You look *really* happy," he stated while we were still embraced.

That relieved me because he'd looked funny when we'd had lunch. "Be very careful and act on your instincts. No matter what. You belong here." He pulled back and stared at me.

I didn't understand why he'd say that, but I answered him anyway. "Will do."

Relief flickered in his eyes as he walked off. My gaze followed Elier's direction. Until I caught sight of Priscilla. She was stealing glances at Jace.

He was talking to a man who was all jeweled up with rings on nearly all his fingers. He looked a little upset as Jace spoke with him.

Jace on the other hand, had his hands in his pockets. The veins along his arms were prominent as his muscles clenched. *He was pissed and trying to control his anger.*

"Dalo, I think I can walk to Jace from here."

"Maybe we should come back in a little while. I thought the meeting was ending, but I was wrong."

"Well, ending or not, I'm heading over to him. He's upset and needs me."

As I got closer to the pair of alphas, I overheard the other man say, "I'm sorry, Jace. I can't help how I feel. I'm just so disappointed. I always envisioned you as my son-in-law." He shook his head. "I just don't see why you couldn't have chosen Priscilla as your mate. She's pretty. She's of royal blood. She's strong. She'd give you beautiful wolflins."

"She's not the one I want. I'm sorry but Priscilla isn't the one meant for me."

"I'll try to accept your choice and get over my disappointment. But my daughter is heartbroken that you didn't mate with her. It'll take some time for us both to accept whom you've selected to pledge yourself to."

I'd heard enough. Jace's distress rose with every sentence out of that man's mouth. I walked over without another thought and placed my hand on his arm right above his elbow. I gently squeezed and he took his hand out of his pocket and draped it over my shoulders. He looked down at me and smiled. "Are you having fun?" he asked.

"Yes. Are you?" I questioned.

"I'm trying to."

"Is this her?" asked the man with too many rings.

"Yes, Jasinda meet Ulises."

"Hello. It's a pleasure," I said with a small bow, then I leaned towards him and planted a kiss on his cheek.

"Well, the pleasure is all mine. I can see why Jace mated with you." Jace went rigid next to me.

"I'm sorry, what?" I said, not sure if he'd said what I *thought* he said.

"You guys are mated. I understand why, now. I thought my daughter was just being a spoiled brat about it. But I get it. You're perfect for him," he said nonchalantly.

"Daddy!" Priscilla cried out as she came into view.

I kept my own anger in check because I wanted nothing more than to punch her in that annoying mouth of hers.

Her father sighed, "Now Priscilla, you have to be a good sport about this. You can't always get what you want. Besides, you know the phrase the humans use- 'you snooze, you lose'. You lost, my little pup."

I wanted to laugh but thought it best not to. She slumped beside him and glared at me. I could *almost* see red in her eyes. Any minute now, she'd have smoke coming out of her ears.

"You're *not* one of us. How is it that *you* got him to mate with you in such a short time?" she shouted.

What the hell was she talking about?

"Priscilla!" Jace's voice vibrated through me. But I just stood there quietly and looked past her, choosing not to acknowledge her. I didn't want this night to be ruined.

"No, let her answer me. I want to hear it from her." She got closer and I felt Jace move to get in front of me. I tightened my grip on him, and he froze.

"What? You can't speak now?" she mocked. "You had plenty to say when you barged into my training session the other day."

"Nope. Sorry, I was completely ignoring you. I was too busy drowning your annoying bratty cries," I calmly stated. "You obviously wouldn't know what courtesy is because you can't hear yourself."

Jace trembled beside me. When I looked over at him, he was trying to stifle his laughter. I looked back at her and just as I'd expected, I'd pissed her off more than I should have. But I kept my hold on Jace, because I was still hearing the word *mated* in my head over and over.

"Priscilla, behave. That's no way to treat your alpha queen." her father scolded.

Alpha queen? How was it possible that Jace and I were mated? Once he mates, he automatically becomes king. Shit, what the hell was I missing here? I kept my cool because I didn't need them to think I was clueless. Tugging on Jace, I began walking us away. I was hoping to get him alone and talk to him about what just happened.

"Where the hell do you think you're going, bitch?" Priscilla roared behind us.

Oh, hell no! The whole world ground to a halt right before me and everyone froze. I mean *everyone* stopped what they were doing to look at her. Jace was already turning around to face her when I pulled on his hand to stop. He obliged and I slowly turned around and walked forward.

"Is that all you've got? Calling me a bitch while my back is turned?" I bit out the 'bitch' part. "What kind of princess are you? Maybe you need to return to princess academy and get educated again. You have *no* respect for your father, your pack or yourself. Not even your alpha. Like it or not, I am his and he is *MINE!*" I yelled.

She lunged forward and I sidestepped her, putting my foot out to trip her. She fell to the ground, anger seeping from her. Hastily, she got to her feet. Her father stepped in front of me with his back to me.

"*Enough,* Priscilla! You're acting like a child. I *won't* have this," he growled.

She smiled. A wicked smile played across her face. Any hint of beauty she possessed disappeared. Something wasn't right. *This* was what Scarlet was talking about when she sensed danger, because the hairs on my entire body stood up at that moment. Priscilla let out a howl. Panic made my heart race. I turned to Jace, who was already reaching for me.

"We need to get everyone out of here," I said firmly.

"We need to get you out of here," he returned even more firmly.

"Jace, you don't understand. Something isn't right. I can *feel* it. Something's very wrong."

He looked me over. A growl ripped from his throat. Next to me, his body vibrated with anger. Canines appeared in his mouth as he turned towards Priscilla. He roared with such a boom, that even Priscilla was scared. I wasn't scared. I was worried. She screamed at him. It looked as though she was challenging him. She shifted into wolf form. Growls erupted all around us. I looked to his pack. Every pair of eyes was glowing. They were all on the verge of shifting, their canines shining brightly in the dark of night.

A few of them moved closer to me, but their eyes never left Priscilla. Others surrounded her father. He didn't look scared, but he too seemed worried.

"Priscilla, don't do this. He's your alpha. If you do this, I'm not able to save you. He has the right to kill you if he chooses," her father pleaded painfully.

Shit. I pulled my hand from Jace's. A pained and confused look marred his beautifully angry features. I walked around the wolves who'd gathered near me. *They must be here for my protection.* I shifted my body in front of Jace, spreading my legs apart in a fighting stance. Lifting my curled hands in front of me, I assumed a boxer's posture. My father had trained me for this. Being the daughter of a powerful man had its benefits. I'd trained with the Mitchell brothers, so I could learn to protect myself against anyone who tried to do me harm or use me against my father. He'd had me train with wolves before, though I never understood why. Now I knew. This would be no different. She's a shifter with more strength than normal wolves. I can figure it out.

"What are you doing?" Jace bit out.

I ignored him. "Priscilla, I know you can understand me. So, I'm going to give you one chance to back down. You don't get to challenge him. You *won't* challenge him!" I yelled.

But nothing. She just kept growling and howling. *So be it bitch. You'll see what my father taught me.* I wasn't going down without a good fight.

Chapter Sixty-Three

Jace

"**J**asinda, get out of the way!" I yelled at her.

"No. We're a team, remember? Trust me, Jace. Let me handle this, woman to woman," she said with a bite of authority in her voice.

My heart jolted at her reminder that we were a team. Perhaps she wasn't that upset at me. *And, since when did my sweet mate possess the ability to go all mean and growly like a wolf?* The last time they had an encounter, she didn't have traits of a wolf. She looked like she was ready to kick ass, but my concern was that Priscilla was in wolf form. A big disadvantage for Jasinda. If she would've stayed in human form, I'd have no problem letting this play out until I needed to step in. I remembered the punch Jasinda had given Miranda the night we'd met and the punch she perfectly landed at Priscilla's face a few days ago.

"You can't get involved, Jace. Your mate just accepted the challenge. You *have* to let them fight it out," Ulises said.

"Fuck no! She isn't a wolf, so those rules don't apply to her. As a wolf, Priscilla has the advantage here. If she shifts back to her human form, then I'll allow it. If she stays in wolf form, then her original challenge to me stands and I'll shift right now," I growled at him. There was no way in hell I was letting Jasinda take on a wolf.

"Let your mate handle this. I'd rather them fight and you stay out of it. At least that way, my daughter lives. Jasinda won't be able to kill her and Priscilla has never killed anyone. I know my daughter. She won't kill your mate. Just let them fight."

"NO!" I roared at the fuckin' asshole.

"Fine. Priscilla, shift back and fight her woman to woman. Show some honor," her father pleaded.

Instead, Priscilla leaped up into the air to attack. I moved to block her but Jasinda lunged forward at the hurtling wolf. With the grace of a fighter, she slid low enough to duck under the blur of copper fur. She grabbed Priscilla's legs, causing her to slam to the ground with a hard thump. Jasinda straightened into the same stance as before. Around us, the pack murmured with encouragement for my mate.

"Damn, enchantress. Don't attack first. Wait for her to attack again. That was wise of you to wait. Keep letting her attack you first," I mentally coached. She looked at me and nodded. She looked different now. Confident she'd win a battle with a wolf. It was amazing. Her eyes blazed with anger, but pain, fear and a deeper rage were in there too. Confusion and disbelief joined the riot of worry and fury inside me. As I watched her, I saw flecks of green flash occasionally in her eyes. *What the hell was that?*

Priscilla was angry, jealous and fearful herself. Desperation swirled around her. She charged at Jasinda, and Jasinda waited for the perfect moment to lunge at her. I was frozen in place as the scene unfolded. Jasinda threw herself forward, right at the wolf. Her hands sunk into Priscilla's neck fur. Then Jasinda twisted her body, flinging the wolf over her. *How in the world?* Then I remembered who her father was. He must have trained her to fight the supernatural. He'd trained her well. Our pack growled in admiration of her skills.

"Nice moves, my enchantress. You can show me more later."

"Thanks, my prince." She smirked at me.

Inside my chest, my heart stuttered. *She'd just claimed me as her prince.*

When she landed, I heard a crack as one of Priscilla's legs broke. Priscilla lay on the ground in a heap, whining. She wouldn't be able to fight now. It took hours for us to heal from broken bones. Unless she shifted a few times to speed up the healing process. With angry strides, I moved towards Priscilla, ready to finish her. I wanted to rip her head off.

"Don't, Jace. Not like this. Give her time to heal and then do what you want," Jasinda said softly. I ignored her sympathy for the injured wolf as it tugged at me. I could hear my mate's intake of breath. "I'm not sure how you do things but that's what I'd want if it was me."

A mate who had sympathy for those who were ruthless. As if I needed anymore confirmation that this divine creation was perfect for me. Balance was always needed in an alpha's life. She needed to bring out the humanity in me. She needed us to show forgiveness, even when we didn't want to. That's what she was doing now.

"Take your daughter out of here before I rip her head off!" I growled at Ulises.

"Thank you for showing mercy," he said with gratitude.

"You should be thanking *her*. Not me." I pointed at my mate.

"My lady. My queen. I thank you for your mercy." He bowed, then went to pick up his daughter.

"You'll want to have a talk with her. She's pissed me off twice already. The third time around, I won't be as nice as I was just now. I'll snap her neck myself. Even if it takes me hours, I'll rip her head off too," Jasinda declared.

Did I say how much I love this woman? Grunts of approval and words of encouragement from the pack backed up her words.

"You won't have her for long. She'll be claimed by another!" Priscilla's voice speared in my head.

"What are you talking about?"

"You'll see real soon. Sooner than you expect. Maybe even now." Her laughter at her own words rang manically in my head.

Her father disappeared with her between the trees. *What the hell did she mean by that?* I stared after them.

A thump drew my attention. A few winged creatures landed right in front of my mate. They almost looked like gargoyles, but they had one huge horn in the middle of their foreheads. Three of them were trying to surround her, but she managed to flee.

Edwin was right there in wolf form. He lunged for one closest to him. *Bullseye!* Edwin landed a perfect bite to the throat, sinking in deep. The gargoyle hadn't even seen him coming.

One gargoyle threw something silver and shiny at her. The other flew at her and lifted her off the ground as I proceeded to chase him. The pack came together, ready to defend their queen. The females grabbed all the children and headed back to the mansion.

In front of me, Jasinda got flung over the river. She disappeared into the woods somewhere just as I caught the gargoyle. *Fuck!* She was a good distance away from me. Those fuckers flew fast. A dark shape leapt across the water. It was Edwin. He disappeared into the woods. Fighting the gargoyle with my clawed hand, I heard a loud scream from where I'd seen them disappear. I was too busy fighting, so I wasn't able to get free. Using my infrared vision, I located her.

Panic engulfed me as I saw her on her knees with some type of cuffs strapped to her wrists. I couldn't make out all the details, but it was as if the cuffs were attached to ropes, and they were pulling her towards something.

She screamed a piercing, agonizing scream. I sliced the gargoyle's face and neck, leaving its wounds wide open. My gaze darted back towards her. A flash of light burst from the cuffs, and she was thrown back a few feet, rolling to a stop on her face.

Dear gods, please be ok. She wasn't moving. Fear wrapped itself like a burning blanket around me.

More gargoyles landed and I was afraid I wasn't going to make it to her. The beast within struggled to be free. If I let that happen, no one would be safe. And right now, I needed to keep her safe from my beast.

"Let me free!" he roared in my head.

I ignored him, knowing I couldn't communicate with him, or I'd lose control. As I watched, Edwin slowly approached her and licked at her face. Thank the gods he'd reached her. He licked and licked until I saw her hands move.

She slowly lifted her head towards him. He knelt beside her and she grabbed a huge chunk of his fur. He slowly lifted himself, helping her get to her feet. I'd never been so grateful for my infrared vision. More and more winged creatures appeared. *Shit!* I was never going to make it to her.

"Free me!" The beast raged.

Should I free him and risk her life? Her life was at risk already. Or should I hold onto my hope for Edwin to save her? My beast couldn't be trusted with the thing most precious to me.

'*She's precious to me too. I'd never hurt her. I love her too. Trust me.*' The beast pleaded.

'*I'm sorry. I can't,*' I said with regret. He was uncontrollable. I couldn't jeopardize her.

Come on, Edwin. Get her out of there.

She used him as a crutch to finally stand. Another flash of light came into view while I ripped one winged creature apart. Silvo and his sister appeared. They came to join in on the fight. Both with swords in hand, they began the bloodshed.

Chapter Sixty-Four

Jasinda

As I leaned against Edwin, a creature approached. It was huge. Like a gargoyle but on some serious steroids. It was purple with black eyes with a horn in the middle of its forehead. A scream no person should be able to make erupted from my mouth. I didn't even know it was me until I felt the vibrations in my throat. The gargoyle flew back at the sound of my scream. So did I.

With Edwin's help, we began walking back towards the river still hidden behind some trees. Through the foliage, I was able to make out figures moving erratically as the sound of metal against metal filled the normally tranquil forest. I gasped as my mind made sense of the sights and sounds. They were fighting just over the river. I froze when I heard the creature behind me. When I turned, he was raising his arm with a chain in his hand ready to strike us. Edwin rushed to attack, but the gargoyle struck out with his other hand and flung him into a tree.

I screamed again in anger, just as his hand with the chain slammed down to hit me. Immediately, I put my hands up in front of my face, making an X with my wrists to try and protect myself as best as I could. A flash of light appeared, then disappeared as I heard a clunk and felt my wrists tremble. I dropped my hands just a little to see what had happened and realized I had blocked his hit and had sent him flying back a few feet. Somehow, my bracelets had turned into an armored shield to protect me. *Holy waters! Now that was amazing.* I'd have to ask Silvo about them later. Scanning the trees, I saw Edwin limping towards me.

"Are you all right?" I asked him.

"You can communicate with me?" he asked, sounding surprise.

I froze, and something shifted in me. A lot of realizations slammed into me at once. *Yes, I could communicate with him, with all animals. I could fight and protect us. I was a warrior princess. I was Jasinda Yol Axlario. Daughter to Leto and Yolalyne Axlario. Princess to my kingdom Merkana.*

I remembered. I remembered who I was and *what* I was. With the memories came the knowledge that I needed a sword to kill the creature in front of me. Concentrating, I tried to will mine to me, but it wouldn't come. *Crap.* My powers were limited right now. *Shit, shit, shit I remembered who I am!*

"Run, Edwin. Run now!" I yelled.

"But what about you?"

"I'll be right behind you. You need to make it over the river," I told him.

"I'm not sure I can leap that far with my injured arm."

"Trust me, I'll help you with that. Now run! When you get close just jump, don't think or hesitate. Jump."

His wolf eyes penetrated mine. *"Ok."*

Hesitantly, he began running out of the trees. I decided to test my powers and make the ground underneath the gargoyle, who was coming towards me, shake. He stepped back a little, trying to balance himself and not fall.

Ok, that wasn't much but it would do for now. He roared, and his breath made the hairs on my skin disappear. In that moment, I ran, following Edwin. He was getting closer to the river. Then I saw them all. The men in the pack were ripping into the last few gargoyles on the ground.

Silvo, Silva, Jace, Elier, Dorik and Scarlet were all standing there looking right at us. My eyes collided with Jace's like they were magnets drawing me to him. Despair darkened his beautiful features. But with each step closer, relief began to creep onto his features. Those glowing green orbs urged each one of my footfalls, as if he could will me to his side. *If only.* A quick glance at Dorik broke my heart. I knew he was reliving watching Lina die. His tough exterior hid a softer side of a man worried for his brother's well-being. In an unfathomably short amount of time, I had bonded to Jace's family. I briefly took in Elier and Silva's expressions. Each of them bore a look of hopeful determination, like they knew the outcome before it even happened. Scarlet was worried and confused. And then I peered into silver pools and saw nothing. Silvo's face was blank, revealing nothing. *Why the hell were they just standing there and not helping me?* Then I noticed the air shimmering on the other bank. Silvo had apparently thrown up a band to keep the rest of the pack and gargoyles from crossing the river to my side. I could see and *feel* the struggle in Jace as he futilely fought the magic that wasn't of his world. The gargoyle was gaining on me, pounding the ground with force.

"Remove the fuckin' band, Silvo!" Jace barked with command.

But Silvo just stood there, watching and waiting. Something in his eyes held mine.

"REMOVE IT!" he roared again at Silvo.

Understanding that Silvo was waiting for me to make the command, I shook my head at Jace. The pain, confusion and desperation that rolled off him slammed into my heart. I wished I had time to talk to him, reassure him.

I locked eyes with Silvo again. At that moment, anger and rage engulfed me. Comprehension dawned on him. He knew I remembered, and I remembered it *all*. He lifted his sword and turned it so that the hilt of the sword was facing me. He knew I needed that sword and that I'd ask for it.

"WHAT THE FUCK ARE YOU DOING?" Jace roared.

"What she needs me to do," Silvo responded coolly.

Sensing my uncertainty at calling for the weapon myself, he drew his arm back and threw the sword towards me. In that moment, Edwin leapt up and I lifted the water like a wave to guide him across to safety. Thank the goddesses for that power working to its fullest and for me remembering it. Closing my eyes, I sensed the sword coming towards me. When the hilt was within reaching distance, I rocketed up in the air, grabbing it with my left hand. Spinning around in midair, I sliced the gargoyle's head off. I landed with a soft thud—my head down, sword at my side and one knee touching the ground. I didn't have to look back to check on the gargoyle. I knew his fate. I knew what I was capable of. I was a weapon.

Drawing in deep, measured breaths, I tried to calm the rage that was fighting to explode. Slowly, I lifted my head and found everyone's faces covered with shocked expressions. Everyone but Silvo, Silva and Elier. The air shimmered for a moment, then the band disappeared with a burst of light. All the gargoyles that had been contained by it, had turned to dust with the death of their leader.

Getting to my feet, I allowed myself to feel Jace's relief and love for a moment. It warmed me and acted as a temporary balm to all the torment swirling within me. Each person gathered on the opposite shore smiled at me, satisfied that I was ok. *But I wasn't.* Silva was on the verge of letting her tears go, but she inhaled a huge breath and made sure they stayed put. With shimmering eyes, she stepped forward, ready to leap across the river. I stopped her with a short shake of my head. One look at Silvo unleashed all my carefully restrained resentment. Ice gripped my heart.

Agony and fury ripped from within me, finding an outlet through an ear-splitting scream. Tears ran down my face as I dropped the sword. Sinking to my knees, I sobbed.

"*Shhh. It's ok, my enchantress. You're ok. Just come back over here. Tell me what you need, my love,*" Jace pleaded with me.

"*I'm sorry,*" I answered in a broken voice.

Covering my face, I attempted to hide the obvious emotions coursing through me. Then I balled both hands into fists and pounded the ground, shaking it a little.

"Jasinda, stop! Please!" Silva pleaded.

The crack in her voice halted me. She and I had been best friends. Like sisters to one another. I'd loved her more than I loved Angie. *How could I have forgotten someone who had been so important to me?* It broke my heart to admit it, but Silva had been my life. Our friendship had been how I'd fallen in love with Silvo. *Shit, I was in love with Silvo. Was I still in love with him?* Shaking my head, I tried to process all the newly established images in my mind. I was the one who had once been married to him. My fingers traced the band of white gold wrapped around my arm. These pieces of jewelry belonged to me. *I was the wife who had left. I was the wife he still loved.*

But I hadn't *chosen* to leave. *They* had chosen this for me. *They* had made me forget. My mother had taken advantage of my state of mind and had altered my memories. *How could they have kept me hidden? How could they have done this to me? How could they have done this to my son? Oh, dear goddesses, my son.* Impossibly, the pain intensified as I thought of my boy and of having been deprived of him all these years. *Where's my son?*

"Jasinda?" Elier said softly.

"I remember," I whispered, knowing they all could hear me.

"I know," Elier whispered back.

"I can't hold it in. I just *can't*!" I said, trying to contain my emotions. The pain of the baby I'd lost, the years robbed from me with my son, my... My breath hitched. It was all just too much ache stabbing one fragile heart at one time. There was no room for anything else. It only held anguish and anger. And those emotions cascaded like a waterfall from the cracks in my heart.

"Then don't... but control it. Remember, your powers can affect our ears," Elier reminded me.

So, I did just that. I screamed with more force than ever before, letting the sonic screams encircle me. At one point, I thought I heard Silvo telling Elier he better run and hide. But it was hard to be certain until I did hear Elier's reply.

"I'm *not* running. Damn the consequences. I'm still her royal guard," Elier screeched through my screams.

Chapter Sixty-Five

Jace

I watched the pain and anger pouring out of her, feeling sick to my stomach. Without our enhanced connection, the sight would have been unbearable. But feeling it with her was the most brutal thing I'd ever endured. I resisted the urge to tap into the memories that I could plainly see filling her mind. The wind swirled around her body in a fury, matching the torrent of emotions she was unleashing into the world.

Her hair lengthened like a cascade down her back and turned black. Her green eyes glowed through the churning debris around her. Her screams punctured me, stabbed me deeply in the heart. I wasn't sure how she'd survive the hurt. How we'd survive. She was letting it all out. Everything that had been done to her. But I sensed something else there besides what they'd taken from her. Grief. A loss of some sort.

"What the hell is happening to her?" I demanded.

"She's remembering it all. The anger, the pain, the happiness and the losses. All her memories are traveling back to her all at once. It's like being hit with a wrecking ball. It just slams right into you," Silvo explained in a calm manner. "She's even starting to get some of her powers back."

"I thought she needed her mother for that," I said.

"Her mom made a provision that would allow her memories and powers to be restored if Jasinda was ever in fear of her own life or the life of someone she loved." Silva recited. "It's the only thing her mother did right."

"Shit," I said. "Can you stop it?"

"No, only she can. It's why I put the band back in place. Her sonic scream will slice anyone that gets near her. It's hard to heal from."

How did he know so much about her? Had he brought harm to my enchantress? Just who was he to her?

Suddenly, she stopped and stood up straight.

Silvo cleared his throat, "Here it comes. It's what I deserve. And I cannot stop it from happening. It's what I regret the most from my last ten years without her," he whispered, as she held the sword in her hand.

Did he just say without her? What the fuck was going on?

She considered the sword carefully, holding it in front of her and examining it. Holding it in her right hand, she closed her eyes, and the sword disappeared into her bracelets. Just like that. Then she faced Silvo, an ache overwhelming her anger.

"Where. Is. My. Son?" she bit out.

That was unexpected. *She had a son?*

"He's safe. We should—"

"Where?" she yelled.

"Niko is with your grandmother."

"This whole *time*?"

"Yes, she was outraged at what we'd done and told me that her grandson would not train with my father."

"Has your father tried to claim him?" Fear made her voice crack and her heart race. This damn band wouldn't let me go to her. I longed to comfort her, to fix all the wrongs that had been done to her. But I didn't understand enough yet.

"Yes."

"Did you challenge him?"

"No, there was no need. Your grandmother took him before my father came to claim our son. He doesn't know where Niko is, and I'll die before I tell him."

"At least you've done *something* right," she said through gritted teeth.

I stood here numbed by what I was hearing. *Her son? Their son?* My heart cracked a little.

"Yol, please let's talk," he tried, as I saw the magic bands expand, holding us even more securely.

"Do you even *know* what you've done to me? *You* voided our marriage. People think I'm missing, or that I left you. Walked away from my family," she spat.

The gasps behind me reminded me that my entire pack was bearing witness to this soap opera.

"But that's not even what I care about. It's the fact that you made this decision for me. My mother and you. What gave you the right? You had no damn right to do what you did? After fourteen years of knowing me and seven years of pledging our lives to each other, you decided something that altered my entire life. You stole from me. My memories, my powers. I've lived ten years without you. Ten years without my *son*. He's thirteen, Silvo!!!! Thirteen! Tell me how that is right." her voice cracked and trembled. But she didn't shed a tear.

My enchantress was strong, even in the face of this unspeakable wrong that had been done to her. *Was she still my enchantress? What did all of this mean for us?* I knew she'd felt our connection, our bond. I'd give her up if that was what she wanted. It would kill me to do it, but if her heart belonged to Silvo, I'd have to do what was best for her.

I stood there in silence because I didn't know what to do. My mind raced with all the information being thrown at me like poison darts, each one aiming for the bullseye on my heart. They had a son together. She was his *wife*. The one rumored to have left him. Apparently, not by her choice. The wife he still loved. That was why he'd given her the jewelry. It was hers to begin with. *How could he have done this to her?*

"Tell me!" she screamed. Each wave of misery from her was another laceration to my bleeding heart.

"I can't, Yol. When I did what I did, I was only concerned with your safety. Nothing else. No consequences."

"Bullshit. We promised each other no lies. *Ever*. You lied. You didn't ask me what I wanted. I didn't want us to be voided. I wanted my husband to be my husband," she whispered. That dart hit the center of my heart. She had never wanted to leave him. She probably still wanted to be with him now. They had a history together. She and I had only had a few weeks together. A few amazing weeks. But just a drop in the bucket compared to a life and family with Silvo.

"Yol, please."

"*No*," she growled. Her fists clenched by her sides and her eyes shimmered with unshed tears. "That's not the worst of it all. That night you told me we were getting our marriage voided, I was coming to bring you *good* news. News I thought would make you happy. Instead we fought about your desire to erase our marriage. You said you wanted your kingdom back. So, I got mad and went to my mother for advice on how to save our marriage."

She took in a breath, as did I. Each truth revealed was a new wound in my heart that only beat for her. Each pain she'd endured wrung more anguish from me. "That's when she altered my memories. That's when she saw fit to do it. But that's also when she realized that I was pregnant with your daughter," she said excruciatingly.

The color drained from my face and I felt cold as ice. My pack murmured to each other, but I couldn't focus on any of their words. I was paralyzed. Paralyzed from head to toe. She had been pregnant with another child. *His* child. *What the fuck had they done to her?*

"I have a niece?" Silva asked.

"Yes," Silvo said, like it wasn't news to him. Like he'd *known* all this time. Turning back to Jasinda, he asked, "Where's our daughter now?"

Worry passed across her face for a moment and then she recovered. But the worry remained in her heart. I could feel it. "I don't know. My mother knows though. I stayed with Mom the entire five months of my pregnancy. After I gave birth to her, I nursed her for three weeks, then Mom sent me to the earthly realm."

Panic engulfed her as she paced back and forth. Everything in me screamed for me to go to her. My mating bands burned around my fingers with the need to hold her. Soothe her hurts. Heal her heart. Love her.

She stopped abruptly and looked down at her hands. A gasp escaped her lips. She held them up to her face.

What the hell was she looking at?

Then she slowly turned and looked at me for the first time since she'd started berating Silvo for what he'd done to her. *Oh shit. The mating bands. When mine started burning, hers must have too.*

Fear and worry floated from her. "We *are* mated??" she asked, breathlessly.

"Yes," I said sheepishly. Guilt wrapped around my throat, choking off any further explanation.

Confusion bloomed within her. "How?" That one whispered word sent chills down my spine.

I didn't want to have this conversation in front of an audience. But I refused to take any more from her than what had already been stolen from her. She deserved the truth. "Yes, that's what I've been trying to tell you."

"*That* was the important thing you wanted to say in the garden?"

A small surge of hope emanated from her. *Why?* Her small ounce of hope was a balm to my soul. I had none myself, other than what little I gleaned from her.

"Yes, and you have every right to be upset. Don't worry we can get my father to void it. If you want to."

"This is what Scarlet was trying to tell me, when she asked me to promise not to run away. To just stay and listen," she murmured to herself and I thought it best not to answer.

Scarlet *had* tried to help me. Glad to know she still had my back.

"*Did everyone else know? Could they all see your name on my finger?*" She asked me as pain caused her body to tremble and her face to fall as she spoke.

I nodded. "*I'm sorry. I needed to be the one to tell you. Don't be mad at them. They were just following my orders.*"

"*I just really hate being kept in the dark.*"

"*I know. And I can't tell you how much I hate that I am a new source of pain for you. I swear, it was never my intention to hide it from you, enchantress.*"

She cleared her throat. "*Do you want to void our mating?*" she asked, pained. Tears pooled in her jade eyes. New hurt radiated off her in waves, slamming into my heart and nearly knocking me down.

The torment behind her question shocked me. I thought she'd be happy to void our mating. *"No, my enchantress. Why would I?"* I admitted.

She stood there quiet, holding onto my gaze. Her relief swooped in and I wasn't sure if that was a good thing or a bad thing. *Was she relieved that I didn't want to void us? Because I'd finally told her the truth? Or something else entirely?* Then she closed her eyes and stepped back. More than anything, I wanted to leap over this damn river and hold her in my arms. Tell her how sorry I was for not having any control. I wanted to tell her that we could figure everything out together.

"I didn't mean to leave you in the dark, I wanted to tell you everything. I was trying to ease you into things. I didn't want to scare you away. I thought you were human." I confessed.

With a smile, she opened her eyes and said, *"Yes, I thought I was too. It's ok, my prince. There'll be time for explanations later."*

She looked at the man standing next to me. Elier.

Tears began to fall on her face as her fear spiked. "What *have* you done?"

"I don't regret it, princess. I'll *never* regret it," Elier spoke with such confidence. *What were they talking about?* The look that passed between them was lost on me.

"You've committed treason. You need to get out of here or he'll kill you." The pain was so surreal; I wasn't sure if it came from her.

I opened my mind to Elier and felt his adoration for her. His love and devotion. The pride he carried for her. I closed my mind back up. I was jumbled from everything I'd witnessed and felt already. I was missing a piece of the puzzle, and with my mind and heart in such a mess, there was no way I could figure out the missing piece. *What the hell?*

"Go. Go now. Please," she pleaded with Elier. "That's a direct order. Just go," she yelled.

With a shimmer and pop, the band holding Elier disappeared. He flinched at her words but spun around and shifted into his wolf form. He ran and disappeared quickly. I tried to move forward but the band still held me in place. *Fuck!*

The water flowing in the river began to churn and a figure shot out. Someone I thought was dead. Someone who looked very pissed. Leto. His eyes were trained on Silvo, shooting daggers for a moment. Then he turned around to face Jasinda. He rose completely out of the water and landed right in front of her. He walked right to her as the water began evaporating from his body until he was left completely dry.

"My daughter, I've been searching for you everywhere. In every realm." The relief that emanated from him knocked me back a little. He opened his arms wide for her.

"Papa, I'm sorry. It was Mom who did this. I didn't mean for any of this to happen."

"I know. Shhh…beautiful child of mine."

"I'm so *angry* she did this," she said as she walked into his arms.

"Her intentions were good. I promise you that. But the way she went about it was absolutely wrong. She was trying to keep you safe and panicked when she got word of Axe being released. He knows about our female line."

Axe? What the hell are they talking about that monster for? What does he have to do with Jasinda? I swear on my life, if he ever comes near her, I'll unleash my beast on him.

'Oh, now you want to unleash me!!!' My beast snapped.

"What about our female line?" she asked him.

Yes, what about it? I wanted to know too.

"Your mother's to be exact. All the females on your mother's side can mate with anyone and yes, I know anyone can mate with anyone. But your mother's line is compatible with all species, making them molduses"

What the hell? I thought the molduse was just an urban legend. A rumor to give hope to a dying species.

"Are you saying what I think you're saying?"

"Yes, my water lily. That's exactly what I'm saying."

"Oh goddesses! This isn't good," fear etched in her voice heavily.

Their voices dropped as they discussed something privately to each other. None of us could hear them anymore, even with our supernatural hearing. Silvo and Silva leaned closer to try to hear, just as I had.

Without warning, her father dove back into the water and disappeared into the shimmering portal that appeared. Somehow, I'd forgotten about the portal in my waters. The portal to other realms.

Jasinda looked at me. The distress that appeared when her father told her about Axe remained. I wish I knew what they'd spoken about privately. Part of me wished I'd tapped into our connection to eavesdrop on their conversation. But I'd never betray her that way. She was holding back her tears.

A tall man with a black, hooded cloak holding a bow and arrow stepped from the shadows behind her. Squinting, I tried to see his face, but it was hidden and he was too far away. Lifting the bow, he took aim right at Jasinda.

Without a thought, I tried to move against the bands. They held tight. "Jasinda! Behind you, by the trees." I pointed.

As she turned to look, the arrow released like a bullet. I couldn't make it to her. I was glued to the fuckin' shields. My heart jolted. I saw Jasinda's body jerk from the impact of the arrow, at least that's what I thought. She whirled around from the jerk, the arrow floating through her hands like a baton. With force, she shot the arrow back at the man in the black cloak and struck him right in the chest. He combusted into black dust and was no more.

Calmly, she turned back to me, unfazed. "I need to go. I need time, Jace. I'm sorry. Please understand. I'll be back. I promise." She dove into the water just like her father and disappeared into her realm.

I just stood there immobilized and not from the magic band because the moment she'd vanished beneath the water's surface, Silvo dropped the band holding us all in place. I was perplexed by her reaction to the hooded man. It was as if he had been no match for her. Not one spark of fear came from her when she'd faced that danger. She'd gone cold.

Emotions warred within me. I wasn't sure whether to be angry or sad. My mate was gone. She was gone and in so much pain. Wounds I wasn't sure I could help her heal. Agony that Silvo and Elier had caused her. Aches her own mother had inflicted upon her and suffering that I added.

"Are you happy? This is all your fault! You and her mother are both idiots for doing this," Silva yelled in her brother's face, then disappeared in a flash of light.

A stab of agony came from Scarlet. "She's the missing princess? The wife you once had? The one I never got the chance to meet?" Scarlet accused.

"Yes." He bowed his head in defeat and let the torment finally show in his face.

"I've been looking for her for nearly ten years in various realms." She shook her head. "And she popped up right here. Right under my nose," she said to herself.

Silvo rubbed his face. "I know. I kept putting you on different trails so she couldn't be found. I altered the images of her in your mind so you wouldn't recognize her. I had orders from the queen that I couldn't disobey."

"*Wow*. This whole time you *knew* I was on the right track and you just led me elsewhere," Scarlet implicated.

"It was what I was supposed to do. For tricking you, I'm sorry."

"Fuck you, Silvo. Fuck you! We're family and this is how you treat me!? When she forgives you? That's when I'll think about forgiving you as well," she finished and stalked off.

He was her family. They were related. *How did I not know this?* I didn't know she had *any* other family members. The revelations just kept coming.

I looked at him then. I could sense his rage, but before I could say anything to him, he disappeared.

What the fuck? Was no one going to explain any of this to me? At least fill in the damn blanks!

I sat down by the edge of the river. The silence behind me told me the pack was waiting on my orders. But I had none to give. My mind and heart had left with her. I couldn't do anything right now. I didn't *want* to do anything right now. Edwin wedged his way into my lap, still in wolf form. His whine told me he missed her already, and he too wished she hadn't left.

I rubbed his fur. "Today you showed true leadership and a whole lot of courage. I'm beyond proud of you, my son."

He nuzzled into me more and I let him. We both needed the comfort. This was going to be hard on the pack. But it was going to be harder on me.

"We'll continue with the Tri Feast. Our alpha queen will return to us. She just needs a little time to get herself together from all that just happened to her," my mother's voice echoed through us all. The pack members retreated to the campsite that was now turned into a battleground.

"Jace? Son?" My mother's beautiful, soft voice embraced me.

"What if she doesn't come back?" I asked her.

"She will. She has to. She's your mate. Your true soulmate. Those are truly rare."

I hoped she was right about that. Because all the emotions that had gushed from Jasinda hadn't been good. It didn't give me any hope at all.

Chapter Sixty-Six

Jace

Three days later...

As I sat riveted by Scarlet's words, I couldn't believe the things she was filling me in on.

"Silvo and Silva are my cousins. Sorry I didn't tell you. I just didn't think it was necessary."

The relationship surprised me, but I could see the resemblance between them now that I knew about it.

"She was right underneath my nose this whole damn time," she mused, still annoyed that she hadn't realized it.

"She was your assignment? You were working for King Leto?"

"Yes, sorry." Her head hung low.

"Don't be. Silvo put you on a different path and you were under your king's orders. Wait, is Leto your King?"

"Yes, he has sworn me in as his tracker and allowed me to live a life outside of his realm. With you to be exact."

"Why?"

"Because I was living a dangerous life and he wanted me to find sanctuary in a steady, safe place. So, he said I could live in a home he would build just for me or I could seek residence with you if you offered it. So, I chose you when you offered me a place in your home."

"For what it's worth, I'm happy you're here. You're family now. Are you returning to her realm?"

"No, not right now. I'm going to wait here until she returns." Hope shined brightly from Scarlet. I nodded because I couldn't speak. "You need to get some rest, Jace. Your office is a mess. Every time it gets cleaned, you mess it up again." She stood, and with sadness surrounding her, she left.

So, Leto was Jasinda's biological father. Now, it all made sense. The colonel wasn't her real father. He had been a ruse to keep her safe. Looking back through this new lens, I understood why she had never been scared by my world. She had embraced it too easily. Scarlet's first declaration that Jasinda was special made more sense now. It was more accurate than either of us could've imagined knowing who and what she was. It explained why my horses had reacted the way they had. *Damn this shit!*

I hadn't slept in three days. Three whole days. Not a wink since she'd left. My bed smelled like her. It hurt too much. So, every night I went to the river hoping she'd return. Praying she'd come back to me.

As I sat on the river bank each night, alone with my thoughts, I asked myself so many questions that I had no answers for. *Did she even love me enough to return? Did she still love Silvo? How could I compete against him? Who could compete against a man who had married her and had left her distraught because he'd wanted to void their marriage while she'd still loved him? What about their children? They had two children together. Would she go back and stay just for her kids?*

My pack searched for Elier. I wanted to know what he'd done. She'd said he'd committed treason. He hadn't wanted to run, but he had. For her. For her, he'd run and had been willing to give up the life he'd built. After all, he was still her royal guard. I shook my head over all the connections I'd missed. Elier was one of her royal guards. That explained why he'd been so adamant about protecting her.

"FUCK!"

I threw a chair at the wall and watched as it broke into pieces. My office was a mess again. For the past three days, every time someone cleaned it, I trashed it again. It wasn't even a conscious plan to destroy things. All these thoughts and doubts swirling in my mind and heart were driving me insane.

I needed her. I wanted her. The warmth in me had died when she'd disappeared beneath the water. But I felt as though I couldn't show my pack any weakness. They couldn't see me like this. She'd completed me, and she'd completed the pack. I knew it, and so did they. Even though she hadn't been their alpha queen for long, or hadn't carried out any official duties, they'd *FELT* it. Just like I had. She was supposed to be with us. With me.

Feeling empty inside, I buried my face in my hands. All the spark I'd ever had died. Snuffed out like a fire doused with a torrent of water. It was the worst feeling, being mated and having my mate gone. Missing her didn't even come close to describing how I felt. Emptiness and no heat. No desire. No passion. No will for anything. Not even my beast was responding to me.

Falling to my knees I yelled, "WHERE ARE YOU?" I pounded my fist against the floor, just as she had that night against the ground.

I froze, sensing a fire in my chest.

"Right here," a voice whispered.

KEEP READING FOR AN EXCERPT OF TRI MOONS:
REVEALED

TRI MOONS: REVEALED

Prologue

Jasinda

10 years ago…

Up the stairs I went, moving toward our bedroom. Silvo said we needed to speak. Maybe he had a quest to take without me. He hated being away from me, so he made sure we spent quality time together before he took his leave. I had some exciting news to share with him. I was hoping I would beat him to it this time around.

I was pregnant.

I felt it when it all happened—when my egg dropped, when his sperm connected. I *knew*, and this time I caught it way earlier than I did with our son, Niko. Enthusiasm filled me at the prospect of divulging this news to him, instead of him telling me. He was the one who told me I was pregnant with Niko before I even knew. I chuckled remembering how proud he was to announce it.

When I entered our bedroom, I went straight out on the balcony. The view was breathtakingly beautiful. Splendid trees cast themselves along the forest in the distance like a shield. The rocks and waterfalls to the right were far off, yet visible from this height, so I could enjoy their beauty. I'd always loved how the water fell from the rocks and into the pond below. It glittered in the sunlight and sparkled in the moonlight. The air was refreshing since technically we lived under a dome of water. Water that aired out for non-merkins. If I walked to the other side of my balcony, I'd have the best view of the castle and the rest of the mountains that made up this realm. Taking myself away from admiring my realm's scenery, I approached Silvo who stood at the edge of the balcony as if he was going to dive off into the shimmering ripples below.

"Dragon heart, guess what?" A smile forming onto my face.

He turned toward me. His face didn't mirror my own. He looked… unhappy? Sad? Angry? "We need to part," he announced.

My next step was heavy, and I swallowed the cry rising within. *Part?* This was a joke. "Forgive me, my dragon, but did you say part?"

"Yes," he hissed, and his eyes went solid red.

"But *why*? Why would you want to…leave me?" *Was there another? Was I not worthy anymore?*

"I want my kingdom back, and father needs me there. I choose to be a *prince* no more. I want to be king. So, I must part with you and merge with Ayana."

I jerked back from his slap to my heart, to my soul and to the love we both had for each other.

"But you *love* me!" I didn't care how weak or foolish I sounded. "I *know* it Silvo. I feel it when I'm near you and when we're apart. You can't hide that from me. I can't hide it from you," I croaked, as the waterworks began descending. "I see it in the way your body relaxes when I'm close. And when you mold us together so we're like one. And when your eyes thaw, and there are no serious creases lining your face. And when you smile at me, knowing I'm the only one you give *that* smile to. You love me! You do! Why are you doing this?"

"Because my people need dragonlins. I *need* to breed a dragon son!" Something in his voice was off.

"Niko will shift into one of our species in time. Be patient. Yours might just be the dominate form. Then you'll know that we can breed more together. I'll give you as many as you want, Silvo. *Please*. Tell me why are you doing this to me? To us? To Niko?" I pleaded.

"We cannot be sure that you'll breed another dragon, even if Niko is one. And he hasn't turned thirteen yet to know what he'll be. But with another dragon, we'll know for sure that my offspring will be dragons."

"I thought that wasn't important to you. You didn't even bat an eye when your father threw that in your face. You stood strong and tall for me when we were fifteen. *Fifteen*, Silvo. And when we were getting married. You told your father that from the moment you saw me, you *knew* I was yours. That I was it for you, and no other would ever delight in your essences."

I came closer, and he stepped back. He looked at me like I disgusted him in some way. It burned my skin alive and shredded my heart. "You told me I was your red dragon," I whispered, my voice breaking as I backed away. Something was not sitting right with me. "I love you, Silvo. This can't be the end of us. I don't want this to be the end, because I feel your love. I feel it." My hand clutched the fabric over my heart.

"This is what I want, Jasinda."

"But we cannot void our mating. It's non-voidable. We blood mated," I reminded him.

"I've found a way, and father has agreed to do it," he said firmly.

"That's impossible," I whispered.

"There's always a loophole, Jasinda."

I turned around and ran from the room, needing to put distance between my ravaged heart and the source of its injury. I leaped down the steps, never touching a step, then rushed out the front door. Once I reached the water, I dove in and swam towards my parents' castle. I knew I looked liked a torpedo in the water and I could only hope my mother would help me.

When I reached the castle, I leapt from the water's slippery grasp and landed on my legs. A new, perfectly dried dress appeared on me as I walked into the hidden side entrance. Once I rounded the corner, I saw my mother standing there as if she'd be waiting for me. "Mother! Oh, thank the goddess you're here. Silvo's acting strange. He said he wants his kingdom back and now wants to *mate* with Ayana. He loves me. I know it, mother."

"You must not fret. He has a duty to his kingdom that needs to be met," she softly replied.

What? Was my mother insane? "If he wishes to be with his own people because his father has put such a heavy burden over him, then let him fulfill it."

"Mother, no." I breathed out. "This can't be." I swayed a little. "He will be king *here*. And I his queen. His people love us no matter what. We are king and queen already in their eyes."

"Jasinda, my waterfly." She came closer and slipped my pendant over my head, settling it around my neck. She'd had it for a few days, because she wanted to add diamonds to it. Said she'd been meaning to since Niko was born and never got around to doing it. Her fingers brushed against the middle. A small light shone on her fingers where it touched her skin. "Forgive me, my daughter, for this is the only way I know." She peered in my eyes. Hers filled with surprise. "A child," she whispered.

And all faded away.

Silvo

I knew it would be difficult. But I wasn't prepared for the depth of pain within. To see her that way. To know the lies that spilled from my lips tore at her. I ripped her heart in a new way. A way I was supposed to never let happen. A way I was supposed to protect her from. Jasinda was no fool. She knew what she meant to me and I to her. She *knew* she was my red dragon, my soul's life force.

How could I be such a fool? How was I going to go on without her?

I was going to lose her forever. *But it had to be done. Right? Was there a way I could have it all?*

Fear became a creation I didn't care to be a part of. Fear for my mate's life and for the universe had been constantly eating at me. The feeling of loss wasn't something to be wished upon anyone.

Slowly, I turned and kept my gaze on the door she fled through. *What in all the gods' names was I doing?* This was all wrong. This feeling of betrayal to her was all wrong. This was a foolish and stupid idea for me to go along with.

I tilted my head back, running my hands over my face. The wetness in my hands was unmistakable. I couldn't leave Jasinda like this. I couldn't leave *us* like this.

Goddesses, please guide my red dragon's heart.

Frowning, I replayed the moments from her entry to her exit. I sensed something different in her…a child! I growled in frustration and raced after her.

I was a fool not to have sensed it instantly. She was with child! *That* was the news she knew would bring me joy.

Once I was outside the house, I knew she was gone. I felt her absence in my heart. I couldn't let this happen to her. We could find another way.

How stupid of me to ever agree to do this with her mother! Jasinda had been my everything since I'd first laid eyes on her. I altered my life just to have her, so that no other could claim her. Closing my eyes, I focused on her essences. I dematerialized and rematerialized in the hall of the king's castle.

Her mother stood there with her head bowed, weeping. "It's been done," she murmured.

"No! Bring her back. Forget all of this. It was a mistake. We cannot do this to her. I cannot go through with this. She's with child, and she needs me. I need her," I strained.

"I know." She looked into my eyes with pain and regret. "You took a blood oath, and I'm not going to undo it, my son. Hate me all you want, but Axe will not find us. I will keep her safe during her pregnancy then send her off into the human world."

"No. I'm her mate, and I have a rightful say in this," I reminded her.

"Not after you took the blood oath. It's for the best, Silvo. Destiny wants it this way."

"Destiny wishes me to be in misery, wishes her to be parted from her son and mate?" I angrily asked.

"Your time will come, Silvo. I promise you that. You will have what was promised to you." She vanished and so did I.

I frantically searched for Jasinda after transforming into my dragon. All my senses seemed to be under a mist. Her essence was nowhere for my dragon to see. The search would've been even more difficult for me as a man. But I could always find her with my dragon.

What have I done? What about my unborn child? I should've left well alone. I roared and blew fire from my mouth. My life would forever be a hoarfrost, without her.

Acknowledgments

To my bestie Krystal Marin, who's been my biggest fan throughout this whole book. Love you for keeping me on my toes.

To my bestie Amaris Pagan, helping me bring my ideas into artistic life and creating the beautiful Enchantress Rose on the back of this book, I love you.

To my husband for putting up with the trio in our home and always answering me when I ask, "does this sound right?" Thank you. I love you.

To my editor Charlotte for being on me about, "dialogue, dialogue, dialogue!" She has definitely taught me a lot and has the patience of an angel. Always answering my questions and giving great advice. I couldn't be more grateful for an editor like you. Thank you.

To my editor Natasha Raulerson for doing an amazing job with my re-edits. Re-vamping my book has not been easy. You took the time to go over it all! Your honesty has gone a long way and has taught me new things. You have definitely shined a light on my work! I love you and I thank you with all my heart!

To my family and friends who have been supportive and encouraging, thank you. Love ya!

To Kristen Martin's YouTube channel, which provides detailed information, thank you. I was able to gain and learn many things that without you would've been very overwhelming. To the Alessandra Torre Inkers group on Facebook and K Street, Thank you all! The Inkers group has been the best group (no offense to other groups) to provide all-in-one and where I found Author friends.

To Michelle Leighton, one of my favorite authors, you were the first person to answer my email within the hour when I asked you a few questions. Giving me all your virtual love in finishing my book. Thank you, for being so wonderful and sweet. You were my first push.

To my ARC and BETA readers, you all rock and are awesome, Thank you! A special thank you to Lylian Aguiar and Cheryl Kodera, you guys are the best Enchanters on my team!

To my proofreaders, thank you for catching the mistakes I didn't. I am grateful to have worked with you all.

To my father and Amy, thank you for always showing your support in the things I love to do.

To my mother who always saw the best in me and saw the writer within. I save you for last because I love you beyond any Enchanting world and I appreciate all that you have done for me.

About Author

Yanette Mantro is *Enchanted* with many stories to write. She fights every day to write so her words can be seen. Even though her first publishing was in 2018, she is excited about the journey she has chosen to embark on. Honestly, she was terrified when she released her first book and still is. Despite her fears, she's quite a goof and loves to laugh. Her writing began around the age of twelve, and she always liked the way the ink looked on paper. Her goal is to entertain readers with her books and maybe with a little of her personality as well. She wants to gain followers who will love her work, crave more of it and see her in her writing. She wants this as her career, because this is what she loves to do.

Make sure to sign up here for her newsletter to find out all the latest and greatest about her writing!
https://landing.mailerlite.com/webforms/landing/m9i7n1

Yanette loves hearing from readers! Email her about Tri Moons: Hidden.
yanette.mantro@gmail.com

While Yanette's website is under construction, feel free to find her in these places!

Instagram

https://www.instagram.com/yanettemantro/

Facebook Group
https://www.facebook.com/groups/348220832344528/

Facebook Page
https://www.facebook.com/yanettemantroauthor/

Goodreads
https://www.goodreads.com/author/show/17887540.Yanette_Mantro

SnapChat
https://www.snapchat.com/add/yanigrl

Pinterest
https://www.pinterest.com/yanettemantro/

Twitter
https://twitter.com/YanetteMantro